EMBASSY

ALSO BY LESLIE WALLER

Fiction

Three Day Pass
Show Me the Way
The Bed She Made
Phoenix Island
The Banker
K
Will the Real Toulouse-Lautrec
    Please Stand Up?
Overdrive
The Family
New Sound
A Change in the Wind
The American
Number One
The Coast of Fear
The Swiss Account
Trocadero
The Brave and the Free
Blood and Dreams
Gameplan

Nonfiction

The Swiss Bank Connection
The Mob: The Story of
    Organized Crime in America
Dog Day Afternoon
Hide in Plain Sight

EMBASSY

LESLIE WALLER

McGraw-Hill Book Company

New York   St. Louis
San Francisco   Toronto   Hamburg
Mexico

Portions of the lyric from "Bye Bye Blackbird" by Ray Henderson and Mort Dixon quoted on page 421 reprinted by permission of Warner Bros. Music.

© 1926 WARNER BROS. INC. (Renewed)
All Rights Reserved
Used By Permission

1 2 3 4 5 6 7 8 9 D O C D O C 8 7

ISBN 0-07-067941-X

LIBRARY OF CONGRESS CATALOGING-IN-PUBLICATION DATA

Waller, Leslie, 1923–
  Embassy.
  I. Title.
PS3545.A565E4 1987   813'.54   86-27235
ISBN 0-07-067941-X

BOOK DESIGN BY PATRICE FODERO

1

London always starts the same way.

For an instant the morning sun sweeps in horizontally while most people are still in their beds, blazes beneath the cloud cover that blankets the city, signals a false promise of lovely weather . . . and vanishes.

Ned tied his running shoes firmly. There was something in the idea of the sun's routine, of the same thing happening like clockwork every day, that struck a deep, melancholy chord inside Ned French. His own life was so much the opposite, so random, so deviously aleatory.

He grinned. "Aleatory" had been one of Chemnitz's favorite words, back in college. Being a German refugee had never stopped the professor from pillaging the daunting corners of the English language.

As for routine, Ned had none. His house in St. John's Wood near Regent's Park, for example, had three exits, one of them concealed. On any given morning, Ned might use any of the three.

He might be dressed, as now, for a jog in the park. Or suited up and umbrellaed. He might walk to the St. John's Wood station of the Jubilee line and take the underground train south to Bond Street.

Ned glanced at Laverne on her side of the large bed, her lush breasts rising and falling slowly. There was such a thing as too-regular breathing.

Paranoia. Ned tiptoed downstairs to the kitchen. He reached to open the refrigerator, then froze . . . studied the door closely. Was it slightly ajar?

Only he and Laverne lived here—their four daughters had left last week for the States—so no sticky little fingers got into the fridge or left it ajar. Gingerly, he gave the door a slight shove with his first and second fingers. The door didn't move, being well and truly closed.

Ned left the house and began to jog down the quiet little street. Something nagged at him still, something nasty and formless and impossible to name.

It was no good joking about paranoia, not in his job. For him it was merely a part of his arsenal, welded to a somber kind of second sight that knew when something bad lay ahead. As he jogged he could actually feel this fear like the onset of a migraine.

Something bad would happen. If only paranoia could stick a more accurate label on it! He glanced at the sky.

This was the magic moment. The sun lighted the east beyond Primrose Hill. To the west, its rays touched with brief fire the plain outline of Lord's cricket ground across Wellington Road. The modern ziggurat of Wellington Clinic sparkled for a moment. Then gray dropped over the scene. Ned had a mental picture of his wife in bed.

Pretending to be asleep?

He paused at the corner of Prince Albert Road. At this hour traffic was still light. He could see, across the trees and the broad hidden trench of the Grand Union Canal, that the crew at Winfield House were already at the flagpoles. Now, in late June, the tree leaves almost obscured the poles.

The American ambassador lived here in a thirty-five-room Georgian mansion set on a dozen wooded acres of parkland leased from the Crown. Most people, British or American, thought the United States embassy was the gargantuan contemporary pile that dominated Grosvenor Square in Mayfair, overlooking the dramatic bronze of FDR in his great cloak braving the storm of history as it reviewed him.

But that checkered Saarinen facade was the chancery of the embassy. Here in Regent's Park, with the momentary glint of dawn sun flashing across the dormer windows of its mansard roof, stood the official seat of power, where His Excellency the ambassador lay him down to sleep and each night prayed the Lord to keep his soul intact, or at least looking good.

Ned spotted his tail car rounding the corner of Macclesford Bridge, but all he could think was:

Why *faking* sleep?

At forty years of age, Edward James French was young to be a full colonel, young to have embassy-level intelligence authority in a city as large and as sensitive as London, too young, he added under his breath, to have a twenty-year marriage breaking up on him. But it was.

He opened his stride to half-speed as he began running through the greenery of the park along the Outer Circle. As he passed Winfield House they unfurled and ran Old Glory aloft. The dull gray morning light tamed the crimson and white stripes to peppermint anonymity and fuzzed the blue field with its white stars to a rectangle of solid, almost nameless hue.

Too bad, Ned thought as he hit his full speed and the embassy fell behind him. Too bad the sun hadn't lasted long enough to ignite that good old flag with a stirring shock of strong, rich color that still had the power to thrill him.

His running shoes thudded lightly along the pavement. Behind him he again caught a glimpse of his tail car, a mouse-brown Ford Fiesta with Moe Chamoun at the wheel, trying to keep his speed slow enough to match the running man's. To Ned's right the burnished dome and minaret of the Great London Mosque appeared and disappeared in an eye-blink. Its swollen gold breast, nipple tipped by a crescent moon, had been dulled by London overcast to a fitful gleam.

His head rang suddenly with that same vision of evil to come. It held him like the talons of some giant hawk. He had these premonitions so rarely that he felt almost helpless in their grip. If only there were a way of putting a name to the evil.

By the time he reached the top of Baker Street he had worked up a sweat and picked up a few fellow joggers. Because of the density of London traffic and the whimsical arrangement of streets and intersections, joggers and bikers alike lived in constant danger from auto traffic and from each other, no matter how self-disciplined they might be. As Ned slowed his pace to conform to the traffic, he moved left toward the curb. It minimized the number of directions from which a vehicle might hit him. Damn all such premonitions!

Behind, his car loitered at a slight distance. The "high" runners were supposed to feel had now been replaced, for Ned, by the closing-in menace of autos and trucks at elbow range. Sharing the road between flesh and steel was, at best, a nervous-making business. But if—

Ahead of him, five or six yards at most, a pale blue Mini Minor swerved to send a jogger sprawling across the stony surface of Baker Street. God, the premonition!

The man hit hard, rolled twice and slammed into the curbstone like a flung sack of cement. Pedestrians froze for an instant, then rushed to his aid. But the Mini kept going. "Hey!"

Yards ahead lay the busy intersection with Marylebone Road. At any moment, when the lights switched to yellow and then green, Baker Street traffic would turn left or right or carry on straight ahead.

"Bastard," Ned grunted. He lunged forward, a sudden shove of speed. His throat ached. Sweat coursed down his face. The lights were turning yellow.

"Bastard!" he shouted, hurling himself at the Mini, his hands outstretched. He could feel his fingers close on the door handle. He was now at his most vulnerable. The car jolted forward.

He twisted hard and yanked the car door open. Then he half leaped, half fell, straight forward. As he dropped, he rammed the car door wide open. The pavement hit him hard at the knees and he gritted his teeth for the painful drubbing that was to follow. In a few yards it could reduce his legs to mincemeat.

But the Mini had stopped dead. Ned realized he had torn the door half off on the driver's side. But what had stopped the car was a mouse-brown Fiesta. Moe Chamoun had swerved ahead of the Mini and forced it to a halt. Ned's shadow had miraculously leaped ahead of him.

"What d'you shits think you're d—?" the Mini driver began in a loud voice.

Ned's right hand blurred for an instant. His first and second fingers, locked together, sank deep into a point above the driver's navel where his vagus nerve was located. The man gasped, unable to move, face dead white.

Ned lurched to his feet and limped back to the fallen jogger. Someone had rolled up a jacket and put it under his bloody head. In the distance, two uniformed bobbies were running toward the gathering crowd.

Ned staggered back to the Fiesta and gestured Chamoun to get in beside him. "Beat it."

"You okay, Ned?"

"Scram!"

The great chancery on Grosvenor Square, with its golden eagle thirty-five feet wide, seems to conform in height with buildings nearby. It is an illusion. While only five floors and a set-back penthouse are visible to passersby, three more floors dig deep into the alluvial clay of London.

In one of the basements Ned French dried himself after a quick shower, rubbed some antiseptic cream on his scraped knees, and began hastily pulling on fresh office clothes. He had barely gotten into the building when he'd been collared by one of the brisk British lads who served as runners, couriers, or, in this case, pages.

"Colonel French, sir." The boy was out of breath. "Mr. Connell wants you immedjitly in his office, sir."

"Soon's I dress. Tell him."

"Immedjitly, sir."

It bothered Ned that less than half of the eight hundred people who worked in this building were Americans. Nearly all the rest were Brits with security clearance of only the most routine kind. When a new one was to be hired, his or her name went to MI5 for vetting, with a secret copy to the Company's Station London office. But the speed with which clearance or disapproval came back from both MI5 and CIA indicated to Ned that the procedures were minimal.

As he buttoned his shirt and draped a tie around his neck, Ned wondered how much more secure a full staff of FBI-cleared U.S. citizens would be. What the hell did security clearance mean these days, anyway? No more than that silly premonition about the accident.

Life was so . . . so aleatory. One minute you were jogging along. The next you were a bloody pulp and your attacker was escaping. He stared into his own dark blue eyes. After a lifetime of games-playing that ranged from simple draw poker to operating agents in hostile territory, Ned knew his eyes gave away nothing, ever. Clearance hereby granted: eyes, general issue, 20–20, one pair, lapis lazuli.

Jane had used that phrase. Not dark blue: lapis lazuli.

He knotted his tie very carefully. When you met with a clotheshorse like Royce Connell you had to be careful not to distract him by a slightly off-center tie. Ned dashed up one of the stairways. It was five floors to Royce's office but a patriot who has just brought down an escaping malefactor ought to be good for a little more effort on behalf of his own, his native land.

"Ned!" Connell indicated an upholstered armchair beside a large coffee table in his office. He sat down at another chair and stared hard at his deputy defense attaché.

"Tell me everything you know about the ambassador's wife, Mrs. Fulmer."

French watched the older man, first warily, then with an appreciation of design, the way he might admire an R-Type Bentley, the stubbier Mark VI model that preceded the start of the R series, or a blues solo by

Art Hodes. Royce Connell was so *right*. It wasn't just that he was a handsome son of a bitch whose head of thick white hair was the only giveaway to the fifty years he'd spent on earth. It wasn't just that he was probably the State Department's best chargé d'affaires with a record of steadily increasing responsibility over a thirty-year career. It was much more the essential rightness of the impression he made: quiet, firm, knowledgeable, well-mannered, well-spoken, and so goddamned well-dressed he could sell you anything from life insurance to chewing gum.

"Born Susan Pandora Morgan," Ned began, "about the last year of the war to Consuelo and Montgomery Morgan of Biloxi, Mississippi. Graduate of Miss Huckleton's School for Young Ladies, employee of the *Tampa Gazette* on general and women's features. BA, Sproull University, Orlando, MA in political science, same august institution. Why don't you get Karl Follett to pull her file for you? It's his turf, not mine. Anyway, there was social clout in this line of the Morgan clan but no cash. My guess is the newspaper paid . . ."

Connell gestured impatiently. "Get to the core."

"Core? If she said to the ambassador," here Ned lapsed into broad parody of a Gulf Coast drawl, " 'Honey, Ah wawnt yoah haid on a silvuh plattah by fahv o'clock, an' don' git no blood awn th' carpet,' poor old Bud would jump in the bathtub and decapitate himself then and there."

Connell's distant look of annoyance was such a considered gesture, never overdrawn, merely the ghost of displeasure, that Ned sat silently for a long moment enjoying it. He liked any masterly performance and in Royce he had a professional trouper of the old school.

Connell's secretary came in then with two cups of coffee, placed them on the table, and asked: "OJ, Colonel French?"

Ned smiled at her. "I missed it at home. Is it too much trouble?"

"Not at all," Royce assured him. The woman went to Connell's wood-grained refrigerator, hardly big enough for more than a few bottles. Ned watched her pour two small glasses of orange juice and leave the room.

Ned had heard the refrigerator door close with a soft *thk*. He knew it was properly closed. Nevertheless he extended his leg toward the box and nudged its door with the tip of his black loafer. The movement made his knee ache. If he thought anything of this, Connell said nothing. Instead he stared into his orange juice and produced a magnificently chiseled frown that in no way distorted the classic beauty of his face.

"Nothing derogatory in Mrs. Fulmer's background?" Connell persisted in his least persistent tone. "Petitions signed? Fund-raising affairs attended? Suspicious friends or acquaintances?"

French shook his head. "She's clean, Royce. What's the beef?"

The deputy chief of mission paused for a moment, much as Ned had, as if contemplating several next moves. Then he picked up a stapled sheaf of papers from the cocktail table and handed it to Ned. "This is her guest list for the July Fourth garden party."

French leafed slowly through the pages, rubbing his sore knees as he did so. There was nothing alphabetical about the order of names. The only principle upon which Pandora Fulmer had made the list, Ned decided, was free association. If she had listed three film stars then she continued to list eight more. If she'd thought of one prominent academic, his name was followed by another five.

Possibly the most prominent Britons and Americans in London, the guests ranged from diplomats, artists, and businessmen to rock stars, clothes designers, and other instant celebrities who appealed to the young. No visiting television or film personality was left out. No notorious mistress or gay escort was slighted. If even half of this list accepted, Ned realized, the garden party promised more photo opportunities than anything short of a natural disaster.

He glanced up at Connell. "What does Follett have to say about this?"

"Follett," Royce responded, waspishly emphasizing the initial letter, "is in Newport, Rhode Island, on one month's home leave."

And now the migrainelike aura of evil clamped down on Ned again. It almost took his breath away, so strongly did he feel it. He tried to calm himself. Easy, now. Nothing to panic about.

"He sure knows when to pick a vacation." Ned frowned. "Wait a second. You're not—in the absence of our security officer you're not dumping this mess in *my* lap?"

"Is there any other lap handy?"

"But, Royce . . ." Ned paused for another long moment. It didn't do to explain too much of the inner workings of the intelligence community to someone who, later, might have to deny such knowledge. "Royce, as you know, people like me, in military intelligence, are not really geared up to handle a thoroughly civilian affair like this one. Since you haven't got Follett, your man should be—"

"Don't remind me who my man should be."

"But it's his bailiwick."

"Wrong." Royce's voice hardly rose above its normal tone. "My responsibility in regard to the security of an embassy event is clearly to pick the best person for the job. Larry Rand is not my choice of best person."

"He'll scream like a stuck pig. A very small, nasty stuck pig."

"He can yodel like a shoat with his weenie in a wringer," Connell remarked in an uncharacteristic burst. "You're hereby in charge."

"Thanks," Ned responded with very little enthusiasm. He sat back and thought: Connell has just made an enemy for me.

Ned finished reading the list, put it back on the table, and sat without speaking. It was hard to know where to begin. In principle there was nothing wrong with inviting prominent people to an embassy celebration on such a typically American holiday. But there was something so devoid of common sense that it qualified as a major disaster. No wonder his paranoia had been working overtime.

"All those celebrities in one place," he muttered.

"All those celebrities in one place," Royce Connell repeated, adding, "like pinning a target over your heart and handing a gun to the nearest terrorist."

"It's the opportunity of a lifetime," Ned responded, trying for a lighter tone. Neither man spoke for another long moment. "Look," Ned said at last, "she'll have to be told she can't do things like this. Maybe in Queen Victoria's reign when life was simpler. Not today."

Connell eyed him silently for a long moment. "Ned," he sighed, "I do envy you military types' ability to ignore political realities. Has it escaped you that the president's political chickens have come home to roost?" A faint look of disdain crossed his face. "He's regressed the nation to before Herbert Hoover. The rich love it, but not the poor or the new poor he's created."

He slowly sipped coffee. Then: "He remains very popular, but his party gets blamed for the pigsty so it desperately needs to stand tall, Ned. July Fourth's only four months before elections. It's our most macho holiday, made for standing tall. And, two weeks ago Exdrec 103 went out to every U.S. ambassador, direct from the Oval Office.

"Stop hiding the flag, the president ordered: Stand tall and let the world know America's not afraid of anything, ever, amen."

Connell put down his coffee cup. "Now, 103 will get bountiful lip service. Ambassadors' speeches will bristle with manly adjectives and daredevil verbs. But few will take it more seriously than that. Our misfortune, Ned, is that the Fulmers are less than a month in service and extremely ambitious activists. Or Mrs. Fulmer is, anyway. Her party plan perfectly fulfills the president's Exdrec. I have no leg to stand on if I try to quash the idea. She has only to wave 103 in my face, or get the president to do it."

The silence that followed had the profound depth of some ancient, abandoned, and highly perilous mineshaft. "There's more," Ned said then. "I can smell it. Not even a politician would be so foolhardy over one stupid public-relations stunt."

Connell seemed to be listening for something, as if Ned had dropped a stone down that endless shaft. He sighed again. "I'm sure you're right," he said at last. "Something clandestine's afoot and needs a brave coat of camouflage paint. We'll get the answer, never fear. But it'll come too late."

"Don't you see?" Connell asked him. For the first time real emotion colored his voice. "Between them, she and the president have boxed us in. And who knows how many other embassies find themselves in the same position?"

Ned's face was grave. He nursed his knee for a moment, then: "Of course, to us military types, as you called me, it's quite simple. The commander in chief says 'Bark!' and we just sit up on our hind legs and go *woof!* Nothing to it. You civilian types have it a lot tougher."

A look of polite disgust showed on Connell's handsome face. "That's because they pay us to think, not react." Instantly he looked sorry. "That was out of line, Ned. I apologize. But I'm really in a funk over this. It's been taken completely out of my hands. She's outfoxed us, and on the highest authority. We can't possibly call off the party. We'd look like fools. We can't do anything but make sure it will be a very well-protected event."

The pause this time lasted more than a minute. Ned had the feeling that Royce already knew what he would say, but it had to be said anyway: "She's set the stakes so high we're sure to have trouble. It doesn't matter who, the Irish, French groups like Action Directe, Spanish outfits like Grapo or ETA, the Rote Armee Faktion or any of the dozen groups who speak for Islam . . . Royce, it doesn't even matter if we're dealing with one of our opposite numbers at the KGB . . . this is a window of opportunity so tempting it *can't* be ignored."

Royce Connell's handsome face had gone slightly putty-colored around the nostrils. He inhaled deeply and then, after a pause, again, as though he had failed to get enough oxygen the first try. His strong jaw set in a hard line. From the side, where Ned sat, it was a chin no prudent man would tamper with. But when Royce turned to face him head-on the rock firmness seemed only a trick of the lighting.

"What I don't get," French said, not bothering to censor his thoughts but speaking abruptly out of anger, "is how she put this over on us. Why didn't we know about this long before she sent out the invitations?"

"I've had Jane Weil keeping close track of her. She hid this from

Jane, too. We're lucky as the devil Jane managed to swipe a copy of the list or we'd be reading all about it in the London *Times*."

Ned sat back in his armchair and let silence engulf the two of them. Slowly, he massaged his bruised knees. He found himself wondering how much Royce knew. Instead of thinking about that silly woman's lethal lawn party he began to watch Connell's face for a sign that he knew what had happened between Ned French and Jane Weil.

Nonsense. No one knew. Laverne had her intuitive wifely suspicions, Ned warned himself, but no one in the entire embassy had an inkling that he and Jane . . .

"Speak up!" Connell snapped. "Tell me we haven't blundered into some disastrous nightmare."

Ned managed a wan grin. "Royce . . . would I lie to you?"

Long after Ned had jogged off into the morning mist that hung over Regent's Park, Laverne French had remained at the bedroom window staring out at the start of another day.

She was young enough—Ned's age—to remember when mornings heralded bright doings. No such feelings now, she thought as she stood there in the same kind of baby-doll sleepwear she had first bought for her honeymoon twenty years ago at the Fort Bragg PX.

These were fussy little tops with puffed sleeves and a bodice elasticized to both support and outline her ample breasts. The see-through batiste was dizzy with cut-out hearts inset with see-further-through ecru lace.

Although he had gone some time ago, Laverne could still picture Ned's retreating body. Of late he seemed to be forever in retreat . . . from her. It certainly wasn't the same marriage, she thought. In the past few years Ned no longer responded to even such unsubtle suggestions as this baby-doll bed costume. In the old days . . .

"Raunchy as a rattler with no hidey-hole," Laverne said. A moment later she was shocked to realize she had spoken aloud. Suppose someone had heard?

But her girls were six thousand miles away, safe in California since last week. The cleaning woman wasn't due till noon. Laverne was alone with the same raw feeling of having been left behind by Ned, not just this morning, but a thousand times in recent years. Ever since Bonn, wasn't it?

She turned from the window and stared at herself in the mirror. The costume was ridiculous. The mother of four nearly grown girls, she told herself, daughter of Lieutenant General De Cartha Krikowski, United States Air Force (retired), herself a captain in the Reserve and wife of a high-ranking army intelligence officer, didn't mope around her bedroom in a whore's come-on rig, moaning about lack of nookie.

Laverne pulled off the costume and stared at her slender legs and full, erect breasts. You will never be anything but top-heavy, she told herself, the pouter pigeon on whom no clothes look sleek. Short blond ringlets covered her head like a cap of silk. "Candy-assed kewpie doll," she said aloud. With that round face and those big, wide-set eyes, she looked like the dumb little kids who used to illustrate Campbell's soup ads.

The look had pleased Ned often enough, she remembered. Even now men's eyes followed her on London streets. At parties there were always some who hung about like stable flies. But Ned was not among them any more. Left behind. With the girls gone and time on her hands, she could see more clearly.

She supposed it had to do with sex. Most things did, or so the women's magazines assured her. Her own upbringing with four huge brothers had been medieval, based entirely on forbidding even the thought of sex. Her mother had been a tormented ray of light during that adolescent ache.

"Verne," she would say, "it's God's will that you grow up in a house full of men, in a camp full of them, too. The only way your father and I can draw a moment's peaceful breath is by knowing that our darling daughter is keeping herself pure in mind and pure in body even though she abides in the camp of temptation because your body, Verne, is a vessel of the Lord's, made for only one sacred purpose, to be fruitful and to multiply his children here on Earth."

The whole thing had sounded like a terrible chore to the teenage Laverne. But in OCS she met the other officer candidates, girls who hadn't had such a repressed childhood. They gave her a crash indoctrination course that emphasized the value of close proximity to male soldiers on those difficult days when one developed "hot slot."

From a chore, sex began to seem to Laverne more of a tax one had to pay one's body. It was with some relief, therefore, that she married Ned and soon realized there could be pleasure in the act.

Abruptly, she turned from the mirror and the sight of her naked body. She could feel the heat in her cheeks. She lay down across the cool bedsheets. Laverne had often wished to be one of those women who pick up "a stray piece of ass" and then discard it as a man would when it had served its purpose. But that was not possible. She and Ned had been joined in the eyes of God, who had blessed her womb both with pleasure and the fruit thereof. Who had now banished her from Ned's needs and desires. Had she done anything to deserve such punishment? Trying to understand this was driving her half crazy.

Not that she'd ever break down. General Krikowski's only daughter was just as tough as her old man. Okay, she wasn't getting much. But there was no way she would ever let it get the better of her. She needed no help, thank you, not from some "frank" discussion with her husband or those bold initiatives they recommended in the women's magazines.

She knew that being unwilling to disclose any of this to him kept it smoldering. It was another source of worry to Laverne that her daughters would be contaminated by the tension, one good reason to have sent them home. There were very short gaps between the four girls' ages. Lou Ann was eighteen, while the youngest, Sally, was nearly fifteen. In Laverne's guilt she associated her liking for sex with a fecundity she found equally puzzling. Ned had only to touch her in those days and she conceived.

It had always seemed odd to Laverne that after Sally, when she stopped conceiving, Ned had never wondered why. Laverne would never confess that she'd had a tubal ligation. She had taken herself off the child-bearing roster for good but not once had a smart man like Ned even bothered to wonder about this new sin she'd committed.

Men.

Luckily her girls were under their grandparents' iron control at Camp Liberty, the wilderness community General Krikowski and his friends had established back home. There would always be men sniffing around her girls, Laverne realized, the way they continued to nose around her. But thank God Camp Liberty was a controlled environment. Thank God it was her father who controlled it.

Laverne rolled over on her back and stared at the bedroom ceiling. She could picture herself suddenly with Ned's tough, wiry body pinning her down as they made love. It was the only way she could enjoy it. He'd talked to her of other things, other things they could do for each other. She wouldn't hear of it. It was something a man might know about—typical of them, wasn't it, to pig up something God had invented?—but she wanted no part of it.

Men.

Downstairs, the doorbell rang. Pulling on a pale gray silk dressing gown that actually belonged to Ned, she padded downstairs in bare feet and switched on the hidden TV camera and speaker that monitored the entrance.

"Yes, what is it?"

The man at the door turned away from the TV lens but not before Laverne could see that he was taller and somewhat blonder and younger than the man who normally delivered the mail.

"Post," the man said, his face virtually invisible. "It's a package too large for the slot."

She watched him closely, playing back in her mind the sound of the word "large," almost like that tree called the larch.

"Never mind. Just leave it on the doorstep."

He hesitated. "Very well." He stooped out of sight; when he reappeared on the TV screen, he was walking quickly away from the house, face still hidden, carrying a small package. He had no cloth bag slung over his shoulder, as British postmen usually did.

So it was without too much surprise that, when she edged the heavily locked front door open, she found no package on the step. Nor had any other mail been delivered.

She relocked the front door and punched up a number on the telephone in the entrance hall. The British rapid double-ring sounded in her ear. After the eighth ring Ned's assistant, Moe Chamoun, picked up. "Defense attaché's office."

"Moe, Laverne French. Ned there?"

"Not at the moment."

"Ask him to call when he's clear. Urgent."

"Can I help?"

She had started to hang up, but could hear Moe's voice. "What's that?"

"I said 'Don't be a hero, Laverne.' Can I help?"

"What gives you the idea—?"

"Your voice. It's got a itty-bitty shake to it."

"That's just the nearness of you," Laverne said and hung up.

Smartass Lebanese bastard. What was the U.S. Army coming to letting handkerchief-heads into the intelligence cadres? Laverne pulled Ned's bathrobe tighter around her waist and padded down a flight of stairs to the cellar. The previous tenant, another embassy spook, had installed a fifty-foot target range, well-insulated to avoid disturbing the neighbors. Laverne twirled the dials on a wall safe and removed the .38 Colt Police Positive six-shot. She cupped mufflike protectors over her ears, loaded the weapon, and switched on the range lights.

Holding the butt in her right hand, with her left cupping the right for support, she hit her stance and carefully squeezed off one shot. Her bare toes dug into the carpet.

The .38 slug tore the heart out of the bull's-eye. Laverne paused, smiled grimly, and put five more bullets through the same tiny hole.

That was close, Bert thought as he walked away from French's house, rounded a corner and, once out of sight, ran two streets to the east. He ripped the address panel off the dummy package and dropped it into a nearby trash bin. It had served its purpose. Risky or not, it had been the only way to make sure of the colonel's entrance defense system. He entered the vestibule of a narrow terrace house that had been cut up into small bed-sit flats. Khefte had rented a place on the top floor with access to the roof.

Although he was contemptuous of French's techniques, Bert remained grudgingly wary of the man as his chief opponent. As he climbed the stairs, he could hear behind him the gradual increase in morning traffic coming down from Wellington Road. It grew louder, more resonant with the strangled howl of heavy trucks and angry red buses.

In the distance, almost overpowered by mounting traffic noises, he could hear the faint cry of the muezzin from the Great Mosque, the first of the day's five calls to prayer. Meanwhile, the great Satan's workweek had begun, as always with a throbbing rush and roar, purposeless hurtling toward destruction, chaos, and death.

He smiled but would have been startled, as he stood on the staircase, if he had seen himself in a mirror. His small face, tanned by desert sun to the same color as those of his Arab comrades in arms, looked almost kindly. Many an Islamic brother had even taken it, by mistake, as a confession of weakness.

It was not. Bert remained, as always, the professional, nerveless and as tough as the hobbed soles of the hiking boots he wore. He continued mounting the stairway, thinking of Colonel French. To Bert and his comrade co-leader, Khefte, French had shown a dazzling variety of exits and entrances, departure times, costumes, vehicles. It had been quite amusing, a playlet entitled "One Hundred Ways to Keep Terrorists Guessing."

The morning roar kept rising in intensity, as if produced by some leviathan tape recording through loudspeakers the size of whales. Bert blinked. The images had come into his mind without his bidding. Big-city stress—he had been in London a month now—always filled his head with these anarchic snapshots.

He could remember, as a child in Stuttgart, playing beside the throb of traffic in empty, weed-grown lots left from the bombing raids of the war. This was before they rebuilt the city into its present commercialized ring maze designed to lure shoppers ever deeper into a pirate's cavern of booty from which there was no release except by overbuying.

He blinked again. Images, words, pictures in his head which he had not asked for. Or perhaps it was the tension of being up against another professional, Ned French. Why, they even looked alike, Bert and the American: the perfect nondescript look, muscular, slight of frame but not of height, with faces that would instantly blend to invisibility in any European city.

Bert had reached the top floor. He paused before the left-hand door and knocked twice, paused, then once. He waited. For such a young man, not yet thirty years of age, Bert waited with the patience of an inanimate object, a valley, a hill. While he waited, he slowly, carefully tore into small bits the address panel of the fake parcel. In time he could hear someone moving behind the door.

"Yes?" Khefte's voice, wary as always.

"*Inshallah.*"

Several of the locks clicked open but when the door edged ajar a heavy forged-steel chain still secured it inside. Khefte's tan eyes were the shiny color of young seal pelt. He undid the chain and Bert slipped past him into the room. Khefte was shorter than Bert, and very clearly Arabic, but there was something about him, a handsome look that made him stand out even when he least wanted to. Perhaps it was the hawk's nose, or the sharp horizontal blades of his cheekbones.

"Your suicide mission is completed?" he asked with sarcasm.

"Do not jest, my brother."

Khefte stifled his next remark, turned his attention to the clipboard in his hand and then looked back at Bert. "I, too, have returned from a mission," he said in quiet, guttural Arabic. "I have made a new weapons inventory. The arsenal grows."

Bert made a peculiar face, as if tasting something he wanted to spit out. "It occurred to me . . ." He broke off for a moment, then went on: "Some of the equipment is used, liberated. Even the ammunition is suspect in the sense that it may have been badly stored. How to test all this? We cannot go into battle with faulty weapons."

"We have before," Khefte assured him smoothly. "None of us have elected security, oh, brother. All of us have placed our worthless bodies in the hand of Allah."

"*Mektoub,*" Bert agreed. "But Khefte, in what holy book is it written that we cannot use our own brains in the name of Allah? I propose we remove samplings of matériel to one of the rural safe houses and test our weapons there."

Khefte was silent for a long moment. In the distance both men could hear someone whistling on another floor of the house.

"It is wisdom," Khefte agreed then. "We shall send Mamoud and Merak. It will be far safer than your adventure this morning with Satan's whore. Do you fancy her?"

Bert grinned. "Hear him. Hear one who himself traffics with she-devils."

"The colonel still acts out his daily charades?" Khefte asked.

"Since he returns each evening to the sex-mannequin he calls his wife, all such charades are useless. You have observed that his bedroom faces to the rear?"

"From our roof I have studied it."

"How long would it take two brothers with a bipod launcher to send a shaped seven-kilo charge two hundred meters through French's bed-room window?"

The look on Khefte's face was sheer joy. He clapped his hands to-gether. "Thus do we observe the truth of the Prophet's teaching. In the affairs of men, women are ever the intruder. See how two brothers work hand in hand when no woman comes between them?"

Solemnly, the men embraced each other with one fierce hug. They paused, drew back, looked into each other's eyes and embraced a second time, even more fiercely.

Bert's arms tightened for a moment around Khefte's muscular shoul-ders. *Heute*, London, he thought, *Morgen die ganze Welt*.

A shiver seemed to wrack his own shoulders for a chilling instant. The tremor was so powerful that Bert felt perhaps Khefte had also shud-dered in the same second. They were truly brothers, blood brothers.

"Today, London," Bert repeated in Arabic as he let Khefte out of his embrace, "tomorrow the entire world."

Carefully, as always, he carried his handful of torn-up address panel to the bathroom, where he flushed the bits of paper down the toilet.

Leaving Connell's office, Ned glanced at his watch: seven forty. He shook it, glanced at an electric wall clock in the corridor that ran the length of the chancery. The true time was just before nine A.M. Obviously his watch had stopped when he'd tried to wreck the Mini Minor single-handed.

He paused, reviewing that moment of idiocy on everyone's part, the guilty driver for trying to run away, his own lunacy for thinking he could stop a moving car. But, damn it, you couldn't let people get away with things like that. Who knew how badly the jogger had been hurt? Ned's paranoia had produced no premonition for that question.

He glanced out of the corridor window that faced Grosvenor Square and noted that the Watcher had arrived.

That was Ned's name for him, a gangling man with a ravaged face, pocked by years of anxiety, who stood bareheaded on the greensward with tall placards bound to his front and back, like a sandwich board.

He had a grievance with the United States but it was hard to know its precise nature. The placards bore in red paint a very elongated U and S down the center. Against a white background blue letters on either side of the U and S formed this message:

NaUSea is
plaUSible when
devioUS men
abUSe the
trUSt of a
generoUS but
frUStrated
geniUS,
oblivioUS to
unjUSt
misUSe,
pioUS
blUSter and
avaricioUSness!
RoUSing
applaUSe
mUSt be
thrUSt on the
crUShing of
rapacioUS
injUStice and
tenacioUS
lUSt!

As he stood there puzzling over the Watcher's message as he had often done before, Ned was distracted by the sound of the great chancery building starting up on a Monday. He'd never mentioned this to anyone, nor would he except perhaps to Jane, but the immense building produced a sound of its own based on a faint hum from the air conditioning, an uneven up and down of voices behind doors, the papery scratching of muted business machines, typewriters, and a faraway, almost astral shimmer created by electronic beeps and buzzes from computers, fax machines, telephones, and the like. You had to stand still and listen hard. The sound was there, now, right now.

On Mondays, once everybody was in his or her own office handling the flood of work that had built up over the weekend, Ned had the habit of wandering here and there, nodding hello, getting the feel of the vast enterprise.

This morning, because of the problem Connell had handed him, there wasn't time for a leisurely tour. Still, French had come to depend on getting that Monday reading. He didn't pretend to be psychic, but he trusted the feel more than he trusted his whole in basket of confidential reports.

This morning, being in a rush, he by-passed Administrative, one of the six sections into which the embassy was divided. There they staffed and equipped the operation, handled finances, transport, personnel, and the security of the building, together with its communications links. It was from Administrative that the security chief, Karl Follett, was missing, on home leave.

The Public Affairs Section he also avoided this morning. After a weekend spate of newspapers and magazines they would all be busy clipping articles. The section worked with news media, operated educational exchange programs, and also sponsored lectures and conferences. It maintained a reference library for those doing research on American politics and current events.

Because they were the heaviest sections in terms of policy, there was no way to make quick social calls on people in the Political Section or the section that handled economic and commercial affairs. Too much went on in these divisions for a fast drop-in chat. The reports they developed and the projects they organized would eventually find their way across his desk in draft form. He could wait.

Some time today, Ned reminded himself, he had to make his routine check on the Internal Revenue Service people, and with the boys who did bank examinations and handled customs. They were the only branches of Economic and Commercial whose work remained confidential and, therefore, of perpetual interest to Ned French.

That left the Consular Section, the one most outsiders dealt with. Through its three branches it issued passports, registered births and deaths of U.S. citizens, notarized documents, gave out voting information, and represented such government services as Social Security and Veterans Administration. If you were a Brit visiting the U.S. you had to get your visa from Consular. Sheltered under this vast umbrella, too, were a few FBI-niks from Justice, quietly doing their thing. The entire operation was handled by the counselor for consular services, a tall slender brunette named Jane Weil.

Ned walked past her secretary and stood in the open doorway of Jane's office. It was a corner room that provided two views of Grosvenor Square outside and the morning throng of office workers strolling to their desks all over this part of Mayfair.

Jane looked up from her desk, keeping her face blank. Knowing her secretary was watching both of them, Ned stayed in the doorway. Jane's hair, long and blue-black as a Sioux maiden's, had been pulled into a loose kind of topknot that kept it under control. "That guest list," she said then. "My God."

He stared glumly at her. "How long did she expect to keep it a secret from us?"

"It's my fault, Ned. I should have insisted she—"

With a very faint movement of his head, he indicated the presence behind him of her secretary, listening to everything. Jane's voice stopped abruptly. "Is it going to be a big problem?" she finished somewhat lamely.

"There's a briefing in the auditorium at noon. Can you make it?"

"Of course."

Shielding his hand from the secretary behind him, Ned pointed first at Jane and then at himself. "It may last a while. We may miss lunch."

"I understand."

His face still hidden from the secretary, Ned gave Jane Weil a big grin. "Thanks for your cooperation," he said, then turned and left.

Only one of the embassy sections remained to be visited. It was his own, the Defense Section, which was officially responsible for liaison with the British and American military commands in Britain. Traditionally, it was also the haven for spooks like Ned. But before he got to his office, he had one other call to make.

The sign on the basement office door read MAINTENANCE ENGINEERING, although it was nowhere near the Administrative Section's office. Ned opened the door to a tiny anteroom equipped for a secretary but always without one. He rapped on the inner door. "Mr. Parkins?"

He could hear strong, solid footsteps behind the door. A moment later the lock clicked twice and the door opened no more than an inch while a pale gray eye regarded him for a moment.

"Oh, it's you. Good morning, Colonel."

The door swung open. P.J.R. Parkins was a good ten years older than Ned and an inch or so taller, well over six feet of oaklike trunk, thick but erect. His close-cut iron-gray hair covered a narrow head with an almost hooked nose and one of those Punch-like chins that, as Parkins often said, "one could hang a lantern on."

Ned eyed the man warily, remembering that he was the highest-ranking British subject on the payroll, fittingly enough, since in this locked back room with its tools and coils of wires and electronic black boxes, Parkins was in charge of maintaining the chancery's vast maze of air, electric, telephone, and computer conduits.

"In the U.S.," Ned began somewhat slowly, "the law takes a dim view of people leaving the scene of an accident. The same here?"

Parkins's strong, almost unlined face looked suitably oaken and non-committal. "So I'm given to believe."

"But," French pressed on, "might it depend on the seriousness of the accident, whether or not the authorities could sort of turn a blind eye?"

Parkins's face wrinkled into horizontal lines of query but he said nothing with the practiced patience of someone used to waiting. But so was Ned. The silence grew.

"I don't understand, Colonel," Parkins finally said, most unwillingly.

"At about half past seven this morning, on Baker Street just north of Marylebone, a motorist knocked a runner sprawling. I happened to see it but, being late, didn't stop. I'm—"

"Gotcher," Parkins snapped. "Leave it with me, Colonel."

"No names."

Parkins's right eyelid slowly lowered. "No names."

Ned made his way up a flight of stairs to his own office but paused to knock at the door next to his. After a moment Moe Chamoun opened the door: "You okay?"

"Will you stop asking me that?"

"Your knees . . ."

"Get me the large-scale maps of Winfield House and grounds. And whatever architect's plans there are, aerial photographs."

"What's up?"

"As usual, we're in deep shit."

Chamoun grinned. "In other words, no time to think."

"Thinking is for sissies. A he-man just starts slugging."

"Our John Wayne posture."

"Right. And naturally, on the—"

"Double."

Ned unlocked his office and sat down at his desk. He put his shell-shocked watch in his desk drawer and took out a newer one, of the digital variety, that his oldest daughter had bought him. He set the time and strapped on the watch.

He had almost the same two-sided view of the square as Jane had, a floor above him. Morning auto traffic tore around Grosvenor Square at its usual breakneck speed. He found himself wondering if Jane was watching it. Had she understood that sign-language? They'd been having lunchtime rendezvous for some weeks but always on the spur of the moment.

Aleatory. Ned sat for a long moment listening to the almost subliminal sounds of the chancery. Even the vibrations of outside traffic couldn't diffuse the familiar, intimate murmur of the great building at work around him.

Then Chamoun came in with maps and the day began in earnest.

2

To Jane Weil the "ten-o'clock" was the core of chancery routine. Perhaps a dozen people, section heads or their deputies and a few wild cards like Ned French or the odd IRS agent, would gather in this narrow room on the penthouse floor.

She glanced around the room, brightly lighted against the dull London morning that, through an expanse of windows, seemed more likely to suck light out than let it in. Anspacher, from Political, sat alone on a divan meant for three. Since he was shorter than Jane and held less prestigious academic degrees, Anspacher avoided close proximity, which was why Jane now chose to sit down beside him.

"Mondays," Anspacher muttered in a pinched voice, his graceless version of "hello."

Jane caught his close-set eyes glancing sideways at her. "And a cheery good morning to you, too," she replied drily. She crossed her long legs with a crisp electrical crackle of skirt and slip.

Across the blue-gray carpet, sprawled in a beige leather armchair, Bill Voss from Commercial gave them the tormented frown produced by a hangover. "Let's keep it down to a college yell. Some of us are dying."

Before Jane could reply, Royce Connell entered, nodded briefly in several directions, and sat down. "Mary?"

The ten-o'clock began with a summary of news from Mary Constantine of Public Affairs. On Mondays, Jane knew, this could use up half the thirty minutes Royce allotted for the meeting. She stopped listening to Mary's voice, rattling off at breakneck speed the weekend's news as reported in British television and press. Instead Jane watched Bill Voss, his eyes closed in a permanent wince.

Bill was AA and thus, assuredly, not hung over. But we're all walking wounded, Jane told herself. It's as if we'd all been hitting the bottle since last Friday and were now paying the price.

". . . interview with Frank Sinatra," Mary was saying, "but it ended abruptly when they raised the usual Mafia-connection charge and Sinatra walked out. However, in *The Times*, we . . ."

The weekend was meant for recovery, Jane thought, from the stress of the workweek. But Americans never forsook stress on weekends as the British did. The higher level of weekday commitment was that much harder to shake off on weekends. Relaxation took as much effort as hard work. So by Monday morning they were all double-stressed by working hard at relaxing.

". . . remind you again that Wednesday, eleven A.M.," Gus Heflin of Administrative was telling them, "we have the regular fire drill and evac situation. Please make a note that . . ."

Bill Voss frowned tiredly at her, aware that she had been staring at him. He shifted uneasily in his chair as if to say: "Stop molesting the animals."

". . . been asked to tell you," Royce Connell said, "that any staff requisitioned for the noon security briefing should also be freed up for the rest of the week. They'll be back on normal section roster next Monday."

"How come?" Voss asked.

"It's a security detail for the Sunday garden party at Winfield," Connell explained.

"So?"

"See me after the meeting, Bill."

"Oh." Voss settled back with a nobody-tells-me-anything look. Jane saw that several other people wore the same expression.

So no one had yet been clued into Sunday's problems. Jane sat up straight on the divan with such force that Anspacher glanced at her in some alarm. If section heads and deputies weren't meant to know, Jane asked herself, who was?

". . . additional possibilities of anti-American demos over the July Fourth weekend," Max Grieves, of her own section, was telling them.

Max's bland job description assigned him to the Justice Department without actually pinning an FBI badge on his chest.

". . . shredders cleared of refuse every day and twice on Fridays. This means . . ."

Voices droned on. Nobody seemed "with" this particular ten-o'clock. No one took notes except Mary Constantine, who liked to shield with a notebook her ordinary breasts which, she had once confided to Jane, she felt were the focus of constant radiological scan by every male in the room. Mary's fantasy probably made no sense, Jane reflected. But if women didn't fantasize, men would be in a sorry state.

Again she sat abruptly upright, disturbing Anspacher's collegiate pose of rumination. At some earlier time in his career he had worked as an academic. He still clung to the boat-neck sweater over shirt and tie, the patched jacket pockets, and the fiercely drilled burn-holes of the pipe smoker.

But wasn't it true, Jane asked herself, that in lateral thinking—which women employed—almost anything was possible, right out of the blue? Thus the plainest man could be ruggedly handsome, the most obese jolly-plump, the nastiest merely nursing a sore paw. Whereas, Jane reminded herself, in male linear thinking, you could only go to B from A and thence in a straight line to C. No wild flight of fancy could break into that iron chain of cause and effect.

It was linear thinking that led devious men like Ned to imagining the minds of their opponents in order to thwart them. It was lateral thinking that led women like Jane to believe that a man like Ned was fully accessible to her, fully detached from his wife and available to make a new life with another woman, moreover, one in his own embassy.

Sitting in this hotbed of stress hangovers, Jane felt a sudden lift in her heart, as if through the London murk a single brilliant pencil of sunlight had touched her like the dazzling forefinger of God almighty. Look at them, she thought, hapless workaholics, their gray routines as leaden as the London sky. Whereas she had a secret garden where she was someone special, lurid, and never gray. The deep pleasure, after years of leaden routine, in something scarlet and dangerous.

"In any event," Connell told them all, "we're practically finished unless one of you has something more?"

He glanced inquiringly around the room, his handsome face all attention and interest.

Oh, yes, Jane told him in utter silence, one of us has something much more. It's the ultimate game of secrets, dear Royce.

She got to her feet, waved to Connell, and left the room, moving with such lightness that she had almost no notion of having gone back to her corner office on a lower floor.

People had to make an appointment to see Jane Weil, unless they happened to be Ned French. The people in her own section had to book meetings with her well in advance. It was unusual, however, for people from two different branches of the section to ask for a joint appointment, her first this Monday. Jane watched the two men for a moment.

One, Gary Leyland, had been her chief passport officer for the past year, a tall, elderly New Englander who still carried around—with a certain stubborn pride—a very strong Maine accent. The other man, new to London, was Paul Vincent, a Californian whose pudgy face was permanently tanned. A lawyer like herself, but fresh out of Stanford, Paul was learning to handle the various legal problems American citizens brought to the section, including questions of citizenship, depositions, and extradition.

"It's this request for passport renewal," Leyland began. He held up a blue passport with its pages fanned open to show the nondescript face of a male.

"Which am I supposed to have, X-ray or telephoto vision?" Jane asked, careful to smile.

"Sorry. A Mr. James Frederick Weems claims he lost his passport shortly after arriving here some months ago. He has a managerial job with an American firm in London, so there's no work-permit problem."

Leyland stopped. Jane waited. Vincent fidgeted. "Do go on, Gary," Jane suggested pleasantly.

"Ay-uh." Leyland examined the passport in his hand as if he had never seen it, nor anything like it, in his entire life. "Y'see," he went on at last, almost unwillingly, "before we issue a new book we telex D.C. to confirm the name, date and location of birth, when issued. Claiming a lost passport is the oldest dodge in the world for having two passports."

"So they tell me," Jane remarked drily.

The older man abruptly realized he was addressing the wrong person and swung his skinny frame around on the sofa to face the young lawyer. "Anyway, back comes a telex from D.C. with a hold order. This bird is in some kind of stateside trouble." He popped the new passport into an inside pocket of his jacket as if permanently imprisoning it. "Which is where Mr. Vincent comes in."

Now the focus of all the attention in the room, the lawyer grinned unhappily, big black-rimmed Porsche spectacles shooting off nervous sparks of reflected overhead light. He pushed them back up on his pudgy nose.

"It's not an extradition order yet," he began in midstream. "It's a preliminary search-and-locate. Some upcoming questions from the SEC is what it looks like."

"Looks like?" Jane asked. "Is that all we know?"

"This Weems is involved in some offshore mutual funds that went sour a year or two ago. SEC is tracking him. Which sort of makes you kind of understand his need for two or more passports."

A nervous giggle escaped him, as if he had said something hilarious. Jane realized she must in some way be intimidating this normally laid-back young man. She smiled at him, hoping that she wasn't encouraging any more feeble witticisms. Then, to Leyland. "Gary, can we get this Weems fellow in for a talk?"

"Out of town right now." Leyland thought for a moment. "We've left messages. Not too many in case we scare our bird away."

"But we know where to lay hands on him?"

"Ay-uh."

"Fine. Your time's too valuable for any more of this," she told the older man. "Let Paul liaise this with Justice. Meanwhile keep the new passport in your wall safe. I can't think of a surer way to smoke Weems out."

In diplomatic circles, E. Lawrence Rand was never introduced by title. This was because his title was station head, meaning he headed the Company's Station London operations or, in everyday terms, ran the local CIA. Of course Larry Rand seldom attended diplomatic functions, being sensitive about his short height and the fact that he looked rather like a Mickey Rooney cookie that had spoiled in the oven.

He glared at the telephone as he waited to be connected with Connell. "Rand here," he started without social preliminary. "Are you for real? Putting Ned French in charge of July Fourth security? There are such things as channels, you know."

"In this case," Connell said coldly, "they flow from me. Any complaints, put them in writing."

"Son of a bitch!" Rand yelped. But he had first depressed the button on his phone, cutting off the conversation. Connell was untouchable at the moment, he mused, but French wasn't. There was only one way to teach a faggot like Connell a lesson. If, by the time the garden party ended, there'd be blood all over the place, Rand would make damned sure some of it was French's.

3

————⟨◆⟩————

At ten A.M., having worked out preliminary plans for Winfield House security, Ned sent his assistant back to his desk to prepare for the noon briefing. Chamoun locked himself into his office and began arranging maps and plans for use with an opaque projector. When Ned French's private phone rang unanswered, therefore, he had to unlock his own and Ned's door before picking it up.

After he finished talking with Laverne French, he scribbled a note on his boss's desk pad and paused to survey Grosvenor Square's last straggling tide of office workers arriving late for their Monday start. Chamoun hadn't been in Britain long, but he already knew there was rarely any point on a Monday in calling people at their office before eleven A.M. or after lunch on a Friday. They simply wouldn't be there.

Captain Maurice Chamoun was far more alert to nuances than other officers his age. The rest of the first lieutenants and captains who had been seconded during the 1980s into embassy intelligence work were the new breed that talked flip, put their feet up on desks, and smoked pot on the sly.

It would never occur to Chamoun, for example, to answer his boss's private line except that Ned had so authorized him. Nor would he have called Laverne anything but "Mrs. French" if she hadn't begun by calling him Moe. These niceties were perhaps not part of a typical Sandusky,

Ohio, upbringing any longer, but in the Chamoun household they had been holy writ.

Ibrahim Chamoun had not exactly fled Beirut in the early 1960s, before it blew apart. But he had not hesitated a moment when his childless uncle, who ran a small Sandusky carpet shop, had offered to make him a partner if he emigrated.

There followed in rapid succession the birth of his son Maurice, two daughters, and eleven more carpet shops in the greater Sandusky area. Uncle Laib had retired. Ibrahim ran the show, served as Chamber of Commerce president and vestryman in the Methodist church, and awaited the day when Maurice would graduate from Western Reserve and assume his rightful role as second in command.

Captain Chamoun closed the door to Ned's office and entered his own one-window room next to it, locking his door as well. He switched on his small desk radio to monitor the next news broadcast. Privacy was a cardinal rule in intelligence work, but two locked doors and a playing radio were also articles of Chamoun's own personal faith. They went with the role he knew fate had dealt him.

He had no illusions that his well-tailored uniform, or the captain's double silver bars on his shoulders, or the discreet row of peacetime ribbons made him a part of a team. He had never been part of anybody's team. His choice of the military/diplomatic/espionage life had been dictated by two motives, one clear, one obscure.

The clearest was to avoid spending the rest of his life flinging Axminsters down before suburban housewives and volubly marveling at the rich thickness of sleazo polystyrene. The obscure reason remained . . . obscure. Not to Chamoun, but to anyone else, even to one who had studied him at some length, as Ned French had.

If Chamoun talked freely to anyone it would be to Ned, whom he counted as his only friend in the service. They had first met in the Rome embassy, not in Bonn, which had been Ned's most recent assignment before London. Rome, with its rich stew of ultraleft atrocities, neofascist massacres, and routine bureaucratic swindling, had brought the two men close together. Speaking freely as a friend to a friend, Chamoun had once referred glancingly to the obscure reason that propelled him. "Being the only Lebanese in Sandusky," he'd said, but never finished.

"Perennial outsider, huh?" Ned had responded.

Chamoun had said no more. Ned had hit it the first time. The feeling of being an outsider would never show up in a normal intelligence vetting.

Although Ned might make something of that trip he'd taken in 1980 on graduating from Western Reserve. Instead of starting work that June in the main store, Chamoun had scraped together his private savings and gone to the one place on earth where he knew he could never be an outsider.

Lebanon.

The irrational lunacy of this urge was apparent the moment he landed at Beirut Airport to be pinned down by crossfire between Druse and Phalangist militiamen. After that, however, things got easier. He walked the bullet-pocked streets of the capital, his slender body, dark coloring, and ripe-olive eyes blending smoothly into the background. His command of Arabic was still that of a beginner, based mostly on listening to his mother and father when they didn't want the children to understand them. Nevertheless, the accent was right.

Or so his Great-Aunt Chana assured him. She had also acquainted him with the family secret. In Sandusky, Ohio, where Uncle Laib had been a pillar of the Methodist Church and Ibrahim had succeeded him, the Chamouns were model Christians. In Beirut they were Jews.

"And here there is no chance of converting," Chana assured him. "People's memories are too long. Here, once a Jew always a Jew, Moisheleh."

He found himself nodding back to her. "And once a Jew," he added, "forever an outsider." So much for Lebanon.

There was a knock at his door. Chamoun looked startled, an animal discovered by hunters. Then, wary as a forest creature blending into the background again, he moved to the door. "Who is it?"

"Open up," Ned French demanded.

Chamoun unlocked the door, but not in a hurry. "Sorry, Ned, but this stuff on my desk . . ."

French surveyed the maps. "Quite right. No, leave the radio on. That message from Laverne. What's so urgent?"

"She wouldn't say."

"Then she'll just have to wait," Ned snapped. Chamoun could see that Ned immediately regretted the sharpness of his tone. Sighing unhappily, his boss sat down on top of Chamoun's desk. "Laverne's the perfect army wife," he said then. "Dear God, does that sound like an epitaph?"

When Chamoun said absolutely nothing, Ned looked up at him. "Did Peter Parkins call?"

"No."

French tried to soothe himself by slowly running his hand across the lower half of his face. "I'm not having much luck wheedling section heads for security people to help with the Sunday clambake. A couple of Feebies and one Customs guy, but the pickings are lean."

Chamoun made an "I'm sorry" face. He knew it was startling, coming out of his usual deadpan look. His lean cheeks and thin mouth gave him a perpetually grave expression that some considered ironic. It was handsome in a Mediterranean way, given to very finely graded contrasts of mood that most people read as irony. It was, Chamoun was aware, an outsider's face, shuttered so as to become unreadable. Except, perhaps, to Ned French.

"Any ideas?" Ned prodded.

"You've notified the Company, of course," Chamoun suggested.

"Of course not." His boss's voice had a faintly acid ring to it. "Those monkeys can find it out for themselves."

"But you have to take the lead," Chamoun pointed out, "if only to make sure Larry Rand doesn't."

This time Ned French's sigh came from much deeper inside him. "Does the Company ever share?"

"Sure, if you bend their arm backward about ninety degrees."

Ned grinned evilly. "And I do need troops." He reached for Chamoun's phone. "Put me on scrambler when I signal you."

In his huge, locked office, filled with electronic equipment and tools, P. J. R. Parkins sat reading a morning newspaper. His oak-firm back, unyielding, made it unseemly for him to bend over his workbench, so he held the paper up in front of him, as if he were nearsighted. As a matter of fact, at age fifty-two, Parkins's eyes still got along without spectacles and missed very little.

His telephone gave a single chirrup and fell silent. Parkins put down the newspaper, swung about in his chair, and jacked a headphone cord into one of several outlets on an ordinary black box. He moved with delicate precision, big fingers unhurried but perfectly targeted. He adjusted two dials and started a tape recorder.

Nice wheeze, Parkins thought. The moment anyone in the building switched a call onto scrambler, Parkins's phone would sound once, alerting him. It wasn't a difficult circuit to arrange because there weren't really that many scramblers throughout the Chancery and most were antiquated models, purely electromechanical, with simple settings, not state-of-the-art computers with a capacity for millions of variations.

". . . how many people you can spare?" Colonel French's voice, unscrambled, was asking.

"I don't play no-win games," the other voice responded after a moment. Parkins recognized it as belonging to E. Lawrence Rand, whom he had reason to believe headed Station London for the C.I.A.

"Larry, that's defeatist."

"Don't shit me, Ned. We're talking realistic projection. Cancel the party. Outbreak of AIDS, herpes, mumps. Use your imagination."

"Will you listen to what's talking shit?" French snapped.

Parkins grinned. He loved nothing better than head-on collisions among the Indian chiefs who ran the Yanks' war parties. From such confrontations a man could learn a lot.

"It's no-win, Ned. Call an abort."

"Too late."

"Never too late," Rand objected. "A tranquilizer dart ought to cool off dear Pandora. Simplest thing in the world."

"Now I know who wanted to waste Castro with an exploding cigar. You people are too high-tech to be believed. Look, I'm offering champagne, smoked salmon, and, later on, real Tennessee barbecued pork. Send me some lads and lassies."

"Serving pork? Clever. That'll keep away the Muslims *and* the Jews."

"Larry," Ned said, "do I have to pull rank?"

"What rank? I don't answer to you, Colonel."

To Parkins, there seemed to be a special note of grievance in Rand's voice, an unusually nasty overtone. It occurred to Parkins that perhaps the usual intraservice jealousy had been stirred up.

"Larry, try not to be so impossible," Colonel French was saying. "I didn't ask for this assignment. It was wished on me, along with Exdrec 103."

Rand's tone was barely civil: "You can take your exdrecs and shove 'em up your ass, Ned. They only apply to shit-eating pogues in the foreign service anyway. They mean less than nothing to me."

"God, you are a fathead," French burst out.

"Off my back, soldier boy."

"Do I have to tell you," French persisted, trying to keep his voice at a moderate level, "how close the Fulmers are to the president? How eager they are to expedite 103 to the letter? What do you want, Larry, a verbal order direct from the White House? Because if you keep on this tack, that's just what I'll arrange for you."

"Amateurs," Rand muttered. "The whole goddamned service is rid-

dled with loony-bird amateurs. When is the White House going to learn
that it can't—" He stopped himself.

"Let's hear it, Larry."

Rand took so long responding that Parkins began to wonder if his
descrambling apparatus was still in order. "I can give you eight men and
five women," he said at last. "But you have to prom—"

"Have them over here at noon today," Ned cut in brusquely. "We're
scheduling our first briefing. Oh, and thanks, Larry, for the Company's
usual helpful cooperation." He hung up.

Parkins broke down the circuit, rewound the tape, and marked the
cassette with an alphanumeric caption. He picked up his telephone and
punched an inside number.

"Message Center."

"Parkins here. Send me a runner, will you, lad? Moorcock if he's
free."

Parkins scribbled a note which he wrapped around the tape cassette
and held in place with a plain rubber band. Someone knocked on the
locked door that separated Parkins's inner office from the anteroom.
Parkins got up to let in a messenger "boy" of perhaps thirty.

"Morning, Major Parkins."

"Moorcock, you silly sod."

"*Mister* Parkins, sir, begging your pardon."

"Take this over to 5."

Once the messenger had left, Parkins made a call on his own outside
line. A man's thick Scottish voice said "Yas?"

"Sending something over, Jock."

"What now?" the man asked irritably.

Parkins settled back in his chair. "What's the gen on a traffic accident
this morning, Baker off Marylebone, about seven thirty, auto versus
pedestrian?"

"Annythin' else?" the Scotsman asked with heavy sarcasm.

"The latest flap over here. The silly buggers have bit off more than
they can chew." P. J. R. Parkins relaxed for a nice secure natter on
perhaps the only outside line in the entire embassy that he hadn't personally bugged.

Jane Weil sat at the back of the small auditorium in the basement of
the chancery building on Grosvenor Square.

At 12:01 Chamoun locked the auditorium doors and drew the curtains
of windows that looked out not on the lush green of the square but on

an airshaft that gave only faint light to the room. Even this was cut off now.

The men and women sitting in darkness—perhaps thirty of them, Jane guessed—were silhouetted against a giant screen behind Ned, who was standing at the podium. Chamoun moved to an opaque projector at the back of the room near Jane. He switched on a brilliant square of light. A blowup aerial view of Winfield House and its grounds appeared on the screen behind Ned.

Jane tried to make out Ned's silhouetted profile. She felt an ache in her throat that swallowing would not ease. "It's gotta be love," she repeated silently from the words of the old Rodgers and Hart song, "it isn't appendicitis."

She seemed to curl further in on herself, like a long, lean, lithe black cat intent on making itself into a kitten. At the podium Ned's voice droned on, spinning out plans. The timbre of his dry Midwest voice affected her, the tone and the rhythm. The meaning could have been gibberish. Probably was, Jane thought.

She had no real business being here. Security wasn't part of her brief. But Royce Connell had asked her to oversee Mrs. Fulmer's activities and she had spectacularly failed to do so. Failed so miserably, Jane reminded herself, that Ned and this whole crew were facing an impossibly difficult job.

No one had accused Jane of failure, least of all Royce, who could if he chose reduce her to tears with a frown. If you had asked Jane Weil at any time in the past two years where her loyalties, her concern, her emotional allegiance—everything but the physical expression of her love—was placed, she would have confessed that she had a full-blown schoolgirl crush on Royce Connell. Didn't everybody?

Now what she felt for Royce seemed only a minor warmth compared to the fire that ran through her. And Ned's feeling for her, she knew, oh, yes, absolutely as fiery.

She made a wry face and tried to concentrate on what Ned was saying. "If only we had perimeter fencing of twelve-foot reinforced Cyclone net," he told the people in the auditorium, pointing to a line of shadow on the screen. "But what we have instead is some kind of vertical steel fluting, stuck together here and there and about as impenetrable as a venetian blind. With that in mind . . ."

Perversely, Jane began to enjoy the hideously uncomfortable position love had landed her in. She found herself wondering if this risk-taking was what happened to women as they entered their late thirties. She had

worked hard. Her next assignment as a foreign service officer fully accredited and appointed by Congress would certainly be as consul in some
small country like Luxembourg, or the Alpes Maritimes section of France.
If she kept her nose clean, that is.

As long as she could stay what she was, plain Jane, hiding her slim
height with flats, her vivid gypsy coloring behind a librarian's preppy
eyeglasses, shirtwaist dresses, and subdued separates from the women's
department of Trippler or J. Press or L. L. Bean back home. She had
dressed no other way since her undergraduate days at Radcliffe and her
years at Harvard Law School.

Somehow she had managed to move upward in the foreign service
by hard, slogging work and no romantic entanglements. Some of this
advancement she owed to a secret "affirmative action" program within
the State Department, whereby the white, Anglo-Saxon Protestant elders
of the tribe allowed token members of other groups to rise from the ranks.
And Jane Weil, with her cum laude from law school, qualified not only
under the category of female, but also of Jewish. It meant she could
never be assigned to the UN or to an Arab country, but that left quite a
few other places.

Then why risk it all with Ned?

Not for the first time in recent weeks, Jane wished for someone to
confide in. She was the older daughter of a schoolteacher mother from
Brooklyn Heights who had married a cutter in the rag trade, expecting
a quiet life, only to watch her husband become the owner of factories
and even mills. Jane had been the model child in both the lean and the
luxurious years, always confiding in her mother. People had said they
were more like sisters since Jane's real sister, Emily, was so different in
every way. As Jane grew up dark and tall, Emmy became blonder and
more bouncy. Jane was the serious, studious girl. Em was the bubblehead,
interested mostly in boys.

It was true, Jane remembered now with nostalgia more than bitterness,
that anything confided to Em was like bouncing a squash ball off an
exceedingly hard corner wall: it rocketed back at top speed on an angle
so skewed it could take your head off.

In the Weil family, as in any other, the squeaky wheel got all the
grease. Emmy's increasingly more serious problems—men and drugs,
usually—drew most of her parents' unhappy attention and, later in life,
large chunks of money paid out to doctors, analysts, and then, sadly, to
institutions, drying-out farms, discreet homes for the prematurely weary.

Sitting in the auditorium now, Jane thought of the ne'er-do-well sister in whom she could never confide. Em would know all about what Jane was going through, wouldn't she? Em had paid her tuition in this particular university. In heartbreak she must, by now, have at least a teaching PhD.

". . . the canal here on the west gives a short run for an infantry-type assault," Ned was saying. "But modern technology being fully available to all, a remote-controlled smart missile can't be ruled out, heat-seeking or TV-monitored. Helicopter assault is another possibility. We're also talking mined kamikaze trucks crashing through perimeter defense or the use of self-destruct aircraft. However, here's . . ."

Jane seemed to shrink even further into her seat. She hated this, hated Ned being involved in it.

They'd reached their lethal rendezvous from different starting places. Ned had come up through the army, which had paid for everything, his master's degree in history and his doctorate in political science. But she had reached this moment via the civilian route, study, examinations, making oneself useful to male superiors who began by resenting her and ended by being her closest friends and protectors. Ned the man of war, she the woman of peace.

The irony was so strong it felt like a knife pressing against her breast. The menace was exciting, the two of them arriving from diametrically opposite points to this battleground they called a United States embassy.

". . . opportunity for ransom is perhaps unequaled in modern history," Ned went on. "To find gathered in one place some of the most expensive and profitable people on earth, each of them connected to some government, some newspaper, some political party, some corporation, some film or TV studio that can, and would, pay millions to save a life. These people . . ."

Jane stared hard at the plan projected on the screen. She knew it was Ned's business to think about the unthinkable and make sure it didn't happen. But surely no terrorist group would be so dazzled by the opportunity as to scratch together in less than a week the kind of tightly disciplined, closely coordinated force needed to take Winfield House and hold its guests hostage.

". . . case you're wondering who might have the nerve and the clout to try such a move," Ned told them, "we know of no single group that could mount such an offensive on such short notice and, by the laws of tactics and strategy, expect to win."

He paused and Jane could feel the tension in the room lessening at what sounded like good news.

"On the other hand," Ned added, "we know of no group of terrorists who has to date showed any inclination to obey the laws of tactics and strategy. We are dealing with people who habitually force their cause far beyond such laws. They have nothing to lose by doing so. They have everything to gain."

4

When Royce Connell took prominent visitors to lunch—diplomats, old friends, or members of the press—he preferred to meet them at a restaurant around the corner. He did not appreciate their arriving at his office. It commercialized the carefully cultivated atmosphere of hospitality.

Moreover, he did not appreciate their arriving at the very moment when his entire security force was mobilizing to fend off the threat of a possible disaster. But all of this was even more disconcerting when the luncheon guest happened to be Gillian Lamb.

God knew she was pretty enough, Royce told himself as he stood behind his desk staring with what he hoped was a benign gaze. Still in her early thirties, Gillian parted her long blond hair in the middle, schoolgirl fashion. It formed flaxen wings around a soft, vulnerable face with British cheeks of pale rose. Her intense eyes, tiger-tawny beneath heavy lids, gave her a smoldering Bette Davis look offset by deceptively gentle features.

Under this less-than-delighted stare Gillian seemed suddenly to wilt. "Darling Royce," she murmured in her bell-clear British voice, each consonant as sharp as broken glass, "have I offended you?"

"What?" Connell blinked, for him the outer limit of a show of surprise. Royce Connell was never surprised, at least not visibly, but life had lately dealt him such a steady battering of shocks that he had resorted to a kind of wincing blink to indicate displeasure. His job, now that he had almost reached the top, was providing less satisfaction and more anguish. Royce was one of those perhaps old-fashioned diplomats for whom peace and quiet were everything. To maintain these conditions, he would perform truly virtuoso feats of diplomacy, in the process making himself even more valuable to his country in a world grown increasingly tempest-tossed. But he could no longer pretend to enjoy it.

"Darling, you're positively glaring at me."

He blinked again, but this time produced his biggest and warmest smile, a smile that engulfed Gillian in a "you are the most important person in the world to me" hug.

"Tell me where you got wind of this, um, Scottish business?" he asked her.

Gillian had not wanted to save her unpleasant surprise for lunch at Gavroche. That would only spoil a good meal. One of her free-lance research people, a local gossip columnist, had phoned her this morning with the news that Ambassador Fulmer's hunting weekend with the Duke of Buchan had been in pursuit of deer . . . out of season.

"He's altogether a dodgy old bird, the duke. No kin to the Earl of Buchan, more of a free-lance pirate. The fact that they were the duke's deer on the duke's eighty thousand acres makes no difference. However," she assured Royce, "my main thrust will be the garden party. It's visual and, after all, TV's supposed to be a visual medium."

"Your entire crew will be at Winfield House?"

"Starting in a few days, to film all the preparations for Sunday."

The deputy chief of mission nearly blinked again, but restrained himself. The idea of Gillian Lamb's TV crew wandering around the rooms and grounds of Winfield House while Gillian dug deeper into some scandal about the ambassador shooting deer out of season, filled Connell with almost as much dread as the idea that the ambassador's wife had caused to be summoned next Sunday a collection of the world's highest-priced hostages.

What had gotten into State, approving the president's choice of this ambassador? Wasn't there a limit to how far up the diplomatic scale a rank amateur could reach by lavish outpourings of cash? Was the work of career diplomats like Royce to be forever sabotaged and made ridiculous by political payoffs each new president forced on State? London was not,

dear God, some backwater South American police state. One didn't
pension off heavy political contributors to London as one did to Tanzania
or Liechtenstein or Greenland. London . . .

Royce Connell frowned and sat down at his desk, avoiding Gillian
Lamb's inquiring gaze. Her great orange irises were like TV camera
lenses. London, he thought, is the trickiest posting on earth. Moscow is
a snap, next to London. Even the devious, egocentric, amoral atmosphere
of Paris was preferable to London. Some day Connell would prepare a
confidential report on London. Running an American embassy here was
ten times harder than in enemy territory. More rewarding, perhaps, in
social terms, and Royce did like his social life, as long as he could afford
it on his salary. Taking Gillian to lunch, for instance, was out of his
own pocket, not Uncle Sam's.

"Darling, you're miles away," Gillian was saying.

Royce nodded slowly. "I'm like anybody else," he said in a somber
tone. "I don't like bad news." He knew his face was much too serious-
looking, so he went on smoothly: "However, I do like the messenger to
be as pretty as you are."

"Don't think of me as a messenger, darling. Think of me as a pal.
An admirer, if you wish."

"And I," he responded gallantly, "of you."

Gillian sat there for a moment in silence, wondering how much bad
news he could absorb in one take. "As a pal," she went on in a quicker
voice, "let me pass on a second bit of advance news before we compose
our stomachs for lunch. It's nothing for me. I'm committed to do the
July Fourth thing. But the newspapers are onto it and one of your Justice
Department chappies should sort it out before it makes headlines."

"Dear Gillian," Royce groaned. "No more calamities, please?"

"Just take a note before we toddle on," she urged him. "It's a com-
patriot of yours called Tony Riordan. Name mean anything?"

"No."

"Name International Anglo-American Trusts ring a bell?"

"Some kind of bucketshop brokerage?"

She nodded. "It's both our glory and our curse, darling, that our
financial center, the city, is run entirely on principles of self-regulation
and good faith."

"So I have heard." Connell felt a faint clamminess across his shoulder-
blades. He hated financial scandals of any kind, but especially those
involving Americans. How was one to keep one's own reputation for self-

regulation and good faith, he wondered, when one's fellow Americans were running unbelievably lucrative scams all over Europe?

"Tony Riordan," he repeated, scribbling a note. "International Anglo-American Trusts. Lovely name. What's the scam?"

Gillian waved a small, pretty hand rather negligently. "Usual fakery. Stock issues for companies that only exist in Tony Riordan's vest pocket. Fake unit trusts. What you call mutual funds. Nothing novel or sophisticated. Just immensely profitable. I think I should add that the cove who gave me this gossip also gave me the story on the deer shoot. There may or may not be a connection to Riordan."

"How much time do we have?"

"Before what?"

"Before . . ." Royce gestured ineffectually.

"Before it all hits the fan?" Gillian asked with widened tiger-yellow eyes. "Oh, days." Her amused glance refocused past him. "Darling, is that a photo of another Fourth of July do?"

Royce turned to the cabinet behind his desk. "Last year's. Just a small affair, embassy staff and families."

"Then this Sunday's is a change?" she persisted. "Pandora Fulmer's idea? Sort of open out the guest list?"

Connell glanced at his watch. "Heavens, we're late." He stood up and so did Gillian. She moved behind his desk and picked up the photograph.

"Who is this dishy gentleman?" She indicated Ned French.

Royce took the photograph from her. "One of our defense attachés."

"The lady beside him?"

Connell had put the photograph away. "I beg your pardon?"

"The busty one." Gillian colored slightly. "I do believe she rather resembles me."

"That would be French's wife. I don't see the resemblance at all."

"The figure, for one thing." Gillian stopped. Her fair face had gone dark with thought. "Darling, I've just realized how little hope there is for me. You simply don't see my discreet charms."

"Nonsense." Smile on! "Sheer nonsense, Gillian. Come, let's not be late. They get so miffed at Gavroche if one doesn't conform to their schedule."

"Sod 'em."

"What?"

"Let's just sit in the square and have a brown bread sandwich." The note in her voice, especially to one as skilled as Connell in reading her music, held a most sinister threat. "You can't escape me," those amazing eyes told him. "Stop all the dazzling footwork," they said, "you're mine."

"Or, better yet, darling, my flat."

A rather tense silence enveloped them. Connell eyed her more closely. Gillian Lamb he had known for some years now. She'd begun as a newspaper journalist, but her bright, abrasive style had gone over much better on television, for which her demure English-rose beauty fitted her visually. "Lamb to Slaughter" was the name of the one-hour program she wrote and produced, last year for BBC, this year for one of the independent channels. Next year it would, he had heard, be syndicated internationally, and had a good chance of reaching an American audience. "Lamb to Slaughter" had one lethally simple idea: Lift the lid on something someone wants covered up.

"They'd never forgive me at Gavroche if I failed to produce the brilliant and beautiful Miss Lamb," Royce said at last.

She laughed softly. "Some day, Royce. Some day . . ."

But, please God, Royce Connell prayed, not this Sunday.

The agentcraft was fairly professional, Ned told himself. If not elegant it was, at the very least, simple.

The safe house was based on, in fact *in*, the immense department store complex called Selfridge's, which occupies an entire block along noisy Oxford Street, only a few minutes' walk from the chancery. Anyone following him, Ned felt, would be baffled by Selfridge's hectic ground floor at lunch hour. A tail would be easy enough to spot after a few minutes and even easier to shake in the densely packed throng.

The second sequence began at the rear of the store, Edwards Mews. There and at its western side toward Orchard Street Selfridge's encompassed a different milieu, a fully-equipped outdoor Shell service station for autos and also a hotel. It was possible—in those days—to get from the store into the hotel without stepping outside. Since the hotel elevators were within a yard or two of the entrance, it was also possible to take the lift to a higher floor without being seen by desk clerks or the concierge. And if, as Ned had done sometime in April, one retained a double room—number 404—in the name of a dummy company which paid by the month whether the room was used or not, one also carried a key to Room 404.

The entire procedure, including weekly electronic sweeps to locate bugging devices, had been arranged as a safe house where Ned could interview contacts. He had actually used it twice for that purpose since April. Only one person, not Chamoun, knew of the place, although Ned felt sure Chamoun would at least have guessed at the existence of such a hideout. Its location remained a secret except to the other person, and Ned was expecting her momentarily.

He slid open the bedroom window of 404. The traffic noise, with the double-paned window open, was quite strong. The roar of well-bred London traffic gets its decibels not from horn-honking but from the sheer accumulation of car, bus, and diesel cab engine noise. Ned tuned the in-wall radio to BBC 3. An actor was reading British poetry in a rich, fruity voice to the background accompaniment of British music, the medieval kind, drum rataplans, bass plunks and the high, galliard scribble of shrill recorder flutes and peculiar fretted instruments with odd names.

He opened the frigobar and poured himself a small chilled bottle of Perrier. Slowly, but more or less in a steady series of gulps, he swallowed the whole thing. Agentcraft made him thirsty, always had, even when it was applied to his own selfish ends.

He stared at the door of the frigobar, then shook his head slowly from side to side. He was *not* going to make sure the door was closed. He walked toward the window to put his back to the small refrigerator. Then he sighed, turned, walked to it and nudged the door shut. He was still shaking his head from side to side, but now the movement was more in sorrow than anything else.

The "thing" with refrigerators would pass, in time. He'd had compulsions like that before and would eventually throw them off, like a lingering head cold. Wrestling with automobiles, however, was a new one. Good thing he hadn't taken on a Rolls.

He slipped off his loafers and lay back on the big double bed. For an instant his mind flipped rapidly through the briefing session he'd just concluded at the chancery, much as one flips through a booklet that animates a movie sequence. Then he put it out of his mind with the thought that he had six days to correct any mistakes.

Jane would have noticed any mistakes. More and more these days, he depended on her to help him through what was beginning to seem a nightmare. Well, after all, he asked himself, what was a nightmare? Something frightening, unacceptable, but linked to the sketchy reality of one's own psyche? Ned adjusted the pillow so that it lifted his neck, the way a Japanese wood pillow did.

Jane was exactly what the doctor ordered, her mind a perfect antidote for the poison in Ned's veins.

Too melodramatic? What would you call the stuff that pumped through his veins, telling him he had spent half a lifetime masturbating for Uncle Sam? What would you call it when a grown man who does his job better than anybody else suddenly realizes he's in a lethal masquerade that serves no purpose? He has spilled his seed . . . on sand.

Because that was what Uncle had been asking of Nephew Ned. More melodrama, huh? The name of the sin was onanism. Onan it was who whacked off into the sand and God took a dim view of it. But if Uncle is God, Ned told himself, then he has clearly sent me directly to Madame Fingers, there to flirt off a few gobs in the interest of making free enterprise and the American way look good.

Oh, Jane, be here!

Be here with your immigrant's view of America, the promised land. I lift my lamp beside the golden door. Jane, tell me it's all for some reason. The fire burns low in us combat-fatigued white Anglo-Saxon Protestant onanists.

Granddaughter of immigrants. But she still has that unvarnished innocence. Land of the free. Home of the brave. I lift my lamp beside the golden door. Send these, your tempest-tossed, to me . . .

Wyckoff had been tossed a little too much that night in Frankfurt. Agentcraft hadn't helped him. Born in Neenah, Wisconsin, where the Kleenex comes from. Died very badly, age twenty-eight, in the thick woods near the Frankfurt *Flughafen*.

Ned readjusted the pillow under his neck and, staring at the ceiling, proceeded to play through the whole mental Wyckoff video one more time.

Nancy Lee Miller found a bench in the shadowless light of a cloudy late June that overcast Grosvenor Square. She sat down, smoothing her skirt but not crossing her long legs in their sheer dark stockings because she would be unwrapping a tuna sandwich on her lap.

It was the usual thin British sandwich: dry bread, pale butter, and almost no tuna. As if to make up for lack of the very filling for which it had been named, the sandwich offered three parchment-thin slices of cucumber.

Nancy Lee longed for the tuna salad sandwich of her native California, a gigantic stereophonic pageant of diagonally cut toast overflowing with theatrically meaty chunks of tuna, celery, scallions, gobs of low-cal mayonnaise, stalks of carrot, curls of green pepper and, over all, a heavy dandruff of alfalfa sprouts, everything lying on crunchy leaves of iceberg lettuce surrounded by half-inch-thick slices of tomato entirely innocent of flavor.

Morosely she munched her mean sandwich, staring idly at the statue of someone in a great cloak. She had often wondered who he was. Some day she would ask one of the other Americans who worked in the embassy. They might have a clue.

At that moment, to the north where the chancery building stood, she caught a glimpse of Colonel French, looking neat in civilian clothes, dashing out the front entrance and turning north along Audley Street. Nancy Lee put down her sandwich on its rumpled square of plastic wrap, dug in her small handbag, and got out a notebook.

She scribbled the date and time on one of the last pages. The notebook was almost filled and she'd been keeping it less than four weeks, ever since Dris had asked her to. The telephone connection had been bad. He'd said he was calling from Beirut and would see her soon. But she'd heard nothing since and all she had now to show for the waiting was this notebook filled with cryptic phrases whose meaning was already fading in her mind. She would soon find it impossible to decipher them just when Dris most needed the information.

That neat Jane Weil, in black-rimmed spectacles, her dark hair piled atop her head, hurried out of the chancery and disappeared along Brook Street. Nancy Lee also noted this in her book. She hoped Dris would be pleased.

Nancy Lee knew she was no brain. She'd barely graduated college and her father had had something sneaky to do with that. There'd been some sort of research grant from his oil company. Always on the go, her parents moved from one oil-producing land to another. She never stayed long enough to pick up a real education from the oil-company schools where the American kids went. About the only thing she could show for such a Middle East childhood was an ability to speak Arabic, not well but well enough.

Dris called her a genius but that was because he was madly in love with her pale brown hair and her small, slightly pug nose and her neat little ears. "Like snails," he would say, nibbling them, his tan eyes burning. He had the habit of nibbling everything on her body, or at least anything he could get his lips or teeth onto.

The last time they'd been together, that really neat week in Rome, she had gone back to London sore all over, nibbled half to death and moving as if in a swoon, drowning in her own orgasmic liberation. It had been almost exactly, Nancy Lee remembered now, like getting sucked

under the trough of a big wave off Santa Barbara and being cast up on
the beach, half dead, pummeled raw, gasping for air, soaked in the wild
salt flush of the earth's great liquid mysteries.

She stopped eating, hot images flooding her brain. Now she tried to
calm herself. There went Royce Connell, "Mr. Catnip" the British girls
in the typing pool called him, with a neat lady in long blond hair who
was obviously ape about him. Nancy Lee made another note.

Being a watcher was not her thing. From the beginning, when her
father had gotten her this embassy job, she had known it would be boring
because it would tie her down in one place and load her with routine
garbage work.

On the other hand, it greatly pleased Dris and she wanted, above all
things on this earth, to please Dris. He had made a woman of her. She
could never repay him fully for this and if the price of serving him was
boredom, then so be it. "Let it be," John Lennon once said so wisely.
Let it be.

Two large white vans circled the square slowly, looking for a number.
Nancy Lee saw them almost every day. They had a funny English name
stenciled on their sides: HODGKINS AND DAUGHTER—CUSTOM CATERING.
Past her bench Londoners strolled singly or in pairs. Nancy Lee found
them a funny lot, the way they dressed and spoke, even their faces, their
big noses and chins, like Mr. Parkins, the maintenance engineer. The
women dressed dowdy, especially the young ones who tried hard to look
way-out sleazy. The men dressed like faggots or tramps, Nancy Lee
decided, but at least they were cute.

She finished her sandwich and unfolded the afternoon tabloid newspaper she always bought because of the horoscopes. "Your weeks of
waiting," she read for her sign, "will close now with love and the opportunity to perform the kind of major service you most enjoy. Saturn's
transit has finally ended."

She frowned. Then she paged forward to the gossip column and made
her way slowly through luxurious hints of low adultery in high places.
Nancy Lee was not a fast reader. When she got to the center item set
off in boldface type it took her quite a while to finish it:

". . . toute Londres buzzing with the event of the season, a giant
Pandora's box to celebrate American Independence Day, courtesy of Mrs.
Ambassador, the social Pandora Fulmer, who's invited a mere five hundred
top people to champers and good ole down home vittels like grilled hawg.
Your invitation hasn't yet arrived? Never mind, ours has, so watch this
space for further . . ."

Nancy Lee felt someone take hold of her right arm, tightly by the armpit. Two men had sat down, one on each side of her. She glanced at the one who held her in such an intimate, painful grip. "Dris!"

"Quiet, beloved," Khefte murmured in Arabic. Then, to the man on the other side of Nancy Lee, "Did I not tell you how beautiful she was? Truly am I blessed."

He pointed at the item in the gossip column and waited, grinning, while Bert read it through twice. The German's pale eyes widened slowly.

Khefte tapped the paragraph Nancy Lee had been reading. "It is written, brother, that we are both blessed. *Inshallah!*"

5

Pandora Fulmer got up quite early when her husband, the ambassador, was out of town. This morning she had been up as early as Ned French; she was sipping coffee when he jogged by in the distance. Pandora often wondered what his job at the embassy really was; "deputy defense attaché" meant nothing, she knew. As she sipped she refined the tiniest details of what would be a sheer triumph for Mrs. Adolph Fulmer III, wife of the chief of mission, ambassador extraordinary and plenipotentiary, personal representative of the president of the United States to Her Majesty the queen.

Tiny details were Pandora's specialty. Some people considered her a tiny detail herself. "You can express me in the numeral five," she often told interviewers from women's magazines. As a former journalist, Pandora knew what made memorable copy.

"The numeral five," she would repeat in her soft voice that had lost its Mississippi accent over the years: "I'm five feet tall. All my clothes are U.S. size five, even my shoes. And, being so petite," she would extend her slender legs for a better view, "I nearly always wear these dreadful five-inch heels. Utterly deplorable, but I'm *so* used to them."

She would immediately break off this self-description to warn readers that such heel height was not to be emulated unless one enjoyed Pandora's absolutely silly lightness of weight, well under a hundred pounds.

"That's seven stone," she would add for the benefit of her British public. Pandora always did her homework down to the tiniest detail.

This would lead the interviewer briefly to the ambassador's contrasting size—Bud was well over six feet and not skinny—but Pandora would gently guide the interview back on track.

The Fulmers were new to London and equally new to the foreign service. As it turned out, however, Pandora needed very little coaching. This morning, start of a week that would end on Sunday with the Fourth of July, was a particularly striking example of Pandora's attention to tiny details, which she hoped would be her greatest personal victory and a real boost for the president.

Pandora knew she was making trouble for the embassy. They would surely wonder why she had waited to mail the invitations so close to the date and why she had done the addressing and mailing with the aid of her own personal housekeeper, Mrs. Crustaker, and Lorna Mae Hodge, her maid. Pandora would have to do some preemptive fence-mending at the embassy, particularly with Jane Weil.

But there was no way Pandora would let the professional diplomatic types play games with her garden party. She might look like a bit of fluff, twinkling about on stalk heels like some forty-five-year-old Tinkerbell, but Pandora Fulmer knew a lot more about playing a loner's game in a big organization than anyone dreamed.

She had had to learn the inner moves as wife of the chief nonexecutive of Fulmer Stores, Inc., the largest single combination of specialty and department stores in the United States. Because he was the chairman's son, her husband had been judged an idiot first by his father and then by management. To be as ambitious as Pandora, but to be married to a man given nothing to do, had been a challenge. She had, however, made capital of the single advantage, money. She had made sure Bud contributed heavily to the Republican Party, so heavily that when the president took office and looked for a way of rewarding the generous and loyal Fulmer, he was struck dumb for only one moment when he heard the price:

"Not London!"

"Yes, London."

His gulp was almost audible. "God," he said then, quite loudly. This was not the first time the deity had been invoked in the Oval Office, but probably never before with such urgency.

Yes, Pandora told herself as she turned from the window and rang the bell for Mrs. Crustaker, she'd have to find a way of keeping Jane

Weil sweet. And she'd also have to break the news of the garden party rather gently to Bud, who hated big social events at which he shook hundreds of strange hands, none of them offering him a drink. Bud had been on the wagon all month because of this ambassadorial appointment. A big party, Pandora knew, was always a temptation to an alcoholic.

The housekeeper opened her bedroom door. Mrs. Crustaker had first worked for Pandora's family, the Morgans of Biloxi, and later for the Fulmers of New York and Baltimore. She was black, not quite as tall as Bud Fulmer, but a lot faster on her feet; very fast for a lady of sixty-seven who also happened to be a great-grandmother.

"Mawnin', Belle, honey," Pandora began in her Biloxi voice. "That phone'll start ringin' 'bout now. You make sure, honey: either you answer it or me or Lorna Mae. I don't want nobody else takin' messages for the party, hear?"

"None of them embassy folk?"

"Don't trust 'em. D'you?"

"Chile, I don't trust nobody but me and you," Mrs. Crustaker said, quoting an old joke between them, "and sometimes I ain' too sure about you."

The two women broke up into soft laughter.

The spotterscope was one of the new enhanced-image types designed for low-light observation but suitable for dull daylight such as today's. Maurice Chamoun stood well back from his single office window and refocused the powerful little telescope on the cloud-shaded green of Grosvenor Square. The Miller girl had been taking her lunch there for several weeks, now that the weather had turned summery. This in itself meant nothing to Chamoun, but the fact that she took notes did.

As he zeroed in on her, Nancy Lee munched her sandwich. At the same time Chamoun could hear Ned French's private line begin to ring. He grunted unhappily, put down the spotterscope and unlocked his office door to let himself into Ned's adjoining room.

On the eighth ring he picked up the phone. "Deputy attaché's office."

"Moe? Laverne French again. He there?"

"Just left the building, I'm afraid."

"I was expecting his call."

Chamoun paused warily. "We have a state of . . . heightened awareness this morning. Ned'll explain." Instantly he was sorry he'd said that. There were rules about sharing office information with one's spouse, even if she was the daughter of that old fossil General Krikowski.

"Then I'm going to have to lay this one on you, Moe," she went on more briskly. "I had a doorbell reconnaisance this morning. Fake postman routine. Crude. I think he was checking our TV surveillance system but also trying to shake me up."

"What'd he look like? Did you get a clear shot?"

"It's on the videotape but it can't be more than the back of his head. If I was lucky I've got a turnaway side shot, but I doubt it. That tape has to be picked up and monitored. I waited here all morning. Now the cleaning lady's here and I have to go out to the market. When can I exp—?"

"Don't leave yet, Laverne." Chamoun made an anguished face. "Anybody we could have sent was . . . occupied this morning. Let me see who I can dig up. But it's lunchtime, so this may take a while."

"I thought Ned would . . ." She let the thought die away.

"He's off on a few chats with . . . contacts."

Her silence began to grow until it worried Chamoun. "Someone will pick up the tape by two P.M., I promise."

"I'll wait." The line went dead. She had to be pissed off, Chamoun thought, and mostly at Ned. But Christ, the opposition was always running its little games. She should be used to this by now.

He glanced out of Ned's window at a Grosvenor Square shadowed by an overcast sky. The Miller girl remained on her bench, knees primly together, munching her sandwich. On all sides Londoners sprawled on the grass, smoking and chatting as if brilliant summer sun flooded their private park.

The tall, gaunt figure of the man with the placards stood off to one side, contrasting sharply with the holiday scene. An odd sort of *cordon sanitaire* surrounded him, Chamoun saw. People enjoying a lunchtime break did not interest themselves in the man's mysterious message. His spare, self-contained air of utter commitment seemed to warn them all off. "Unless you are prepared to join me," his stance seemed to tell them more strongly than words, "keep your distance."

Ned French had had the FBI check him out, the old codger Ned called the Watcher, but they'd never found anything worth mulling over. Strolling by, two uniformed bobbies, a man and a woman, eyed the cryptic placard and moved on. Nobody was interested.

No, wait.

Off to one side of the Watcher three young men sloped idly on a bench. From this distance, and without his scope, Chamoun could only see them in rough outline, scrawny, spotty, but kitted out in the latest fascist yobbo style: heavy black stomping shoes, skin-tight black pants, imitation black leather jackets studded with metal, and soup-bowl haircuts under back-tilted black porkpie hats, bought one size too small.

Their interest in the Watcher had to be the product of boredom, Chamoun decided. Boredom and the keen interest sadists naturally take in the isolated and potentially weak.

Chamoun wondered if this were something the embassy ought to keep an eye on. The Watcher was protesting something American, but it wouldn't do to have him roughed up right at the doorstep of the chancery. And when a true British yob got to work, really started feeling his way into creative aggro, out came the steel knucks, chains, and lead-weighted saps. At football sluggings, even a few kitchen knives made their appearance. Likes his gore, Mr. Brit.

Chamoun returned to his own office and locked himself in. When he picked up the spotterscope and zeroed in on Nancy Lee Miller she had company. Carefully, Chamoun examined each of the two young men. The good-looking Arab was new to him. But the other face . . .

The three people on the bench got up and walked off, the Arab's arm circling Nancy Lee's waist proprietarily. Chamoun grinned. The girl was a typical airhead, but conditioned toward Arab men. Benefitting from his own appearance, Chamoun had dated her twice and scored both times, a pleasant experience if you could stand listening to the bad Arabic she insisted on as pillow talk.

The other face . . .

Chamoun paged through drawers of dossier files, each file including photographs. The face of the other man was not to be found.

He unlocked a drawer of his desk and removed some floppy disks, totally uncaptioned. He switched on his micro and fed it a disk. On the screen appeared brief biographies and small photos, often a blurred snapshot. Chamoun scrolled through the disk, then a second time, more slowly. Finally he settled on one photo that loosely fit the face of the other man with Nancy Lee. He transferred some information from the screen onto his calendar pad. He had completely forgotten about the three yobbos.

His quick scribble was in English. But the information on the disk had been in Hebrew.

At the western edge of Greater London, to the south of Ruislip with its underground tube station, lies a large patch of open green farmland bisected by the A40 highway that leads eastward into the heart of London.

Here the RAF's Northolt Aerodrome provides uncluttered landing space for flights of a confidential nature for which the public bustle of Heathrow would be too risky.

The queen's flight lands here after voyaging back from across the seas. But the private Learjet which arrived from Aberdeen contained only two passengers, neither royal. Although one was accompanied by a contingent of three bodyguards, both passengers were consigned to a normal black Fleetwood Cadillac limousine. With a Ford Escort following and two British motorcycle police leading the way down the A40, the motorcade passed through Ealing and Shepherd's Bush and, via the Paddington Flyover, progressed toward Regent's Park. Adolph Fulmer III, ambassador extraordinary and plenipotentiary, had returned.

His companion, Jim Weems, was not a guest of the embassy at Winfield House nor a personal friend of Fulmer's, although he did serve as the new European manager for Fulmer Stores, Ltd. It had been his company's Learjet. Weems's exit from the Fleetwood as it came to rest in the driveway of Winfield House was abrupt. He barely had time to shake hands with the companion who had shared a weekend of shooting in Scotland when the security people hustled Weems to a waiting taxi and his hotel in Mayfair.

Bud Fulmer watched him go with no great feeling of loss. He barely knew Weems, who had presumed on his recent Fulmer Stores connection to arrange an invitation from the Duke of Buchan, Weems's pal, not Fulmer's. Bud was ill at ease except in the presence of truly old friends. Since none were to be found on this side of the Atlantic at the moment, the only people with whom he felt comfortable were Pandora and Mrs. Crustaker.

To tell the truth, Bud often mused, basically he was the last person on earth to be appointed anybody's ambassador. He honest-to-God didn't like mixing and mingling with people. The whole ambassador thing basically had been Pandora's idea but he was stuck with it.

He stood for a moment at the columned portico of the Georgian house, whose two-story pilasters supported a triangular pediment that rose to the level of the mansard roof and its dormer windows. Fulmer was a big man without being a fat one, big-boned and big-muscled, thick but not paunchy. His unlined face fit someone in his forties, but Bud Fulmer would be sixty this November. Over the years that slablike face, deeply tanned by outdoor living, had furrowed only slightly, barely enough to project an expression. As Pandora often said, his smile and his frown were interchangeable. Bud had a typical Bud Fulmer solution to offer:

"It doesn't matter if I'm smiling or frowning, honey, basically you do whatever you think's best."

This diffidence had been part of Bud's personality when they married, in the 1960s. With the passage of time it had only deepened, if this was not too strong a word to describe whatever feeling Bud Fulmer had. This despite the fact that he came across as a real man's man, devoted to fishing and hunting, wilderness backpacking and the like.

In Scotland, where the rude old Duke had treated him as a rank amateur, he had surprised everyone by dropping his first buck at nearly two hundred yards with a clean heart shot. He had surprised them even more by turning diffident again. "No, no more. That's it. Thanks a lot. Let's get back to the house."

It had puzzled Pandora in the first years of their marriage that a man with such a forceful appearance, such a pleasantly deep, booming voice, and such keen hunter's eyes, was in reality shy, retiring, unambitious . . . in those days the word "wimp" hadn't come into use. Later, when she understood why Bud was as he was, Pandora would never have used that word to describe him. But plenty of others did.

His three-man security squad escorted him up the stairs to the suite in which the Fulmers lived. Somewhere phones rang.

A month before, Royce Connell had wanted to assign an experienced British valet but Bud Fulmer had reacted badly. "Pandora does that," he'd explained.

It wasn't, Bud knew, that he was helpless without his wife. After all, he'd gotten along for nearly forty years without any wife at all, much less a cute little powerhouse like Pandora. It was that he didn't expect to rise any higher than what he already knew he could handle, with her help. In his life expectation loomed small.

"I'm back, honey!" he called, barging from room to room, hearing the ring of telephones, until he tracked her down in the sunny dayroom where they usually had breakfast together. She was rising from the long table at which she and Mrs. Crustaker had been working.

Moving fast on high heels, Pandora ran to him. He lifted her up in the air and kissed her somewhere between her ear and her mouth, several satisfying times. "What're you two cooking up?" he demanded.

She was high above him, as light as a child and easy to hold. The telephone rang again. "Put me down, sugar. It's the Fourth of July picnic. You remember." She watched him for a moment and saw that he didn't. "Have you had lunch?"

"Not hungry." He set her down. "What picnic?"

"It's traditional. The ambassador gives one every year. And I thought, 'Great! Here's a chance to do the president some good.' It's turning out beautifully, Bud."

He sat down across from Mrs. Crustaker and gave her a wink. "Belle, what's she into now?"

The big black woman indicated dozens of sheets of paper lying about. "This here's the guest list. Only five hund—" The telephone rang and her long arm darted out for it. "Winfield House," she said. "Can I help you?" As she listened she ran a pencil up and down several lists, found what she was seeking and made a check mark. "We are looking forward to the pleasure of your company. Thank you." And she hung up.

"That's two hundred sixty yesses so far and eleven no's."

Bud Fulmer sat back and listened again to his wife's explanation of how promptly and thoroughly they were responding to the president's urgent request to stand tall and show the flag. Of how much goodwill they would be creating on the president's behalf at a moment when he sorely needed it. The telephone rang again and as Belle answered it, a second call came in. Pandora picked it up.

Idly, Bud Fulmer watched the two women checking off their lists. Nobody had ever warned him what a vacuum life basically was, how much dead space a person had to get through each day. The weekend in Scotland . . . endless. The duke and Jim Weems half in the bag from breakfast on, chuckling over financial hanky-panky they'd pulled off, patronizing him as some sort of duffer, trying to get him to sneak a drink. Then drunkenly impressed by his easy shot. Then drunkenly insistent he kill more, more.

Fulmer grunted softly, something like the ruminating noise a steer makes, nothing to do with his temper but only the state of his digestion. As if he *liked* killing. Christ, what did it prove? Basically that the poor stag wasn't carrying a 30.06 Husqvarna 6000 with scope sights? In a duel with equal weapons, Bud would have loved to watch the stag drop the duke.

He smiled, knowing that the flicker across his face would not be noticed by either woman. The telephones kept ringing and they kept up a bright, impersonal, friendly stream of chatter.

He couldn't do that for five seconds, Bud mused. Come to that, basically he couldn't do much of anything except drop a buck at two hundred yards if the light was right. Dad's big mistake, he recalled, was his insistence that Bud be kept clear of Fulmer management. Not that it had affected the business an iota. In the fifteen years since Dad had passed on, the enterprise had expanded from some two hundred shops and stores to more than a thousand throughout the U.S. and, now, Western Europe. No thanks to Bud Fulmer. Thanks, instead, to a series of salaried managers, kitted out with stock-option benefits and profit-sharing plans, basically men like Jim Weems, with his shady contacts in high places like the Duke of Buchan, who had murdered his first wife —the one who brought him his fortune—under the guise of a hunting accident.

Why Dad had kept him out of all this was a question Bud had rarely asked himself in his early manhood, when he had been encouraged to piss away decades in aimless sports, womanizing, draw poker, and booze.

Bud watched Pandora now, neatly inscribing something on one of her typewritten lists. Slowly it began to percolate through his mind that a hell of a lot of people were saying yes. He pulled over a sheet of names and scanned them. A frown failed to distort his face as he realized even he had heard of most of these folks. Basically, it was who's who in London. No wonder Pandora was so excited.

This would be exactly the sort of star-studded shindig, Bud knew, that had first attracted her to the idea of a goddamned ambassadorship. He grinned at her as she ticked off another name on her list. "It's getting on for three hundred yesses, sugar," she told him, reaching for another ringing phone.

All those celebrities in one place, the ambassador thought. And him without his Husqvarna 30.06. Too bad. He'd be able to bag himself a cabinet minister, maybe, or a movie star. A broad smile crossed his face. But so could somebody else, he thought then. Basically they might even bag him.

The smile faded to a worried frown. But no one noticed the difference.

6

The wall radio in Room 404, still tuned to BBC 3, throbbed with endless neo-Debussy loops coming to no resolution except, after a pause, when the announcer attributed the work to Delius and then announced Ralph Vaughan Williams to follow.

Ned groaned. "BBC has a deal with every British composer living or dead, talented or not, by which his slightest effort gets regularly aired."

Jane Weil rolled her long body off him and smiled at the ceiling. "Look on the bright side. You're guaranteed Purcell and Elgar. Do we have to go back to work?"

He watched her for a long moment, the slim sweep of her naked body with its ivory skin and small breasts, the narrowness of her waist and the rich thicket of black pubic hair.

"Of course not," he assured her. "We have no proof anybody will be interested in Pandora's Sunday jamboree. Relieved of that angst, we have nothing to do but try to run an organization that Pandora has already shown she can outrun without even drawing a deep breath. Jane, don't tempt me. The way I feel I'd like to barricade the two of us in Room 404 for eternity."

"That frigobar only has one bag of peanuts and some potato chips. And I've already finished the chips as lunch."

He glanced in a veiled way at the electronic clock on the bedside table, hoping she wouldn't notice. "One thirty," she told him. "We have fifteen more minutes before we go our separate ways. French, you're very preoccupied today. It can't be the Fourth of July party because, from what I could tell at the briefing, you've got the thing neatly contained. Or hope to."

He failed to reply, knowing that she had by now gotten used to his slow responses. But some things you told no one, not out of a sense of privacy but because you didn't want to load them with this kind of burden.

"You and Royce," Jane was saying, "I know you both feel I should have headed off Mrs. Fulmer before she mailed those damned invitations."

"We've been up against devious ambassadors' wives before. I remember once in Bonn . . ." His voice died away.

After another long pause Jane turned on her elbow to stare down at his face, retreating from her as its shutters closed, one after another. "Once in Bonn," she echoed. "What happened . . . once in Bonn?"

"Once in Bonn," he began in a rush, since hustling it out into the open was the only way he would ever expose it, "I made a prime professional mistake. I'm from Wisconsin. Did you know that?"

"Dear me, that *is* a mistake."

Ignoring this, Ned went on:

"You probably think I'm from Chicago because I went to the University of Chicago, but that was after the army took over my life. No, a little town at the foot of Lake Winnebago called, oddly enough, Fond du Lac. This agent was a kid named Wyckoff and he came from Neenah, which is at the top of the lake, where they make Kleenex. I was running him in a game with Oleg Protoklitov. Oleg was to get arrested so that he could have an excuse for coming in without letting K know he'd been planted on them ten years ago. Am I going too fast? Oleg was ours. But we had to make it look like he wasn't. Wyckoff, the kid from Neenah . . ." His voice broke badly. He covered up by coughing.

Neither of them spoke for a long moment. When Ned resumed, it was in a carefully normal voice: "It was a setup. Wyckoff was to claim Oleg had made advances to him in a gay bar in Frankfurt. None of us knew it was some kind of neo-Nazi SM leather joint. We all assumed it was your average harmless gay hangout. Wyckoff started an argument with Oleg, as planned. Then something went wrong. I have never . . ." His voice broke again, this time with a faint tremor of pain.

"Let it go for now," Jane suggested.

"Hell, no." He coughed briefly, then a second time. To gain composure he stared at his bruised knees and lightly rubbed them. Then he reached for the bedsheet and pulled it up over both of their bare bodies.

"The scene got out of control," Ned went on then. "I mean out of Wyckoff's control. Oleg ran for it but Wyckoff went down in a hail of chains and cudgels and whips. They found—" He coughed again. "There's a forest near the airport at Frankfurt. This body was found handcuffed with its arms yanked around behind a tree. I believe it was an oak. With a circumference of . . ."

He stopped once more and considered the featureless ceiling for a long moment. "In the frigobar is another bottle of Perrier."

Jane brought it opened, but instead of getting back under the sheet with him, sat on the edge of the bed and watched him swallow the entire eight ounces of charged water in one slow series of gulps.

"That was Wyckoff's body?"

"They had cut off his head."

"Ned!"

"His cock, too, but you might have expected that. Will you make sure that fridge door is closed? You see, every serviceman's fingerprints are on file, but it took us a while to get a positive ID back from the States. In this case fingerprints were what we had to go on. I keep saying 'we' but it was only me. I had cooked this up and sent Wyckoff into it. Oleg wouldn't surface so there was no we. That refrigerator door . . ."

He glanced down at his hand, holding the empty, bowling-pin-shaped bottle. Gently, with no seeming force, he threw it across the room. It hit the frigobar door and shattered into several green chunks.

"You think that's easy to do?" Jane asked. "Those bottles are practically indestructible."

"It's all in the wrist," Ned explained. "I am so sick of this story."

"Tell it a lot, do you?"

"Not ever."

"Save the rest for some other time," she suggested. "It's tearing you up, Ned."

"There's almost nothing more left of it. A week later in our apartment in Bonn. Laverne was out that evening with the girls at a Disney movie. English language, German subtitles." He glanced at her.

"Laverne speaks Disney, does she?"

"And also World War II GI slang."

"Roger," Jane responded. "Wilco. Over and out."

"So when I got home from the office there was this note from her telling me dinner was in the microwave. The apartment had been without occupants for several hours. I opened the refrigerator for—" His throat seemed to clamp shut.

"A bottle of Perrier," Jane finished for him.

"And there he was."

"What?"

"His head. They'd managed to keep the eyes open till rigor mortis set in. Wyckoff was staring at me."

"Good God!"

"Imagine if one of the girls had found it first?"

"Good God."

To give herself something to do, Jane got up from the bed and, on hands and knees, picked up all the pieces of the shattered bottle and deposited them in a wastebasket. Then she opened and closed the frigobar door, making sure Ned saw her do it.

Ned watched her with an abrupt sense of pleasure. Somebody was doing something useful, he thought, an act without shades of gray. It is always pleasant watching a tall, naked woman kneel, as if posing for an artist, so that her back curves in a beautiful arch and her slender arms extend this way and that. Jane's long, dark hair, usually pulled up on top of her head in a knot like a French chambermaid's, had long ago come undone in a cascade of black rivulets in which faintly blue highlights shifted like the blue flame of a coal fire.

As quickly as he had broken up, Ned felt himself come together, at least for now. Telling it had helped, but the healing was only temporary. When the wound is permanent there is no healing.

"I do remember reading something about it," Jane said, returning to the bed and getting in under the sheet with him. "God, you're freezing!" She jackknifed her long legs around his midriff. "But I don't remember it having to do with any American embassy."

Ned nodded. "We had to arrange for the head to be found somewhere else. But it wasn't fair to Wyckoff's family just to let the kid go down in the annals of the unexplained. They . . . I told . . . This is confidential, Jane. On home leave before reassignment to London, I went back to Wisconsin, just a buddy of their son's, telling them some lies. Both of them were school teachers, intelligent people and confused. You live your whole life imparting unshakeable truths to kids, so the truth of your son being dead, without any rational explanation, strikes deep."

"My mother's a school teacher," Jane said. "My father insists that his driver take her in the morning and pick her up after school. She's still teaching in a Brooklyn elementary full of horrible little delinquents."

"How often has she been mugged?"

"Never. With the driver and the car the kids figure Mother has some kind of Mafia connection."

Both of them laughed softly for a moment and then fell silent again. "Wyckoff's mother," Ned said at last, "had guessed what her kid was up to in Germany. But nobody's wildest fantasy could match the reality. I'm still not sure myself. Did some of the nasties in the bar take him apart for fun? Was the game hijacked by one of the neo-Nazi organizations? There isn't a great deal to be made out of a head in the refrigerator except the obvious, that I was guilty of Wyckoff's death."

"But you weren't," Jane said quickly.

"We're all in agreement, the butchers and I. By the way, it was someone with practical experience butchering meat who did the decapitation. I spent months working that line without . . ." He sighed. "Besides, Wyckoff wasn't the first kid I've sent out to be killed. Just the first from Neenah. Anyone in the services, even in peacetime, understands that the authority to command implies the authority to kill."

Jane retreated slightly from him. Her body lay perfectly straight now on her side of the bed. "So, in the army the smart thing," she murmured, against mewing sweeps of Vaughan Williams music, "is to get as high up the ladder as one can."

"There is always someone higher." He laughed and then started to cough. "I didn't want to load all this on you, Jane."

Jane turned, a bit unwillingly, toward him. Her lustrous dark eyes, huge under full eyebrows, swept across his face, side to side, questing. Then: "French, this is one incident of many. It mustn't obsess you. Unless there was something special about it?"

"I liked the kid. That was an error. But he was simply part of the daily body count. It's a crude game. To keep score we use bodies so the people back home can say, 'Oh, hey, boy, our guys are really giving the enemy a shot in the ass.' And the people who run the game can say 'Look how the citizens lap this up. We're good for another four years in office.' And the idiots like me who play their game for them can say 'Boy, I really scored, huh? Another promotion for me, sure.' And everybody rests content for a little while longer."

At the wall, the radio music ended and, after the announcer announced what had been played, there was a pause. A series of beeps led up to the time check and news.

". . . have a dampening effect on the disarmament conference scheduled to begin next week at Geneva, where . . ."

"French," Jane began, then stopped.

"I know, we should have left the hotel long ago."

"No, not yet." Her big eyes seemed locked on his. "What is 'the game'? A figure of speech? A euphemism for espionage?"

Ned slid off the bed and went to his clothes, draped neatly over the arms and back of a long upholstered sofa. He pulled on his underpants and socks, then stood, distracted by another piece of news from the radio.

"Your knees! You've got to have them looked after."

"Nothing."

"Jogging in traffic," Jane told him. "French, you fool. Has the nurse looked at those knees?"

He draped his shirt over them with fake coyness. "Not lately."

"Stop being a hero, French."

"It's supposed to go with the uniform."

She jumped up from the bed and stood facing him defiantly. "We're at peace. If people like me have anything to do with it, we'll stay at peace. We don't need heroes."

The pause that followed had such sudden tension that Jane finally smiled, although a bit shakily. "Well, here I am lying again." She took his shirt from him. "I do need a hero. You'll do." She kissed him lightly on the mouth, turned him around, and helped him into his shirt. "Did you put something on those knees?"

Ned nodded absentmindedly, listening to the radio news. ". . . will no longer stand idly by accepting the insults and political aggrandizement of the West, the mullah told reporters. There was a time, he warned, when southern Europe from Spain to the Balkans was under the control of Islam. He also warned . . ."

"Charming," Jane commented. "Is he part of the game, too? Or don't I understand the meaning of the term?"

Ned pulled on his trousers. "Jane, look, nobody dares attack. When you lose everything politicians no longer have anything over which to wield power. Even the corporations that support them have no one left to sell anything to. So our greatest peacelovers are in Washington and Moscow. Don't smile, Jane. If we keep playing the game, body count is tiny compared to nuclear holocaust, so who's to say that the game isn't a brilliant device to save all our bacon?"

"Oh, shut up, French."

Reaching for his jacket, he paused in mid-gesture, leaning forward, as if snapped by a camera. He gave her his number-one interrogator's scowl. She hesitated for a moment. "How long have you felt this way?"

"Quite a while." He picked up his jacket. "I date it from that poor Wyckoff kid but his death was just the straw that broke this camel's back."

She glanced at her hair in a mirror and ineffectively pushed the long strands up into their normal topknot. "It's a sort of elastic circle," she said then, "black with little glitter bits."

Ned stared at her, thunderstruck at how unconcerned she was by his own immense failure of faith. He suddenly laughed out loud. "The demise of French will have to wait," he asked, "till we find Weil's hair thingie?"

Locating the elastic, she started trapping and shaping her hair upward, arms raised in a posture Ned felt sure she knew made her look like a teenage girl again. "You see," Jane said in an absentminded tone as she tucked strands here and there, "there are those who mistake a job for a divine calling. Such a man, and there's one here in Room 404 with me right now, sets himself up for a crisis of faith, like the minister who suddenly doubts the existence of God."

She had all the strands under control now and encircled them with the elastic. She let them droop slightly into a blue-black mobcap. "I know our charlatans want only to stay in office. I know the Soviets have the same kind of Neanderthals running their country. But people like us who serve them must never give ourselves airs. Otherwise we end up disgruntled and angry and burned out. Like you, French. Like you."

"Indeed." From behind her he was stroking her sides, moving down slowly from her breasts to her hips, going over again and again the inward curve at her waist. Her skin reminded him of some impossibly smooth fabric, barely protecting the firm flesh and jutting swell of her pelvis. "Burned out?"

"Leave now, French. Leave at once. If I run into you at the chancery this afternoon, keep your distance." She was watching him in the mirror. "And don't look so disconsolate. Please?"

He tried on a clown's grin. "Better?"

"Go back to being morose." She turned around in his arms and held him for a moment. "Are you all right?"

"There is something you do for me, without even trying, that makes it possible for me to go on."

Her startled glance searched his face for a moment. "That's dangerous, too. I'm beginning to see who I've fallen in love with. You're all or nothing at all, aren't you?"

"Never thought much about it."

"Once you were all patriotism. Now you're all cynicism. And whatever you and Laverne had went out the window during that change."

"It happened long before I met you."

She nodded. "Yes, all right. But listen to what I'm saying, French. I'm being very selfish, analyzing you this way. Because you and I are putting everything we have on this . . . this turn of the cards. This gamble." She paused. "I wanted to get lighter, not heavier, because we both have to be back at our desks within seconds. And here I am sticking probes into you. Into us."

He was silent for a long time. Then he kissed her on both cheeks, lightly but firmly. "I love you, Weil. Like everything else, this will have to be continued . . . later."

"Yes." She started dressing. "Later."

Not far from Lowndes Square, where Knightsbridge meets Belgravia, stands a sizable house in white with black trim built just after the First World War. Number 12's style, now called Art Deco, is again the rage, and the building changes hands regularly, doubling in price. Recently it went for almost nine million pounds, to an Arab, of course.

Not just any Arab, a few of the kindlier neighbors would hasten to add. Dr. Hakkad is a prominent ophthalmologist in his native land, whatever it is, and something of a multimillionaire man of mystery. Well, after all, who else could pay cash for Number 12?

Since it is a rated building, he is powerless to alter the exterior, but the inside is afire with hot purples and oranges, flocked walls, sunken baths, golden faucets, and immense beds with filigreed headboards. A true *Arabian Nights* decor hides in the heart of staid Belgravia.

The color scheme gave Bert a headache. No, truly. He would never have mentioned it to anyone, and certainly not Khefte, if the American girl hadn't said something first. She had been lolling around the top-floor apartment at Number 12 all afternoon, smoking kif and drinking arak.

"Something funny happens in between orange and purple, Dris," Nancy Lee had complained sleepily. "It makes my eyes shiver."

Khefte-called-Dris had been painstakingly paging through her notebook, asking questions and making his own notes. Usually Bert had to make do with second-rate material in these ventures. But in Khefte he had a well-trained professional. Bert found it hard to believe Khefte wasn't German, like himself.

It was well known how fragmented and multi-sided Islam could be,

Bert mused. The world knew of the Palestinians, and of the several currents at war with each other within the PLO. There had also been publicity about the Shi'a brethren and the various splinters, the Hezbollah, the Amal, the Jihad sects. The Sunni were also to be reckoned with, as were the Druze.

But this was merely to name organized groupings. For each there were a dozen more without names, perhaps with only a tribal affiliation, or a common ancestry in a certain region. In Khefte, Bert knew, Islam had someone who understood these conflicting currents, loyalties, religious ideals.

"It is true," Bert said in English, unable to contain himself. "There is an optical conflict where these colors meet."

"Where in life, oh my brother," Khefte intoned in Arabic, "does conflict not exist? Beloved," he turned to Nancy Lee, "you have logged Colonel French out and in every day or two at noon or thereafter. You have logged him back ninety to one hundred minutes later. The same is true of the Weil Jewess, and on the same days." He glanced at Bert. "Does not Allah smile upon us?"

Nancy Lee giggled. "You, like, talk funny." Her eyes closed.

Khefte smiled. "In today's newspapers we have read accounts of this truly foolhardy event planned by the ambassador's wife. Brother, the question must have crossed your mind a thousand times, was this a trap of Satan or a gift so magnificent that it could only have come from the hand of Allah."

Bert glanced uneasily at the American girl, but it was obvious that Nancy Lee was dozing on the long flame-colored divan, her head resting on an octagon pillow of violet and silver spangles. He and Khefte moved to the windows at the far end of the room that overlooked Belgravia Square in the distance.

The two men watched London's evening traffic jam. Cabs, cars, buses, vans, and large trucks waited silently in order to move forward a few car lengths at each traffic light change. "How disciplined the British are," Khefte breathed softly.

"How like sheep," murmured Bert.

"If we had a month!" Khefte spat out like a curse. "But from tomorrow we have only five days."

"You are right," Bert agreed, using his normal tactic with Arab co-workers, the quick affirmative response. No Arab liked to be told no, Bert knew. "Still . . . there is another way."

For the first time, Khefte's pale tan eyes swung toward Bert. "Explain."

"Do you agree," Bert began, "that it is within our military capacity to stage a surprise assault on the mansion?"

Khefte thought a moment. "Yes."

"But how long can we hold Winfield House during days, perhaps weeks, of negotiation?"

"Precisely."

"During which," Bert swept on almost without pause, "the enemy city surrounds us with infiltrations and further subversion of our forces."

Both of them had abandoned Arabic and were speaking in terse English, softly, so as not to waken the sleeping girl. "Khefte," Bert asked in a voice as near triumph as he ever allowed it to get, "do we defeat Satan only by emptying his pocket? On what tablet of stone is it inscribed that we cannot shame Satan before the world by executing his bloated, elitist guests?"

Behind them, the girl turned over and began to snore. Khefte took a long time answering. Bert could almost see, behind the café-au-lait irises, the tortuous process of thought disturbing Khefte's brain.

They were an autonomous cadre, but did Khefte understand the difference between their own rather opportunistic group and one dedicated in the home country and sent out to the west, targeted like a missile toward a single task? Their cadre had no such simple mandate. It was required, in effect, to live off enemy territory until a proper target presented itself. That was why it was financed by a "sponsor" like Dr. Hakkad. He it was who paid their bills, monitored their progress, and participated in their decisions. In this humiliating way, he was their superior. And who was Hakkad if not a banker, a usurer of the kind specifically proscribed by the Koran?

Bert's small mouth pressed into a thin, grim line. The inconsistencies of Islam, the diametric differences between sects, had always bothered him. He could see even now, in Khefte's hesitation, that he too was confused by the endless complexities of ends and means. Hakkad would have no such hesitation: ransom would be his goal. But a political statement that shook the four corners of the earth would have more impact if divorced from profit. Would Khefte understand that?

In Khefte's eyes a strange look shimmered. Bert thought that perhaps the queer dusk light had touched off some murky layer behind the Arab's tan irises. It could as well have been a look of admiration.

"Either way," Khefte breathed with deadly softness. "Oh, yes! Either way. How . . . lovely."

*   *   *

Ned French left the IRS offices in the northwest basement corner of the chancery, several flights down. He had been chatting with one of the agents about a long drawn-out field audit she was trying to bring to a close with an American businessman now stationed in London.

"He's strung us along nearly five years," she had complained. "Fellow named Weems. He's changed jobs twice during all this."

"What's it look like to you? Unreported income?"

"We always begin like that," she said, grinning like a small shark. "Whether it's true or not, that is. It's called 'guilty till proved innocent.' "

Feeling sorry for Weems, whoever he was, Ned made his way along a corridor to the lair of P. J. R. Parkins. After the usual delay with locks, the big, treelike fellow stood bulkily in his doorway, blocking anything but a brief glance at the carefully confused mess of his office-cum-workshop. "You'll be wanting to know about that accident, Colonel?"

"How is the runner?"

"Concussion, sprains, and a broken thumb. He's expected out of hospital once they're satisfied about the old coconut." He rapped the iron-gray hair on his head.

"And the driver of the Mini?"

Something behind that oaken façade seemed to be struggling forward—something, Ned thought, faintly humorous? "The driver's in nick. It's his third offense. He's a proper villain, that one."

"Good. I was hoping he hadn't got away."

"Hadn't got away?" Parkins echoed. He started to emit a sound like the chuffing of a faraway locomotive. "Hadn't got awa-a-ay?" he repeated, having trouble containing his mirth. "The bastard's still trying to catch his bloody breath!" He barked out a single guffaw and went wooden-faced again.

"That's as far as the Bill is taking it, Colonel," he added, referring to the police by the slang term in use among both coppers and crooks. "They're not looking for any witness. Or any Ford Fiesta."

"Thank you."

"Not at all, Colonel."

"Good night."

Parkins glanced at his watch. "Why so it is. Quitting time already. Another Monday, finished at last."

Ned French decided against saying anything more than some bland social cliché. His relationship with P. J. R. Parkins was extremely delicate. It was based on neither of them admitting who the other really was.

Slowly Ned mounted the stairs to his own floor, then paused at a corridor window to look out on the square. Late-working people were going home. The pace of London crowds fascinated Ned. Neither going to work nor coming from it did they ever actually hurry. No more, he reminded himself, than they rushed to answer a telephone; they always let half a dozen rings go by. One would have to find some Mediterranean city to duplicate the pace of leisurely London.

As it often did toward the end of the day, the sun now came in under the overcast, sending a flood of pink light across the city. The Watcher's elongated shadow spread far along the greensward, scarecrowlike, almost as if he had been raised in effigy. Or, Ned thought, crucified.

The placards that rose above the Watcher's head produced a squared-off shadow that resembled a top-hatted Abraham Lincoln. Or could it be the battered plug worn by Baron Samedi, the voodoo god of the dead? No, wait. With his red, white and blue placard . . . Uncle Sam!

No one paid the poor old guy any attention, Ned saw. However, three National Front thugs hunched together on a nearby bench, lighting three cigarettes off one lighter with the angry concentration of religious adepts miming a ritual. Once smoke floated freely, the biggest one, no taller than the other two but chunkier, with no neck whatsoever and biceps like kegs, got to his feet and sidled off in such a casual, "who me?" manner that Ned's suspicions were instantly aroused.

He watched the thick punk circle the Watcher and take up a post on the far side. Having done this, he gave his two brothers a thumbs-up sign and a gigantic wink. At once they began to shorten the distance between them and the man with the sandwich board.

The scene reminded Ned of one of those forty-year-old movies that came back on TV now and then from World War II, in which Conrad Veidt was always beating Jimmy Cagney or Paul Henreid with a riding crop. People huddled around clandestine radios in crummy old clothes, living in fear of the midnight pounding on the door.

Ned's thoughts shifted abruptly to Aaron Chemnitz, his old philosophy professor at the University of Chicago. Funny how the mind worked. Ned had begun the day remembering one of Chemnitz's pet words, "aleatory." The old refugee had permanently tattooed Ned's brain with odd tidbits like that.

Funny about the Jews, stormy petrels. Always at the eye of whatever hurricane there was. Even J. C. himself, stirring up trouble for Pontius Pilate. The only peaceful Jew Ned had ever met was Jane. The rest seemed cornered in tight places, as if they had been elected the cutting edge of whatever was going disastrously.

Chemnitz would easily understand what was about to happen down there in Grosvenor Square. He wouldn't see it, as Ned did, as sadist jackasses inflicting pain on someone too weak to fight back. Chemnitz would create a whole philosophical construct equating the condoned and open use of brute force with the deepest requirements of entrepreneurial anarchy.

Down below in the square, passers-by were few and far between. In minutes the yobs would have loony old Uncle Sam all to themselves.

He glanced at his new digital wristwatch. What the hell business was it of his if some elderly nut got punched up by native fascists? A passing Brit should intervene: they'd be *his* fascists. It happened all the time in Britain, the old being savaged by the young, either for their money or for the sheer hell of being able to beat them up.

By those rules the man with the sandwich board looked fair prey. Ned saw the beefy thug move closer. His mates were now less than a yard away.

Who is the Watcher to me? Ned asked himself. Other than a persistent pain in the ass, that is?

Ned watched the beefy one slide a two-foot length of one-inch pipe out of his right sleeve. "Christ," Ned grunted. He jumped down the chancery stairs two at a time and burst out through the front door.

Off on the greensward the heavy yobbo brought the pipe back for a sweeping sidestroke into the Watcher's kidneys. The other two had already divested him of the wooden sandwich signs and were contentedly kicking them to splinters. Ned dashed between moving cars, ran out onto the square and put on a burst of speed as the big thug began to hammer the elderly man's back.

"Hey!" Ned shouted, closing the gap. "Hey, you!"

None of the yobs looked around. One kicked the Watcher's knees from behind and brought him to the ground. All three began kicking him.

"Oi!" Ned yelled. "You lot!"

This time the language got through. The beefy hoodlum grinned wolfishly as Ned jumped for him. He launched another wide-swinging blow with the pipe, this one aimed at Ned's face.

Ned ducked, sidestepped, smothered the yobbo's right arm and twisted the pipe out of his hand. Wielding it like a lance, he jabbed the end

into the heavy lad's midriff. The two scrawny ones looked shocked as
their bulky comrade doubled over onto the grass next to Uncle Sam and
began to puke. They ran off.

A moment later the beefy thug staggered to his feet and followed
them. From a safe distance of a few yards he twisted around, face bone-
white, and squeegeed vomit off his lips with the back of his hand. "We'll
get you bloody Yanks!" Then he continued his timely escape.

Ned kneeled beside the Watcher. "Old-timer, you okay?"

The man's voice sounded squeezed with pain. "Hands off me."

Ned heard the American accent, or perhaps a Canadian one. The
man was as old as Ned's own father, but totally down and out. Ned
glanced around the square, looking for someone to help him carry the
old man or call an ambulance or something. But for the moment the
square was empty.

The Watcher stirred and dragged himself to his knees. "Look what
you did to my sign."

"Those hoodlums did it. But that doesn't mean I'm unhappy they
wrecked it."

"You're from the goddamned embassy."

"Yes, I am."

The old man's gaunt, deeply lined face seemed to set in stone. He
started to get to his feet. When Ned reached out, he shook him off.
"Don't need *your* help," he muttered. Slowly, despairingly, he began to
collect bits and pieces of his sandwich boards.

"Can you tell me something?" Ned asked then.

"Not likely."

"What's your beef with the U.S.?"

A bitter noise, like a hoarse crackle of rage, squeezed out of the
Watcher's tight-pressed lips. "Jesus H. Christ," he gritted. "If that isn't
the ultimate insult!" Holding onto his ruined signboards, he limped off
into the gathering dusk.

Ned stood for a long moment. The stage was almost empty now,
yobbos and victims, passers-by, everyone on his way elsewhere. Disgusting
world, wasn't it? Sorry, Professor Chemnitz. Disgusting people. Ned felt
like an idiot saving Uncle Sam's ass for him.

On the other hand, Ned reminded himself, if he's a genuine U.S.
citizen, I guess I owe him one.

Feeling rumpled and out of breath, Ned went back inside and mounted
the stairs to his office. He saw that Chamoun's door was open. A messenger was just leaving. Ned sat down across from Chamoun as the captain

locked his door. Ned closed his eyes for a moment. When he opened them, Chamoun had patched a video player into his micro VDU.

"This is a cassette Laverne sent. Your front-door monitor."

Ned nodded wearily. "Don't let me stop you." He closed his eyes again. "Pretend I'm not here." After a moment, he slowly reopened them as Chamoun slit the envelope and removed the tape cassette he'd had picked up. Ned watched as Chamoun touched the keys of his computer and waited for it to boot up. Then he switched on his video and watched the tape run. The picture was shot through with horizontal white flashes but it was still easy enough to see the man's short-cropped blond head, turned away from the lens. They watched him stoop down out of the frame, then stand up and walk quickly away without, as Laverne had noticed, a postman's bag. Or one of those peculiar dirt-gray smocks some postmen wore.

Chamoun's face looked unhappy. This was always the trouble with the lo-fi equipment used for entrance security. It was too easy to defeat. There'd been a case in Rome, Ned remembered, where the intruders had come armed with a can of black paint to spray the TV camera lens and make the householder believe his system was simply malfunctioning. "Try one of those first frames," he told Chamoun.

He rewound the tape and started it again. There had been one or two frames at the very beginning where . . .

Chamoun flipped to freeze-frame and backed the tape up slightly. There! Ned wondered if he could get a graphic printout of the image. He squinted hard at the electronic picture. The face was unfamiliar, so far. "Who dat?" he asked.

"Dat?" Chamoun rubbed his hands like a magician. He inched the tape one frame farther back, to its very first image. The head was still mostly turned away, but the ear, with its fleshy lobe and individual shape, was something to go on, as was the faint tip of a small nose and just the suggestion of a corner of mouth and eye. It wasn't, properly speaking, a picture of anything much.

"Dat," Chamoun told Ned, "is a lad called either Bertolt Heinemann or Charles Hutt or Ben Idris Wakil. Take your pick."

"Gee, Moe, I love 'em all. Why are we interested in the sucker?" Even as he asked, Ned got that same sudden premonition. He waited for Chamoun's reply, but he already knew the answer.

Part 2

TUESDAY
JUNE 29

7

Laverne had awakened before Ned. These days, with the four girls just
gone home to the States and little for Laverne to do this early, she usually
slept until nine A.M. But here it was, seven. She could hear Ned showering
upstairs. In a sleep-drugged burst of unaccustomed activity, Laverne had
turned out an immense breakfast, the kind with which her mother had
fed four hulking boys and a baby daughter.

Laverne had made sour-milk pancake batter from scratch, fried rashers
of bacon, kept slices of buttered toast on hold in the warmer, and, at the
appearance of her husband, would set flapjacks and eggs a-fryin'. Enough
coffee for eight people, enough maple syrup for twelve, enough orange
juice for sixteen and enough butter for twenty-four were standing by as
potential accessories to the crime of the Great American Breakfast.

She heard Ned shut off the shower upstairs. "What do I smell?" he
called down the stairwell. "Verne, you up?"

"Breakfast's ready when you are."

"Soon's I shave."

Laverne sat down at the bay window in which she was growing pots
of chives and sage and other herbs—or rather was baby-sitting herbs
potted by her oldest daughter, Lou Ann. This was the second week that
there were just the two of them. Laverne had stopped cooking much,

Ned's hours being so uncertain. When she did it tended to be Mother's grub, meat-and-potatoes Gothic, no foreign stuff with garlic.

Ned came into the kitchen, rubbing his chin. He was dressed for the office today, minus his suit jacket, and Laverne could see that, although he had instantly taken in the immensity of the breakfast display, his too-sharp mind had already moved on to other matters. "I asked Moe Chamoun to pick me up."

Laverne nodded. "Flapjacks?"

"N-no. Toast and a strip of bacon."

"You've got to be kidding, Ned. Look at this spread."

"How about this spread?" he responded, patting his absolutely flat belly as if it protruded.

She poured two pancakes onto the griddle and watched them spit fussily for a moment in melted butter. "A man who puts in the hours you do," she said then, "needs a proper breakfast."

Ned shook his head from side to side as he carefully laid the smallest piece of bacon on the smallest triangle of toast. "I don't smoke any more. I only run once or twice a week. I haven't had a tennis racket in my hand for a year. I'm a sedentary, desk-bound pogue, Verne."

Her head swung sideways in unconscious mimicry. "Everything seems to be changing," she murmured almost under her breath. "You can't tell the players without a scorecard."

"That's endemic to this business."

"You mean epidemic." She flipped over the two pancakes. "Is Royce Connell serving a big dinner tonight?"

Ned frowned. "Tonight, is it? No, just his usual class-act buffet."

She turned off the flame under the griddle. "Do you like Royce? Really?"

Ned munched his spartan meal, using the mouthful to keep from speaking. Then he sipped his coffee, black, no sugar. He stared down into the dark depths of the mug and remained silent.

Laverne sighed softly. "I miss the girls." Her voice had a softer quality to it.

Ned looked up suddenly, as if hearing a strange voice. He watched her for a moment. "Me too. When are they due back, early September?"

Never, Laverne answered silently. Not if I can help it will they ever stray from the safe little nest my parents have made for them. She watched Ned's face, feeling a rare and lovely twinge of malice. He wasn't the only one who didn't have to answer questions: two could play.

"I miss them," she said then, "because when they are around for breakfast, you make an effort at conversation."

"Do I?"

She watched the faint flicker of interest in his eyes die out as his brain switched back to whatever it was already brooding about. He went to the refrigerator-freezer, a double-door affair too big now for just the two of them. Without hesitation he opened the fridge door, got out some orange juice, closed the door. Laverne noticed that he had no trouble pouring off and drinking a small glass of juice. "Big white box no spook Kimosabe?" she asked, smiling.

He glanced unhappily at her. "You caught that, huh?"

"Hard to miss. You've been fridge-shy since Bonn. That's more than a year."

He put the glass in the sink and ran water into it. Then he glanced at his watch. "You . . . haven't mentioned it to anyone?"

"Why should I? So it could go into your dossier?"

He nodded, still not looking at her and still not sitting down at the table with her. She transferred the pancakes to her plate, put two pats of butter on them and added some syrup: "Sure you don't want one?"

He turned to see what she was talking about. "They smell great. But no." He checked his watch again. "This is the one Lou Ann gave me, I can't get used to no hands."

"Better sit down," she advised. "Moe Chamoun is never late. But he's never early, either. What do you see in him, anyway?"

"He's a first-class intelligence officer."

Frowning again, Ned stared at the empty chair as if pondering the most important decision of his life. Finally, he picked up the second-smallest strip of bacon and began nibbling slowly at it like a squirrel with a nut. It saved conversation.

"Ned."

"Mm."

"Chamoun mentioned something yesterday about, uh, heightened awareness. I suppose that's officialese for 'no time to help the wife when she's had a run-in with Commie provocateurs.' I had videotape for you that'd still be hanging around the house if I hadn't damn near ordered Chamoun to pick it up. Is that what we're now calling 'heightened awareness'? And speaking of provocateurs, what do I do next time? Or doesn't it concern you that your wife is some kind of target of opportunity? Because it does kind of concern your wife. The next bastard who tries anything gets a .38 slug right through the brisket. Does that do anything to heighten your awareness, Ned?"

He continued to munch the bacon until it was gone. Then he gave her a rather sour smile: "Cool down, Verne. I'm sorry about yesterday. I apologized fully last night."

"Without explaining anything."

He sighed and nearly glanced at his new digital watch one more time, but choked off the gesture. "I suppose," he said in an absolutely neutral tone, "that you've established need to know with that little speech about wasting commie intruders? But just to keep your trigger finger frozen, let me explain."

He outlined the Pandora Fulmer garden party without describing any of the measures he was mounting for the defense of Winfield House. Laverne began cutting wedge shapes in her pancakes with the edge of her fork but without actually eating. "We're invited to the party?"

"Of course. But I'm not going to be able to hold your hand. You'll be on your own."

"Does that make for a change?"

"What?"

"Does being on my own, without you, constitute a change?" She pushed the plate away from her. "When were you going to tell me about the party, the night before?"

"Leave it to you," Ned snapped, allowing the anger to show, "to somehow distill out of a major potential disaster the juice of personal affront."

His wife nodded agreement. "Wives do that. Especially abandoned ones. Especially when the abandonment has been sort of covered up. Live home, sleep in the same bed, but not really *be* here!" she finished in a shout.

"Great." He glanced at his watch openly. "I'm going to wait outside for Chamoun. He's a young, impressionable bachelor. No use poisoning his fantasies about wedded bliss."

"What about mine?"

"I beg your pardon?"

Laverne could feel her breath surging in and out almost painfully. She had never intended to get into this kind of argument. It wasn't her style; it smacked of whining. General Krikowski's only daughter never whined. Whining was the act of an inferior.

"My fantasies of wedded bliss," she heard herself say. "Do you have any idea of what I—?" She stopped herself just in time.

It was none of Ned's business—he had made that quite clear by his phenomenal lack of interest—what she had done to make sure there would be no more children. It was a sin against God and her marriage vows but, at the time, it had seemed the right thing to do to make sure they weren't inundated with children. She no longer went to church every Sunday and it had been more than a year since she'd taken communion. But she could still remember what the priest had said to her that day ten years ago when she had confessed to him about the tubal ligation. His reply had echoed inside her head through the years until she finally saw it as a small masterpiece of bullshit. But she supposed the priest had heard that particular confession often enough to have a pat response ready.

"A heavy burden on your soul," he said, "but you've brought it to the One who specializes in heavy burdens. Leave it with God. And I want you to do a full novena during Lent."

"And every year since," Laverne burst out.

Ned stared at her. "I beg your pardon?"

"Ned. You're like all the rest of them now. You don't even talk American. 'I beg your pardon?' They get at all of you, even the best of you, and they turn you all into wimps."

"Verne, you're babbling."

"Am I? It's from being left behind."

"What?"

"I'm glad I remembered that. Left behind. I was thinking about it yesterday morning when I watched you leave. You're *always* leaving, Ned. Since you eventually come back, you can't be *said* to have left. But the effect's the same, on me. I'm something *left behind*. Do you read me?"

"Even the italics." He looked at the kitchen clock. "Is this something that can only be aired at the start of my working day? Was I supposed to be so groggy after a monster breakfast that you—"

"Oh, sorry about that. I can't imagine why I rustled up all this grub. I must be lonesome for the girls." She began playing with the cut-up pancakes again. "Suppose your Lebanese buddy likes flapjacks?" The doorbell rang.

"Here he is," Ned said with such an obvious look of relief that Laverne's eyes went misty for a moment. General Krikowski's only daughter didn't cry, either. No moan, no whine, no cry.

Instead, General Krikowski's only daughter got to the front door ahead of her husband and invited Moe Chamoun inside. "Take five minutes for a cup of coffee, Captain."

The dark, slender young man smiled pleasantly. "That's a terrific idea, Captain."

Laverne became aware that her thin cotton robe was showing a lot of cleavage. She carefully readjusted it. "How'd you know my grade?"

"We know everything," Chamoun said in a mock tone of mystery. "Morning, Ned."

"Let's go."

Chamoun's progress toward the kitchen and the welcoming smell of fresh coffee halted in mid-stride. "We're in a hurry?"

"We're always in a hurry," Ned rasped, pushing past him to the front door.

"Sorry about the coffee," Laverne said.

"Not as sorry as I am," Chamoun told her.

"Don't answer the door to anybody, Verne," Ned called as he disappeared outside.

"And that's an order," his wife responded with some irony. "But will it help?"

"Seriously," Chamoun said, his dark eyes flashing sympathy, "we're only a phone call away. Don't be a hero."

"On the double, Captain." She made a whooshing gesture. "Out. Out. Out."

She sat down at the kitchen table and listened to the departing purr of the mouse-brown Ford Fiesta. Slowly she began cutting the pieces of cold pancake into even smaller fragments.

When the young girl who would become Queen Victoria first lived there, the Kensington section of London was countryside, small produce farms and wayside villages on the great coach routes north and west.

What she would have said of Max Grieves's neighborhood today is not recorded by history. At Kensington High Street rises a cliché tourist's hotel facing out over the gardens where Victoria cavorted as a child, if Victoria ever cavorted anywhere. In this hotel, as befits a bachelor in a foreign land, Max Grieves rents a mini-suite and sends the bills each month to the Department of Justice, Washington, D.C.

On Tuesday morning he left the lobby at eight, not lingering in the porte cochere to eavesdrop on the comical conversations of fellow Americans visiting London. It would be wrong to say that after several years here Max Grieves was blasé about London. It would be truer to say that he had long ago had his fill of dumb tourist wisecracks.

Besides, he was in a hurry and feeling quite inadequate. In the pecking

order of the embassy, as one of the handful of FBI agents quartered on
Jane Weil's department, he could expect to have a private chat with
Royce Connell almost never, leaving aside the access they all had to the
deputy ambassador at the ten-o'clock meetings each morning. So when
Royce had phoned him the previous night to ask Max to "ride in" with
him this morning, the day shimmered with hope.

Contrary to the comic-book version of a federal agent's daily routine,
it was often quite dull being an FBI man. The fact that Royce had
something to convey in his limousine, under supremely secure conditions, gave Max hope that the assignment was special.

He strode south along Victoria Road into the congeries of dead-end
and one-way streets that make up this residential area, designed to baffle
vehicular traffic in any direction. He turned west in time to see Royce's
bobtailed black Cadillac pull up to the broad entrance stairs of a buff-
colored building bearing a discreet plaque reading CORINTH HOUSE.

Such a huge place, with its staff of servants, assigned to just one man.
Royce must rattle around inside much as Max did in his infinitely smaller
hotel suite. The FBI man stood by the black automobile, nodding to the
chauffeur although they had never actually met. After a while Max began
to examine himself in the tinted windows of the Cadillac, making sure
his appearance was everything it should be. Meeting with Royce Connell
had that effect on most people.

Max looked seedy and inadequate. And first impressions were everything, weren't they? he asked himself. He hadn't come this far, however,
without learning a little about appearances. He gave himself a reassuring,
squared-jaw look in the mirrorlike Cadillac window. Insecure he might
feel. But like the rest of the world, or the successful part of it, he had
somehow to look secure and in control. Not easy.

For one thing, Max told himself, he was a poor excuse for an FBI
man. Grieves had come directly out of a Midwestern state university's
graduate school with an MA in law enforcement. Most of his study had
been in bookkeeping aspects of crime fighting. Max Grieves was one of
the post-Hoover breed hired after the Director's death had released the
bureau from nearly fifty years of make-believe. Freed from the pious
idiocies of the Hoover past, in which it carefully avoided bringing a single
serious case against any member of organized crime, the new bureau was
headed in the opposite direction now. Although it still spent taxpayer
money reinfiltrating the thoroughly blown organizations of the Left, it
had now begun to function as a true federal law-enforcement agency,
taking on a nationwide criminal conspiracy for the very first time.

Max frowned at his reflection in the dark-tinted bulletproof glass of the Cadillac. He looked pasty-faced, his rather long, narrow head pinched and distorted as if by a hangover or a sleepless night. He really was losing his hair, wasn't he? The dark strands inched their way backward almost visibly. He'd benefit from wearing a hat, wouldn't he? Did men wear hats these days? What would Royce say? Did Royce wear a hat? He was so rarely visible out of doors.

And my eyes, Max told himself: not trustworthy. Bloodshot equals shifty. And too light a hazel for a brunette. Christ, everything about him looked wrong this morning. Inadequate.

"Admiring the view?" Royce Connell asked.

Max whirled. He could feel his face burning: "Caught in the act. Good morning, sir."

"A little healthy vanity never hurt anybody," Royce responded, eyeing him slowly, as if for fleas. "Hung over?"

Max winced. "I don't even have that alibi for looking so ratty. You'll have to excuse me this morning. Maybe it's the light."

Royce looked up at tentative patches of blue overhead. Max noticed that the minister, as he was officially called, seemed to have dressed today to match Corinth House behind him, in a sort of oyster-tan summer-weight suit, cut tight in the British tradition, with an almost black tie and heavy black-framed spectacles. By way of matching Royce, Corinth's buff facade sported black window frames and trim. Not by any sign, certainly not a flag, did it advertise what it was the permanent residence of the embassy's number-two in London.

"Shall we?"

They got into the rear of the Cadillac. The chauffeur closed the door and slid behind the wheel. He pressed a button that raised a heavy sheet of plate glass—bulletproof, Max decided—between the driver's part of the car and the spacious rear seats.

Royce locked both rear doors from the inside and sat back as the Cadillac surged forward and into the park where the vast stretch of greensward divides Kensington Gardens on the west from Hyde Park on the east.

"Max," Connell began at once, "does the name Tony Riordan ring a bell? American stock promoter?"

Grieves shook his narrow head. "I'll check the files."

"Do that. Be discreet. I've learned privately that he's about to take a big fall in the city, casting the good name of American financial enterprise even lower into the muck and mire. What I'd like to do is avoid headlines.

I guess what I'd really like is for Riordan to disappear off the face of the earth. But barring that there must be a way for your people to put the arm on him for something he did back home and rush him to the States before all this London stuff, uh"—he recalled the phrase with a faint smile—"hits the fan."

"Can do."

"It's delicate, kidnapping an American citizen. Illegal, too. Please be careful."

Max felt a preliminary tremor of fear jangle his breathing and heart-beat. Cloak-and-dagger stuff! He glanced nervously out the window as the heavy limo turned north along the inner road that fed into Park Lane. They would soon be at the embassy and this highly privileged, horribly dangerous interview would be at an end. Max's mind darted here and there from one worry to another.

"Naturally," Royce was saying, "you're going to have to juggle prior-ities on this one. I want you to give Ned French all the help you can with the garden party. But I want Riordan bagged and shipped within twenty-four hours."

"Wearing two hats . . ." Max's mind wandered again. "I don't suppose anybody wears a hat in summer any more," he was shocked to hear himself ask. "I mean I . . ." He gulped.

Only a world class diplomat knows when not to hear something. Royce Connell seemed to concentrate entirely on smoothing out a crease in his pale tan trousers. When he looked up again, it was to see the environs of Brook Street as the Cadillac drove toward the embassy chan-cery a street away.

"You get out here," he said, rapping on the front window. The driver halted for a moment and Max hopped out of the limo.

"Twenty-four hours," Royce called pleasantly as he shut the door and signaled the chauffeur to drive on.

Max stood for a moment on the corner of Upper Brook and Park Streets. He watched the limousine turn right into Blackburne's Mews. From there ramps led down to subterranean parking levels where the chancery stood. Hot behind it Moe Chamoun's brown Fiesta made the turn. Everybody in motion! Life in the fast lane! Up and at 'em, Grieves!

Not for the first time, Max's narrow face pinched with worry. What was wrong with the bureau, taking on somebody as inadequate as he? Couldn't they have weeded him out long ago? What business did he have on such delicate, illegal stuff?

Grimly, he squared his shoulders and his jaw. He marched off toward
the day's work.

In the garage space at the rear of the chancery Royce Connell's driver
had swiftly brushed down the car, using a large fluffy mitten that deftly
swept away any motes of dust. He checked the ashtrays in the rear of the
limo and found them clean. Then, glancing around the garage to make
sure he was alone, he inserted his right hand palm down under the slight
gap that ran from the passenger part of the car forward to the space under
the driver's seat. His hand came out with a glossy black box the precise
size and design of a John Player Specials cigarette box.

The chauffeur flipped open the box as if to extract a cigarette but
there were none inside. Instead a small tape recorder turned slowly,
silently. Squinting, the chauffeur stopped the tape, pressed a rewind
button and the tiny cassette reeled backward. He tucked it in the breast
pocket of his dark gray whipcord jacket, put a fresh micro-cassette in the
recorder and slipped it into his side pocket.

"Morning, Hopchurch!"

The chauffeur whirled guiltily around, to find P. J. R. Parkins watching him closely. The big man made absolutely no noise walking up on
his prey. "M—mornin', Major."

"Morning, what?"

"Sorry, sir. It's bloody hard to think of you as a bloody civilian, isn't
it?"

"Just once make that mistake in front of the wrong bloke," Parkins
began in a hectoring tone.

"I know, sir. I do indeed, don't I? Most sorry." Hopchurch dug into
his breast pocket and removed the tiny cassette. He and Parkins glanced
around the garage before the small item, the size of a thin matchbox,
changed hands.

"A Mr. Grieves, sir."

"Gotcher."

Parkins about-faced in a manner so military that no trained observer
needed to hear him accidentally referred to as "Major." He moved off
as silently as he had come, heading back through the chancery building
to his small office filled with electronic equipment.

Behind him, much relieved at escaping a real verbal hiding, Hopchurch got out a small spray bottle and began polishing the Cadillac's
windows, inside and out. One of Major Parkins's men he might be, but
he was also quite a professional chauffeur as well, wasn't he? He'd worked

for half the foreign embassies in London, hadn't he? Damned well knew his business, didn't he?

Smiling slightly, he polished the glass to a beautiful sheen.

The Fiat Fiorino is perhaps the smallest European-made van on the road today, now that most corrugated-hut Citroën 2CV's have rattled their last. This Fiorino, sprayed bullet gray over blisters of pocked rust, fed deftly through the Hyde Park roundabout traffic and headed toward the Thames. It crossed the river where the Battersea Power Station's four great Art Deco smokestacks dominate the flat landscape of parkland and warehousing. Passers-by had time to spell out the maroon lettering on the Fiorino's flanks: WELLINGTON NOVELTIES.

Bert drove under two railway bridges, then swung sharply left into one of the many dreary industrial wastelands Hitler's bombs left standing in South London. U-STORE–U-LOCK read the sign on the large brick building.

Bert braked to a halt before high Cyclone fence gates. He eyed his two companions. If the strategy was for them to blend inconspicuously into the milieu as ordinary working-class types, their preparations had been ambitious but not thorough. The dingy overwashed jeans with rubbed knees, yes. The tattered sweatshirts, yes. But the hair: Bert and the two Arab men had recently had haircuts. As London laborers, their hair was much too short.

When Bert signed in, the girl who controlled the entrance gates barely glanced at them. It really wouldn't concern her, Bert decided, that they were an ill-matched threesome.

He, tall and blond, contrasted sharply with Merak, a short, famine-wracked lad of perhaps sixteen with scruffy black hair and dark olive skin, and Mamoud, who had the kind of pale grubby look produced by an overdose of cigarettes and not enough baths. Of a lighter complexion than Merak, Mamoud showed faint lines of sweat-dirt in any crevice that would accumulate them, under fingernails and even at the desert-squint corners of his steady, pale gray eyes.

Bert steered the tiny van into the alleyway that served the warehouse. He was all too aware that raw recruits like these gave Khefte major training problems. Six months ago—six weeks in some cases—they had been desert or souk rats living on a mouthful of couscous and scrounged cigarette butts. They had no idea of how to behave in a Western ambience like London's. They could only mimic a role model like Khefte, whom they adored. As a result, they tended to move like a male dance team, executing a choreography of stance and motion dictated by tough para-military discipline.

Bert parked the Fiorino near Area G. In the distance at Area J they could see a police van from which two uniformed bobbies were unloading large cartons. This had happened before during Bert's visits here; he already knew that several local precincts used this warehouse to store their outdated paperwork. But the sight of blue uniforms caused Mamoud's steady gray eyes to flare wildly, and skinny Merak to stumble as he left the Fiorino. Then, picking up cues from Bert, they added to the flow of their choreography an extra measure of utter nonchalance.

For them this had been the hardest of Khefte's lessons to learn. It was difficult to change the habits of a stealthy young lifetime and teach recruits, fresh from Heathrow Airport with their student visas, to emulate the stunned and gelid ennui of the young British worker. This was es-pecially so when a burning thirst to slash open each white's guts and watch them ooze steaming mauve into the gutter inflamed these young-sters with luscious fantasies of hot blood.

Bert opened the small van's rear door to let Merak and Mamoud remove a rack of brilliant turquoise dresses wrapped in clear plastic. They wheeled the rack into an elevator that took them two floors higher, where they rolled the dresses down a long corridor of locked doors. They stopped at one with a drop-forged vanadium-steel padlock.

Bert inspected the dial to see if anyone had tampered with the com-bination. He always left it set at 14. Since only he had the combination, it was his responsibility to make sure of the impenetrability of this lockup space. He had asked Khefte to keep a copy of the numbers, but the handsome young Arab could not be bothered with such details.

Bert was well aware that almost any lock can be removed, given time and the proper equipment. This one was far too tough to be sawed or burned by any normal welding torch. A thermic lance would be needed. But Bert also knew that with police and other users of the warehouse coming and going regularly, there would never be enough privacy for anyone to force the lock. Whoever had its combination, however, controlled about a hundred thousand pounds worth of ammo and weap-ons.

He ushered the Arab youths into the cubicle and bolted the door behind them. Around the three of them lay wooden crates stacked four and five high. "The police dogs below," Bert murmured in Arabic. "Do you think they noticed us?"

Mamoud had already opened the nearest crate. He stared down almost lasciviously at a battered Ingram M-10, naked-looking minus its magazine and fat barrel silencer. "Let them," he sneered. "With this we conquer cities of police."

Bert reached past him and lifted out the Ingram. "A wise choice, Mamoud," he went on in a tone of praise. He flipped open other boxes and assembled the Ingram's components, carefully choosing the most heavily used silencer and a tattered steel magazine that rattled loosely with its load of cartridges.

He placed it in Mamoud's hands, locking glances with the steady gray eyes. "Test it well, brother," he cautioned. "If such a much-used weapon as this works properly, so will the rest. They were bought in batches. If the worst of them works, so will the rest of the batch."

He opened another crate and removed four grenades at random. Merak's thin fingers snatched at the corrugated gray-green eggs and clutched them to his bony breast.

"These will be a problem for you," Bert advised him: "As Khefte has explained, you must make sure the noise of the explosions goes unnoticed." He unpacked a Kalashnikov and snicked in its curved magazine, battered and dented with much use. "But we have arranged for you to use one of Khefte's safe houses outside London. It is in a deserted rural setting but close to the underground tube. And, as you will see, thanks to the stupidity of the great Satan, it is an ideal place to test weapons."

Mamoud took the AK-47 from him, hefted it, and turned toward a row of eye-shatteringly orange women's dresses hanging on a wheeled clothes rack. He slid the weapon inside the plastic covering and managed to attach it to the hanger in such a way that the dress hid it completely. He glanced up coolly at Bert, not seeking praise but quite ready to entertain it.

"Very good, Mamoud," Bert enthused. These Arab youths were hardly more than children, but children with bulging male egos that responded to praise like crops to rain.

Eagerly, Merak began tucking grenades into the pockets of a flame-colored silk jacket. "Excellent, Merak," Bert said. "Now I understand, brothers, why Khefte in his great wisdom chose you two of all the rest."

At the far end of the Metropolitan underground line sits the suburb of Amersham-on-the-Hill, spawned in the 1930s when the Metropolitan line first came through. It looks down on Old Amersham, the true village that dates back to the Saxons, if not the Romans, and to this day boasts Tudor, if not Elizabethan, pubs, houses, and barns. Bert had taken it on himself to drive the Fiorino and its small cargo of weaponry to Amersham, there to pick up Merak and Mamoud after they completed a practice run on the subway train.

They swaggered out of the station now as if they had endured and conquered an immensely difficult task. Mamoud, who had established domination over the smaller Merak, claimed the front seat beside Bert while their starved comrade rode in the back like merchandise.

"You must remember the way," Bert cautioned Mamoud. "When you have completed your tests you must telephone London at once, walk back to the station, and take the next train to London. Understood?"

Mamoud's pale gray eyes stared straight ahead at the road. The Fiorino was moving briskly now past the seventeenth-century façades of Old Amersham. After a moment they were on open road with the Chiltern hills gently rising on either side, covered in alfalfa fields and copses of trees. Sheep nibbled at great green fields. Crows swarmed in small, nervous flocks.

"Here," Bert said, slowing after a mile to turn left at the sign LITTLE MISSENDEN.

The Fiorino rattled between small cottages and past two pubs. There seemed to be no other store of any kind. After turning off onto even narrower roads past a church, Bert backed the van into a squeezed garagelike lean-to that supported the end cottage of four, dilapitated but still standing in all their Tudor whitewashed stucco and black cross-and-slant timbering.

Even this late in June, the empty house had a chill to it that made little Merak shiver as he carried in the weapons and stowed them in the cramped kitchen with its late-Victorian furnishings.

Bert laid his finger on his lips. "Listen," he whispered.

The three of them stood silently for a long moment. Then, not far away, someone seemed to fire two shots. Merak flinched, but Mamoud stood his ground.

"Listen again."

The chilly interior of the old house lay as still as a grave. The three waited patiently, Bert checking his wristwatch. Again, two shots, but from a slightly different direction.

"Did I not say that this place was ideal for the testing of weapons?" he asked the two boys. "There are crops. There are crows. And, there are these machines that use a cannister of propane gas to make the sounds of explosion, a double explosion, as of a shotgun. *Boom-boom!*"

"And the crows fly away?" Merak asked.

"Exactly." Bert touched his lips again. They waited. Two more shots from a new direction.

"They begin at dawn, these insane machines," he explained. "There are at least half a dozen in this area alone. And they stop when the sky grows truly dark. This time of year, between nine and ten P.M."

"How stupid the whites," Mamoud sneered.

Putting aside his own skin color, Bert nodded vigorously. "But what a gift from Allah." He paused. "Do you have any questions?"

Merak shook his narrow head, the scurf of his scalp showing through thin black hair. Mamoud looked away, steady and cool in his new leadership fantasy.

"Let me suggest," Bert told them both, "that south and west of this village lie rather extensive woods surrounded by crow machines. Do your testing there between nine and ten o'clock. Understood?"

Again Merak nodded agreement while Mamoud failed to reply. "Do not wait until later, when the pubs close. The English, wandering home in a stupor, are dangerously unpredictable. Do your testing between nine and ten P.M. And there will still be trains back to town, at least until midnight. Is that clear?"

He watched Merak's scruffy head bob twice in agreement. The mulish look in Mamoud's steady eyes grew, if anything, more recalcitrant. The sooner Bert left these two to their task, the sooner Mamoud would stop acting out anti-white ego tricks.

"Good fortune, brothers," Bert said, heading for the side door to the lean-to. "Stay inside until dark. Then, to work! May Allah guide your hand."

8

Within the great chancery building Tuesday had begun to accelerate its tempo in crisscross rhythms, people fresh from their private lives shifting to the public affairs of the embassy. They relied on the throat-clearing routines of opening mail and gathering notes. But for two men this hour before the ten-o'clock was anything but routine. Like willful slashes of paint, flung in anarchic swirls, the two made their rounds in a manner too concentrated and much too deceptive to be called routine.

And both kept carefully out of each other's way.

Ned French had by now visited several departments as he went through his usual sniffing of the air. Although he had talked with a lot of people, he found that he wasn't listening well. His mind was still on the morning altercation with Laverne, if one could describe her outburst that way.

Trying to get the whole episode out of the front of his mind, Ned saw that the reason he was having difficulty was that the outburst was such a rarity. Laverne was not a complainer. Ned had listened to enough gripes about army wives over the years to know that his own rarely gave that kind of trouble.

It had to be something quite powerful, a grievance of heavy emotional charge, to spark such a scene. Which he had handled about as badly as possible, Ned told himself.

He paused at a turning of the stairs, considering the situation from this new viewpoint. The very idea that his life with Laverne was creating a problem for him here in the chancery was a sign of such outrageously bad management that, if it had happened to an officer under him, Ned would have had to reprimand him severely.

As he stood there, he saw a thick, tree-trunklike torso silently round the stairs a landing below: the estimably stiff-backed P. J. R. Parkins, pacing as quietly as a cat. Ned drew back out of sight. It was not the first time they had nearly met, each on his morning round. But, like all their other near-encounters, this one had been deftly stage-managed to avoid confrontation.

The thought of old Parkins padding about the building filled Ned with a mixture of chagrin and amusement. He had no doubt the man was MI5 or Special Branch. His job gave him the excuse for prying into any crevice of the chancery. What bothered Ned much more was his suspicion that Parkins's work was so easy to spot that it might well be a bluff. The British war effort in World War II had been stuffed with deliberate duplicity, fake armies and airfields, double agents at every turn, elaborate spoof campaigns and the like. Any foreign intelligence officer who worked with them knew that bluffs had always been a hallmark of the British style. But, if this were so, what was being covered up?

Ned walked quickly toward his next drop-in talk, not even aware that thinking about Parkins had neatly moved Laverne out of the limelight and almost backstage. The old boy had his uses.

At nine thirty Ned French moved up the stairs to the floor where Jane Weil worked. He glanced out of the windows at Grosvenor Square below. Late-arriving office workers moved at a leisurely pace toward their destinations. The day was mixed, patches of blue hurrying past at high altitudes, followed by rolling clouds.

Ned stared out at the scene, wondering why he didn't move on. The square looked . . . wrong?

The Watcher wasn't there.

Well, of course not, Ned remembered. Those punks had gotten in some heavy blows and kicks. A man the age of the Watcher would be nursing painful bruises. Ned found himself wondering how old the man was. Sixties? His own father's age? Hadn't he asked Max Grieves to check him out a few months ago? There ought to be a file.

Detouring on his way to Jane's office, Ned stopped at Grieves's shut door. He knocked, paused and entered. Max's long, narrow face looked surprised and squeezed out of shape, as if it had just emerged from a wringer.

"Morning, Ned." The FBI man's voice was almost a groan. "What's the latest on the July Fourth thing?"

"Never mind that. What hit you this morning?"

"Do I look that bad?"

"I've seen worse in a bottle of formaldehyde up at London Clinic."

"I've got a—" Max stopped.

Ned had always found this man's face easy to read. "I've got a problem," was the import of the choked-off words. Ned nodded, as if in answer to a question. "You remember a few months back I asked you to run a check on that old geezer with the funny sign who hangs out in Grosvenor Square?"

Painfully, Grieves tried to shift his attention from his own unvoiced fears and doubts to what he hoped was a nonthreatening request. "Yeah, sure. What's up?"

"Can you give me a look at his file?"

"Yeah, sure. What's up?"

Ned frowned at him. "I mean like now."

"Yeah, su—" This time even Max heard the panicky repetition. "Old geezer with the sign." He turned in his desk chair to the computer terminal set on a right-angle table leaf. He switched on the machine, then paused, fingers poised over the keyboard.

"All the latest high-tech, huh, Max?"

"Yeah, sure. What the hell was his name?"

"You can't access it without a name? What kind of data retrieval system is that? I mean, could you try a keyword?" Ned suggested. " 'Protest'? Uh, 'dissent'? 'Complaint'? 'Crank'? 'Loony'? Max, does somebody else in your office have a better access code? Max?"

Grieves shook his head very slowly from side to side. "You don't understand, Ned. In this office, I am the computer officer. I am the one they sent to computer school. I am the one who set up all our data programs."

Ned was silent for a moment. "And you entered your dossiers only one way, by subject name?"

"Is there some other way?"

This time Ned didn't speak for a much longer time; he was busy calculating the cost of four or five terminals and a secure heavy-duty mainframe computer dedicated only to the work of this office.

"Hey, look," Max burst out. "Give me the bastard's name and I can lay his whole life in your lap inside of a tenth of a second, Ned."

"Terrific."

"Burnside!" Max screamed.

"What?"

Grieves joyously punched away at the keyboard. True to his boast, within less than a second a paragraph of three lines appeared on the monitor tube, glowing bright green letters that Ned bent down to read.

BURNSIDE, AMBROSE E., the dossier began. AGE: 66. MALE. CAUCASIAN. CURRENT ADDRESS: 60 GOODGE ST, EC2, LONDON. NO KNOWN RECORD.

"Where's the rest?" Ned asked.

"The man has no record, here or back home, Ned."

"That's admirable," Ned responded. "If a man has no record you can't develop any more information than this?"

"I followed him home myself. I got his name from his landlady. It's a collection of bed-sits above a pub with a funny name. Nobody in the pub knew him except as the guy with that crazy sign. He didn't frequent the pub. He didn't talk to anybody. Half a day of my time, it took. A transient neighborhood over there, Ned. Students at London University. People who use the British Museum. It's Bloomsbury, for Christ's sake."

"Calmly, Max."

"I'm calm," Grieves assured him. "I checked him with all the master files, here and back home. Came up blank."

"Clean bill of health, then?"

"Did I *say* that?" Max moaned. "He could be Joseph Stalin resurrected. All I know for a fact is he has no record."

"But you're wrong, Max. Ambrose E. Burnside was a very famous Union general during the Civil War."

For a long moment Grieves stared owlishly into Ned's eyes. Then, testing: "Some relative, maybe?"

"Great-grandson, maybe?" Ned helped out.

"Maybe."

"Maybe an alias, maybe?"

"Aw, shit, Ned."

The two men observed another lengthy silence. "Shut off your dumb computer, Max." Ned French sighed. "What'd it set us back, the whole damned thing, half a million? Is that what private industry charges Uncle Sam? Double the market price? Latest state-of-the-art software and you program it for an alias that wouldn't fool a schoolkid of twelve."

"These things happen, Ned. You know that."

And at least you didn't end up with your head in my refrigerator, Ned added silently. He scribbled Burnside's address on a slip of Grieves's paper. "Thanks for all your help, Max."

When Ned turned toward the door, Grieves cleared his throat. "Ned, I'm administration. I'm not a hotshot field guy. I mean, when I tail somebody like Burnside, we're lucky if I don't lose him in the first few streets."

"Now, Max, don't be endearing."

"Listen, you asked for help and I did what I could." Grieves held up his hand. "Which wasn't much. Okay, agreed. But now you have to help me. The name is Tony Riordan, American con artist, stock promoter. I have run him through the computer five different ways and nothing shows up."

"There are five different ways of spelling Riordan?"

"At least. Ring a bell?"

Ned shook his head. "Maybe his real name is Am—"

"—brose E. Burnside. Very funny. I'm waiting for the dayside to come on duty back home at the Bureau. Maybe he's in their file."

"Quarter to ten A.M. here? Quarter to five A.M. in Washington, D.C. The dayside doesn't come on for a while. Try telexing the night guys."

Ned left Grieves's office and made his way along the corridor to Jane's room. He kept wondering how many government jobs were filled by amiable idiots like Max Grieves. You couldn't stay angry at them. But you couldn't get a day's work out of them, either. Or, if you did, it was a churned-up ball of mistakes that someone else had to untangle.

Jane's secretary was away. Ned moved past her desk and knocked on Jane's open doorway. "I have a complaint about one of your people, Miss Weil, ma'am."

"Why, Colonel French, sir, you did startle me."

They stared at each other without speaking. Then Ned moved a few paces inside the door. "Stop right there. You look good enough to eat," Jane said. "And I'm due at the ten-o'clock."

"No time for even a snack."

"None. What's the complaint?"

"I know you don't run Max Grieves, but—"

"Such a sweet young man. But between here and here," Jane said, indicating her left and then her right ear, "pure Philadelphia cream cheese."

"What is this obsession with eating things?"

"Never mind. What's for lunch?"

"I think I can promise you some dry-roasted peanuts, if the hotel's restocked the frigobar."

"Usual time?"

"Let's start a half hour late, just to break the routine."

She nodded, her glance going past him. "Amanda, did you finish that Xeroxing?"

"I'm on my way," her secretary called. Ned listened to her heels click off into the distance. He mimed a small kiss, then turned and left, making sure Amanda caught sight of him right behind her.

"Yes, Jock," P. J. R. Parkins was telling the man at the other end of the telephone line. "No need to send it over. I've wiped it. Just noteworthy for the name of Tony Riordan."

He sat there, planted firmly in his chair as if both he and the chair had been carved by the same craftsman out of the same thick log.

"Yas?" the Scotsman asked in his usual irritated tone.

"Riordan," Parkins repeated.

"Is that s'posed t' tairn me on?" Jock inquired acidly.

"If it doesn't, maybe I'm wrong."

An awkward pause followed this. Then Parkins stirred himself. "Do you have the file on that jogging accident from yesterday?"

"Do I? I do not."

"It seems to me the poor lad who got hit by the car was called Riordan. Or the bastard who drove the car."

A yawn came down the line. "Warrk it out, Peter, warrk it out." The line to MI5 went dead.

It was physically possible for Parkins to lean forward or back in his chair; it was, however, culturally encoded in his genes that while one was seated one's upper trunk remained at a strict ninety-degree angle to the floor. So, to get some ease now, after his rebuff by the Scotsman, he got to his feet and began pacing the narrow area between tables of electronic equipment and tools.

He'd have to phone around. He'd have to ring up the duty sergeant and get the first name of Riordan. Name. Nationality. It was probably a total coincidence. He was probably neither a Tony nor a Yank. And he could even be a Peardon or a Dearden, Parkins cautioned himself, because the report he had gotten yesterday was by telephone, not in writing.

But if he were Tony Riordan, of American extraction, then what kind of game was the crafty Colonel French playing?

*   *   *

The young man in the loose, student-type clothing lay on his stomach, legs spread, elbows crooked in an infantry position, head erect and eyes peering through extremely powerful binoculars of such magnification that they required a small tripod of their own to keep the images steady.

He lay in what seemed to have been a small bedroom, long deserted, on the third floor of a modern building which the British would call a "purpose-built block," an apartment house. Situated in this leafy glen amid the lush summer greenery of Regent's Park, the house might at one time have been a dormitory for students and the young man one of its legitimate occupants.

But the business upon which he seemed thoroughly embarked—he kept a thermos of hot coffee and some candy bars by his side—would hint that there was nothing legitimate now about his presence in this place.

At this height his line of sight just cleared the rather thick stand of bushes and trees planted across the street to shield from prying eyes Winfield House, home of Ambassador and Mrs. Adolph Fulmer III. The street that intervened between watcher and watched was called Outer Circle. At this hour of late morning, very few autos used it as a thoroughfare south.

It was along Outer Circle, in fact, that Ned French had jogged yesterday, seen Old Glory unfurled and, a moment later, the muted gleam of the central London mosque. This Islamic temple lay just south of the dormitory-style building in which the watcher continued to survey the windows of Winfield House and the two entrances that led into it from Outer Circle.

One entrance, directly across from the dormitory, would have had a clear view of Winfield House's west flank and south façade. But it had been chained shut, its great iron gates boarded over with plywood to foil the stares of passers-by. The other entrance, a few yards to the north, remained open, but guarded by a gate house. The few vehicles that came would pause to be identified, then swing left along gravel paths to the rear of the mansion or, alternatively, to the parking area behind the greenhouse and tennis courts.

The man with the binoculars glanced at his wristwatch, saw that it was eleven o'clock, and reached for a rather bulky walkie-talkie.

"Tango-two for Charley-one."

The radio transceiver crackled. "Speak to me, oh observant one."

"Usual traffic. Gardener's van. Also Hodgkins and Daughter, Caterers."

"You have made my day, oh eye of Allah."

"Ten-four."

The young man pulled over a clipboard and scribbled a line on the printed sheet of paper after the number eleven. Then he resumed his watching. Abruptly, the walkie-talkie made gravelly noises again. "Tango-two, Tango-two, visitors."

"Say again, Charley-one."

"Thou art bless-ed above all men," the man's voice intoned. "Gotcher shoes shined, soldier? Ten-four."

Puzzled, the man with the binoculars stared at the silent radio. Then the meaning of the message came through to him: someone arriving on an inspection tour. Well, so what? He was where he was supposed to be, doing what he'd been ordered to do. No need to panic.

"Don't get up," a voice barked behind him.

The young man writhed sideways, grabbing for the nasty little Uzi submachine gun that lay next to the walkie-talkie. Then he froze. "Ulp," he managed to say.

"Ulp you."

A small man, as compact as a fire hydrant, stood in the doorway of the room. At first glance he looked somewhat like an unfriendly Mickey Rooney, but a Mickey Rooney who did fifty press-ups a day. There was much the same elfin face, now jowly, but the sparse iron-gray hair wasn't teased forward into elf-locks. It bristled defiantly in a strict fifteen-millimeter crew cut.

"As you were," the small man yapped. "Back to the binoculars, Schultheiss."

"Yes, Mr. Rand."

"Much going on?"

"Routine, Mr. Rand. Delivery trucks."

"Lorries, Schultheiss, lorries. Keep to the local chatter. You don't stick out as much."

"Yes, Mr. Rand."

"You heard about Sunday's disaster plan?"

"Mr. Croft briefed me. Some sort of celebrity bash?"

"It's an abort, Schultheiss."

"Huh?"

"No go. No bash. We're disestablishing it."

"But I understood this was a personal project of Mrs. F.?"

"Well, disunderstand yourself, Schultheiss."

"Yes, Mr. Rand."

The exchange of flat American voices in the unfurnished room sent up a faint clatter of echoes, as if the conversation was being conducted from a much greater distance over extraterrestrial wavelengths. The antiphonal response, "Yes, Mr. Rand," tendered at intervals, had a most soothing effect, as if the colloquy might have been carried on between the altar and the extreme rear pew of a very large cathedral.

"So pack up and follow me," Rand told the younger man. "We're going to enhance our electronic surveillance by an incremental factor of two, you and Dietrich. Everything in and out gets taped and transcribed."

"Even the stuff on Mrs. F's lines?"

"Especially."

"Yes, Mr. Rand."

The short, gray-haired man stared down challengingly. "Get going, man." He watched Schultheiss pack away his gear in a plain canvas duffel bag, which he zipped shut as he got to his feet.

"All set, Mr. Rand."

They looked an odd pair, Schultheiss still resembling most of all a student. With his duffel bag he was now a student on his way home for summer vacation. And Larry Rand, who ran Station London for the Company, looked like anything but. Retired jockey? Athletic coach? Something sports-oriented? There was a strongly aggressive forward-leaning stance to him, an indomitable, bulldoggish, "get in there team and *win!*" look that went well with the clipped, order-giving yap and the air of total self-assurance.

Rand swiveled around and led the way out of the room to a larger area where a long table bristled with eavesdropping equipment. Several young men, student types, all wore micro-light earphones and appeared to be listening to their normal diet of Top 40 pop recordings. But from time to time they scribbled notes.

Once in motion, Larry Rand lost the bulldog look. He was extremely light on his feet, swiveling, backing and sidling like an adept sheepdog or terrier. And, like a small dog or a jockey, he seemed to have mastered the trick of conquering the world. Perhaps he knew it instinctively, that it took only the proper flick of a riding crop, or the well-timed paroxysm of yapping, to force great massive things to obey.

He sat Schultheiss down at one end of the long table and indicated a pair of headphones. "The interceptions are assigned automatically," he explained. "When your control panel lights up, snap to and be god-damned sure you code your notes accurately as to time received, down to the split second. Otherwise we have a hell of a time matching notes to tapes. Understand?"

"Yes, Mr. Rand."

"Get going."

Rand sidled up to the window. In the top floor of Winfield House, working away at one of the dormer windows in the mansard roof, a housemaid squirted too little liquid on the glass and polished it half-heartedly. Rand's face grew scornful. Half-assed performance bothered him far more than nonperformance. You paid a maid to clean. If she didn't you fired her. But it took years to catch up with the maid who gave it a lick and a promise. Meanwhile, she was stealing your money like a thief.

He turned and glared at the group of young men. They seemed to be studying for an examination, gathered at a long library table where electronic information slowly nurtured their minds. Well, it *was* an exam, Larry Rand reminded himself. Every day the enemy threw curves you had to be able to handle. The exam never stopped, life-and-death questions to which you had to know the answer or pay the supreme penalty.

He moved to a corner of the room where a plain telephone lay on the dusty concrete floor. He picked it up and dialed a number. "Henning," he snapped after a moment. "Give."

The man at the other end began with a few throat noises of the "I'm not sure" variety. "Too early to tell, Mr. Rand."

"Is it?" Rand barked. "Or is that just an excuse?"

"We just started an hour ago. About half the people haven't yet answered their phones."

"Alibis, Henning. Who did you connect with so far?"

"In person just two: Rupert Maine and Gillian Lamb."

"Who?"

"He's some honcho at Granada TV and she's got a TV show of some kind. Women's news? Something."

"Spare me, Henning. What's the bottom line?"

"Maine caved instantly. He's not coming and he's yelling at any of his people who were invited not to come. But this Lamb bitch wanted to know who I was, speaking for what organization, et cetera, et cetera."

"No alibis. What's the bottom line?"

"Mr. Rand, what we did was make damned sure this woman will be there Sunday. She says controversy's her middle name. Some gobbledygook about lambs to slaughter."

Larry Rand stood silently for a long moment, listening to the faint shushing sound of voices in half a dozen pairs of headphones as his crew continued eavesdropping on Winfield House. "Keep at it, Henning," he snapped then. "What luck have the others had?"

"About the same. Fifty-fifty."

"Here's an order: You get another tough nut like the Lamb bitch, you're authorized to issue threatening letters from terrorist groups. Got it? Go to condition red on cranks like her. We'll see how much controversy she really likes."

He hung up and stood, half-turned away from the listening crew. He didn't know if Gillian Lamb were American or British. If the former, he'd institute a search-and-destroy mission, the works, and call in the IRS to audit her tax returns. If British, he'd hint that he could get the same aggravation mounted by Special Branch and Inland Revenue. He couldn't, so poor was the state of relations between the Company and its opposite numbers in Britain, but Lamb wouldn't know that. Anyway, in the odd case where Rand might actually have to squeeze some pinko celeb to the wall, he could always blackmail the Brits into helping. It gave away points but so be it.

Like some of the staff recruited after the wartime OSS was phased out and the peacetime CIA was created, E. Lawrence Rand had been a student at Brown University. His academic career had been C+ but he had managed the fencing team, a post that, like coxswain of the rowing team, belonged to diminutive students. In any event, after graduation in 1960 he went on active duty with the Company and rose steadily in its ranks.

This was due to two factors, the first a sheer accident. One of the founding fathers of the CIA had been E. Henry Rand, not related at all, a fact Larry managed to keep quiet. Sharing an initial and a last name might seem too obvious a bit of juju in even the most primitive society. But in the corridors of the CIA at Langley, Virginia, especially after the death of the founding Rand, it worked like a charm.

The second reason for Larry Rand's steady rise to power within the Company was by no means accidental. It had to do with character. Station London, by way of illustration, had always been a plum assignment for any career spook edging toward retirement. It usually went to a man ready to leave the fast lane for intensive cultivation of his rose garden.

But in recent years Station London had become a tough case, loaded with nasty surprises and requiring, as station head, a real ball-buster, someone who could be a bastard without the faintest qualm.

Larry Rand came naturally to mind.

What he was doing now, "disestablishing" Pandora Fulmer's party, a pride and joy more precious to her than a child, would earn him her undying hatred if she ever found out who was intimidating her guests. It wouldn't go down at all well with cryptofaggot comsymps like Royce Connell, either, much less his seeing-eye dog, Ned French.

But not for one second did a man like Larry Rand doubt that he was doing the right thing. That was the secret of command, utter confidence. Yes, his intervention might have an opposite effect with a junkhead journalist like Gillian Lamb. It might create a hard core of dipshit knee-jerk liberals who rallied around, constituting a target of opportunity for a few Mick or Muslim murderers and giving Ned French a hard time after all.

Never mind. When you know what the right thing is, you do it over and over again. And again, until at last you reach Larry Rand's level, where *whatever* you do is the right thing. At the last minute, when hordes of guests failed to show up, his own people assigned to French would make sure the ambassador and his asshole wife were protected. The rest were expendable.

Especially Ned French.

One of the problems a tough man has, once he is respected as a ball-buster, is that his more finely honed instincts go unpraised. For all his swagger and yap, the diminutive Larry Rand had an almost paranoid ability to spot character flaws. His antennae were infinitely more sensitive than most Company yahoos and never more so than when his jungle instincts were aroused.

In the jungle, the animal that shows weakness must be brought down. Basic triage instincts demand this. But there is a special knack to recognizing such beasts. One must be aware, for instance, when an animal like Ned French is about to leave the herd. One must anticipate his first lurch, his first stumble, and file that information away against a rainy day.

That was the art of intelligence as Larry Rand saw it: files bulging with such detail, he could stand off any attack by any other bureaucracy. That was his highest priority as head of Station London, to protect it from bureaucratic sabotage.

Did some birdbrain like Connell want to bypass the Company, assign

a different man and service to a job that was rightfully the Company's?
Then the man had to be smashed before Connell's eyes, dramatically,
dangerously. That was the only way such an important lesson could be
taught.

As for French, tough titty. He knew the rules of bureaucracy. If he
hadn't learned them by now, then he deserved to be wasted.

9

Normally, Ned scheduled his rendezvous with Jane for about half-past twelve. Having set the time closer to one P.M. today, Ned left the chancery at five minutes to the hour, moving briskly in the sporadic sunshine, looking neither left nor right as befits a man giving the impression that he does not, could not, and will not conceive of being followed.

Like so many outward aspects of Ned French, this was an illusion. Years before, in his parents' home in Fond du Lac, Wisconsin, a rambling frame house with broad veranda and cool basement, Ned and his friends had whiled the hot summers away playing table tennis in the cellar. It had developed, in some of them, a hacking cough caused by too many illicit cigarettes and, in Ned, an amazing degree of what ophthalmologists called "peripheral vision," together with the other table tennis attributes of instant, almost visceral reactions and decisions.

Even this extra ability did nothing to quell the uneasy feeling he had today that all was far from well. Perhaps it had been Laverne's outburst this morning, or the silliness of Max Grieves, or any of a dozen other minor disturbances, all of them combining to stir up an overarching premonition of larger failures to come.

Even so he marched resolutely eastward along Brook Street and doubled back via the pedestrian thoroughfare called South Molton Street, past small boutiques going in and out of bankruptcy and even tinier but more solvent eating places where, one day when all this uneasiness calmed down, he and Jane might manage an out-in-the-open lunch devoid of the angst of the present.

One day, when all this calms down, Ned repeated to himself. When all the angst evaporates. How would that come about? he wondered. How would Laverne be persuaded to let him go? How would he and Jane openly display their feelings for each other and not draw down instant, if veiled, disciplinary action?

Behind Ned, pausing to stare into narrow shop windows displaying scrawny punk-styled trash, a young student more or less kept pace with Ned's progress. By the time they had reached the noise and crowds of Oxford Street the young man had closed the gap, in approved style, to about thirty yards. In the parlance of agentcraft, Ned noted, he had escalated from a long to a short tail.

Pausing at the congested thoroughfare, Ned faced this way and that as if watching for a bus, without once turning to look directly at the student. But in the swings of his head his remarkable peripheral vision picked up yet another pedestrian with a strikingly similar itinerary. He had spotted the young fellow as far back as the post office at the corner of Blenheim and Molton, a weedy lad with too-short dark hair and a nose, as Ned's father had put it, "I'd like to have full of nickels."

Feeling somewhat like the grand marshal of a parade, Ned waited for the lights to change and moved across Oxford Street. His cortege followed at appropriate distances, Student within thirty yards, Nose holding back at fifty. As far as Ned could judge, being prohibited by caution from a direct inspection, neither youngster had spotted the other.

While being tailed was not yet another of the day's minor failures, it did contribute to the generally doomed ambience of the day. No good would come of Tuesday, Ned decided. Another famous French foreboding?

Ned paused again to let his goslings regroup while he tried to decide what to do. He had a lot of faith in his ability to lose anyone in the madhouse that was Selfridge's ground floor. But two followers?

A long file of buses inched steadily eastward now, people swinging on and off the open rear decks with such ease that it was possible to believe this common London habit was a safe one. Indeed, Ned knew, it was not; the person jumping on or off rarely got hurt, but some small, elderly, law-abiding grandmother patiently waiting for the legal moment to board or leave the bus was usually crushed instead.

Annoying, Ned thought. Two tails, one of them from the Company

and the other, most likely, an associate of the much-traveled Bertolt
Heinemann to whose existence he had been introduced only last evening
by Moe Chamoun. The technique of eluding surveillance was by no
means cut and dried. There were no laws about it. But instinct told Ned
that his chances of success dropped alarmingly with two men on the job.

He would have to abort the rendezvous. Jane had left her office some
time ago. His best bet was to call her directly in Room 404. It wasn't all
that risky, was it, compared to the rendezvous itself? They had been
tempting fate and relying heavily on agentcraft for some months now.
This would be the first time they'd had to call off a meeting. Pretty good
performance percentage. But daunting as an omen. So the day's malign
promise was already fulfilled. Black Tuesday, damn it.

Ned moved into Debenham's department store in search of a telephone, thinking of one of those comfortably small eating places he had
just passed on South Molton, where he and Jane might one day . . .

But, of course, the relationship would be completely different without
Laverne. Whether she knew of it or not, it was a threesome and always
had been. Her existence sparked off the illicit thrill. Without her it would
merely be scones and tea on South Molton.

He found a telephone, waited four minutes for the woman using it
to end her call and at last phoned the hotel that was part of Selfridge's,
asking for Room 404. Automatic, insistent ringing began. Ned could
picture Jane's alarm. Eventually, the phone was picked up but she said
nothing.

"Jane?"

"Dear God! You frightened me half to death."

"Jane, it's no go. Half the spooks in London are on my tail."

"Charming."

"I'm not any happier about it than you."

"I know. Bye."

He hung up and turned around so rapidly that he found himself
staring directly at Nose, a mere dozen yards away, who then affected a
sudden spurious interest in pantyhose. Student, better trained, was planted
before a bank of elevators, as if waiting for one.

For the next half hour, Ned led his entourage into and out of record
shops on Oxford Street, from Marble Arch to Tottenham Court Road.
In each he spent some time finding the one clerk, usually the oldest
graybeard in the place at perhaps age 26, to inquire after albums of piano
music.

"The early stuff from the thirties and forties," Ned would explain.

"Pinetop Smith. Art Hodes. Joe Sullivan. Jimmy Yancey. Jess Stacy. Any of the boogie-woogie people like Albert Ammons or Pete Johnston or Meade Lux Lewis. No duets or trios. Just solo stuff."

In no cases did he actually find an album but he did run across a few tapes, suitably encrusted in awed devotional slogans like "all-time classic greats" and the like. These he bought, not because he didn't have the performances. In most cases he actually had them on 78-rpm shellac discs now more than half a century old and irretrievably lo-fi. He had dragged these platters with him through most of the past twenty years, Laverne helping haul this millstone from one army post to the next.

"They can't get too hot or too cold or too damp or too dry," she would point out. "They get better treatment than the girls."

It was just as well, Ned decided now as he bought tapes, that if he and Laverne broke up their happy home, some of the piano performances should be as portable as these cassettes.

He watched Student flipping through a stack of records. Nose paced disconsolately outside on the Oxford Street sidewalk. They had by now realized that they were tailing the same man and that he, in turn, was leading them a useless trail. When both youngsters returned to their HQs, their controls would have a merry time trying to sort out what had actually happened. Or not happened.

He started back toward the chancery. When he turned off noisy, exhaust-choked Oxford Street and moved south on Duke Street, Student gave up on him, recognizing the way home. Nose persisted until Ned disappeared inside the immense building. Ned stood well back in the foyer and stared out the plate glass at Grosvenor Square. He saw Nose in hurried conference with another lad of Arabic mien. They dashed off together, gesticulating as they talked.

Mournful, miserable day of ugly little failures, unredeemed by seeing Jane alone. He had come to depend on their rendezvous. Deprived, he was suffering withdrawal symptoms, infantile ones at that. Mean, nasty day.

Ned left the chancery again, to wander alone with his melancholy. He still had half an hour before anyone would expect him at his desk. Perhaps luck would be with him and he would run into Jane on a similarly depressed ramble.

He kept away from Oxford Street bustle now, delving in and out of small quiet ways until he found himself in Hanover Square and subsequently well into the area of Soho's sex shops, strip joints, and news agents' shops, windows filled with small advertisements for local torture mistresses. Wherever fate took them, whatever fortune yielded, people could always stage-manage their own devotion to pain. Time passed.

He glanced at his watch. He had somehow used up the unhappy half hour without examining any further his own pained entrails. It was the mark of a hardened intelligence agent, Ned knew, to avoid introspection.

In any event, he had no true grievance with Laverne. She had been a good army wife, God knew. Twenty years ago, in that almost forgotten era when they'd married, she had seemed to him an ideal choice. She was attractive, rarely complained, raised four great kids, and backed him up with good home cooking and sex. Wasn't that all a man wanted? No need for frills like being on the same side, politically, or seeing the world in the same way.

He sat for a moment in Soho Square, tired of himself and his awkward probings into what was left of his marriage.

Yes, true, a split had opened between them over the past few years. Laverne, with her military turn of mind, had this morning correctly analyzed the movement: he had *gone on* while she had been *left behind*.

What could you call it? Philosophical differences? Political ones? Degrees of commitment? Laverne had never budged from the blind fundamentalist my-country-right-or-wrong dedication of her father. But the rest of the world had. And so had Ned.

He watched an elderly gent inching slowly along the inner path of Soho Square with a small Jack Russell terrier on a lead. The old man was not begging. But the cute little white-and-black terrier would stand on her hind legs and make paddling motions with her forepaws until people sitting on benches parted, smiling, with a few coins. These the old gent neatly accepted in an upturned cap as a form of entertainment tax.

Ned's thoughts wheeled abruptly to Ambrose E. Burnside, the man with the grievance. Striding rapidly north along Rathbone Place, he reached Goodge Street a few minutes later. Number 60 was, indeed, a pub, as Max Grieves had promised. It bore the welcoming name One Tun. A side door offered a stairway up.

On the second floor, as the British called their third, Ned paused in front of a closed door. Behind it he could hear someone coughing between volleys of light tapping, as of a shoemaker nailing a sole to a last. Ned knocked at the door.

The tapping stopped and so did the coughing. Far below, from the depths of the One Tun, Ned could hear the astral beeps and synthesizer hoots of a coin-operated gambling machine, as if pixies or space invaders were giving the customers a floor show.

"Mr. Burnside?"

He could hear locks being undone, the squeal of an iron bar being removed. The door edged open a few inches. The old man's eye was inflamed by a garish mauve-violet bruise, the sclera shot with a net of tiny exploded blood vessels.

"You!"

From far away came the chuckling, tittering noise of elves in the gambling machine, peep-peeping like chicks from another planet.

A resemblance existed between the two men at the corner table at Boulestin, the Covent Garden restaurant much favored by newspapermen who were being taken to an expensive lunch and didn't want to run into other newspapermen. Boulestin's slightly jaded air fitted their own appearance, while Boulestin's pricey menu accorded with the fat lunch-buying budgets of those who cultivated journalists.

In Hargreaves's case the man paying for lunch was another journalist, but nobody paid too much attention to that. Gleb Ponamarenko was officially accredited to the Soviet news agency Tass, but his expense account told cynical hacks like Hargreaves otherwise.

Strange, Hargreaves mused, the odd feeling he got when he stared across the table at Gleb putting away a neat ounce of Beluga caviar in four greedy gulps. The British journalist had a vague feeling of watching himself. There *was* a certain resemblance, damnit, no denying.

Gleb, whatever job he really did for the Soviets, was nobody's idea of a Russian spy. Across his face—Gleb would be in his mid-forties, Hargreaves guessed—spread the haunted lineaments of the Old Queen's Romanov–Hapsburg–Saxe-Coburg spawn, flung across the nations of Europe in the last century to rule and to ruin. Those baggy eyes! That florid, high-cheekboned face, that narrow nose with its questing nostrils, that self-indulgent lower lip. And, enclosing all, those deep-biting calipers that sequestered nose, mouth and mustache in an ironic parenthesis.

Hargreaves had quite forgotten what they were talking about as he stared at Gleb, a lunching pal of some years now. That was one of the Russian's more mysterious accomplishments, wasn't it? Staying on? He'd been in London a decade at least while all around comrades were being transferred everywhere else. A prodigy of bureaucratic finagling.

"Amazing," Hargreaves muttered.

Gleb looked up from a bit of lemon he was carefully squeezing over the last ragged remnants of the caviar. "This is by no means our highest quality," he assured Hargreaves. "The restaurant is economizing, I'm afraid."

The Briton listened to Gleb's English accent, a solid Oxbridge one, never the telltale *w* for *v* nor the giveaway loss of articles before nouns. If one listened long enough it was possible to know that Gleb was not a native-born Brit, but it was impossible to know what he actually *was*.

"No, amazing that in all these years I haven't noticed your facial resemblance."

"To what?"

"Damn it, to me."

The Russian frowned as he studied the older Hargreaves's booze-ravaged face, temple veins in high relief, scarlet network of blood vessels exploded across the nose, an unhealthy puffiness of cheeks. "Don't be insulting, Nigel," he purred. "I am a handsome man often mistaken for the young Cedric Hardwicke while you are a clapped-out alcoholic who writes the best gossip column in town."

"Handsome? You? You've got that damned Victoria-and-Albert look, especially today when you haven't pruned that great roach-haven of a mustache for weeks." Hargreaves squeezed lemon on his portion of caviar and spooned a bit of it onto a curl of toast. "Damn it, who, in fact, are you, genetically speaking? We've eaten a meal together often enough for me to ask."

Gleb shrugged. "My father was the celebrity, not I. A short little man"—Gleb indicated a height from the floor of less than a yard— "who was nevertheless for seven consecutive years chosen top Stakhanovite welder in the Dnepropetrovsk Basin. He—"

"Stakhanovite? What the labor lads call a damned speed-up artist?"

"Precisely. My father died in the defense of Stalingrad, as did so many others, but he left my mother behind in her eighth month of pregnancy. My eighth month, you might say."

The Russian stopped to watch Hargreaves demolishing his own caviar at a steady pace. "They tell me you are moonlighting for that terribly attractive Gillian Lamb. Is it true?"

"A man must eat," Hargreaves admitted past a mouthful of toast and fish eggs. "Gillian's TV production company pays damned well and doesn't interfere with my schedule at the newspaper."

"Congratulations. She is lovely."

Hargreaves's ravaged old face suddenly flushed. "Nothing to it, old man, I assure you."

"Not yet. But I know your reputation with women."

Hargreaves dusted the tips of his fingers together. "Gleb, you can get anywhere with flattery, except with damned old Hargreaves."

"I had no need to flatter you, old man," Gleb responded. He signaled a waiter to clear their plates. "In fact, it is you who must flatter me," he went on. "On the accuracy of my spy network." His eyes widened alarmingly, as if to warn Hargreaves off any wisecrack. "No, truthfully, I am told you've started digging dirt on that whole gang over at Winfield House. Something to do with next Sunday's garden party?"

"Not dirt, damn it," the Briton assured him. He sipped his steely dry Muscadet, still well iced although it had been poured some time before. " 'Lamb to Slaughter' does not deal in dirt."

"Excuse me. Background material."

"Just on the few sods who've caught Gillian's interest."

"I am told only Royce Connell interests Miss Lamb."

"You're damned well told quite a bit, eh, Gleb?"

The Russian waved the remark away as if it had been a compliment. He and Hargreaves had been fencing like this for years. The scenario was always the same. In the early part of the meal, as the journalist tanked up on whiskey and white wine, he played hard to get. During the mid portion, lubricated by a mellow claret or burgundy, he began to slip information—not all of it accurate—like an overladen ship in stormy waters. By the cognac he was spilling such intimate items that Gleb, out of a sense of shame, would call a halt to the striptease. No, not shame, he told himself now, but only the innate conversational tactics of a trained angler. Do not remove too many fish from any given pool; it alarms the rest. Do not strip damned old Hargreaves too bare or he'll remember . . . and regret.

Angling, after all, was Gleb's profession. Well nearly, he corrected himself. In the KGB's First Directorate, Gleb's section was devoted to general animal husbandry, the cultivation of high-ranking defectors. One must first have the knack of recognizing such rare beasts. Then one must create the special avenues by which they are induced to leave the herd and lurch off on their own.

He realized he had been staring too closely at Hargreaves. With a pointed finger, he asked the waiter to refill their glasses, finishing the Muscadet. "Another bottle?"

"Heavens, no. Some of that Figeac you had him open will do me."

When the main course arrived, both men surveyed it with pleasure. Whatever a Boulestin dish tasted like, it was always well presented, this one being thin rare slices of Charolais beef arranged like autumn leaves with stems formed by parsley fanned out across green leaves of Kos lettuce on a soft gravelly bed of cubed beef aspic and mille-fois cornichons, crunchy and tart.

"No, as a matter of fact," Hargreaves said, beginning now to spill information under his own power, "you'll never guess who Gillian's most interested in."

"Other than Connell."

"Other than Connell, who is, after all, a known quantity, wot?"

The Russian's forehead contracted slightly in a row of furrows. He had the kind of face in which furrows came and went in varied and startling places, a face made for hearing every kind of news, good or bad, and reacting accordingly. "Some unknown stranger?"

"One of these muffled mystery men who stalk the shuttered streets of London," Hargreaves said in a burst of fanciful language. Modern-day British journalists, whether concerned with gossip or harder news, tended to rely on the fustier phrases of their native tongue, particularly those florid phrases of the Victorians, if only out of nostalgia.

The wrinkles disappeared from Ponamarenko's face. "Ah, then I am sorry for the lady," he said. "This town . . ." He shook his head, but whether in sadness or wonder it was impossible to tell. "You know, Hargreaves, perhaps better than I, that there are some cities in this world that seem destined to attract and breed a certain type of adventurer. Singapore, eh? Hong Kong. And in the West, certainly Vienna and Zurich and Lisbon and London. Yes, your own London. This town has become an entrepôt of intrigue." He smiled at the phrase. "If you do a column item on it, no credit, please, for that last bit of fustian."

"Intrigue?" Hargreaves managed, despite what he'd drunk so far, to resemble a lopsided caricature of Gleb Ponamarenko, but considerably more seedy. "Tell all, damn it. If anyone would know it'd be—"

"Not so." The Russian raised a cautionary finger. "I'm aware of the sinister character you hacks have pinned on me, an honest member of your own profession, if that is not a contradiction in terms. But I assure you, I am a known quantity, just as Royce Connell. The men I speak of are ciphers. Shadows. They flit in and out of London ceaselessly on adventures that beggar the wildest imagination. Well, of course, that is not strictly true. They revolve around money, preferably cash. But in this they differ very little from the rest of us poor grubs, eh?"

"Tell me more, damn it. I'm starting to salivate."

A look of total unconcern came slowly forward on that corrupt face of Ponamarenko. "Can I trust you not to turn violently around and stare?"

"At what? Yes, of course, damn it."

"Slowly, now, and only when I tell you to do so. There is a man sitting at the very best table, the far corner, the one I never book because I do not like to be the cynosure of all eyes. Get ready but don't look yet. He is listening to his luncheon companion and his eyes are roaming the room. He is a youngish man, not yet forty, overweight, with extremely protuberant eyes and a high forehead that ends in very kinky, coarse hair. A virtual mop of hair. Now!"

In the most offhand manner in the world, Hargreaves pointed to a detail on the ceiling where it met the wall and, moving his finger and his glance at the same time, as if tracing some invisible architectural feature, swiveled slightly until he was looking directly at the man in question.

He saw someone just as the Russian had described, yet with an ominous nonappearance, as if haunted by other images. He had a spiky mustache, something like steel wool, and an unhealthy, gray-white complexion that never seemed to see the sun, an easy matter in rainy London. But that was not what made the face seem haunted. It was as if it had been assembled by committee, Hargreaves realized. It was not one face, but the physical embodiment of several identities.

He turned back to face his host. "Damned strange face, old boy. Now you see it, now you don't."

"How astute of you, Hargreaves. Most people would judge that a weak face, the sign of a weak character. But you and I know better. It is the face of the day, so to speak, that a very strong character has chosen to wear."

"Tell me more, you damned tease."

"But that's precisely it. I know very little more. I know men like that exist. They are a new breed, Hargreaves. Whereas you and I are hopeless romantics who work and strive only for art's sake, this new breed has in place of a heart one of those arrays of silicon chips that directs every move in terms of pounds, pence, dollars, and cents."

"Never rubles and kopecks?"

Ponamarenko shrugged. "Do I know? I only know they have no heart, in any but the crude medical sense of the word. They are programmed to instigate, or hijack, any profitable venture they uncover. Take charge, pervert its original aims, whatever they might be—political? cultural? military? economic?—and turn it firmly in the single direction of their own profit."

"I'm damned if I get you, Gleb."

"Here. Here is an example from not more than six yards away." The Russian's eyes hooded slightly as he prepared to shift around names and identities to protect his own security. "Here is a team of equestrian experts from Hungary. They arrive in London bearing the most favorable advance notices. Everyone in this horse-mad island wants to see them. Amateurs and professionals of dressage queue up at the Albert Hall box office and, I am sure, in Edinburgh and Manchester and Birmingham. They pay a tenner apiece to watch the celebrated Hungarians jump, ride, put their famed horses through their paces. From the Hungarian point of view, this is very good for foreign exchange. The team can gross fifty thousand pounds a night. Say ten performances in the U.K. Half a million pounds, not forints. Hungary is most pleased. A man called, if I am correct, Aldo Sgroi—can there be such a name?—a prominent Italian film producer, offers to make a documentary of the triumphant tour. He is an ordinary young man, a bit flash, but solid, real, sincere. And he will ask only for ten percent of the profits. The deal is signed. What a brilliant idea to increase the earning power of the team! By the last day of the tour Sgroi is one of them, practically speaking Hungarian. Are they blood brothers? *Igan!* Will they ever betray each other? *Nem!*"

The Russian stopped and carefully polished off some of the beef on his plate, ignoring the presentation, while Hargreaves openly chafed at the delay. "Come on, you sod!" he urged.

"All in good time." Chew. Chew. Swallow. "The receipts have been deposited in an Eastern-bloc bank down in the city. Which shall remain nameless. On the last day the team manager is swamped with detail: plane tickets, visa matters, getting the horses properly crated and loaded, to say nothing of the team, the grooms, the handlers. It's a small Hungarian army that must be mobilized for departure. It is understood that the bank will forward the credits to Budapest as soon as the team leaves. But here comes one of the team—or perhaps it's one of the film crew, hard to tell them apart this past two weeks—with a note signed by the team manager. He asks for a certain executive in the bank, hands over the note, and ten minutes later has the Hungarians' half million in fifty-pound notes packed in a brief case. Off he goes!" Gleb clapped his hands together. "Now you see it, now you don't!"

"I'm damned!" Hargreaves chortled. "I'm bloody damned!"

"And mind you, old man," Gleb went on, "this Sgroi is just one man. There are dozens of his type stalking the shuttered streets of London, looking for a going money-maker to steal away for themselves. If this magnificent game had been played by, let us say, CIA agents, can you imagine the language to be heard in Budapest? But there is nothing political about these mystery men. They are the hawks and vultures who wheel overhead, waiting for likely prey. And you tell me one of these has excited the lovely Gillian?"

The glow of evil glee suffusing Hargreaves's face slowly died away. "Dear me, no," he said at last. "Nothing that mysterious."

"Then, tell me."

But instead of answering, Hargreaves surreptitiously peeked around at the far corner of the room and examined the plump, pasty-faced man with the pop eyes. Amazing, wasn't it, what kind of outward appearance lent itself to producing an air of confidence? Film producer indeed! In the popular mind—Hargreaves firmly believed that anything he believed was also believed by the popular mind—the typical confidence man was suave, smooth, well-dressed, rather attractive to both men and women, and certainly quite free of any odd or disturbing characteristics that would warn off a prospective victim.

Amazing. Hargreaves sighed. He might himself have made a good confidence trickster, if he'd had the nerve. But about the only con jobs he ever successfully pulled off were on young and impressionable women who needed his help in publicizing themselves. He sighed again.

"Your mind, such as it is," Gleb pointed out, "is wandering."

"Yes. Just marveling at the rough clay that can be molded into such a damned masterful intrigue as the Affair of the Hungarian Team."

"You spoke of the fair Miss Lamb's curiosity. In whom," the Russian asked with magnificent control of English, "is she interested?"

"Some U.S. embassy spook called French."

"Called French?"

"Yes, you see . . ." the journalist launched into a stumbling explanation of what he felt sure had confused his host, that the bugger wasn't actually French, only called French. Gleb wondered how best to dam the flow of unnecessary explanation.

"Ned French," he finally said. "The jazz buff."

Hargreaves stopped in mid-word, mouth still open. "Beg pardon?" The flush now completely plated his face with rosy warmth.

"A jazz piano freak, like me."

"You know him?" Hargreaves's fingers were delving clumsily inside his jacket, trying to pull out a pen. "Plays piano," he muttered, inscribing the words in a small notebook.

"Not at all. Just a fan, like me. Although, mind you, I don't believe we like the same artists." Gleb paused and waited while Hargreaves scratched a line through his previous note. "I'm told he dotes on an obscure Chicago pianist called Art Hodes." Gleb made an odd, almost fastidious face that contrasted with the faintly libertine cast of his Saxe-Coburg look. "Very spare, blues-oriented performer. Funky."

"While you?" Hargreaves urged.

"I? My taste lies with the immortal Oscar."

"Wilde?"

"Peterson." Gleb watched the journalist write this down. "Not me, you silly sot. Gillian doesn't want background on *me*."

"Quite." Hargreaves scratched out the note. "What else can you give me on French?"

Gleb sat back and began carefully dissecting the rest of his forest glen of leafy beef. He chewed some, found it too dry, then glanced up at his guest. "On the contrary, old man, what else can you give me?"

If Colonel French took lunch early, Captain Chamoun dined late, and vice versa. But if Colonel French forgot to tell his deputy when he was lunching, Maurice Chamoun was trapped at his desk, unable to decide when, or even if, to go out for a bite. As life normally went, this presented no major problem. But today, for personal reasons, Chamoun particularly wanted to take lunch outside the chancery. He flipped on his tiny transistor radio to try and get a news broadcast on the hour. Nothing but music. He turned it off.

With no sign of Ned being back at his desk, nor anyone who remembered when he'd left the building, Chamoun stood at his windows overlooking Grosvenor Square and tried to decide what to do. It wasn't like Ned to leave so invisibly that not even the entrance guards remembered. But, lately, he'd become somewhat slippery at midday.

This morning Chamoun had placed a telephone call from a phone booth before he got into his car and picked up Ned.

As a result of that call, he was now in some distress.

He stared at a long-legged girl sitting on a bench outside, Nancy Lee Miller, without a sandwich or an Arab lover, but still writing in her damned notebook. Even at this distance Chamoun could see she was using a new book, which argued that the old one was being studied by her control. Chamoun had a sudden idea, not a good one, but born of necessity.

Outside, the day had a fickle, on-and-off quality to it, Chamoun noticed as he circled the greensward in order to come up behind Nancy Lee. The sky was alternately cloudy and then patched with blue, threatening either rain or sun and delivering neither. People moved through nervously, eyeing the sky—and perhaps each other, Chamoun brooded—with an air of misgiving.

He moved in behind Nancy Lee's bench. She was actually reading a book. A paperback lay open in her hands but her small spiral-bound notebook was hidden beneath the novel. In literary taste, if in nothing else, Nancy Lee proved patriotic, the novel being one of a series of pornographic runaway bestsellers produced by an American writer who lived abroad.

"Shame, shame, Nancy Lee," Chamoun murmured in her ear.

The girl actually jumped as if physically assaulted. She let out a strangled squeak and then saw the source of her torment. "Oh, you! You scared me, Maurice!"

"You dig that real raunchy stuff?"

Her face reddened. "I didn't notice anything goody-goody about your tastes."

He patted her hand. "Free tonight?"

"Afraid not."

"Tomorrow night, then."

"Not this week, Maurice." She managed to add a certain aura of invitation to the refusal, but so awkwardly that Chamoun wondered if he had the stomach to see this one through.

He took the novel from her. "Which are the hot parts?"

"Buy your own copy."

"Why should I if my girlfriend owns one?"

Her blush deepened. "Maurice, since when did I get to, like, be your girlfriend?"

"Only in my dreams," he murmured dramatically. He reached for the notebook and idly flipped through it, back and forth. "Writing your own porno, Nancy Lee?"

"Give it back."

"Here." But he didn't return the notebook till he had located the line "12:55: French out." He grinned at her as she retrieved the all-important book.

They were silent for a moment and the girl's glance wandered around
the greensward. It came to rest on the bronze statue of a man in a great
navy cloak, storm-tossed but resolute.

"Oh, yeah," she said then, remembering to ask. "The old guy in the,
like, coat? That one?" She pointed.

"FDR? What about him?"

"F D. Who?"

"Franklin Delano Roosevelt. President of the United States during
World War II. During the Great Depression. If I remember right he was
elected president four times." Chamoun watched her more closely. "You
know you've heard of him, Nancy Lee. You know they taught you all
about him in school."

"They did?"

"Nancy Lee," he began after another pause, this time in a faraway
tone as if not actually wanting to be here asking these questions, "how
old are you?"

"Over eighteen."

"No, seriously. Are you twenty-one yet?"

"Sure. Why?"

"Nancy Lee," he went on, taking both her hands in his. "Can I say
something very personal to you? About sex?"

She laughed nervously. "Why not?"

"Did you ever hear of female circumcision?"

There was a slight, awkward pause. The color of her cheeks lightened
considerably. "Is this some kind of, like, gag?"

"It's also called clitoridectomy."

"Maurice!"

"Nancy Lee, Arab guys won't be satisfied till they cut out your clit.
Don't tell me you haven't heard that before."

This time the pause was much longer and more awkward. "You've
been spying on me, Maurice."

"I'm jealous as hell, that's all."

She let out a whoop of laughter. "You want to eat your heart out?
We spent a week in Rome with him like trying to bite it off!"

There was something infectious about her laughter. Chamoun found
himself giggling. She eyed him for a long moment. "I can't tonight,
Maurice. I've like got a big thing going at eight."

"Whatever happened to five thirty at my place? I'll have you back on
the dot."

She sat silently, playing with her notebook. "You don't know this guy, Maurice. He's . . . what I mean is, I like owe him and he's not shy about getting his. He's like insane if another guy even gets near me."

"Five thirty, corner of Audley and Grosvenor. I'll be in a little brown Ford Fiesta. You'll be wherever you're supposed to be by eight P.M. precisely."

"I don't know, Maurice. I wish I could."

"This guy is already getting a little bored. And you're tired of owing him all the time. With me it's a fresh start."

Her lips had parted slightly. She stared at him with such intensity that she let the notebook slide off her lap onto the grass.

"And afterward?" she wanted to know.

"Up to you, Nancy Lee. That's how crazy I am about you."

"Well . . ."

"Five thirty. Audley and Grosvenor. It's a date."

One of the few boutiques that didn't go bust regularly along South Molton's walking street stood at the corner of Blenheim. It seemed to Chamoun the shop had always been there. Under the name Bricktop it featured fairly normal women's clothes and accessories of the sort worn by stylish middle-income women. The place had been named after the famous woman whose Rome nightclub had attracted so many celebrities. But there was another reason for the name. After he left Nancy Lee, Chamoun walked over to South Molton and stood for a moment at the corner, staring into the windows of Bricktop.

Then he moved on toward one end of the street. At a coffee bar he ordered a buttered crumpet and a pot of China tea. He sat for perhaps fifteen minutes, studying the top of the table and wondering whether the appointment he had made this morning for one thirty would be honored at two thirty, the time it was now. He sat, neither alert nor relaxed, but much aware of the passage of time. Suddenly there was a slight noise at the entrance to the coffee shop. He looked up.

The owner of Bricktop was fat. There was no sense calling her plump. She was a good fifty pounds overweight and, in a woman of her modest height, this was a crucial three stones plus. But she did have bright orange hair and had taken the nickname as her own. She did have the greatest pair of breasts south of Oxford Street, Chamoun reminded himself. North of that boundary, naturally, Laverne French held the cup. Cups.

Bricktop sat at a table behind Chamoun so that when she spoke softly to the nape of his neck only he could hear. He heard her strike a match.

A moment later she blew cigarette smoke at his neck. "*Nu*, boychik, you took your time?"

He nodded. Carefully, he began writing something in pencil on one of the coffee bar's cheap paper napkins.

He and Bricktop went back a long time together. "Back to when I was skinny," as she was fond of saying, although Chamoun's recollection of her was that she had always been buxom and, in the vernacular, "zaftig."

He recalled with some clarity their first meeting in Tel Aviv that day he'd arrived by bus from Beirut. He'd just graduated college then, in the good old days before the shooting got out of hand, but even then only his U.S. passport had gotten him through, Chamoun remembered, in a coffee bar not unlike this one, trying to order in English.

"Hey, Yank, you need an interpreter with a Wellesley degree?"

Bricktop—she had a name like Miriam but Chamoun had lost track of it over the years—had been born in the States, but migrated after college to a kibbutz north of Jaffa. She was ten years older than Chamoun and, even then, already held the rank of captain in Mossad. Not being a native-born Sabra, she didn't qualify for the internal intelligence service, Shin Bet. But Mossad, being a worldwide army service, fitted her formidable talents much better.

As Chamoun sat there now and carefully wrote his brief note, he wondered if she might not be a colonel now, like Ned French. After all, running Station London for Mossad was one hell of a job.

Especially for a woman.

10

"No, sir! If Abe Lincoln had only backed him up, instead of dumping him for that bastard Joe Hooker, the war would've been over by the fall of 1863."

Ned French sat in a quiet corner of the One Tun on Goodge Street, listening to Ambrose Everett Burnside III, defending his grandfather, the butcher of Fredericksburg.

It was a pleasant, old-fashioned place, the One Tun, with an immense three-sided central bar to which scores of customers could happily belly up simultaneously.

The old man had in the last half hour made a remarkable comeback on the strength of one small whisky and several cups of strong coffee.

"You have to remember one thing, young man," Burnside was cautioning him. "Grampaw made the mistake any honest man would. After all the outcry—well, twelve thousand Union dead and only five thousand Johnny Rebs—Grampaw told Lincoln straight out: "Sir, sack the insubordinate bastards who did me in—that was Franklin, Sumner, and Hooker—or sack me. It didn't matter that at Fredericksburg Grampaw was up against generals like Robert E. Lee and Stonewall Jackson. No, sir, Lincoln just relieved him of command and sent him off to Tennessee. And later didn't Grampaw save Knoxville from Longstreet? You can bet your boots nobody back home in Rhode Island thought any the less of him. They elected Grampaw governor three times. And they sent him to Washington as senator. Y'see, young man, the name I bear is an honorable one. And *that's* what makes this whole thing so godawful hard to bear."

Ned tried to think of a new way to ask this strange old man what his grievance was against the United States. "Tell me about yourself, Mr. Burnside."

"In 1940 I volunteered, before Pearl Harbor, young man. They put me in the air force. In those days the air *corps*. We all transferred into the U.S. Army Air Force in 1942."

"Pilot?"

"Master mechanic. I came over here to England with the first group of 17s. Six-striper."

"And you were mustered out here?"

"In 1950. I was married by then." The old man fell silent, his gaunt face tightening in cords of gristle.

Ned supposed it was time to establish his own military credentials. He produced an out-of-date AGO card that showed him a lowly lieutenant. He found this grade easier to use when talking to enlisted men. Being a colonel only put their back up.

Burnside's banged-up eye swiveled sideways to view the identification. "Shavetail, huh? Don't kid me, young man. You're too old for looey."

"What does it matter? You know I work at the embassy. If you've got a legitimate gripe, I can help you."

The old man sat back slowly, as if Ned had handed him an unlabeled pill that could either kill or cure. "Yeah," he said at last, his voice suddenly grittier in tone, "I married a British lass. Vickie, cutest little Wren you ever saw. I worked for one of the aircraft companies here before it went bankrupt. That's been my career. Each company that hired me went under within a few years. No way could they take on Boeing or the rest. So Vickie and I ran a little corner shop in South Kensington, cigarettes, newspapers, candy, sub–post office. They bought me out two years ago for a lump sum."

"Well, that's good news."

"It's a pasta joint now."

"And the money?"

"We had just enough to live on, what with my pension and Vickie's. So we put it into one of those unit trust things. It was American. The fellow who ran it was American and what it invested in was American companies. 'Get your guaranteed share of Uncle Sam's riches!' It appealed to Vickie and me because we sure weren't going to invest in British concerns, were we?"

"What was the name of it?"

"International Anglo-American Trusts."

"Sounds English."

"That was the company name. The name of the trust we bought was North American Freedom Fund Growth Shares. 'Join the growth miracle of the 1980s!' "

Burnside grew abruptly agitated. "I've been hollering at the god-damned embassy for two years now and nobody's heard me. Twenty thousand pounds down the drain! That's thirty thousand dollars, young man. Vickie always had a bad heart. She needed a bypass operation, two hundred twenty-seventh on the national health waiting list. If she'd lived three more years they'd have her in the operating room for sure. I wanted to pay for a private operation but she wouldn't have it. And then, over-night, the company and the fund folded up and sneaked away."

Burnside's breathing had quickened. The bruised skin around his bad eye grew darker and more livid. His gnarled fingers stretched out to grasp Ned's arm above the wrist.

"I kept the news from her. But a week later she was unwrapping something and saw it in an old newspaper. She came to me. 'Luv, is it true? All our nest egg?' I had to stand there like a great dummy and nod. Her pretty blue eyes turned up in her head, the way a doll's would. She fell to the floor right in front of me."

He tapped a thick forefinger downward on the tabletop and then couldn't stop tapping. "Right there at my feet, young man. Rushed her to the hospital. Never regained consciousness. Stress, the doctor said." *Tap, tap, tap.*

Ned sighed heavily. The boozy air of the pub soughed in and out of his lungs as he watched the ruined face of General Burnside's grandson, a credit to his nation and the Eighth Air Force, a man undone by . . .

Ned delved into his inside breast pocket and came up with a pen and an old envelope. "Give me the name of that fund again?"

The old man's forefinger was relentless, punishing the tabletop in lieu of punishing those who had transgressed in the name of America. "Never mind the fund name." *Tap. Tap.* "It's the rotten crook who ran the whole shebang. And him an American, too."

"Name?"

Tap. Tap. "Name of Tony Riordan."

Ned scribbled furiously on the envelope. "Let's make it eleven A.M.

tomorrow. You come to the main entrance on the square and ask for Mr. Grieves," he said, writing it down. "Here."

He pushed the scrap across to the crotchety old man and watched him read it with suspicion. Once again he saw a strange resemblance between this messy old man and his own neat, well-groomed father back in Wisconsin. "Grieves? Don't like the sound of that name one bit."

"And for God's sake," Ned went on, "fix yourself up before you get there. Wash up. Shampoo your hair. Comb it. Shave off that stubble. Look sharp, soldier."

Ned retrieved the scrap and wrote on it: "SHAMPOO! COMB!!" He tucked it into the frayed breast pocket of the old man's jacket. "Come on, soldier, let's get to a drugstore right now. We're going to buy you what you need."

"Don't need charity," Burnside said in a huffy tone. "I've got my pension money."

Ned stood up and glanced around him. "There's sure to be a drugstore nearby. Boots. Underwood. One of them. Buy yourself the works because I want you looking sharp when you show up tomorrow."

"What's so important about this Grieves fella?"

"He's trying to lay hands on your old buddy Riordan, the one who did you in. You're a valuable witness, old-timer. But you have to look respectable. Get it?"

Burnside seemed to consider this for a long moment. Then he nodded, almost reluctantly. "Sit down," he ordered. "I think maybe I owe you a beer, son."

At three thirty, Jane Weil picked up her desk telephone and dialed Ned French's private number. On the sixth ring she hung up, knowing that by now she would only get Maurice Chamoun. Her heart seethed with irrational resentment against Ned. Only calmly talking to him could relieve her peculiarly unhappy state of mind.

It wasn't just having their lunch date canceled at the last moment that triggered this black feeling of despair. After all, she told herself for perhaps the tenth time since it had happened, there stood at the heart of their relationship an implicit fail-safe procedure that governed them in any situation. Neither of them should betray the other by suddenly getting emotional about it.

Everything was a game, she repeated savagely to herself. Ned's cloak-and-dagger life was a game in which, as he put it, they kept score with a daily body count. Hadn't he told her just that only yesterday in their sad, prim little hotel love nest? By the smallest of extensions in his mind, their own affair was equally a game and, as such, had rules.

The primary one: Don't give the game away. Jane's expression went even more grim. And certainly don't complain or explain. Dear me, never.

She got to her feet and started out of her office, then stopped in midstride, realizing that Ned was not at his desk and, even if he were, she had to have a cover story if she wanted to drop in on him.

Jane returned to her desk and placed a call to Winfield House, using the number Pandora Fulmer had given for RSVP messages. The powerful, smooth voice of her housekeeper, Mrs. Crustaker, answered the ring. "Winfield House. Can I help you?"

"Mrs. Crustaker?"

"That's correct."

"Belle, this is Jane Weil from the embassy."

"Miss Jane! Nice to hear your voice," the elderly black woman responded in extremely cautious tones. "Mrs. Pandora's not here at the moment."

"And I know the phone must be ringing right off the hook."

"Calmer today. You know how these things go," the housekeeper said with easy expertise. "There are a whole slew of folk who don't know what RSVP means, or don't care, or told their secretary to phone and she forgot. You know."

"So it's easier for you today. What're you up to now, over three hundred, I should think."

There was a very long pause at Mrs. Crustaker's end of the wire, which was all Jane needed in order to know that Pandora Fulmer was staying clear of her out of a guilty conscience. Finally:

" 'Bout that," Mrs. Crustaker admitted.

"Say three twenty?" Jane persisted.

Another cautious pause. Jane could hear a hand go over the telephone at Winfield House. Voices sounded faintly. The line cleared. "Three ten, Miss Jane," the housekeeper admitted with a more open air. "I just did my sums. Three ten."

"Thanks, Belle. Please give Mrs. Fulmer my apologies for not being out there this morning to help, but we have a lot of last-minute security work here today."

"Beg pardon?"

"Security, Belle. Do you have any idea what sort of precautions we have to take for Sunday? All those important people in one place?"

The idea seemed new to Mrs. Crustaker. "That so?"

"Tell Mrs. Fulmer not to worry about that end of it," Jane added with some malice. "Just don't worry her pretty head about it. We're coping."

"Isn't that marvelous?" the black lady enthused. "Bye now."

Jane put down the phone in an even worse mood. She now had a story to cover her visit to Ned's office. But did she really want to see him? He'd cut her off dangling today. The shock of hearing the phone ring in their illicit little hideaway! Not knowing whether to answer. And then being chopped off with a few curt words, hardly an explanation. An emergency, grant him that. But it was now hours later and not a word of apology or commiseration.

To hell with him, then. She phoned his office again and let it ring until Chamoun picked up: "Captain Chamoun, it's Jane Weil."

"Yes. Colonel French isn't—"

"Can you take a message? I've been in touch with Winfield House. The RSVPs have slowed down to a trickle. They've got three hundred and ten affirmatives."

Chamoun mumbled something under his breath as he made a note of the message. "Anything else?"

"Bye." Crisp. Hang up. Efficient Miss Weil.

And to hell with Ned French.

The Company's communications center had only recently been moved to within a few hundred yards of Berkeley Square. Although it was under his direct supervision, Larry Rand hated the place.

Nothing personal; the area was handy enough, little eating places in Shepherd Market, hot and cold running tarts parading all day, classy discos in the evening and a few even classier restaurants, top hotels nearby, and for the culturally inclined this corner of Mayfair was near enough to the art galleries on Cork Street, the Royal Academy on Piccadilly, and a brisk ten-minute walk to the theater district.

The latest state-of-the-art equipment had been installed, truly bug-proof systems that could reach out to any spot on earth. No, the reason Rand detested the place was because it was a *place*. It had a location. He was too experienced at this not to know that eventually it would be bugged to a fare-thee-well by everybody from the IRA and the KGB down to dear old MI5 and 6. It was in the nature of any *place* to be vulnerable.

And yet, Rand reminded himself as he moved briskly along Curzon Street toward the center, what other way was there to handle communications? He had started with the Company as a field agent. Way down deep he would always think like one. Your pocket was your office. The nearest phone booth was your miracle state-of-the-art bug-free communication. You thought you were blown? You scrammed. A goddamned communications center had nowhere to go but stay put.

He disappeared inside an extremely old-fashioned storefront that sold tortoiseshell combs and big badger's-hair shaving brushes to the quality. Most gentlemen in search of such arcana went to the long-established shop further along on Curzon. This rival emporium had been established all of six months before. You wandered into the rear where the gent's tummy-tuck girdles and mustache-training bras were discreetly displayed. Then you kept on through an unmarked door that was an elevator. You shot up, in Rand's case, to the second floor.

Rand's short, stubby body moved this way and that, eyes darting as he passed through the windowless network of glass-partitioned work areas whose walls didn't quite reach the ceiling. Young men and women worked computers, typewriters, code machines, and other equipment. A muted babble of sound overlaid the great blind room like the workaday rustle of an active hive.

At the rear, two offices had real floor-to-ceiling walls and doors that closed. One belonged to Henning, one of Rand's deputies for communications. The other office Rand used on his infrequent visits here. It wasn't just that this place was a *place*, he complained to himself now, it was that, to save the Company money, everything channeled through here, radio, satellite relay, telephone, telex, fax, computer lines, everything. This wasn't just a place, it was a goddamned prime target.

"Henning!" Rand jerked his head at the private office. He sat down behind the desk reserved for him and waited for his deputy to arrive.

If the majority of the Company's employees these days looked and dressed like college students, Henning, who had worked for the Company almost as long as Rand, resembled one of those superannuated permanent graduate students who parlay overlapping fellowships and grants into lifelong careers of studenthood, acquiring one new PhD after another. He had the permanently strained eyes fronted by heavy-framed glasses that betrayed decades of close reading, but his longish hair, untinged by gray, still had the lively, almost unruly look of youth. So did his face, as if unmarked by life. You had only to look at that unlined face, Rand thought peevishly, to know you were looking at a man who had never in his life worked anywhere but behind a desk.

"Give me the latest on Operation Intercept."

Henning sat down across from Rand and produced an unhappy sigh. His tongue worked away for a moment at something stuck in his front teeth. His spectacles magnified his weak eyes like something out of a horror movie. Then, knowing the impression he made, Henning whipped off the heavy glasses and rubbed his eyes. Then he rubbed the lenses.

"You'll let me know when you've run out of time-wasting maneuvers?" Rand asked.

"I'm not stalling. It's just that you're not going to like what I have. We're still running about fifty-fifty."

"Half say they won't come and half say they will?"

"That's about it."

"Did you do what I told you? Mention threats from terrorists?"

"Nobody gave me the kind of trouble that Lamb woman did."

Rand nodded. "As of now, if you run into opposition of any kind, tell them we can't guarantee their safety because of these threats. Lay it on heavy. Oh, and by the way . . ." Rand paused, knowing that however blameless Henning might be, that sort of opening was always unhappy-making. No reason Henning shouldn't be as unhappy as he was, right? Rand grinned unpleasantly. "By the way, do you really mean to tell me you don't know who Gillian Lamb is?"

He watched Henning's face go white. This morning neither of them had recognized the name but Larry Rand had since done his homework and Henning had not. "Don't you ever watch TV, Henning?"

"Not often."

"She even told you the name of her pinko, rabble-rousing show, 'Lamb to Slaughter,' and you still didn't tumble. And, what's more, she's scheduled to film the whole fucking disaster on Sunday. She has a crew coming. No wonder she got so curious about you. And no wonder a lot of people are determined to show up. It's their big chance to be on TV and they wouldn't miss it for the world."

"Jesus Christ."

Rand nodded as if approving this call for help. "So you and your team start using the terrorist ploy as of now. We'll see how many of these publicity lice still want to attend." Rand reached for a red telephone. "This circuit ready to go?"

Henning was on his feet. He turned back with a dazed look. "Always."

"Close the door behind you. And, Henning."

"Yes?"

"The next time we talk I want all new numbers. 'Fifty-fifty' you can stick up your ass. Understand? Out."

Rand watched the door close. He wondered if he'd been too soft on Henning. He was one of those time-servers you had to prod or whip. Keep his ass full of red welts and he performed nicely.

He punched four numbers into the red telephone's keypad. It was connected to something new the Company was trying, a kind of scrambled intercontinental PBX system in which certain offices could ring through securely to other key offices anywhere in the world with a minimum of time-wasting. The random pattern of the scramble was determined by a computer. So far only twenty of these phones existed.

After a third ring a man answered. "Yeh?"

"Mac, it's Larry."

"Yeh? What's up?"

"I need some Pentagon material."

"Kinda scarce here in Langley."

"Anything you can get me on an intelligence colonel named Edward J. French."

"Yeh. How's that Sunday clambake coming?"

"Where'd you hear about it?"

The man at the Langley, Virginia, end of the line paused for a moment. "Shock waves travel fast. Nobody expected any ambassador to react that strongly to Exdrec 103."

"That's the trouble with amateurs," Rand grumbled.

"Still, Connell could've called you in."

"Bastard chose not to."

"Do not," the Langley man intoned in a sepulchral voice, "speak ill of the dead. You're going to make Connell pay, or I don't know my E. Lawrence Rand."

"Something like that," Rand muttered unhelpfully. "That's why I need the stuff on French." He paused. "Any other embassy planning anything stupid?"

"Number 103 only hit a bull's-eye in London. But you know how it is, Larry, there's always more to these things than meets the eye."

"What?" Rand snapped. "What? Stop holding out on me."

"Me? Hold out on you?"

"Come on, give," Rand demanded. "What's coming up?"

"Just as soon as we've established your need to know, sonny-boy—"

"Aw, shit," Rand yelped. "Give, will you?"

"Hey, we all have our hole cards to play, Larry. I'm sure you're holding a few, especially for that Sunday clambake."

Rand sat silently for a moment, unwilling to beg for information.

"That's why they're called hole cards, Mac," he said with fake breeziness. "You don't see 'em till I show 'em. Till then, let's just say I'm up to my *cojones* in damage containment."

A mean cackle sounded at the U.S. end of the conversation. "And what about French's *cojones?*"

"Well," Rand said, "do-or-die crunches have only two ways to go. Either way French looks bad."

"You sound like you don't care which."

"How soon can I get the stuff on French? Tomorrow?"

"Yeh. On this phone."

"*Do svidaniya, gospodin.*"

"*Proshchai, tovarishch.*" The line went dead.

Still smarting at the hint that something was in the wind, something Mac wouldn't tell him, Larry Rand held the phone away from himself and stared glumly at it. Then he shrugged. He almost, but not quite, smiled. Old Mac could be as mean and nasty as they come. So be it.

Rand's broad, hammered-down face looked almost good-natured for an instant. Old Mac got the drift fast enough, he mused as he hung up the red telephone. The object of Sunday's exercise was to put French behind the eight ball. With luck he might even get killed. At this point Rand hadn't made up his mind which. All he knew was that the Sunday garden party was a golden opportunity for him, without spending too much effort on it, to bring French down in small, bleeding chunks while Connell looked on in horror and learned his lesson.

Rand had a nose for these things. Like the KGB's own brand of headhunters, he knew when an animal had to be cut out of the herd. It might not actually be necessary for French to die. That was partly up to whoever started shooting, wasn't it? But if it came to that, death had a lot to recommend it. Connell would never forget the lesson.

Nor would French.

At 5:25 in the afternoon, Captain Chamoun got the mouse-brown Fiesta out of its parking place. He merged into the traffic moving around Grosvenor Square past the chancery, keeping on Brook Street and moving east toward New Bond Street.

Just before he reached it, however, as he passed South Molton Street, he turned left into a narrow, high-walled enclave called Haunch of Venison Yard. He killed the engine.

Chamoun waited for only a few moments in the deserted area. Then a fat woman with orange hair walked into the yard from Blenheim Street.

She paused, puffing on a cigarette, until two younger women, laughing at something one of them had said, cleared out of the area. Then the fat woman threw away the cigarette, tipped forward one of the Fiesta's front seats, and got into the back.

One moment Bricktop was there at Chamoun's car, the next moment she had disappeared like a magician's assistant. Despite her girth she had managed to curl up on the rear floor space and pull some sort of dark blanket over her.

Chamoun started the engine. "Five thirty on the dot," he announced to the air.

"*Sei gesündt*," a voice responded from the same air.

"You've lost weight, huh?" Chamoun asked as he reversed the car out of the yard and continued east to Bond. "You don't show at all back there."

"Sarcasm at this precise moment?" the disembodied voice complained.

"Heading south on Bond. Coming back to the square on Grosvenor, just the way we planned."

"Spare me the blow-by-blow account." Her voice had a breathless quality to it.

"You breathing all right?"

"Drive, *schmendrick*."

"Okay, I'm at the corner of Audley turning left. There she is, my little Arabian *nafke*."

"Don't get a swelled head, Maurice. Just because the girl's waiting for you it doesn't mean you're God's gift to women."

"No? Then what does it mean?"

"It means this girl is truly, terminally stupid."

Chamoun grinned as he braked to a halt and swung open his left-hand door. "Hop in, baby."

Nancy Lee Miller looked both ways before getting into the car. "If my boyfriend ever knew . . ." she immediately began on an off-putting note.

"He'd sew up your entire pussy, clit and all."

She burst into giggles. "Maurice, you're, like, impossible."

The small car moved quickly south, paralleling the edge of Hyde Park a few streets away. When they reached Hertford Street, Chamoun turned right and then left onto Park Lane. Although traffic was at its height and the roads were clogged with autos, trucks, and buses, he counted on being at Bricktop's number-three safe house in Chelsea in half an hour.

"Where do you have to be at eight o'clock?" he asked.

"Belgravia."

"Where in Belgravia?"

"He'd like cut out my tongue, Maurice. I swear it."

"So how am I going to get you back there on time?"

"You'll put me in a cab at quarter to eight."

"Got it all figured out, huh?"

She giggled again. In the traffic noise neither of them could hear the faint sound of a bottle of ether being upended into a handkerchief. But a moment later the pungent smell of the solvent was unmistakable. Nancy Lee's lips parted to say something. The handkerchief clamped down over her nose and open mouth. It felt so cold it seemed to burn. Then there was no feeling at all.

"Open up your window, Moishe," the red-haired woman said as she filled a hypodermic syringe with Pentothal. "Otherwise all three of us are going sleepy-bye."

11

On any weekday night in London, thousands of parties are under way, mostly modest ones devoted to drinks, dinner, and, perhaps, cards. Others may be more modern, the screening on home video of a rented film cassette or the selling to a group of neighborhood women of sexually arousing undergarments and other aids. But tonight two concerned Ned French's life.

The first took place in the magnificent Art Deco house called Number 12, where Dr. Hakkad had arrived by air this morning. It was hard to know precisely what role he played: host, fly on the wall, guest of honor? But that sort of deliberate role confusion was normal for Dr. Hakkad.

As host, for instance, he was lavish, adept, and glib in the nonverbal language of hospitality. Through Western eyes he seemed too much. Western hosts are expected to have endearing flaws and make jokes about them: forgetting a guest's name or running out of ice. They are expected to be well-groomed but not so as to make male guests feel grubby or females to wish with their very soul that they had worn real pearls.

For, to tell the truth, Dr. Hakkad, who was a noted ophthalmologist, nearly blinded his guests with his own resplendence and the languorous brilliance of his home. Unfortunately, his fat wife and his children—five fat girls and a fat boy—rarely accompanied him on his London visits. Instead his sister, the delightful Leilah, served as hostess. Ten years

younger than her brother, she carried her full-blown beauty like a blossom
from Allah, full-lipped, full-eyed, richly fleshy without being fat, and
clad in a swirl of hand-loomed fabrics as sheer as tissue paper and as
colorful as a desert sunset.

"Breast of mutton, *en papillote*," one Western journalist guest had
murmured, but he was perhaps driven to malice by the fact that, like
any worthy Muslim hostess, Leilah paid nearly all her attention to the
female guests.

In any event, Muslim parties are usually overwhelmingly male. Bert
and Khefte moved through from room to room, as did several other fit,
muscular men and a few male waiters. A French attorney and his chic
wife moved independently of each other, as did a chubby, unhealthy-
looking Italian film producer and his mistress, who only spoke Italian
and wouldn't stop.

Three Fleet Street journalists nearly went into shock on arrival when
they saw guests sipping orange juice. But Bert led them into a side room
where whiskey and gin awaited them. The other guests included a pair
of professors named Margarine, an elderly married couple who specialized
in oil-bearing rock strata.

With Leilah, there were four women. It was easy to see that they
were wildly outnumbered by the men present. The appearance of Nancy
Lee Miller would have helped redress this imbalance. But here it was,
eight thirty, and no Nancy Lee.

As if to highlight this, Leilah had gathered the women in a small
circle at one end of the living room, where they tried, in three languages,
to find some common ground. The only man to try breaking into this
sodality was the film producer. From time to time he would stand behind
Leilah and put a small, pale, moist hand on her richly endowed shoulder.
His peculiar exophthalmic eyes stared like a frog's, as if sucking in visual
information. Then he would leave the women, letting his hand feast on
Leilah's flesh to the last possible moment before breaking contact.

The party Ned and Laverne French attended was at Corinth House,
the mansion in Kensington where the United States embassy's number-
two was quartered.

The last man to hold Royce Connell's job had been married with
three children. Even so his family had barely filled one of Corinth's
floors. Whatever the place had been before the United States bought it,
its ground floor was made for entertaining. Extremely high ceilings looked
down on two very large rooms, a kind of all-purpose ballroom-reception

area to the left as one entered, and a comfortable library to the right, with bookshelves mounting skyward to a height that required a rollable built-in ladder.

Unlike Dr. Hakkad, who dressed up for a party, Royce Connell had long ago learned to dress down. He would pick some elderly, faintly tweedy marmalade suit, elegantly hung on his spare frame, or perhaps dove-gray trousers and a navy blue blazer, its breast pocket spouting a flared fountain of blue bandanna that took more time to arrange than any other part of Royce's carefully casual attire.

And he paid a lot of attention to the male-female balance. Any married embassy guest, like Ned or Bill Voss from Commercial, was expected to bring his wife. The president of a prestigious Ivy League university back home had arrived alone, his wife being indisposed, so Royce had paired him with Mary Constantine from Press who had to be there in any case because several journalists were expected. Two United States representatives had broken loose from a congressional junket passing through town and were, fortunately, of opposite sexes, making a couple in Royce's mind, this one interracial.

Since he had also invited Gillian Lamb and particularly did not want anyone to think she was his partner, Royce had instructed Jane Weil to "dance me close" and be his official hostess, *in loco uxoris*. Which left Royce with the problem of finding a man for Gillian. An old college chum of his, David Doyle, if anything more handsome and devoted to the elegant single life than he was, had just arrived to start shooting a TV series for BBC. "Latch onto La Lamb," had been Royce's orders.

It had all been done in such an offhand way that Royce was never quite sure if his Noah's-ark maneuvering had in fact produced perfect pairing or not. These once-a-month social events were deliberately underplayed for several reasons, some quite Machiavellian.

But underplay had always been Royce's style. People tended to drop their guard at parties that seemed not at all grand but rather homey and off-the-cuff. This was especially true of parties that seemed to have no theme, no purpose, except spontaneous good fellowship of the most casual kind. Royce counted on Jane to maintain this light touch but to make sure that everyone knew everyone else, not only their names but what they did in the great world outside Corinth House.

Inside, as always, the catering was as Ned had described it, a class act. The ham and the turkey had both been flown in from Virginia, baked to an old Connell family recipe and sliced in big, thin portions. The vol-au-vent pastries were done on the premises and filled with something creamy, tasting of crab and asparagus. For the occasion, Royce's normal staff of an English butler called Fishlock and five Filipinos was augmented by London's most popular Irish bartender who could not only remember what people wanted but whether they liked a strong or a weak drink. Noonan held court in the library, where the long buffet table was set up. It was extras like Noonan, whom Royce paid for out of his own pocket, that kept Connell's personal budget in the red and his savings nil. But Noonan was worth it.

"Mr. Hargreaves himself," he murmured discreetly as the gossip columnist approached him. "Your goodly host has some Chivas Regal awaiting your approval."

Hargreaves, who had not yet recovered from lunch but was ready to kill for a drink, shook his finger negatively. He and the bartender were old friends, the Irishman being hired for all the best freeloads in London.

"Noonan," he said in a voice several notes lower than normal, "if you know me at all, you damned well know I loathe and detest fancy Scotch blends. A single-malt, well and good. For sipping, like cognac. But for your heavy-duty journeyman tosspot, give me the damnedest whiskey you've got, the kind that brings a rip to the throat and a tear to the eye."

"Dear God, Mr. Connell wouldn't give it house room." Dubiously, he produced some Whyte and McKay. "I happen to like this one. Is it too smooth for you?"

Hargreaves watched him pour a stiff jolt. "We'll just have to experiment, Noonan. We'll have to employ scientific research. It's the only damned way the human race will ever know." His voice dropped to a murmur as he took the drink from the bartender. "Speaking of knowledge . . ."

Noonan's eyes narrowed. "I've one or two likely bits for your column, Mr.—" He stopped. "Yes, madam, a bit more of the white Bordeaux? Was it chilled enough for your delicate palate, madam?"

Hargreaves wandered off, sipping the whiskey with an extremely unscientific approach that actually resembled gulping. Although this was his first drink since his very alcoholic lunch with Ponamarenko, he managed somehow to stumble headlong into Ned French. During the apologies Hargreaves was horrified to realize that his glance had not once locked sincerely with Ned's but was riveted instead on his wife's breasts. Laverne was wearing what she normally wore to Royce's parties, something full and blousy that minimized her bosom, but there was no way mere fabric could be arranged to fool old Hargreaves.

*   *   *

In the interests of pan-Islamic solidarity, Bert kept away from Dr. Hakkad as the ophthalmologist slowly and thoroughly made his rounds of the guests. If any of the younger men were to travel in his penumbra, Khefte had explained to Bert some time ago, it must be one who, to put it as delicately as possible, could be said to look like a son of the prophet, not of a Stuttgart auto mechanic.

This suited Bert well enough, since he was on hand mainly to take care of those of the Doctor's more alcoholic Western guests who were inclined, when drunk, to say things and do things no Muslim could forgive.

Bert had been in the movement more than half his life, having begun as a twelve-year-old in the Frankfurt rail yards surreptitiously sneaking past dozing trainmen late at night to throw a switch and send a freight train crashing disastrously into a line of standby commuter cars. From his experience with the Western and the Islamic personality he knew that, when not guarding his mouth, the typical Westerner could not help but make some remark, no matter how harmless it seemed, that could be relied on to make Muslim blood boil. It was literally true that, in the words of Marx, capitalism did contain the seeds of its own destruction.

Of all his boyhood comrades in the movement, Bert alone had ended up working with Arab cadres. He hadn't really planned it that way. Nor had his old friends planned their lives. Bert seldom thought of them any more, or of their motivations.

What drove Bert had remained essentially unchanged since childhood, a primitive and perhaps mismatched amalgam of ideas. From his grandmother, who had raised him, a gentle old lady who could remember the aborted hopes of German workers' communes after World War I, he had picked up an idealistic feeling for the downtrodden of the world. To this Bert had fused the knowledge that only violence works. His father, a nasty drunk with ready fists and weapons, had always got his way in a fight. To a child's mind, searching for some central secret of life, it seemed obvious that he who struck more violently and with less regard for others would always win.

In the cadres of Arab youth he found widespread acceptance of this secret. He and they seemed made for each other. Both could contemplate with equanimity the idea that only violence could set them free. In his current work with Khefte, this conviction had so far been expressed mostly in words. But as soon as next Sunday it would be expressed in bullets.

At the moment, however, the words were still flowing in every direction. Dr. Hakkad had cornered a man from one of the tabloids who, already in his cups, had made the mistake of referring to Islam's current goals as being "mainly this jihad business, you know, some sort of holy-war type thingie."

"Dear sir," Hakkad began, moistening his faintly bluish lips as a virtuoso violinist might rosin his bow before attacking Paganini, "one must, after all, eventually rise above the level of the typical tabloid headline." He smiled pleasantly. " 'Shock Horror as Mum, Eighteen, Eats Her Own Baby' sort of type thingie."

"Yes, b—"

"One must, after all, *aspire higher* as my saintly father often told me. It does not rhyme in Arabic, but no matter. One must think of journalism as a profession, indeed a calling, several notches above sewer worker or pickpocket."

"But this jihad thingie is—"

"A way of stating the obvious goal of all religions, an Islamic version of your own Christian outreach, your *opus Dei*, your—"

"I am not a practicing Christian."

A faint frown crossed the doctor's slightly beaded face. He patted his forehead with a brilliant orange handkerchief of thinnest muslin. "Khefte, my brother," he murmured, suddenly realizing that if this hack were not a practicing Christian he might be a Jew, "will you see if Mr., uh, Mr. . . . our friend would like another drink?"

"Mr. McNulty, another drink?" The journalist shook his head.

Hakkad rolled the rather spikey Celtic name about in his mind for a moment. Jews often changed or "streamlined" their names, but he had never heard of one masquerading as Irish. "Mr. McNulty," Hakkad went on smoothly, "has it ever occurred to you or your publisher that in the five articles of Islamic faith are contained the key to world peace, an end to hunger, and the start of truly global democracy?"

"I can't actually s—"

"You have heard the phrase, 'the five pillars of wisdom'?"

"I believe I m—"

"We begin with *As-Shahadah*, which is our declaration that there is only one god, Allah, and that Muhammad is both his servant and his messenger. Nothing peculiar in that, eh, dear sir?"

"I am not a p—"

"Yes, of course. The second pillar," Hakkad rolled on, "is *Salah*, the five daily prayers every Muslim owes to God, his Lord and Creator. *Sawm* is the third, simply the fast or Ramadan, a holy month during

which from dawn to sunset one abstains from food, drink, sexual inter-
course, and all evil and malicious thoughts."

"I'm not really talking ab—"

"Fourth is *Zakah*, by which we tithe two and a half percent of our
wealth to relieve those less fortunate than ourselves. This is no more
revolutionary than your own Church of England's poor box. And, finally,
the fifth pillar for the truly devout is *Hajj*, a pilgrimage to the Ka'ba in
Mecca at least once in a lifetime." Hakkad stopped and smiled beatifically,
as if daring McNulty to find a flaw in any of the pillars.

In the background, Bert caught Khefte's eye, then tapped his wristwatch and made a gesture with his head. Khefte backed away as McNulty
began a long tortuous explanation of the fact that he was a lapsed Catholic
of Marxist leaning who . . .

"It is nine o'clock," Bert murmured in Khefte's ear. "When does that
woman of yours arrive?"

Khefte's tan eyes went dead, devoid of any expression at all. "As for
her being my woman, she has forfeited everything by this betrayal."

"It is of no importance, brother," Bert said in an almost soothing
tone. He had recognized, in the few months he had worked with Khefte,
that the man was at his most emotionally upset when his face was totally
unmoved. "I am more concerned about Merak and Mamoud." Bert
glanced at his watch again. "Just about now, or within an hour, they
should complete their testing. I worry about those two."

". . . relationship between certain norms of Marxist practice," Hakkad
was telling the journalist, "and the operation of our own Islamic laws
has not escaped your attention, I am sure. For qualified journalists seeking
in-depth answers, there are rather generous research grants. It is not always
possible for one who works on a tabloid newspaper to qualify for such a
grant, but I have been instrumental in the past in helping several . . ."

"Not at all, Colonel French," Gillian Lamb was saying.

Her long flaxen hair, middle-parted, framed her face like a pair of
fine-spun curtains. Her tiger-orange eyes, entirely surrounded by white,
focused intimidatingly on Ned.

She had the trick of seeming to use one form of intimidation while
actually using another. The startlingly pretty face, the grave, all-seeing
eyes, backed by a reputation for merciless reportage, seemed to give her
the cunning of a jungle cat. It was odd in a media person, such fierce
independence, as if she did not depend on the cooperation of her subjects
but could strive beyond the symbiotic back-scratching that modern jour-

nalism had become. It was almost, Ned mused, as if she didn't need the job in order to live. But if he were to surrender to her manipulation, Ned knew, it would be not out of fear but something quite different.

As one who had often interrogated those hostile to him, Ned had sensed this different feeling, akin to what lay at the heart of the sado-masochistic relationship. Bear down hard enough on someone, he recalled, and you steeled him to the point of total rejection, dogged silence.

But come at him as Gillian did, sideways, flanking his guard, smiling with sureness and knowledge and power, and soon a feeling would creep over the one being questioned that all this tiresome, endless interrogation was beyond him and so thoroughly in the hands of the knowing interrogator that one might as well give in to domination, let all such matters rest in the hands of the dominant one . . . and relax.

Gillian Lamb did well as an investigative reporter, Ned decided, because, perhaps unaware of her power, she could coerce the kind of capitulation a slave gives a master.

"Not at all," she was telling him. "Not for one moment would I want to know the extent of your preparations for Sunday, or their nature. I simply wanted to get a kind of, um, parametric sketch of things."

"The big picture?" He smiled slightly.

"Is that what the Americans call it? Broad strokes. Background briefing?"

His smile broadened. "No luck, Miss Lamb. In fact, not even an admission that we have a problem on Sunday."

"But surely . . ." She stopped. Her perfect cheeks grew slightly rosy. "That is, I had been led to believe . . ." She cut herself off again. This time her startlingly tawny eyes widened as she glanced around the huge room. In one corner, at the buffet, Jane was helping Laverne to some salad. Ned averted his glance hastily. He felt Gillian's small, soft hand take his and lead him to the front windows. They were alone for the moment.

"You may not be able to tell me anything," she murmured softly so that he had to lean closer to her, "but I'm not quite as chary with help as you." Again her intimidating glance swept the room for eavesdroppers. "I had the most amazing telephone call today from someone who claimed to be speaking on behalf of the embassy security staff."

"Only one man can authorize that, and he's on home leave in Rhode Island." Ned eyed her more closely. "What did he say?"

"He said they were unofficially warning guests that they couldn't take responsibility for the security of the party."

"What!"

"And when I started quizzing him he hung up."

"That's incredible."

"Even more incredible, he rang back an hour later and told me they had received threats from known extremist groups. Didn't I want to change my mind? So I hung up on *him*."

"Lovely."

She paused, her eyes returning slowly to his face by way, first, of his hands and then his arms. The impact, when her glance locked with his, was formidable. He waited, knowing what she wanted him to say but absolutely determined not to be dominated by her.

"Is that your official reaction, Colonel? Lovely?"

"It's what we say when even the most amazing eyes in London are urging us to say more."

"Do I ask for more?" she begged innocently. "Isn't it enough for me to have met my match? I can see why Royce feels as he does about you."

Ned's smile returned as more of a grin. "You really don't give up, do you?" She was still holding his hand and he gave hers a light, friendly squeeze. "Try me on some other topic, Miss Lamb."

"And lo, it will be like Jesus striking the rock? You will positively gush forth?"

"Was that Jesus?"

She gave him what could only be described as a dirty look. "Very well, Colonel, since you won't be drawn on specifics, even when it might mean that I could help safeguard my crew in case of emergency, let's assume there is no trouble on Sunday. Let's assume—in fact let's get down on our knees and beseech—that all goes smoothly and some three hundred celebrities enjoy the hospitality of your nation and undergo the indoctrination of your president, via his close friends, the Fulmers, who . . ."

"Hold it."

". . . consider this social event a prime political opportunity to present the president's side of several ideological battles he happens to be fighting with Congress, the Senate, and a good third of the governors as well. Let's—"

"Hold it."

"Hit another no-go area?"

"Where did you hear the Fulmers would be doing this?"

"A source." She gave him a sweet English smile.

"Unnamed?"

"Would I be as unfriendly to you as you are to me? No, the source is Mrs. Susan Pandora Fulmer."

He was squeezing her hand too hard now. Instead he dropped it. "Sorry. Didn't mean to get that violent."

She glanced sideways at Laverne, deep in conversation with Jane Weil. "As long as Mrs. French doesn't mind, why should I?"

The fat woman with the orange hair had propped the blindfolded Nancy Lee Miller in a plain kitchen chair and tied her wrists behind her back. She could see that this bothered Maurice Chamoun. "They're not tight," she assured him. "But you'd be amazed what a little touch of bondage does for these dumb types."

"Brick," he told her, "what could she know? She's just a kid who's been sexually liberated by some Arab stud."

"From what you tell me," the head of Mossad's Station London said, "there's a lot she knows, whether or not she knows she knows. Follow me?"

"Could anybody? What did you inject her with?"

"Pentothal."

"Should she still be knocked out? You overdosed her."

Bricktop nodded and lighted a cigarette. "I don't usually handle this field stuff myself. But since my number-two got himself smeared all over the Channel hovercraft last week . . ."

"That was Dov?" Chamoun sounded horrified. "The newspapers didn't give his real name."

"Dov and his wife and one of his two kids. They were on a weekend drive to Holland. Go look at the tulips, I told him." Her voice faltered and she took a long drag on her cigarette. "And four other passengers," she added in a lower voice. "That's what two grenades will do, wired together on one detonator."

"This Miller girl is not important enough to waste your time on. When I called you, all I wanted to do w—"

"Never mind what you wanted, Moishe. I have plans for this girl. They don't concern you or your Colonel French. I don't even want her to see you here when she comes to."

He watched her take another long drag and blow smoke into Nancy Lee's blindfolded face. "I thought from what you told me she'd be pretty," the redhead remarked. "She's merely cute."

"Nice body."

"Listen to him. I know about men, Moishe. In fact, you could say

I know more about men than it's safe for a woman to know." She lit a second cigarette from the first. "In fact, if you ever wondered what makes a lesbian out of an average chubby American yenta, you could say it was a plethora of information about men."

Chamoun almost flinched, but managed to control the involuntary movement. "You're . . . ?"

"I'm," she stated.

"That's funny."

"No it's not. What I really am is bisexual, so watch your ass, baby." He laughed nervously. Then: "She's coming out of it."

"And you're leaving."

"This is going to get sort of steamy, huh?"

"What do you care?" Bricktop asked.

"Like leaving the fox in charge of the henhouse, right?"

She puffed a great cloud of smoke in the air between them. "Get out, Moisheleh. It's time for the grown-ups to take over."

Hargreaves was trying to convince Royce Connell that the big radio at the rear of the reception room would certainly serve for a little dancing. "We don't dance here at Corinth," Connell said, trying not to laugh.

"Mrs. French and I would adore to dance."

Connell eyed his flushed face and tried to estimate how drunk Hargreaves was. "I'll tell you what," he said then, "find me two more couples who want to dance."

Hargreaves immediately returned to Laverne, who had gotten off in a corner with Betsy Voss, Bill's wife. The two women had known each other for years without ever being friends. They were part-time allies who clustered with each other at parties where they either knew no one else or weren't confident enough to talk to others.

"Miz Betsy," Hargreaves said in what he believed to be a Midwest farm-boy drawl, "Miz Laverne, ma'am, I'd shorely be honored if . . ." He blinked, having lost the thread of his request.

"Daddy don't 'low no dancin' round here," Laverne murmured. "Right, Bets? Can you see Royce Connell rolling up the rug and—"

"Cutting it?" Hargreaves put in eagerly. "You know, cutting a rug?" He blinked brightly.

"As a matter of fact," Betsy Voss said, "he happens to be a very smooth dancer indeed. Very professional."

Laverne started to say something but seemed to think better of it. Hargreaves's arm was around her waist now, his fingers nervously edging northward under her bra. "Look, Hargreaves," she began, pronouncing it "greeves" when he had twice made a point of explaining it was pronounced "graves." "You have got to stop trying to cop a feel."

Betsy Voss looked shocked. "Laverne?"

"He's drunk and disorderly," she explained, stepping out of Hargreaves's grasp, "so he thinks he's cute. Actually he is, but not in the way he thinks he is."

"Cute as a bug's ear," Hargreaves responded Midwesternly, but from such a spiritual distance that he might have been speaking to someone else. "Frankly, it's a compliment I wouldn't extend to many ladies. You and Miss Lamb, in fact, but she's off-limits," he babbled.

"And I'm not?"

"You personally?" the gossip columnist asked. "You personally are a lovely old dear, Mrs. French. In another life on another planet I might ask you to marry me or at least sit on my face. But here, tonight, you have been dragooned into the general PR effort of one of Royce's monthly dos."

With an angry look, Betsy Voss flounced away. "You just insulted her," Laverne pointed out.

"I spoke only to you."

"That was the insult."

"Whell!" he exploded softly, "fancy that. But you're not insulted, me old darlin', are you?"

"Do you get far with that 'sit on my face' line?"

"Be amazed." He hiccupped solemnly. "Shall we dance?"

"Didn't Royce say you needed two more couples?"

"Some such condition."

"Well, then, get him to ask Jane Weil to dance. She's got a crush on him the size of Mount Rushmore." She thought for a moment. "And Doyle, that good-looking college chum of Connell's. I'll bet he's equally peachy as a dancer."

"Really? You're sure."

"Hargreaves, where did I ever get the idea that gossip columnists had to be men of the world?"

"No, Mahmet," his sister Leilah said in such a small voice that it could only be heard by Dr. Hakkad, "it will definitely not go down well. Madame Lussac might not mind. After all, the French are liberal in these matters. That so-called film producer is only too eager to desert his talkative girlfriend. You can see by those frog-eyes that he is an ogler of women. But Professor Margarine—the wife, not the husband—is too old-fashioned. She would be hurt if you invited her husband and not her."

"But, Leilah, you know about this place in Golders Green. It is entirely for men."

"Then make your invitation privately, and only to those of our blood."

"Too late. I have already spoken to McNulty and one of the other newsmen. The cat is out of the bag. All I ask is that you round up the women—there are only three—and escort them home in one of the limousines. Is that such a shocking request? You have already said that only Professor Margarine—the female Professor Margarine—might be insulted. Well then."

"I have no idea how the filmmaker's woman will take it. She speaks Italian so rapidly I haven't understood one word in ten."

"Leilah, enough."

There was a long pause. "Yes, Mahmet." She turned away from him in a gorgeous swirl of colored fabric and made for the corner of the room where all three women were trying to keep up some kind of conversation in French, Italian, and English. Professor Margarine—the female one —was trying to explain what she and her husband did in the desert for months on end, two elderly academics living the life of the bedouin, but with Land Rovers and seismic apparatus.

"*Nous*, ah, we, ah, cause these *petit* explosions?" Professor Margarine was short, stocky, with bobbed gray hair and bangs. She dug her fingers down into the thick pile of the carpet and then flung her fingers into the air with a loud "*Boom!*"

"*Brava!*" the petite Italian woman said. "*Tu sei molto carina.*"

"Ladies," Leilah began tentatively, "I'm afraid this hasn't been your typical London party. It would be more typical of Damascus or Riyadh, and now my brother—he is such a scamp—has invited the men to one of those belly-dance parlors in North London."

When none of them responded, Leilah turned to the filmmaker's mistress. "*Gli uomini, capisce, gli uomini vanno fuori senza donne.*"

"*Ma, perché?*"

"*Perché c'è uno spettacolo con*, um, *ballerine*, yes? *La danza di stomaco, capisce?*"

The Italian woman burst out laughing. "*Bene! E le donne? C'è vino, no? C'è qualche cose da mangiare, no? Benissimo!*"

"What is she saying?" Professor Margarine—the wife—asked.

"The men will be going out. She says, good. We'll stay here and drink wine. Why not?"

Madame Lussac shrugged. "Not much of a change there, eh?"

"And later, ladies, I will take you all home in my lovely Daimler." Leilah was watching the female geologist closely, as the only one who hadn't spoken her mind. Pale eyes looked out from under the thick gray shelf of bangs that gave this woman, who might well be in her late sixties, the look of a small boy.

"Fine," she said, turning to the Italian woman. "Explosions, *capisce? Boom!* And then *guardiamo il* seismograph to see . . ."

It was not a party to which P. J. R. Parkins had been invited this evening. More of an informal booze-up among his oldest mates in the Special Branch. This section of the Metropolitan Police was officially limited to investigating clandestine activities that threatened the well-being of the nation. Unofficially, of course, like secret police anywhere, they investigated whatever they pleased.

It was when he was leaving the pub at nine P.M., early enough to get home and share a cold supper with Mrs. Parkins—his mother, P. J. R. being a bachelor—and catch some of his favorite TV, that Parkins remembered the jogger and the Mini.

As he was about to descend the stairs to the underground at Warren Street, his big, stiff torso wheeled about for a moment, as if he did not have the gift of swiveling his head on his shoulders but had to move his entire body. As he tried to remember which police station had the information he needed, Parkins's usually unfurrowed forehead wrinkled.

The accident, he recalled, had been just north of Marylebone on Baker Street, which put it here in NW1 district. So it was the boys at the Albany Street Station who carried the affair on their books. Swinging about to the west, Parkins strode massively to Albany Street and turned right for the stationhouse. The duty inspector had actually trained under him at Hendon nearly a dozen years ago. "Jampot!" Parkins called at a strapping lad in his early thirties with a magnificent scowl.

Jampot whipped around, glaring, then saw who had called him by the nickname he had over the years made quite an effort to lose. "Sweet Christ, Major Parkins. You did give me a turn."

"There's a good lad. See here, Mulvey. I won't call you Jampot if you don't call me Major."

Mulvey laughed and led the way into his office. This being a real office in a real police station, he did not offer his visitor a mug of coffee, tea, or any other beverage, but got right down to business. "Anthony X. Riordan," he remembered at once. "U.S. passport. About thirty-five years of age. Contusions, lacerations, and abrasions. Broken thumb. Concussion."

Parkins suppressed a smile. "Which thumb?"

Mulvey glared at him. "Left hand, wasn't it?"

"And, on a busy manor like this, what makes you recall poor Riordan so accurately, then?"

"Because the bugger's gone missing from hospital, hasn't he?"

"Bloody hell!"

Mulvey nodded, still glaring, but not at Parkins. "And also because you've been on us since the moment it happened, haven't you? And there's the mysterious Ford Fiesta, isn't there? And the avenging jogger as well? And you're not the only heavy lad asking questions. Some sod flashing dicey ID from U.S. Naval Intelligence, *he* said. I reckon the CIA prints up those fake cards by the gross, don't they?"

Parkins shook his head in commiseration. "This month they're using fake Internal Revenue Service ID. Wouldn't you half faint dead away if one of the prats showed you real ID? And the stuff they want to know about fair takes your blood to the boil. I had one snooping around last month some perfectly ordinary British computer firm. Asking all kinds of niggly political stuff. Any socialists on the payroll? That kind of thing. Nasty business, eh? He didn't seem to know we'd had a socialist government for bloody years, did he? And what business is it of Uncle Sam if some British concern has a few people who vote Labor, I ask you?" He sighed and seemed to calm down. "So," he went on, "Riordan scarpered. On his own?"

"At four A.M. with a bandaged head? Not likely, is it?" Mulvey tried to soften his perpetually angry expression. "Are you telling me this is an SB case?"

"Don't come over all official with me, Jampot. It's two plods, talking shop."

Mulvey nodded. "Because my brief in this is nil. Riordan's not a native. He's accused of nothing, is he? Letting yourself out of a hospital is only an act of desperate self-defense, isn't it?"

Parkins sat for a long while looking at him. Mulvey was refusing to chase down Riordan and he was right, of course. And he, Parkins, had no right poking into the case either, since poor Riordan was now the object of both the FBI's and the CIA's attention. As well as the interest of that tricky, lying little sod, Colonel French, who was up to his neck in it. In fact, Parkins realized suddenly, a disappearance from the hospital was precisely what Royce Connell had asked of his FBI man, Grieves. Parkins got to his feet.

"Thanks, Mulvey. I think, at the end of the day, we're both well advised to stay out of this one. In fact, I'm sorry as hell I was conned into pulling out Yankee chestnuts from their own fire."

But as he walked back to the underground station, Parkins remembered that Grieves had gotten his orders around eight thirty this morning, hours after Riordan had disappeared. The damned thing was more complicated than it looked. Best to sleep on it.

The two representatives, Jane decided, were about equally balanced, as symbolizing the awesome yang and yin of the American republic. Chuck Gretz (Republican, South Dakota) was a skinny plant biologist who had gone broke farming in the 1960s but had since found quite a lot of success as a congressman. There was much to be said against the idiocy of making representatives run for reelection every two years, Jane knew, but anybody who had survived two decades of this kind of legalized massacre, as Gretz had, deserved respect.

His "date" for the evening was a black woman, Mrs. Kathryn Hearns (Democrat, the Bronx, New York), now on her third term in the House of Representatives, a chubby mother of three who had earned her law degree nights while cleaning rooms at the Sheraton Hotel days. Known as Katy, even to political enemies, her voting record almost precisely opposed that registered by Gretz. Anything Katy was for, Chuck was against.

"Hilarious, isn't it?" Gretz asked Jane.

"But you're buddies."

"We are more than buddies," Katy explained. "We are mortal enemies." She gave Gretz a powerful hug.

"Is this what they call the great game of politics?" Jane asked in her best noncommittal, career-diplomat tones.

She was watching Ned in conversation with that gorgeous Gillian Lamb and his own wife, Laverne. There was a physical resemblance between the women, Jane saw. They were both short, like her bubblehead sister Emily, and blond and big-busted. And attractive. Jane was still unhappy about the canceled lunch date and inclined not to idolize Ned at the moment.

Abruptly she realized that Gretz had actually responded at length to her question but she hadn't heard a word he'd said. "That's fascinating," she managed to respond.

"*Fan*-tastic!" Katy Hearns remarked, and sent her buddy Gretz into paroxysms of laughter. "You know that joke, Miss Weil? These two black gals know each other from high school. They meet after ten years. The better-dressed one says 'Oh, my, yes. Hubby is very rich.' And the other gal says '*Fan*-tastic!' And the first one says 'We own three homes and four Cadillacs.' And her friend says '*Fan*-tastic!' And the rich gal says 'And what about you, dawlin'?' And the other gal says 'I been going to chawm school.' So the rich one wants to know what they taught her in chawm school and she says 'They taught me to say *fan*-tastic instead of bull*shit!*' "

Katy's eyes closed down tight as she dissolved in mirth. Then they opened very wide and focused hard on Jane. "Whatever my old buddy Chuck tells you about the democratic process, Miss Weil, I have my answer. *Fan*-tastic!"

"Meaning there is no democratic process?" Jane asked.

"Meaning the House is a club, same as the Senate. A back-scratching club. Chuck's farmers need subsidies. Did you ever know a farmer who didn't have his hand out for a subsidy? And my voters need welfare money. They always will. Never mind who deserves what or whether the federal government can afford it. If I help him with his farmers he helps my welfare folk. And *that's* the democratic process."

Gretz coughed nervously. "I can see by the look in your eye," he told Jane, "you're thinking, here's a pair of freeloaders who have hijacked the system to keep on being reelected."

"Not I," Jane assured him. "I'm not paid to think anything of the kind."

For some reason this sent both representatives into gales of laughter, during which both accepted fresh glasses of Jack Daniel's and 7-Up from Noonan the bartender, now cruising the party for drink orders. It was a hallmark of Noonan's brand of service that he knew Gretz was on his sixth and Katy Hearns her third. But if asked, even by his employer, he would feign total ignorance.

"Miss Weil?" he asked Jane.

"Nothing, thanks." She waited till he was out of earshot. "Listening to you two is intoxicating enough. It's a good thing you're not from the same state."

"We'd murder each other," Katy responded.

Jane watched Ned French excuse himself from his two blond bombers and head her way. "Colonel French, you've met our lawmakers?" Jane began in a cool voice.

"I've been watching you three enjoying yourselves. It occurred to me that we have some TV and newspaper people here you might want to talk to."

"That's thoughtful of you, Colonel French," Mrs. Hearns responded, "but it's wasted on us."

"What Katy means is," Gretz explained, "the only journalists we're interested in are American ones."

Ned smiled. "Not too many of your constituents living on this side of the ocean?"

Katy Hearns poked her finger into Ned's unyielding ribs. "Does my heart good to see what smart folks we have working for us overseas. Chuck, you ever see a brighter pair than these two?"

"It's a shame we can't spend a few more days in town," he said by way of an answer. "Can't even stick around for the Fourth of July garden party."

"Not even invited," Katy added sweetly.

"Really?" Jane reacted. "But that's only because Mrs. Fulmer didn't know you'd be in town."

Chuck Gretz produced a sour little smile. "Our committee isn't a very powerful one. Only insiders have ever heard of it, not an ambassador who's new to political life."

"Now, a Senate committee," Mrs. Hearns suggested. "That'd cut more ice." Her plump face grew serious. "It's just a shame people new to politics haven't learned the rules."

"Rules?" Ned asked in his politest way. "The only one I know is 'Get elected.' "

"That's rule one. Rule two is 'Get Reelected,' " Katy explained. "And rule three is 'Take care of your friends.' "

"And your enemies," Gretz added softly. "Which implies a fourth rule. 'Never forget a favor or an insult.' " He flashed them a toothier version of his smile now.

There was something seductive about all this insider talk, Jane realized, something that made one drop one's guard. Otherwise why would Ned have said what he did next?

"I'm told the Sunday party is going to be heavily political," he told the representatives. "Lots of support for the president's side on various issues."

"Yeah?" Gretz snapped. "These Fourth of July things are never political. But never."

"Not till you Republicans get hold of 'em," Katy Hearns retorted, her grin something ferocious. "Don't pay us no mind, you two. We're worse than a pair of boxers in training. Chuck, come over here, will you, dawlin'?" She led him to a private corner.

"Should've kept my mouth shut," Ned muttered.

"Don't kid me, Colonel French."

"What's that mean?"

"You *like* stirring up the animals," she pointed out in a tart tone. "I watched you stirring up La Lamb. Which got me all stirred up. I never thought of you as a deliberately provocative man. But you seem to have the gift. And, considering your true feelings about politicians, you absolutely used those two nice people, didn't you?"

"What were you and Laverne talking about so long?"

Jane shrugged. "Maybe she'll tell you."

"Now who's being provocative?"

By midnight Professor Margarine—the husband—and also Maître Lussac, the French lawyer, were yawning cavernously despite the most abandoned contortions the belly dancer could produce. Only the self-styled film producer, one Signor Aldo Sgroi, remained fascinated by her orgiastic wriggling. His protuberant eyes, as Leilah had predicted, were the sign of a tireless ogler. Twice since eleven o'clock Bert had induced Khefte to ring his own number. One of his lieutenants sat waiting for a call. But Mamoud and Merak had neither telephoned nor arrived.

Khefte pretended to take this in his stride, and Bert knew why: to show anxiety in front of his sponsor, Dr. Hakkad, would be to lose face. But no such restriction operated in Bert's mind. He was worried and he didn't make much of an effort to conceal the fact from Khefte.

"It is always thus with unseasoned fighters," he whispered to Khefte when Dr. Hakkad had turned his attention elsewhere.

"Comrade," Khefte smiled, "you begin to sound like an old woman. A seasoned commander has mastered the technique of waiting."

"Don't lecture me." Bert's temper almost leaped ahead of his self-control. Instead he managed a laugh, not much of one, and joked: "You are right, brother. Waiting is an art that takes much waiting to master."

The journalist McNulty had been fast asleep in his chair for at least an hour, lulled into peace by the hypnotic pulsing music and possibly more raki than was necessary for human nutrition. Bert watched Khefte help bundle guests into the two limousines. "I'll be along later," Bert promised.

He watched the limos depart, then went back into the restaurant and phoned for a cab to St. Johns Wood, where he picked up the small bullet-gray Fiat Fiorino van. Pushing the tiny vehicle at top speeds over empty highways, he reached Amersham in half an hour and made his way more slowly past the station where both the British Rail and Metropolitan underground trains stopped. There was no sign of Merak and Mamoud.

Bert headed into the open countryside a mile or two and turned off along the darkened main street of Little Missenden. Both pubs were closed and shuttered. No lights showed anywhere along the row of Tudor cottages that led to the ancient church. Bert switched off lights and engine and drifted. Peace lay softly around him.

The silence was soothing. In the distance something said *prroo?* At this hour all the crow machines were quiet. Farther away, miles perhaps, a heavy lorry or a two-car train went by with no more than the sound of tearing paper. Bert sighed with uneasiness.

Mist lay close to the ground. There was a river nearby, Bert remembered, although he couldn't think of its name. The small van slowly rolled to a stop within ten yards of the end cottage where Bert had left the two boys this morning.

The moon was nowhere to be seen. But just over the eastern horizon the clouds shone faintly silver. To the west, over London, hung that curiously salmon-pink gauze that shrouds the city at night.

Prroo? Pp-proo?

Bert stepped very softly, avoiding the gravel for the grassy yard of the cottage. He moved silently from window to window, trying to see inside. He could feel his heartbeat quicken, then chided himself for being, as Khefte had accused him, an old woman. But surely the cottage was empty. Surely those two stupid boys would long ago have done their job and gone back to town? All around him the night lay peacefully.

Very softly, Bert inserted a key in the cottage's side door. The lock turned noiselessly and he stepped inside. Silence. He took another step. Why such caution? Here the countryside lay sleeping.

Something snicked. The bolt of a weapon.

Bert dropped to the floor and rolled silently back out over the threshold. The silenced bullet made a choked, waspish noise. *Thrp.*

Thrp.

He rolled sideways over gravel. The noise he made was hideous, shattering the peaceful night. *Thrp. Di-di-dit.*

Bert scrambled loudly to his feet. He ran, crouched over, toward the Fiat.

Di-dit.

Ahead of him a cobweb of shattered glass appeared in the side window of the van. He crouched lower, ran around to the other side, jumped into the Fiat.

The Ingram opened up with a full, silenced burst. *Ti-di-di-dit!* One of the guns he had sent the boys to test.

He started the engine and roared off through the sleeping village. Lights out, foot down hard on the gas pedal, heart pounding, mouth dry.

The Fiat howled as it shattered the utter peace of the sleeping countryside. In their beds, villagers and farmers stirred but no one woke. The van's tires shrieked as Bert rounded a turn at top speed and roared down the highway toward London.

Then the countryside went back to sleep again.

Part 3

WEDNESDAY
JUNE 30

12

Early Wednesday morning Chamoun placed a call from a booth on his way to Winfield House. It rang a dozen times before a sleepy woman's voice, a thick purr still clotted with dreams, said: "Yes?"

"Brick, good morning."

"You woke me up. And in answer to your unspoken question, she's still alive but fast asleep unless you woke her up, too."

"Get anything out of her?"

Bricktop produced a noise somewhere between a chuckle and a snort. "Is that your version of 'Getting much?'"

"Come on, Brick, I'm in a rush."

"When did I say I wanted anything out of her but her pure white body?"

"Ah, screw you." He started to hang up, but heard her voice. "What?"

"I said you should be so lucky. Are you going to be anywhere meetable this afternoon?"

"If I have to."

"Same as before."

"Right. You sure she's okay?"

"You're going to hate this, Moisheleh, but this girl wakes up today a better human being than she ever was before. You understand? I have awakened this godforsaken chick. I have turned her on. I have lighted her fire. What other 1960s jargon can I use to describe the fact that she has been done to a turn and, boychik, has she turned."

"Don't kid yourself," he said in a dour voice. "Between her ears is so much air there isn't anything solid *to* turn."

"But that only makes it easier. I don't have to displace much."

"Save it. Save every drop of it. I'll buy a bagel to smear it on."

"Meanwhile, since your conscience seems to be noodging you, let me give you my personal guarantee this girl is neither diminished nor hurt. She has been enhanced!"

The pudgy young lawyer from California, Paul Vincent, looked worried as he sat in the anteroom of Jane Weil's office this Wednesday morning. He had not been in consular work very long, but he did understand that of all the ways to keep one's superior abreast of a rapidly changing situation, the worst was to take up her time with your personal fears. A memo or phone call was far less time-consuming but the plain fact was, Vincent was over his head. The longer he delayed laying his fears on Miss Weil's desk, the less happy she'd be with him.

"She'll see you now," her secretary told him.

Vincent prodded his thick black Porsche spectacles back up his nose to a more efficient level and went into Miss Weil's office. He saw her glancing at her watch as he came in.

"I've got the ten-o'clock in a few minutes."

"Maybe I should come back later." Vincent's voice quavered faintly. He was sure only he could hear it.

"Sit down. Let's give it a fast try."

The young lawyer sat and began paging through a folder. "This is about that Weems business," he began.

"I assumed as much. What's the problem?"

"You remember when we met with Mr. Leyland on Monday, you—"

"I remember. What's the problem?"

Vincent frowned. He'd been warned she was tough, but no one had thought to add that this morning she had clearly wakened on the wrong side of the bed. "It's just that . . ." He heard that damned waver again, stopped, swallowed. "I seem to have . . ." He stopped again and glanced at her in a panicky way, trying to unscramble what he knew from what he was afraid of.

"Is something the matter?" she asked in a somewhat softer voice. "Are you all right?"

"Yes, I . . . You have to . . ." He took a deep breath. "I've hit a
brick wall," he said. Then, as if explaining it in more detail, he added,
"I've hit a brick wall."

"You mean you've hit a brick wall?"

He peered at her and was relieved to find her smiling. "Somebody
is p-pulling strings, Miss Weil." This time the quaver got the best of
him. She couldn't possibly ignore it. "I mean first it's surrounded with
a brick wall. Then it's a whitewash job, pure and simple."

She nodded politely. "Whitewashed brick. Got it."

"I know I sound upset," he confessed. "I hate to put this sort of thing
on your desk, but . . ."

In the silence Jane Weil cleared her throat and examined her watch
a second time. "But there's nowhere else to dump it?"

"Let me tell you what's happened."

"Would you? That would be most kind."

He winced. "I'm sorry. But this thing has me spooked. Right after
our Monday meeting I telexed D.C. for a dossier on this Weems. Tuesday
D.C. telexed back negative. No known anything. It seemed strange. If
you remember, we only got interested in Weems because, when Mr.
Leyland was looking to reissue a passport, Justice put a hold on it. Now
Justice was claiming they never heard of Weems."

"In just those words?"

"No. But they might as well have. So I got on the phone. You were
already gone for the day. I phoned D.C. and talked to the office that
had put the hold on Weems. They told me I was nuts, forget it, didn't
I have something better to do on Uncle Sam's time, et cetera. So . . ."
He paused as if reluctant to go on.

"So?"

"I did something maybe I shouldn't have. I went outside channels.
A buddy of mine at Justice. We graduated law school together. I got him
at his office and asked him what the f— . . . what was going on. He
called me back an hour later and this is the spooky part."

He could tell Miss Weil was using all her willpower not to check her
watch. "He told me to call him later, 'like the good old days, when we
proved I was right.' "

"That spooked you?"

"When I remembered what he meant." Vincent pushed his glasses
back in place again. "When we were at school we were always phoning
home for money. He said when you called your old man you paid the

bill. I said you had to call from a phone booth collect. It dramatized the hardship of your case. And I proved I was right."

He saw that she was smiling again, and went on quickly: "So I got to a phone last night when I knew he was home and placed a collect call. The first words out of his mouth were, 'Are you in a phone booth?' So I realized what it was all about. He was afraid his office phone was tapped. Or mine!"

He flipped through his folder and stopped at a page of penciled notes. "He said this Weems and one other guy, his associate, were untouchable. I reminded him nobody was untouchable. He said it had been made very clear to him by his superiors that Weems and the other guy were CIA."

"What?"

"Agents or contractees. He told me flat-out he didn't want to risk checking it any further. It was a matter of national security, and that was good enough for him and it should certainly be good enough for me. Meaning us."

"Meaning there is no more hold on a new passport?"

"Apparently."

She sat in silence for a long time. "But what we actually have at the moment is the original hold order."

"Right."

"Nobody has rescinded it officially, either in writing or orally?"

"Right."

She got to her feet. "Then here's what you do," she said, gesturing to him to get up. "Listen closely."

"Yes?"

"Do nothing. We will continue to operate under the original hold order until something comes through to change our direction." She led him to the door and ushered him out. "If this is truly a matter of national security and the CIA desperately needs a new Weems passport, we'll hear further. Otherwise we can assume that someone in Washington is just blowing smoke."

"Okay." Vincent felt relieved. "And the other guy?"

They were walking along the corridor now, Jane Weil heading for the ten-o'clock. "The other guy?"

"Weems's associate. A fella called . . ." Vincent paged through his folder again as they walked. "Called Anthony X. Riordan."

Burnside woke tired and hung over. He rarely drank since his wife's death, but talking to that young embassy fella yesterday had given him new hope. When the guy left, Burnside had tied on quite a few before staggering upstairs to his hole in the wall.

From somewhere nearby a church tolled the hour, but Burnside had long ago given up listening to its sound. He had to be somewhere this morning. The young fella had told him to . . .

Burnside found the scrap of paper in the breast pocket of his coat. "11 a.m., Mr. Grieves, U.S. Embassy. SHAMPOO! COMB!!"

Burnside looked hopelessly around his tiny bed-sit. He hadn't had a piece of soap on hand for a week, much less shampoo or a comb. He'd have to do what he said he'd do, go out and get some. He threw on a jacket over his bare chest, took three fat round-pound coins from the top of his dresser and moved slowly, still quite unsteady, down the steep flight of stairs, past the closed pub and around the corner.

The Boots pharmacy was a new place, very modern, with salesgirls who looked askance at nasty old men like him. Never mind. Soap. Shampoo. A comb. He pushed open the big glass door and wandered into Boots. This early in the morning the place was half empty, except for a few young mothers pushing babies in strollers. Ah, here were combs!

He began to wander aimlessly, hoping to come across what he wanted with the same accidental success that had led him to the shelf of combs. But this was a big store. It stocked everything from small TV sets to garden tools. He stood in front of a computer display for a moment, watching the green letters skitter across the screen. He strolled out a side door. Then he stopped to reorient himself. Which way was Goodge Street? A young woman in a blousey sport jacket and high boots stopped beside him.

"Pardon me, sir."

"Hm?"

"I believe you took a comb at Boots and didn't pay for it," she remarked, not in a questioning tone. "I'm the store detective. Would you accompany me back to the manager so we can get it sorted out?"

"I . . ." Burnside frowned with the effort of remembering. His hands began to delve desperately in and out of pockets. "Did I?"

"Oh, yes. This way, please."

"But, I—"

"It won't take a moment, sir. Not a moment."

The security office inside Boots was a tiny room with two TV monitors. A chubby girl sat watching the two screens as cameras in the store kept switching back and forth to different views. The young woman who

had stopped Ambrose Everett Burnside III had telephoned the store manager and the local police station.

"I am not a shoplifter, young woman. I forgot I had the comb with
me. That comb is important. I realize appearances are against me, but
. . . I'm due at the embassy in an hour. I need my comb. I can't sit
around here. I haven't done anything. I've got money. Here," he began
to shuffle through his pockets.

"Please wait. Save it, please."

Abruptly the small room grew crowded as two young uniformed police
entered, with a nervous young woman, the assistant manager, in tow.
"This is the gentleman?" one officer said. He had bristly blond hair and
smiled at Burnside with an odd air of complicity as if he recognized him
from some prior arrest. The manager refused to meet the old man's
indignant glance and kept turning as if to leave.

"It's up to you, miss," the blond man told the manager. "We can
give him a caution and release him. Or you can prefer charges. Then
we have to take him to the station."

"What happens there?" she asked in a small, "I'm not here" voice.

"If this is his first offense, he gets a caution and he's released anyway.
But we will then have a record on him."

"Will you excuse me?" she mumbled. "I have to make a call."

The tiny room seemed just as crowded after the manager had left.
The policeman with the dark hair started chatting up the store detective
while the other examined the comb.

"Forty-two p?" the blond one asked Burnside. "I ask you? Is this a
job for the Metropolitan Police?" He smiled in that same insinuatingly
knowing manner, as if he and Burnside were old associates. "And you
didn't help, if I may say so, kitted out like a right dosser. Looking as you
do, anybody'd run you in."

Someone knocked on the door. When he opened it, the manager
stood there and beckoned both officers out of the room.

They returned looking embarrassed. "You don't have to," the blond
one told the other. "It's not automatic. Her boss tells her to go the limit
because Boots has been suffering lately, but that isn't an instruction
to us."

"Wait a second," Burnside said. He started to get to his feet. "You're
railroading me. I need my comb. I have some rights in this."

"Sure you do. You'll get them at the station." The policeman opened
the door. "This way, Mr. Burnside. Mind that step, will you?"

*   *   *

Ned French sat back in the heavy wooden captain's chair and glanced around the long dining table at the rest of what was called, for lack of a better name, his "committee." Max Grieves was there, representing Justice. Moe Chamoun served as Ned's second in command. Harry Ortega was in charge of Winfield House's extremely small security staff, barely a dozen men, some of whom had other duties in the gardens or garage. Kevin Schultheiss looked too young to be deputizing on behalf of Karl Follett, who was on vacation in the States.

A motley group with radically mixed allegiances. Max was of course honor-bound to report back to the Bureau, but that was a known quantity. Schultheiss was another matter. He was, indeed, one of Follett's two deputies. But he was also one of Larry Rand's hidden ears inside the chancery. Like a number of other employees, Schultheiss was a Company plant. It didn't bother French one way or the other as long as he did his job properly. But it made Ned think twice before saying anything in front of Schultheiss that he didn't want Rand to know.

This sunny room had been allotted to Ned's committee just for the morning. Normally, Mrs. Fulmer's housekeeper had assured Ned, this was the master control center of the space ship, from which the mighty midget issued her orders.

Schultheiss ground on with a critique of what they had seen this morning, most of it a shock except to Ortega, who knew at first hand how poorly perimeter defense was set up. Ned glanced out the window across the trees. He could see some sort of dormitory building across the road. He caught a faint glint of light, not the flash one gets from a flat pane of glass, but the bright dot that comes from curved glass. A lens. Someone watching them. Probably also reading off their conversation by bouncing a laser off the intervening windows. Lovely stuff.

Ned got up and opened each window, letting in a warm rush of late-June air and making it impossible for the eavesdropper to read vibrations from the glass. As he sat back down he smiled politely at Schultheiss.

". . . perimeter fencing that anybody with an oxyacetylene torch could get through in twelve seconds," the younger man was saying.

"You don't need anything that fancy, Kevin," Ned cut in blandly. "A two-by-four will spread those uprights apart enough for someone to squeeze through. Or if you really want to let in a body of men, you could create a gap two feet wide with nothing more state-of-the-art than an automobile jack."

"So you agree it's not possible to defend this place?"

Ned shrugged. "It depends on the attack. Suppose the only guests were a popular rock group. And Winfield House was besieged by five hundred inflamed subteens thirsting for autographs and souvenirs. Then you'd worry about perimeter fencing. But just who are we expecting? Tell me that and we can begin to guess their MO."

"Sorry, Ned, my crystal ball's no better than yours." Schultheiss had a kind of brainy student look about him and the faint smile that went with baiting the professor.

"Part of the answer's simple," Ned told all of them. "Our danger comes from either end of the terrorist spectrum. Either a big group, well financed by Arab bankers, that could actually mount a paramilitary offensive. Or some small screwball bunch that is not afraid to die and more or less welcomes it."

"Or both, on a good day," Moe Chamoun added.

Harry Ortega snickered. "And you're gonna stand off these bastards with a pick-up crew like ours? I mean I don't know who else you've got, Colonel French, but what I'm volunteering is a pack of jumped-up gardeners and guys who know how to roll a tennis court."

"You're right. I'd have panicked a long time ago and called in three companies of MPs to surround this place inch by inch. Mean mothers with automatic rifles and submachine guns. Give me, say, three hundred of them and my panic is over. I'm cool. But it does give a very olive drab look to the party."

Schultheiss nodded. "The more I hear the more I wonder why you haven't called it off."

"My orders—and if Karl Follett were here, he'd get the same orders—are to protect this event with everything we've got, short of turning it into a NATO training exercise."

He gave them all something of a smile, or at least an upward tensing of the mouth. "Now let's start functioning like real security people, okay? What sort of caper would we dream up if we wanted to make Uncle Sam look like a sap and cream off a lot of ransom money? Let's assume we're blind to risk and have unlimited funds." He glanced at his watch. "Max, remember, you have to be back at chancery in an hour to meet that guy Burnside."

Grieves nodded. "No sweat. But, Ned, why do we assume anybody is going to stage such an attack? What proof have we got that somebody's stupid enough to try?"

"Good question. Anybody else want to answer it?"

Schultheiss's prof-teasing smile came and went. "Is there an answer?"

"Sure. We assume what we assume because *that's our job*. We're paid to prepare for the worst. You don't need any other answer than that."

"Okay," Max went on. "Why do we assume they'll go the ransom route? Why not just bomb the bejesus out of Winfield and call it a big victory?"

"Another good question. The answer is that you don't get such a lucrative opportunity every day of the week. We have to assume, politics aside, that plain, simple, criminal greed might trigger an assault."

A door at the far end of the room opened slowly and the petite Pandora stood there, twinkling at the seated men. "Don't let me interrupt," she called. "Colonel French, may I see you for a moment?"

Ned got slowly to his feet. "Certainly, Mrs. Fulmer, as long as you're not interrupting." His glance fastened for a moment on Chamoun. "Explain the two scenarios, airborn and infantry. I'll be back."

He followed Pandora Fulmer out of the room and closed the door behind them. "How long will you be using the room?" she began at once in a low voice.

"Another, oh, hour or less. Is it needed?"

"It is."

In her heels she came up to Ned's breastbone. She was wearing a very tight beige wool skirt split up the side with a burnt orange sweater over it and a lemon scarf around her long, slender neck. "I'm sorry, Mrs. Fulmer. We can hold this conference somewhere else. The basement? One of the garages?"

She blinked. "Don't get fresh with me, Colonel. You're only here because Mr. Connell has scared the life out of the ambassador and he's gone along with the general hysteria."

"I don't think it's hysteria, Mrs.—"

"Call it what you will but get one thing straight, Colonel. This party will not be swamped with goons in uniform. It will be a free and open expression of our nation's democratic institutions and a tribute to the talents and tenets of our president." Her eyes sparked.

Pandora had small, bright eyes of a kind of Copenhagen blue, but when she was angry, as now, the color grew muddy and greenish and hard as a stone. Ned watched her respiration rate mounting and wondered if she were doing it on purpose or couldn't help it.

"Please calm yourself, Mrs. Fulmer. My only thought is to make sure your party is an uninterrupted success."

"Yes? That's not what I suspect."

He listened to the hardness in her voice, the sudden cutting edge of sibilance like a snake's hiss. "What do you suspect, Mrs. Fulmer?"

"As of yesterday three hundred and ten people had said they would attend. Normally more would have RSVP'd affirmatively. Now we're getting cancellations. Our expected total is down this morning to about two seventy. Someone is playing games with this, Colonel. Someone has decided that my party is going to be a minuscule flop so it can be protected without any real effort. That person, whoever he is, is my enemy, Colonel. I have a few ideas about his identity. The moment I can prove it, he'll find out what an enemy I can be."

Ned shook his head sadly. "Hard to believe anybody could be *your* enemy, Mrs. Fulmer. Uh, did I hear you mention something about the talents and tenets of the president?"

Pandora's dirty jade eyes raked sideways across Ned's face. "Every party must have a theme."

"Isn't the Fourth of July enough of a theme?"

"Not dramatic enough. I've had material shipped in from the States, pamphlets, several videocassettes . . ." She went vague. They stood there for a moment in silence.

"Videocassettes? Will you have TV monitors at the party?"

"Does that have anything to do with the security arrangements, Colonel?"

"Only to the extent that we need to know everything you've planned. There can't be any sudden surprises."

Pandora produced one of her doll-like gestures, refined and delicate. "I'm sure you know that the president has caused a number of video presentations to be made on his various positions. They've been broadcast in the States on TV. There is also a tremendous grassroots movement to screen them in people's homes."

"Positions?" Ned persisted. "On intervention in Latin America? Nuclear disarmament? That sort of thing?"

"I believe so," she replied with a certain elegant fastidiousness, as if the subjects of the videos were of no importance.

"Do you know if anyone else has made such videos?"

"I beg your pardon?"

"Congress? The Senate? Any other branch of government besides the executive?"

"Colonel French, I haven't the faintest notion. Is it necessary to know?"

"I'm thinking of the effect on the press, Mrs. Fulmer. Quite a few will be on hand, with the notion that this Fourth of July garden party is like the others being held by U.S. embassies and consulates around the world. To the world our embassy represents our entire government, not just one branch of it."

"Surely that's not for you to decide, Colonel?"

"You're quite right. It lies with the Political Section and, of course, the ambassador and the minister." He eyed her speculatively. "Mr. Connell *does* know of this?"

In the silence that followed, Ned saw something change in Pandora's pretty face. One wouldn't have thought there was room in that tiny area for anything major to shift. But there was now a certain set to the jaw, Ned saw, that resembled the sudden hardening of concrete. In some way he didn't have time to analyze, he had risen to the top of Pandora Fulmer's shit list. He was being held responsible for the Company's disestablishment of the guest list. And now he would be held accountable for pointing out that politicizing Independence Day was simply Not Done.

Her sweet little chin took on the firmness of steel and her eyes, dusty green, grew almost as opaque as obsidian:

"I haven't the faintest notion," she repeated, "whether dear Royce knows of this. But if he does, I'll surely know who told him. Won't I?"

When Dr. Hakkad awoke after a night of dissipation, he did not have the same burnished look of sleekness that his guests would recognize. This was a puffier, more dyspeptic version of himself, with sparse hair rumpled in all directions and deep dark smudges around each eye; the doctor would really not come to life until he had finished several small cups of espresso Leilah made fresh for him in the kitchen of his apartment at Number 12.

He sipped his second cup while reading the morning papers and calling out tidbits to Leilah, who remained in the great reception room, carefully servicing her fingernails.

"It's the Sudan again," Hakkad called to her. "The silly buggers are planning to invade Ethiopia."

"*Inshallah!*" Leilah intoned in a voice that narrowly avoided mockery.

"And Yamani is still waffling on the price of crude. He must know by now that his strongest move is silence."

"*Bismillahir,*" Leilah responded.

"And the idiots in Iraq . . . impossible!"

"*Al-Rahman.*"

"Stop that, Leilah. Reciting the names of Allah is meant to sound pious." He returned to his reading of the morning newspapers.

In truth the Arabic news was rarely to Dr. Hakkad's liking. Although one faith bound together nearly one billion people living on the shores of the Mediterranean, the Red Sea, and the Persian Gulf, as well as dozens of other lands around the world, no single way of dealing with the affairs of the world was shared by these lands or peoples. Each had its own fears and dreams. To the man who could bring them together politically and, it went without saying, militarily, would go power and riches unheard of in this mundane and nasty century.

The road to this power did not lie in conventional politics. This the young Hakkad had learned early on after several expensive and disastrous attempts at seizing political power in various countries. In today's complex world with its instant lines of communication and computer-stored information, it was possible to stand at a power crossroads, holding all the lines in one's own hands, and enjoy ultimate power by being the medium through which it all had to flow.

None of this was easy. With Iraq and Iran at loggerheads, with Turkey allied to NATO, with African lands like Libya and Egypt at odds and disruptions even among the Malaysian and Indonesian peoples, the ambitions of a man like Dr. Hakkad were constantly being tested, thwarted, accepted, ignored, embraced . . . it was no work for a nervous man or one who lacked supreme self-confidence.

"Will you look at this," he suddenly implored his sister, "the Soviet Union's border with Islam, from Turkey to Pakistan." He was staring at a map under the headline MUSLIM SOVIETS KEEP KREMLIN PLANNERS ON THEIR TOES.

"*Al-Karim,*" Leilah intoned.

"Stop it, girl! Allah is not mocked. Bring me my appointment book, will you?"

Silently, his sister retrieved the book from the hall table and brought it to Mahmet with a deep obeisance. "I am warning you, sister. Your attitude is not exemplary."

The doctor scanned the two pages that described his Wednesday itinerary. In the afternoon he was due down in the city to speak with an Arabic merchant who could prove very important to him. Hakkad was used to taking risks of the kind represented by Khefte's cadre. But only risks that could be highly profitable. The merchant could help ensure that profit.

Dr. Hakkad glanced up at his sister and saw that she had not moved but stood statuelike as if awaiting his next command. Even as a girl she had been able to communicate irony without words. He sighed again.

"More coffee, Leilah. And get me that young firebrand Khefte on the telephone. In this busy day I must yet speak privately with him."

"Al-Razzaq."

13

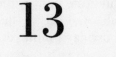

Bert got off the Metropolitan train at Amersham, the last stop, at about noon. It had been a long time since he felt as buffeted by fate as he did now. He glanced around the small town without really seeing it. The sun, hidden behind a cloud, oriented him to directions. After a moment he struck out on foot for the old town and the road to Little Missenden.

Nothing was going right, he thought as he trudged rapidly downhill. From the first day when he and Khefte had been brought together to form this cadre, he had sensed in his Arab comrade a mental barrier that would make total cooperation difficult.

So it had been Bert who gave in constantly, smoothing over differences in opinion. Only ideology held him to his Muslim brothers and, eventually, there had to be more than that.

Ideology or not, the whole operation was in danger. Two boys were missing. Had they been the ones to stage the ambush? If so, it was directed against Bert, probably by Mamoud. But Khefte had not accepted this explanation and, to tell the truth, neither had Bert.

Something else had happened. The boys had been diverted. Captured? If so, by whom? Police?

Nothing made sense, but everything menaced the outcome of the entire plan. In the still darkness of the countryside last night that vicious ambush made no sense. It was as if Bert had dreamed a nightmare, the ultimate one, betrayal by one's own. But there were three bulletholes in the Fiat. And its right window was shattered.

It was dangerous to come back in broad daylight, but nightmares must be laid to rest. Bert had to find out what had happened, find the boys, discover what this hidden threat was.

As punishment for letting it happen—Khefte's nasty turn of phrase —he had refused Bert any backup. This reconnaissance had to be made alone. Perhaps it was just as well, considering the bitterness Bert had begun to feel for some of the less political members of the cadre, who hadn't the sense to appreciate the unselfish help Bert had always given their cause.

The long road curved as he dropped from the new to the old town. What did the British call this? Twee. Little curio shops and antique stores bearing dates in the late 1600s, cross-timbered Tudor pubs, tea rooms, and gourmet delicatessens. Bert paused to note in one window a display of cheeses. There, with a little sign stuck onto it, lay a delicious wedge of Muenster, its pale body pocked by tiny holes, its spine a brown oxidized layer.

In his grandmother's kitchen in Untertürkheim, near the Daimler Benz factory, the seven-year-old Bert would be left alone to amuse himself. A real coal fire kept the big cast-iron stove hot. He would toast bread and lay paper-thin slices of Muenster on it—that thin so no one would know he had helped himself to it—and watch the cheese melt and sink slowly into the toast. The invisible Muenster would change completely from a cool, bland nonentity to a hot, savory taste he could inhale even before munching it. The toast would transcend mere bread and cheese. It would become a brilliant secret, something the boy alone had created.

Bert's jaw set in a firm line and he willed himself onward, out of Old Amersham. He, of course, did not miss his childhood. Naturally not. But every once in a while a sentimental pang would override his rational mind and for a sick moment he would feel despair engulf him like a dank wave of seawater.

Ach! He had barely slept at all last night. In this condition anyone was prey to the silly, romantic illusions of childhood.

Now that he was out in the countryside again, Bert opened up his pace. Soon the new rhythm overcame his weepy outbreak of sentimentality. To his left, beyond that grove of trees, lay Little Missenden. He would not be such a fool as to enter town as openly as he had last night, floundering straight into an ambush.

"Stupid!" Khefte had described it.

They had argued most of the night, he and Khefte, until finally, seeing the obscurity of the situation, Khefte had dumped it all in Bert's lap. "Your idea . . . your plan . . . your ambush . . . you get to the bottom of it. And fast."

Khefte then turned away with magnificent disdain to become a character in a different fantasy. The telephone had rung at ten this morning and the traitorous American whore had sung a sad song that touched Khefte's male pride. She had been kidnapped. Yes, truly, perhaps by the CIA. Who knew? They had given her truth drugs. She had told them nothing. She had been tortured. "Dris, wait till you see the bruises!"

Bert reached the edge of the woods and saw that they were dense, but not extensive. With any luck, they could be searched rather quickly. Overhead fat black crows made raucous sounds. They rose like a cloud, ten or fifteen of them, shuddering noisily in the air. They came to rest beside one of the crow-scaring machines. Bert grinned as the crows settled down amid rows of peas to dine off the maturing pods in the very shadow of the patented noise machine.

Bert moved silently into the coolness of the woods. Small pale blue flowers in clusters on long stems speckled the undergrowth as he moved in the dense shadows. He had seen them in the wooded heights above Stuttgart, as a boy. They were called . . . what?

He sat down on a stump and pulled out a bright red bandanna with which he wiped his forehead. The forest had chilled his damp brow.

Bert took a deep breath of the humus smell and stood up. As he did so he spotted the short cylinder of brass. Then another. Then five more.

Here! They had tested the weapons h—

His throat closed over. Up through the humus-rich soil, thrusting past the small blue flowers, a hand grasped for his leg. Up through the *Glockenblumen!*

He jumped back. The hand was motionless. Even now he could see the dirt engrained in the knuckles and the pressure lines that circled the wrist.

Mamoud's hand. He of the pale skin and disdainful air. Bert dropped to his knees and began digging at the loose-packed soil dog-fashion, blindly, fiercely. The arm came into view. Then the other arm and, finally, the face. In the distance the crows seemed to be laughing.

In a sudden, and rare, fit of helpfulness, Kevin Schultheiss offered a lift back to chancery and Ned took it, leaving Chamoun behind to settle some details with Harry Ortega. Before he left Winfield, however, Ned placed a call to Jane Weil. Her secretary put him on hold and when, several minutes later, he still found himself in this position, Ned hung up.

He was sitting in the passenger's seat now as Schultheiss maneuvered his elderly Mustang through fairly heavy traffic down Baker Street, discoursing all the while on the idiocy of noncareer diplomats in dealing with the great world outside their own environment. Ned found Schultheiss's small, precise lecturer's voice terribly depressing, even apart from the half-baked opinions he was reeling off as firsthand. He was obviously, and not too well, doing that very American thing, filling "dead air." Ned had often been guilty of it himself, mindlessly babbling on to avoid any significant talk.

Instead of listening, Ned began to rehearse the various reasons why Jane didn't want to speak to him, starting with the possibility that she did but had been prevented by circumstances. He ended at the opposite pole of speculation with the fear that she was well and truly angry. If so, he wasn't at all sure why.

His experiences with women were quite limited, considering how long he had been in the thick of the amorphous, multilayered intelligence community, with its agents, counteragents, moles, sleepers, and all the rest of the bric-a-brac. Women moved as freely as did men in this milieu and the love affair or, at any rate, the sexual relationship was a central factor, often used as a weapon of enticement and blackmail.

Being married half his life didn't qualify French for any higher expertise with women, nor did fathering four daughters. Experience of the kind that would help him read the signals Jane was sending out could only be gained by long, diligent, and persistent promiscuity. Jane, alas, was actually the second serious relationship of Ned's life.

Even so, he agonized as Schultheiss nattered on, were women that much different from men that one couldn't decipher their thinking?

". . . little lady really runs big Bud Fulmer," Schultheiss was saying. "And nobody runs her."

"Hmm?" Ned turned toward him.

"I can imagine the earful you were getting from her."

"And for nothing," Ned agreed. "She seems to think I'm the one disestablishing her clambake."

"How's that?"

"Larry Rand is trying to trash the whole guest list," Ned said, sending the message directly back to the Company as he did so. "He's telling them threats have been received from terrorist groups."

"No shit?"

"No problem for me," Ned went on carefully. "The fewer guests the better. But that dear little lady thinks I'm the villain and she's out to castrate me."

"Did Mr. Rand tell you this?"

"Does he ever tell anybody anything?" They were crossing Oxford Street now, heading south to the chancery. "My only hope is that this isn't another of the Company's fairy tales. If some real threats were received we'd have a clue to who the enemy was."

"Uh . . . I see."

"Do you?"

Schultheiss's cheeks had gone faintly pink, but he stared straight ahead as he steered the Mustang into the back entrance of the chancery. "Do I what?"

"Nothing, Kevin. Thanks for the lift."

Ned sprinted up the stairway to the floor where Jane's section lay. As he passed Max Grieves's open door he was hailed. "Hey, Ned. Your fruitcake never arrived."

Ned backtracked to peer around the edge of Grieves's door. "You sure? He was all primed for this."

"I even phoned the guards at the entrances. Nobody of his description has showed."

"Burnside really needed support from us. He needed to know the U.S. cared what happened to him."

Grieves stared blankly at him. "Some loony old coot with a signboard? Since when is that part of our workload around here?"

Ned stood without speaking for a moment. There was no sense coming down on Max with the full force of a two-by-four to the brain, because Max didn't really have enough brain to warrant drastic rear-rangement. Still, this was what old Chemnitz had called a "learning moment."

"Max, what do you think we *should* be doing around here?"

The FBI man looked suddenly doubtful. "Whatever drops into the in basket?" he asked on a note of hope.

Ned smiled in spite of himself. "Max, why does the government have embassies and consulates? To create jobs for you and me? Or to help its citizens overseas?"

Max brightened up. "I get it." Then doubt returned. "But genuine crazies like Burnside?"

"Is that what he is? Or is he an elderly American who's lost his wife and his life savings in one fell swoop and doesn't know what to do except stage a weird kind of placard protest."

Ned glanced at his watch and moved on to Jane's corner office. No secretary guarded the portals. He saw her talking into a telephone as he came to her open door and knocked on the jamb.

She glanced up rather coolly, he thought. Without any change of expression, she continued into the phone: "I agree, Royce. It is definitely foul play. Have you spoken to Colonel French about it?"

She stared straight ahead as she listened. "Where did she get the idea he was behind it?" Another long pause and, this time, her glance moved slowly to Ned's face, treating it as if it were another form of woodwork. "He seems to have made quite a hit with Mrs. Fulmer. I'll see what I can find out, Royce. Yes. Yes. Bye."

Slowly she replaced the telephone. "I see you've added yet another blond to your list of conquests. Mrs. Fulmer has just demanded your head."

"And a good good morning to you, too."

He sat down across from her desk. "Why are you mad at me? I couldn't help what happened yesterday."

"No more than you could have called me all afternoon or evening, or taken me aside at Royce's dinner and whispered a few sweet words of longing or commiseration or even some bland Britishism like 'Jolly bad luck, wot?' or—"

"And what is this about blonds?"

"The man is hip-deep in them. Busty, blooming blonds."

"Pandora Fulmer is busty?"

"Obviously the odd titless brunette now and then is a temporary aberration." She watched him for a moment. "I am trivializing this, aren't I? It goes deeper than hair coloring."

Ned let a long time go by in silence. "What is it today? Why is everybody I talk to using code? Why is everyone carrying a secret portfolio? I don't seem able to connect."

"You should be used to that by now, French. You've spent half your life in a world where nothing's what it seems. And neither are you."

"Oh, look."

"The French I knew was a figment of my woman's fantasy. The real French may be a lovely fellow, but he's not to be relied on for anything. Ever."

"One date screwed up! One time!"

"Get your mind out of the hotel bedroom," she advised him. "Wasn't there more to us than that?" Her big, dark eyes seemed to grow larger as she stared at him. Finally: "There may be two or more Frenches in this world, even a dozen. But the current me doesn't much like the current you. No, she doesn't."

"Come on, Jane."

She shook her head slowly from side to side. He caught her profile for a moment, outlined by light from the windows overlooking Grosvenor Square. She had a strong face for a woman, and at the moment it was set in the firm lineaments of rejection. His fate, Ned thought, was to be surrounded by strong women.

"Not only strong," he said aloud, "but stubborn."

Her great eyes slowly returned to gaze at him. "You don't really understand despair, do you? In your experience it's always rational and connected with an actual event, like the death of that poor young man from Wisconsin. But there is a despair that can be triggered off by something trivial, even a canceled date, but which expands to fill every corner of a relationship and choke it to death."

"Jane," he said, "I find all this angst hard to believe. I mean, one postponed date?"

She watched him in a brooding silence for a while. "I have moods," she said then. "Perhaps you've never seen me like this. But I watch you with your sexy little wife . . . your sexy Gillian Lamb . . . your God knows who or what else. It's a whole, rich life you lead out there . . . *without me*. Few and far between there are the moments when our social lives crisscross. And even then they are never occasions for behaving naturally toward each other. Instead we have new moments for further lying, further dissembling."

She paused and took a long, slow breath. "Ned, lying is a major ingredient of your bloodstream. It might almost be said that they pay you to lie. I won't pretend there haven't been times I was called on to lie. But I find it very difficult. I find it depressing in public life and degrading in my private one. But the worst of it is when, having managed to commit a great many lies, all I produce is a stolen moment *that never happens*. Then what I feel . . . is angst!" Her voice grew suddenly sharp. "Don't tell me ever again that you find that 'hard to believe,' Colonel French."

His face had grown very grave, an older version of the somber look Chamoun often wore, as if they were watching the dissection of some family pet animal. "Don't say anything, Ned," she told him. "It's not that I wouldn't believe you. It's just that . . ."

Silently, they stared at each other.

Once the police van had deposited Burnside and the young woman store detective at the stationhouse, new officers began to take charge of the case. The detective was taken off by the young constable who had been flirting with her at Boots. The elderly man, looking even worse for wear than before, was left to sit on a bench facing a young sergeant who was busily filling in forms and even more busy not looking up.

It's like being a pebble in a cement mixer, old Burnside thought. He couldn't actually say that anyone had been rude. Unless you counted the Boots manager who didn't need to prefer charges but stuck it to him anyway.

"Is that what I think it is?" an inspector asked, looking over the sergeant's shoulder. "When are they going to stop playing games?"

The sergeant shrugged. "It's too demoralizing for them, going after real thieves. Can you imagine? A forty-two-p comb? While their own employees steal them out of house and home?"

The inspector, who looked to Burnside to be about fifteen years old, made a face. "Can you imagine what a ratbag that'd be? Nobody'd work for Boots. Take his statement, check his record, give him his caution, and let's move on to greater things, eh?"

"Like lunch," the sergeant said. He looked, if anything, younger than the inspector. Neither of them looked at Burnside. It was as if he weren't even in the room.

"Right. Mr. Burnside? Would you step up here, please? This won't take long."

The sergeant proceeded to relieve him of his change, a wallet he carried with nothing in it but his Social Security card, his house keys, and a scrap of paper that said: "11 A.M., Mr. Grieves, U.S. Embassy. SHAMPOO! COMB!!" Painstakingly the young officer searched Burnside's pockets and patted him down for a weapon. "We have to do this, Mr. Burnside," he remarked.

Then he spent about fifteen minutes itemizing everything, after which he handed it all back except the keys, which he placed in a plastic bag, labeled, and sealed with a patented device. "Would you sign this here, please?"

Burnside stared at the printed form with all his worldly possessions entered on it. "Why?"

"It just says these are all yours and will be returned to you. It doesn't commit you to anything beyond that." The sergeant watched him sign. "And here." He pointed to another line. "And over here. This won't take long."

Hearing a commotion behind him, Burnside turned in time to see the female Boots detective and the young policeman laughing as they left the stationhouse together. He stood there, shifting from one foot to another while the sergeant continued filling out the four-page form. Time passed. Phones rang and were answered. Everybody else's life went on. More Boots employees stole from Boots. More innocent shoplifters were arrested, for all Burnside knew. More time passed.

"You can sit down, Mr. Burnside," the sergeant said at last. "This won't take long."

Burnside dozed off and on. Finally an officer came in and murmured something in the sergeant's ear. He went into a back room and fought with the combination lock of a wall safe. Having opened the door, he removed a plastic bag and ripped it open. "Are these your keys?" he asked the elderly man.

"Sure. I think. Maybe. What about my comb?"

"Sign here," the sergeant said, pointing to yet another line on the form. "I told you this wouldn't take long."

"But now I've got a police record for something I didn't do."

The sergeant looked up at him. "If you ask for a trial this gets held over. The whole thing can take as long as a month or two. Or you can take your caution from me, right now, and walk out of here."

"What sort of chance would I have in court?" the old man wanted to know.

"You need a really top barrister to prove a history of failing memory and a few other things. Otherwise you don't have a case."

"Or the money to pay a barrister."

"Yes, well, they do say justice is blind." He managed a lopsided grin. "Sign here?"

"Have you got five minutes, Colonel French?"

Ned looked up from his desk, where he and Captain Chamoun were examining some charts Maurice had just brought back with him from Ortega, the Winfield House security man. They were detailed blueprints of the mansion's electrical circuits, burglar alarms, and telephone wiring.

In Ned's doorway, unannounced and arriving as silently as a cat on velvet, stood P. J. R. Parkins, his hooked nose as rampant as a scimitar.

His upper trunk thrust forward in a rather aggressive posture. "You know Captain Chamoun?" Ned suggested.

"Yes, well, er . . ."

Ned glanced at Maurice, who rolled up the charts and left the office without another word, closing the door behind him. "Well-mannered young man, that," Parkins remarked. "May I?" He hovered over the visitor's chair.

"Please sit down. What can I do for you?"

The silence that followed was the usual one between two men who were used to waiting. Ned sat back in his chair and decided he'd let the old boffer have his little touch of drama. He waited.

"Riordan's gone missing," Parkins said then.

Ned frowned. The name of Riordan, so far as he knew, had never before passed between them. It was better, at this point, to play dumb. "Riordan?"

"Anthony X. Riordan, the bloke whose life you may have saved Monday morning when that Mini sideswiped him."

"The jogger was called Riordan?"

"Oh, dear me." Parkins found a similar relaxing pose in his chair and the two of them played at being entirely at ease for another whole minute. Finally, Parkins cleared his throat, a very small sound but heavy with power. It reminded Ned of something a Mercedes salesman in Bonn had once told him when trying to get him to buy the car. "Remember, only a truly powerful car can go really slowly."

"Dear, dear me," Parkins echoed. He looked entirely at ease and so did Ned, two life masters in a body language tournament.

"If I may digress momentarily," Parkins began then. "I don't have to tell you that we get all kinds of villains in this town. I mean New York may set more horrible records for crime, but we do get some right twisters on our own. We especially attract financial villains from all over the bloody world. They come zooming in on our city with their teeth sharpened like ruddy vampires. They'll drain the lifeblood out of any enterprise. There are some stories I could tell."

He stopped and settled into an even more comfortable pose. "We reckon this Riordan bloke is one of that stripe, looking for likely earners to take over and drain dry. You wouldn't credit what they get into. We have more than a notion that one of them with a smooth line of Irish blarney has even hijacked one of the Sinn Fein groups that specializes in very profitable kidnaps."

"Anything to make a quid," Ned remarked.

"Exactly. Nothing t'do with politics or freedom for the Emerald Isle or what have you, just plain ordinary loot. Now Riordan being an Irish name, the two wires have started to cross in our minds, don't you know?"

Ned nodded sagely. "I can certainly see why."

"Can you?" Parkins pounced. "I'm extremely glad to hear that, Colonel. Anything like this, with an embassy connection to it, is very worrisome to all of us. Even if there's nothing to it, the possibility of bad publicity is enough to add a few gray hairs." He rapped his skull.

"You're absolutely right," Ned agreed. The two of them watched each other warily, but no longer with such overt opposition. It was hard to tell which of them had engineered the change in atmosphere.

"I must be forthcoming with you, Colonel. Unless you object, I'll be away from the chancery for the next few days and my assistant, Loveapple, will be handling any technical problems."

"Loveapple? Do I know him?"

"Short, squat Yorkshireman. Very little hair."

"And he's competent?"

"Quite," Parkins assured him.

Ned wanted to ask why the Riordan "case" required Parkins to take a leave of absence. But he wasn't about to blow off the landscape the nicely calibrated cloud of mist he and the Briton had managed to puff up around themselves.

"If you approve Loveapple, he's got my approval, too," Ned said in a solemn tone.

Parkins smiled pleasantly. His oaken face, while virtually motionless, somehow conveyed an aura of thanks, gratitude, good fellowship, and that most sacred of attributes, trust.

"Colonel," he said at last, "you and I have always got along. In the year you've been here our paths have never crossed in any negative way. Am I right?"

"Are you telling me they have now?"

"Something is going on with this blasted Riordan chappy. Sinn Fein, or what, is all a guess, but his case has grown quite worrisome what with him disappearing himself and all. And the only connection I have is you."

It was on the tip of Ned's tongue again to ask Parkins why an employee of the embassy responsible for electrical and other conduits had been seeking "connections" in the Riordan "case." Instead he let Parkins keep on talking.

"Now there's no need for the two of us to collide head on," the older man assured him. "There's every reason for us to handle this as discreetly as possible. I'm sure you agree?"

"I do indeed."

"Then can you tell me what the bloody hell you were doing jogging next to that man on Monday morning?"

"Ah." Ned sat forward and presented a very forthright façade, all willingness. "I certainly will if you'll tell me who was driving the Mini and what's happened to him."

"A minor villain called Chalky Fetters with a long record of aggro assault. He's a cove you hire to rough somebody up . . . or worse. Naturally, he's out on bail. But we've got him cold when it comes to trial and if Riordan turns serious we might nail him on a capital charge."

"And Riordan is actually missing? Left the hospital?"

"With or without help. Willingly or otherwise. We jolly well don't know. Now that's enough out of me. Let's hear from you, Colonel."

"Precisely. But let me begin by warning you, Mr. Parkins. You will find most of this quite unbelievable."

Two vans, one large and one small, pulled up at the entrance to Winfield House. The guard at the gate came out to glare at them. "What's this now?" he growled.

"Albion," the driver of the lead van called. He delved into the glove compartment and came up with a wad of papers.

"Albion what?" the guard asked unpleasantly. With some reluctance he accepted the papers and backed off to squint at them. "Rentals? Rentals of what?"

"TV equipment, mate."

"Don't know about that," the guard responded in a mulish tone. "You lot just hold it right there." He disappeared inside the gatehouse and was gone for some time. When he emerged it was still with great reluctance. Every line of his face indicated that he was against the whole idea. Nevertheless he jerked his thumb off to the left.

"Pull 'em in back of the house. Nice and quiet, now."

The two vans moved around the corner to the left and soon were lost to sight. At that moment a small white Metro appeared with Gillian Lamb at the wheel, looking soft and silvery in a snow-white jumpsuit.

"Good Lord, is it you, luv!" cried the guard.

"It's me, luv," she called.

"They should've sent you in ahead of the vans." He winked and waved the white car through. "Am I goin't'be on the telly, luv?"

"And why not, a handsome devil like you?"

He cackled and watched the car turn left and follow the vans out of sight. Then, whistling good-humoredly, he returned to his gatehouse.

Pandora Fulmer received Miss Lamb in one of the formal ground-floor rooms, much too big for two people but evocative of the sheer physical size of the American world presence, which Pandora was not. Although she was still angry at what seemed to be a conspiracy behind her back to ruin the Fourth of July party, Pandora had as always done her homework when it came to dealing with the press or TV.

She gestured to the walls, covered in intricately hand-printed Chinese paper, and then indicated a pair of silk-upholstered love seats set at right angles to each other. "We're lunching in the garden," she told Gillian Lamb, "but I thought we'd have our drinks here and get to know each other."

Gillian sat down and smoothed out the rather wide legs of her one-piece coverall, of a chic so advanced and *sportif* that it instantly made fuddy-duddy a Sino-Victorian room decor that had cost the earth to install. Pandora, who knew the room generated more than enough fussiness on its own, had also dressed "down," but in the manner of a white Southern belle, 1950 college coed style, in flared skirt, long-sleeved shimmering white shirt, two strands of pearls, and, in place of her usual high-heeled sandals, plain red-rubber-soled buckskin saddle shoes with contrasting laces. As she well knew, she looked from a slight distance like a twelve-year-old. Gillian did not.

The Englishwoman smiled prettily and teased one long straw-bright strand of hair away from her cheek. Her startling orange eyes swept around the room. "This is lovely, Mrs. Fulmer."

"Thank you, Gillian. I had absolutely nothing to do with the decor. And please call me Pandora."

"Not Susan?"

"The only person who ever called me that was my mother." Both women laughed. "What would you like to drink?"

"I'm not much of a drinker when I'm working. A Coke?"

"That's fine." Pandora pressed a button. When Mrs. Crustaker appeared, Pandora said: "Two Cokes, Belle. By the way"—she got up and stood beside the tall black woman—"Mrs. Belle Crustaker, my housekeeper. This is Gillian Lamb, who's doing the TV."

Gillian stood up. Though she was not a tall woman, she and Mrs. Crustaker nevertheless caused the twelve-year-old almost to disappear.

They shook hands. "You don't like a lot of ice in your Coke, Miss Lamb?" the housekeeper asked.

"Not too much."

"Belle is a great-grandmother," Pandora announced.

"No! That's hard to believe," Gillian responded.

"Even harder for me," Belle said and disappeared.

When the drinks arrived and Belle had left them, the two women wandered around the room, Pandora explaining the name and provenance of each ornate Chinese vase or other object. It began to be obvious that she could do an equally accurate job anywhere else in the house. At about the same time it also became clear that Gillian was less than fascinated by objects.

"It's a people program," she said for the second time, describing "Lamb to Slaughter."

She sat down in the love seat, mostly to bring the museum travelogue to a close. "Viewers think of it as a program about issues, but it starts and ends with people. Sometimes you, or I, might not think much of them. But the world only holds a limited number of Nobel winners. What fascinates us all is the average person, especially in an unusual situation."

"Does that describe Sunday's garden party?"

Gillian nodded at the implied demurrer. "I don't think anybody who becomes an ambassador can be considered average or ordinary. And you certainly haven't invited an average group of guests. Nor is your Independence Day an average event. Especially not when it's celebrated in the very land you fought to become independent from." She smiled sweetly. "But to the average viewer we all have our parties, our picnics, our outings. There is something riveting about the way the great ones go about doing the same thing, on a greater scale. Does that make sense to you . . . Pandora?"

Glowing with satisfaction, Pandora nodded several times. And, although she herself had been a journalist, no warning voice sounded in her inner ear, cautioning her that this kind of soft soap, while traditional, could turn out as slippery as a banana peel, and just as upsetting.

When Captain Chamoun said he was going out and asked if he could bring back a sandwich and coffee, Ned decided instead to break office protocol and go with him. This seemed to bother Chamoun but Ned was far too engrossed in his own problems to notice.

They strolled away from the square toward Oxford Street, and within a few hundred yards both of them had spotted Student, following at an approved distance. "A shorter, darker lad with a Cyranose," Ned muttered, his hand in front of his mouth. "Can you make him, too?"

"Just behind Student. He's turned away to look in that estate agent's window," Chamoun said in an undertone. "Why are we mumbling? They can't possibly have parabolics on us in this crowd."

"They were on me yesterday, both of them, till I finally dumped them."

"I wondered where you were yesterday afternoon."

"You remember the Watcher? The guy those National Front goons beat up? Paid him a visit. Let's double back to the square and sit down. No reason we can't rest our butts while they stand up."

When the two intelligence officers got back to Grosvenor Square they were still being followed. "Got any idea," Ned wondered as they sat on a bench, "why I have suddenly sprouted not one but two tails?"

"Student is a Company man. You can spot it in his style of surveillance."

"That kind of answer only produces more questions. Why is Larry Rand having me tailed?"

"God, I don't know." Chamoun yawned and stretched. "Why haven't you told Royce what the Company's doing to the guest list?"

"Pandora bent his ear this morning, blaming me. I'm going to let Royce stew till he's hopping mad, then blow the whistle on Rand."

"And what about her idea of having little monitor TV sets all over the place running presidential videos?"

"Holding it in reserve, mah boy," Ned said in a gruff W. C. Fields voice. "Never give Pandora an even break." He stood up. "You go east. I'll go west. Let's see who Student loves the best. If you do get to a coffee shop, it's a roast beef on brown bread with lettuce. Coffee black. Chocks awaaaaay!"

He started west as rapidly as possible. Chamoun watched both shadowers follow him. Smiling very faintly, he moved some streets east until he was standing at the corner window of the boutique called Bricktop. Then he made his way to a coffee shop nearby and sat toward the back of the long, narrow room. It took Bricktop almost half an hour to arrive. The fat woman stood at the counter with her back to Chamoun. He examined at leisure the truly immense female spread presented there while she gave the counterman an order to go.

"Nancy will be back in the chancery tomorrow," the woman with the orange hair said in a low voice. "She'll look roughed up. Ignore it. It's makeup. Don't contact her. If she needs you, she'll say so. Do what she asks."

"As a favor to you?"

"The girl is out on a limb. That *momzer* Arab has taken her back. She needs a friend, Moishe. Be a good boy, will you?"

"Brick, you take a lot of chances . . . with other people."

"That's why I'm Station Head and you're just a mole." Her big body heaved with laughter.

"What's the joke, Brickie?" the counterman asked.

Returning to Ned French's office, paper bag in hand, Chamoun saw him reading the jacket liner of a phonograph album. "You lose that pair?"

Ned nodded. With his left hand he gave the album to Chamoun. *Art Hodes: Chicago Blue.* Chamoun examined the photograph of a small, elderly, elfin gentleman pounding the keyboard of an upright piano whose front sounding board had been removed to let strings and hammers show.

"You dig this stuff, Ned?"

He nodded, still without talking.

"It's beyond a simple Sandusky boy like me," Chamoun said, putting down album and paper bag. "If you need me I'm in my office."

Ned French nodded a third time. As Chamoun left, closing the door behind him, Ned's right hand, which had been well below desk level, came into view holding a large manila envelope in which the phonograph album had been delivered by hand just a few minutes before. The album was one he had been searching for most of his adult life, with no luck. In his hand, too, was a small white business card, engraved neatly with a name over which a message had been scrawled in bright blue ink:

"Happy listening."

French turned the card over. There was nothing on the back except the very faint indentations that show a card has actually been printed from a costly engraved plate, not by the cheaper thermographic process.

"Gleb Ponamarenko," the engraving read. "Correspondent, Tass News Agency."

14

Most passersby, seeing a Rolls moving sedately through the narrow, clogged streets of the city, a white chauffeur at the wheel and a resplendent Levantine as sole passenger, would assume vehicle and driver were rented by the hour. But in the case of Dr. Mahmet Hakkad, they would be wrong.

Pan-Eurasian Credit Trust could afford it. Twenty years before, when Hakkad was a young, successful ophthalmologist in Beirut, he had founded the trust when he saw the possibilities of midwifing the Islamic conquest of the world. The company had begun its life exchanging currency at a small premium, or a large one for customers who required absolute secrecy. Its extensive credit operations had made it, by now, possibly the leading bank of the Arab world and certainly one of the few to have profitably weathered the violent ups and downs of the oil market.

This afternoon the good doctor had been driven eastward into the walled fastnesses of the city, that square mile of unregulated thievery in which he was as much at home as a piranha in the Amazon.

The man he was about to see offered a magnificent opportunity to unload a risky venture and in the process insure a profit. This man controlled the new liquid riches of several Middle Eastern lands, not the green-brown treasure of oil but the transparent riches of water. For it was true that in many places within the Islamic world, where sharp cuts in oil price had impoverished the day laborers, local agriculture had suddenly risen to prime importance. When there is no oil money to buy food, one returns to growing it.

And for that, one needed Elias Lateef's water.

Lateef was a small man, terribly thin, with a face whose bone structure dominated design. The high cheekbones of the barely hidden skull created dangerous knife-edges. His dry lips, and his tendency to peel them back when smiling, exhibited teeth down to the gingival tissue—dismaying teeth, horsy and powerful. The eyes nestled far inside the skull's eyeholes in a dry, papery nest of wrinkled flesh.

Hakkad was suddenly struck by the *desiccated* quality of the man who controlled so much life-giving water. It was said that even Allah had to obtain a Lateef franchise before causing rain to fall.

"Please," the skeletal man said, indicating a carafe and two glasses. "It is only, er, London water, but I have had it filtered three times to remove the, ah, clay."

Both men laughed politely and then Lateef, setting aside his glass, got down to business at once. "It is of funds that I am forced to speak," Lateef explained. "I need not describe to you the, er, special taxes placed upon businessmen of the faith, taxes of an, er, special nature and designated for special use."

Hakkad nodded. Depending on which lands one did business in, private contributions of cash had to be made to each government's "emergency" fund. No accounting was ever made. Like everyone else, Hakkad considered this a simple business tax and cared not whether it ended up in the pockets of politicians or funded terrorist groups.

The ophthalmologist spread his manicured hands out in a graceful, palms-up gesture, as if releasing some great sea bird. "All is not lost, my friend. Pan-Eurasian is not without special resources. I do not refer to cash assets as much as to hidden reserves of"—Hakkad pursed his lips delicately—"of manpower."

The water-merchant's flesh-draped eyes seemed to widen and move outward like the flexible stalk eye of a snail. "Is this possible, in Britain or in our own lands, where unemployment is rife, that reserves of manpower are anything but, er, an unwanted liability?"

"I do not speak of British workers, who for generations have practiced on-the-job sabotage of the deadliest kind." Hakkad reversed his seagull-releasing gesture as if enfolding the bird of good fortune back into his embrace. "No, I refer to active young men of our own faith, available here in Britain for good works."

"Of a kind one can reasonably expect to produce, er, cash?"

The good doctor smiled broadly. The hook was set. He had for some time been wondering how to offload Khefte's heavy expenses. He had been blackmailed by his own government into financing the cadre here in London, which he accepted as yet another business tariff. Well and good. But backing a commando of terrorists produced only debit entries in the ledger.

He would, in effect, "sell" Khefte to Lateef for the promise of millions in ransom money. The transaction would go down in Pan-Eurasian's books as a short-term loan, easily repaid, even with exorbitant interest, if Khefte was successful. Like a bookie who "lays off" big bets among other bookies to share risk, Hakkad was taking out a financial insurance policy, with Lateef holding the bag. The details would trouble Lateef. But his need was strong, so the remedy had to be stronger. That, Hakkad reminded himself, was the cost these days of doing business in an ever more chancy world.

It was always simple, Ned reflected, to get in touch with Gleb Ponamarenko, Tass's brilliant London correspondent who hadn't filed a story in years.

While he might lunch or dine at various restaurants about town, the Russian was always to be found between five thirty and seven in the evening at one of two Knightsbridge bars. It was, like most of Ponamarenko's agentcraft, simple to the point of elegance. Those who wanted to meet him "accidentally" knew how to arrange it.

Nor did the strategy fail this evening when, at about six, Ned found Gleb in a rather upmarket eatery on Pont Street meant for Sloane Rangers and their male companions. No one Ned knew ever actually ate there without suffering acute food poisoning. But it was perfectly safe to drink at the bar.

"Just as long as you don't nosh the hors d'oeuvres," he murmured in the Russian's ear as he slid onto the next barstool.

"Never! In fact, I had such a lunch that I may not eat again till breakfast."

"No civil servants tonight to stuff with blini? No newspapermen to slather with caviar?"

"Is my work that crude?" Gleb asked in a huffy tone, turning his depraved, aristocratic face to Ned. The fierce calipers that enclosed his mouth seemed in danger of breaking apart in a grin.

"Not when it comes to phonograph albums," French confessed. "How did you get onto my passion for Art Hodes?"

"I have my ways."

"And one of them is putting a tail on me during my lunch hour while I stroll from one record shop to another freely confessing my addiction." He decided to let the Russian have both barrels. "That studious fellow works so much by the book I thought he was one of Larry Rand's."

Gleb's face displayed bewilderment, not a lot of it, because its natural design was far too knowing for innocence, but enough to convince Ned French. "Not yours?" Ned asked. "Then the young lad whose mother seems to have been an anteater?"

Ponamarenko made *tk-tk* sounds behind his front teeth. "You have the advantage of me, as the bishop said to the chorus girl."

"Neither?"

"French," the Russian said in a tone of heavy irony, "an album you have been looking for since God knows when? On the strength of one lunchtime shopping spree I suddenly produce it from my top hat like a rabbit?" The bartender arrived.

"Scotch, soda, very little ice," Ned told him.

The bartender went away. "I, too, nourish a passion for jazz piano," the Tass correspondent admitted. "I won't tell you my favorites, too schmaltzy. You're a devotee of that spare, wry, funky style. But let me tell you: People who collect solo piano records are basically loners. Did you know that?"

"With the combined strength of every worker's, artist's, housewife's, agronomist's and dog-catcher's Soviet collective massed solidly behind you, you call yourself a loner?"

"Far from the madding crowd." Gleb nodded several times. "Here's your drink." He took it from the bartender and placed it in Ned's hand. "To us," he said, clinking his martini glass against Ned's drink.

"Us loners?"

"Us professionals." Ponamarenko eyed Ned as he sipped his whiskey. "And the work-related dysfunctions to which we are heir."

French frowned at him. "That sounds like a bad translation."

But Gleb was shaking his head negatively even before the words had been said. "The French call it *le cafard*. In Vietnam your soldiers called it the thousand-mile stare. Sailors call it cabin fever. Businessmen in the States refer to it as mid-life burnout." He laughed softly.

"So what's your dysfunction, Gleb?"

"I don't often confess it." He finished his martini and signaled for another. "If I tell you I never want to leave London, that I have found my lifetime milieu and won't be parted from it, you'd tell me that was old news."

"And if I told you my leaves were getting slightly brown around the edges with this life we lead," Ned pointed out, "that would hardly qualify as a hot scoop, would it?"

"Don't minimize something that could be serious."

"Oh, my God, Gleb. Don't tell me you've got your eye on me? You're hoping to stampede me into your corral and change the brand on my hide?"

The Austro-Moldavian-British face looked only slightly upset, Ned saw. An agent like Ponamarenko always worked in depth and with an eye to the long view. If the Hodes album had been a bribe, in advance, for a private interview, or merely a way of piquing Ned's interest, then Gleb had gotten value out of it. He had *delivered his message.* From now on, even if he'd been rebuffed, it would become increasingly easier for him to raise the subject in a dozen subtle ways.

"And if I am?" the Russian asked. "Do you blame me for wanting to work with quality material?"

"Put it out of your mind," French told him. "I don't mean on the back burner or the deep freeze. I mean expunge it from your gray matter, Gleb. I am not for sale"—he held up his hand to stem the tide of indignation before it started to flow—"not even to swap for more Hodes albums. But I will make you a deal: Tell me where you got that album of *Chicago Blue* and I'll buy you a drink."

The parenthesis of lines around the Russian's nose and mouth bit deeper into his skin as if being engraved by acid. "My mother has an old wives' expression, Colonel French. 'To a tough steak comes a sharp knife.' You've heard it before?"

"No. How is your mother?"

"Fine."

"Thinking of having her visit you?"

"I don't know which of us would enjoy that less." His new drink arrived. "Your parents are well?"

"Very."

"They tell me the Wisconsin winter was very hard this year. Lake Winnebago froze over."

Ned grinned amiably. "Gleb, I'm deeply chagrined that I can't re-count for you how many beets your mother grew in her little garden in the Crimea. I'm also flattered you bothered to work up this much gen on a lowly cog in Uncle Sam's mighty intelligence machine. I am sorry it's a dead end for you, but I would still like to know how you got that album."

"The information wouldn't help you. Not unless you knew our Station Head in Chicago."

Both men stared at each other and broke up laughing. Perhaps, Ned thought, Ponamarenko was genuinely amused, perhaps not. But there was no question that Ned French was trying his best to hide the queasy feeling of being targeted by someone as astute as his fellow drinker.

Le cafard, was it? One of those psychosomatic ailments that could kill you faster than bullets.

Tonight being one of the rare times they weren't invited out to a large dinner, Ambassador and Mrs. Fulmer were enjoying a small snack in their own kitchen at Winfield House. The servants had been dismissed for the evening. Even Belle Crustaker had left for a visit with a remote cousin of hers who lived in Stoke Newington.

Moving about the immense kitchen like one of those pretty but useless insects that decorate a summer garden for a few brief hours, Pandora Fulmer was putting together the simple ingredients of toasted cheese sandwiches, half a dozen of them.

"Too late for coffee, Bud?" she asked.

He was seated in his shirtsleeves at a long table usually used for preparing food. Only someone his size could use such a high table for reading a newspaper. He looked up, first at his wife, then at the wall clock, then at his own wristwatch. It seemed to take forever for what he had been reading to leave the front of his mind and be replaced by the concentrated thinking required to make a caffeine decision.

"Just tea, honey. Is there any of that Earl Gray?"

"Lots. Sugar?"

"No. No milk, either."

"I mean you, sugar. Did you ever meet that security fellow, Colonel French?"

Bud Fulmer's mind shifted heavily from caffeine to French. Every scrap of what he had been reading about—the safety of nuclear reactors—had drained completely out of his mind. "Don't think so.

Maybe shook hands once. He's got that cute wife with the . . . um . . ."
Bud's flat slab of a face changed shape very slightly in what only Pandora
knew was a lewd grin.

"That's the one," she told him. "You don't miss much, you old
goat."

"Just lookee. No touchee."

Pandora laughed. "That man will be the death of me, Bud. He's
singlehandedly wrecking my party." She sat on the table beside his newspaper, took one of his big ham-sized hands in both her tiny ones, and
recounted her bill of particulars against Edward J. French.

Bud sat in silence after she had finished. "You want me to have him
taken out and shot, honey?"

Her eyes went wide with anticipation. Then reality took over. "Oh,
if only you could."

"I'm bigger'n him. You want me to punch him out?"

"Stop teasing me, Bud. What can I do about this horrible man?"

"Well." Bud laboriously shifted his brain into the new gear, one of
those low-low ratios useful for climbing steep grades or getting out of
loose mud. "First of all, nothing much between now and Sunday because
my understanding is if we don't have him, we don't have anybody. But,
second, nothing you told me would hold up in a court of law. It's what
they call circumstantial. You don't actually know he did all these things.
If you can prove it, honey, I'll have his scalp handed to you on a silver
platter. And that's a promise."

She picked up his hand and kissed the big knuckles. "Oh, Bud.
Whenever I have a real problem, you're the only one who . . ." She
stopped, choked up. "What a terrible waste it was for your father to . . ."
She couldn't go on.

"Honey, please."

"So unfair. So wasteful. What a horrible man."

"He was a genius, honey. He only made one mistake and you're
looking at it." Bud Fulmer glanced down at the open newspaper. What
had he been reading before? He sniffed. "Honey, those sandwiches."

She hopped off the table and rescued them from under the broiler.
Slipping on a dainty padded glove, she arranged the open-face sandwiches
on a large platter and sprinkled a bit of paprika for color. Then she added
some slices of cucumber as a decoration.

"A beer'd go nicely with that," Bud mused aloud.

"Maybe after the first of the year you can go off the wagon."

"I know. Lookee. No touchee." He placed a triangular half-sandwich in his mouth. His jaw moved slowly and the whole thing went down in one swallow. "Have one, honey?"

"He treats me like an idiot, Bud."

A second half-sandwich disappeared almost as quickly. "Well, honey, just between you, me, and the kitchen sink . . ." A third morsel followed the others. Bud's throat pulsed up and down. "I mean, that guest list." He laughed. "Between the two of us, honey, you *are* an idiot."

"Bud Fulmer!"

He lifted her onto his lap. "Come on, now," he said, poking a triangular snack at her lips. "Eat your din-din."

Ned turned into a phone booth and called his wife. "Running late, Verne," he announced. "Better eat without me."

"It's just snacks." She was silent for a moment. "Will you have eaten when you do get home?"

"Don't know."

"You sound peculiar."

"Don't I always?"

"Are you all right?" she asked.

"Fine. Something funny happened just now, but that isn't news this week. See you later."

He hung up without waiting to hear her response. He hadn't actually lied to her, nor had he told her the real truth. Gleb Ponamarenko's feeler was disturbing but easily dealt with. What bothered him much more was why it had come at this time. What sort of vibrations was he giving off that a sensitive soul like Gleb could recognize? Perhaps the thing between him and Jane had come to the Russian's attention? But why read it as a confession that French was starting to crack up? Only one person could read it as that. It would have to be a person who had bugged Room 404 of Selfridge's Hotel.

But that, too, wasn't possible. Ned swept the place personally once a week, sometimes more often than that. Any listening device would have been spotted. And anyone trying to read the windows of Room 404 with a remote-control laser was wasting his time. He'd get equal proportions of traffic noise and Radio 3.

It was often said among intelligence people when they discussed agentcraft that none of it was worth much if you didn't have the gift or the luck of outguessing the other fellow. A boxer or fencer or tennis player, anybody in a one-on-one sport, knew that anticipation or mind-reading was the most important trait a player could have.

Gleb Ponamarenko was not an old adversary. He had come to Ned's attention only a year ago. Then why in hell, one was entitled to ask, could Gleb outguess him? Only one reason: he had the gift, the nose. Very discouraging.

Ned was strolling now along the quiet side of Cadogan Place, past Cadogan Lane, heading south in the general direction of Chelsea. The evening was settling in. But dusk did not have its usual calming effect; its deep mauves tonight could not beguile his thoughts away from anything as filled with misery as Gleb's new interest in him. It would not go away. Once the Russian had convinced himself he was right, the damned information would follow Ned wherever he went, even if he resigned his commission and opted for early retirement.

The ludicrous thing was how little Ned knew that might be of value to the KGB. Names, yes. And possibly the West German circuits hadn't changed much in the year Ned had been gone; this might merit some effort on the Russians' part. But of the British side of things, Ned was sure nothing he could divulge would be of major interest.

It was usually like that in the intelligence community. One tended to know less than was commonly assumed. Like joining a secret society of any kind: the awesome secrets, the initiation ceremonies and handshakes turned out to be dull stuff, if not downright laughable. It was all to the good that each agent knew only a small amount. As for the extent of his own current operations in Britain, he had been forced, by having to replace Karl Follett on this Fourth of July party, to transfer things to others. An intelligence major stationed in Medmenham had been saddled with two ongoing operations and another in Manchester was temporarily looking after a third. These were low-level circuits, nothing earthshaking. Gleb would have a nice yawn over them.

Ned was strolling now along the little branching streets behind the department store called Peter Jones, many of them bearing names like Cadogan Gardens, Cadogan Gate, Cadogan Square and Cadogan Street. He realized, abruptly, what he was doing, something he had never done before. He was looking for Jane Weil's house.

He had never seen it. The place was too small for her ever to have invited a lot of people over for an office party. In any case, both had agreed it would be a very foolish idea for him to visit her there. He only remembered that it had a silly name, something like Possom or Mossop, and it was somewhere in this area. He had looked at a large-scale street map once and seen that where she lived, Number 37, was a very tiny triangle of not more than two or three buildings.

Dusk had shifted imperceptibly toward night, although the sky was still bright in the west where an unseen sunset turned the bottom of a low-lying bank of clouds orange. On this street he was striding along, Milner, roads came in at odd, dark angles whose vistas rapidly faded into darkness.

This was silly. He had no clear idea where her street was, just his normal professional skill at remembering what he had seen once, on a map. Even sillier, she might not be home. And what gave him the idea she'd be pleased to see him? Well, only for a moment, then, he rehearsed. A quarter of an hour?

He was pacing along a street called Denyer now, the crooked extension of Milner, when he suddenly realized—professional training again—that he'd overshot. He turned back. The intersection was so loosely delineated that he didn't see Mossop until he actually found a street sign. But there was Number 37, painted a very pale pink, or so it looked in the tricky illumination of streetlamps and the fading orange overglow from the west.

Lights on in the ground floor!

It was a child's drawing of a house, one big window and narrow door on the ground level, two windows on the top floor. But there was a light!

He rang the bell. From inside he could hear music and, as he noticed this, the volume suddenly decreased. Suppose she had a guest? He could hear footsteps, then the sound of locks being fiddled with. No embassy person at her level had missed any of the security lectures from Karl Follett about entry-door procedure. Ned could hear her setting the chain. The door swung open three inches.

The door closed and, unchained, reopened wide. "Come in."

She avoided his glance but looked past him into the quickly darkening street. Then she shut the door, chained it, and shot the bolt. Her tiny entry hall was barely big enough for both of them. He had paused there and created a traffic jam. He turned back to face her and she threw her arms around him, hugging him hard.

"Ned. My God." She was a tall woman, strong enough to hug him so hard it almost hurt. He found himself embracing her just as fiercely, as if they were trying to weld themselves together with such pressure that nothing could separate them.

"Oh well," he said. "That does answer the first question I was going to ask." He bent his head until he could kiss her. It was some time before they left the tiny entrance hall.

"It's amazing you've never been here," she said. "Whisky?"

He nodded, surveying the room. It had an odd shape, as did a lot of the older houses in London, neither walls nor corners nor floors quite plumb. The room seemed to grow slightly larger as it went away from one. The walls had been painted a very pale taupe to match a slightly darker shade of carpeting. Along the far wall a narrow chimney breast separated the room into two sections fitted with bookshelves, hi-fi equipment and the like. Pouring whisky into two glasses, Jane's hand moved sideways and cut down still further the volume of the Mahler sweeping through the small room from two exceedingly large speakers.

"Is everything . . .?" She turned with a glass in each hand. "Are you all right?"

He nodded, took a glass, and clinked it with hers. "Good luck to the house," he said then. "The first drink of the first visit is always to the house. My father taught me that."

"It's amazing, isn't it? In the old days people of our age had already lost their parents. But yours must be, what? Late sixties?" She knelt and lit a gas flame in the fireplace.

"Mid-sixties. Dad had to take early retirement at sixty. It wasn't what he wanted. He'd taught chemistry in the same high school."

"Ned, you never told me you were a teacher's son."

"I've been thinking about him today. You remember that old horror with the sandwich sign? He reminds me . . . No, it's just they're the same age. And the old guy called me 'son.' " He smiled guiltily.

"You're blushing. Don't tell me."

"My lips are sealed."

"Sharp blow to the heart, French." She got hold of his right hand and kissed the palm. "So I was wrong, wasn't I? You do actually have a heart . . . for elderly tramps and titless librarians."

"There you go being physical."

"I have lived the life of the mind for so long," she told him, "that I have almost forgotten how to live the life of the body. And I don't give myself airs. I'm no intellectual."

Ned stared into the flickering gas "coals," beginning now to grow red. "I had a professor like that at the U of C, called Chemnitz. Taught philosophy."

"Aaron Chemnitz?"

He nodded. "Died last year. We used to write each other every six months or so. I had the gall once to write him a note from Bonn in my dog-German." He was being hypnotized by the small gas fire. "There are only a handful of his kind left. We don't need them any more. We only need medicine men. Political shamans. They tell us: 'You elect me and you can ask me for anything.' Which is where the fraud begins."

She frowned. "Ned, most people realize it's only rhetoric. He can't give them *anything*. Most people know that."

"Right. If the pols were content to leave it at that, it'd be fair enough and still tilted a bit in their favor, like the gambling odds in a casino are always tilted a bit toward the house. But what pol can leave a good thing alone?"

"I don't follow you at all." She was massaging his ankles. "Let me take your shoes off."

"Any time. Are you listening or being physical?"

"The latter."

"Why can't he leave it alone? Because he has to tilt it still further in his favor until the basic deal goes fraudulent, everything to him and nothing to the voter."

She had slipped off his black loafers. "And the name of the game becomes 'fake issues,' " he added.

"Right, French. Right."

"I mean," he wandered on, "real issues never get on the ballot: poverty, disease, pollution, unemployment, aging, poor education or shelter or care or food. Do pols address themselves to those issues? Shit, no. They have a whole grabbag of fakes to distract the voters. The evil empire of our political opposites. The rising tide of pornography. A quick return to capital punishment. Gun control, closed-shop union contracts, fluoridization, welfare cheats in Cadillacs, the frightening rise to secret power of blacks, Asians, Hispanics, women, Masons, homosexuals, and atheist longhairs. The pols wave these issues around like red flags and the voters, like maddened bulls, lunge at the fakes and get impaled on the real issues."

"Do you mind if I take off your socks?"

"Huh?"

"And stuff them in your mouth?"

"Ah, Weil, you wild animal, have you no time for the life of the mind?"

He slid sideways out of the chair on top of her. They wrestled quietly for a long time as the coals slowly faded from bright orange to a strong, hot rose.

The small French carriage clock on her mantel emitted seven discreet pings.

*   *   *

The cab let Ned off in front of his house. He paid the driver, let himself in past the armed burglar system, shut it off and re-armed it. As he worked the switches on the wall box hidden in the front closet he caught sight of a note Laverne had left in the most likely spot for him to see it.

"P. J. R. Parkins called 10 P.M. Call him any time you come in," followed by a London telephone number.

Ned glanced at his watch and was horrified to find that it was nearly midnight. He went to the hall telephone and punched in the number Parkins had left, hoping he wasn't waking him. After a long time someone answered in a careful voice: "Inspector Mulvey."

"Is Mr. Parkins there?"

"Is this Colonel French?"

"Yes, it is."

There was no sound on the line for a long time and then, quite like a bobby in a pantomime, Parkins came on the line with a cheery " 'ello, 'ello, 'ello?"

"Sorry to ring so late."

"We're all up at this end, Colonel. You know that long and very acceptable story you told me about your accidental relationship to Mr. Riordan?"

"Yes?"

"Well, I'm afraid it won't do any more."

"Please explain."

"Can I ask a favor, Colonel? Can you get down here to the Albany Street station?"

"At this hour?"

"You see, the Bill has located Riordan."

"Oh?"

"And he's quite dead."

Part 4

---◆---

**THURSDAY
JULY 1**

15

Professional courtesy, Ned French thought. I'm being extended professional courtesy. If P. J. R. Parkins and Inspector Mulvey had been undertakers, they would be charging a reduced burial fee to a fellow mortician.

It was now somewhere between three and four on the morning of Thursday, July 1. They had crisscrossed the St. Johns Wood area several times, twice viewing Riordan's body *in situ* while measurements and photographs were being taken and the hotel suite dusted for fingerprints, and once more when all that remained of Anthony X. Riordan, U.S.A., was the chalk outline of his body on the worn wool pile of the hotel-room carpet.

Dismal business, Ned thought, designed by these two to wear him down. It would never occur to them to believe his story of being simply the jogger next to Riordan, quite accidentally. In their place he wouldn't believe it either. And, now that Riordan was dead, a new set of rules prevailed. This was now a potential murder investigation and the kid gloves were off.

Riordan had lived at a large, modern hotel just south of Lord's Cricket Ground. By a misleading coincidence it had an excellent view of Winfield House and the Great London Mosque, as well as Lord's and the peculiar ziggurat shape of Wellington Clinic. Quite a tidy location, Ned realized, and one guaranteed to keep both cops convinced that there was much more to Riordan's death than met the eye.

At first glance it seemed that Riordan had sustained no injuries exceeding the original damage of the accident. The police surgeon had been very clear and also, under questioning by Parkins and Mulvey, distressingly vague about that. Yes, the demise was consistent with the kind of lethal cerebral embolism often associated with concussion. Yes, the only marks of violence were those originally noted after the traffic accident. No, he couldn't swear to any of that, not a word of it, till after the postmortem examination. No, really. He had heard of grievous harm done by exacerbating—he repeated the word portentously—existing injuries.

Ned knew he would be well within his rights to call a halt, go home, and have what was left of a night's sleep. But this was not advisable. He hadn't yet explained where he'd been earlier Wednesday night when Parkins had called him at home and left a message. More to the point, it was in that particular period of time, say seven P.M. until Riordan's body was found at nine thirty by a chambermaid coming in to unmake the bed, that the murder, if that was what it was, had been committed.

Under the unwritten rules of professional courtesy, at no time did Parkins or the rather churlish Mulvey ever merge these facts into a blunt question along the lines of: "Can you account for your movements during the murder period?" Because this question hovered constantly in the air without ever being voiced, Ned felt it would be awkward suddenly to stand on his rights and leave.

Moreover, at this point, he really didn't want to return home to Laverne. She would surely wake and want to know precisely what Parkins wanted to know, but for different reasons. At this point Ned wasn't about to give anyone his alibi for anything. It wasn't necessary, was it? He had nothing to do with the luckless Riordan, other than the original encounter on Monday. Poor Riordan.

A good-looking fellow, even in death, Ned remembered. On the Albany Street Station wall the electric clock jump-clicked to 3:59.

But, Ned supposed, if Riordan were the consummate con artist everyone said he was, he'd have to have charm, blarney, physical attractiveness. Even in death.

"So, whilst we're waiting for Forensic," Parkins suggested, "what else can you tell us about poor Riordan?"

"I wasn't aware I'd told you anything. I don't really know anything. I did, as you asked, identify the corpse as the fellow who'd been sideswiped by the car on Monday. But you already knew that. More than that, as I've said, I do not know."

Perhaps, Ned thought, this might be the time to ask P. J. R. Parkins for an explanation of who he really was. On the other hand, as an embarrassing question, it would unleash a few from Parkins. So the situation remained at standoff. Having worked with the police of many countries, however, Ned knew that in a murder case even the most tactful or corrupt cop eventually got around to the embarrassing questions. No wonder they were all waiting for Forensic to declare it either accidental manslaughter or murder.

And, if the latter, how long would it take them to ask straight out where he had been earlier in the evening?

No, Laverne told herself, it just wasn't possible to go on living like this.

In her rare bouts with insomnia, lying awake next to a sleeping Ned, during those small hours when nothing is ever possible except disaster, Laverne had often yearned to be with her daughters and her parents in Camp Liberty, California. Tonight—or this morning, she amended, glancing at the faint red digits of the bedside clock-radio—without Ned on hand to fill their bed with more irony than she needed, the situation looked even more impossible. They just couldn't go on like this.

To begin with, who the hell was Parkins to him? Just one of the embassy staff, if she remembered rightly. She had come downstairs at midnight, having heard Ned return, only to find that he'd left the house again, and had placed her note about Parkins on the front hall table with an added scribble:

"Emergency. Sorry."

She had thought of calling the embassy's night number but decided that this would be a breach of something or other. Security. And yet, if Parkins were involved, how secure could any of this be? Lying sleepless in bed now, Laverne supposed that it had somehow to do with the Sunday garden party. Who cared?

She was tired of being a good little soldier. She was tired of being a left-behind spare wheel.

It had been a mistake, sending the girls home to California. They had filled her days, no question about it. She should have gone home with them. Then Ned could stay out all night every night and she'd never lose an hour's sleep over it. But there was a danger, if the five of them left Ned alone in London, that he'd never come home. Laverne recognized that, to an intelligent man, Ned's world was very seductive in the challenging way that a difficult puzzle is seductive.

That was the true separation between them, she thought. He was off in his own habitat, the intelligence establishment, about as tricky and devious a place as the foreigners who populated it. All Europe was tricky, all Asia devious. They had never been posted anywhere outside the U.S. that wasn't, in her opinion, hostile territory. Never mind how the treaties read between, say, the United States and Britain or West Germany or wherever. Hostility had nothing to do with treaties. It was a state of mind.

Either you felt among friends, Laverne told herself, or not. And, with the exception of another Army wife or woman officer, she had never warmed up to any foreigner. The ones here in England came closest, but could you trust them?

Tuesday night's party at Royce's was a perfect example. She felt more at home with Betsy Voss, stick-in-the-mud Betsy, or Jane Weil, than she ever would with a charm-chick like Gillian Lamb or even that funny Hargreaves fellow, sincerely panting down her decolletage. Jane she especially liked, a genuine American girl who couldn't get Royce to see her as romantic interest.

Well, that was Jane's problem. Laverne recognized her own problem in military terms as being "overextended from base supply."

All this foreign duty might look glamorous to some, but it was chickenshit to her. Naturally she had to go where Ned was posted. He was a career officer. A successful dossier depended on being happily married to a stable wife. Laverne knew how these dossiers were compiled. A man whose wife keeps running back home, or even contemplates living with her parents and daughters rather than her dear career hubby, is a liability. General Krikowski's only daughter was not going to be a liability to her hubby. Not in this world or the next.

But in fact she had reached the end of her tolerance for life abroad. This country, where they talked a stilted, prissy version of English and wasted their time with all sorts of let's-pretend memories of former greatness, as if they still had it, gave her a severe pain in the ass anyway. None of them were sincere, just a nation of actors, good ones, maybe, but only believable as an actor is believable, within a framework of artifice.

Let's face it, Laverne thought as she stared sleeplessly at the bedroom ceiling, now easier to see as the sky outside grew faintly lighter. Outside her window a blackbird awoke and began serenading her. She wasn't supposed to be the big brain in this family, Laverne thought, but you had to be a moron not to see that size was everything. All the small businesses got swallowed up by the big ones. Among the giants, mergers daily reduced the number of rivals. And the same thing applied to countries. They didn't call it a merger because in these little pipsqueak countries they never called anything by its right name. These banana republics. These mini-nations. These little stages, peopled by cunning actors.

She began to call the roll of the foreign places she and Ned had been stationed and it wasn't till she came to Moscow—where they'd spent eighteen months—that she found a land real enough to be considered a nation.

So that's it, she thought, the United States and the two Commie countries, Russia and China. Forget the rest. And, among these three real nations, was there any choice of where to live? She glanced at the bedroom clock: 4:06. If you rolled it back eight hours to California time it was . . . eight o'clock in the evening. Dinner would be over. It was all so reassuringly predictable. The girls would be doing their homework. Mom would be watching TV or writing letters. Dad would be . . .

She twisted sideways to the telephone and punched in a series of numbers so quickly—fourteen digits were needed to call her parents' private line at Camp Liberty—that she had no time to consider the good or bad of what she was doing, only the need to talk to someone she loved in a place she loved in a country that meant something and had the size to back it up and whose people were sincere, not actors.

"Hello?"

"Lou Ann? It's Mom."

"*Mom!*" The shriek nearly deafened her across six thousand miles. "It's Mom! Hey, it's *Mom!*" The screaming sounded like a mob gone wild but the smile on Laverne's face was sweetly relaxed and happy for the first time since the girls had left London.

The first thing Bert felt was an agonizing ache at the back of his head, the knobby part just above the neck. He had the illusion it was this that had awakened him from slumber with its excruciating pain. But as soon as he opened his eyes he saw his mistake.

They had wired him to a chair with copper-colored baling wire twisted tight enough to bite into his flesh and cut off superficial circulation. They had worked over his face, too, so that he could, with the tip of his tongue, feel where teeth had snapped off.

Finally, because he was naked in the chair, he could see the livid bruises and gashed skin around his penis and scrotum. The pain from all these had awakened him, not out of slumber but from coma. As soon as they realized he had come to, they would begin the interrogation again. He closed his eyes.

How had he not suspected the existence of such an elite group? With what supreme arrogance had he and Khefte assumed they were alone in circling their prey? Alone in targeting the supreme opportunity?

But these were troops he would be proud to serve with, Bert realized through waves of pain, if they hadn't been mercenaries. These professionals made Khefte's cadre seem like sullen schoolboys. They had held him now since late yesterday without once letting him catch even a glimpse of a face beneath the ski masks or hear more than the few words addressed to him in German, curt, brutal demands for information. He still had no idea who these troops were, even their nationality.

A new breed, these troops, mercenaries without an ideology. It was obvious, now, that when he had brought Merak and Mamoud up here from London, he had led this enemy directly to Khefte's safe house. Having survived the ambush that followed that first mistake, Bert had compounded his error the next evening by using the gent's room at the Red Star pub to wash up. There the elite troops had found him.

Everywhere, he thought, these money-grabbers shoved aside the political cadres. Mammon replaced Marx. And with such greedy capitalist efficiency! He wanted to know more of their origins.

Since he had refused to answer any questions at all, the interrogation hadn't gone far enough to reveal, by its direction, what the enemy was up to. It only disclosed that, in his ability to stand up to torture, Bert was as professional as they were. Perhaps, if he gave them a few lying answers, Bert decided, he would learn more about them.

It was hard to know, however, what he would do with such information, once it had been bought. After all, he was under no illusion that he would ever leave this place alive.

With one part of his brain, Bert understood this without feeling any emotion at all. He had been harshly interrogated before, but it had always been in open pretense of legality, by interrogators who, if caught, had to answer to a higher authority under democratic control. These elite troops were autonomous and honed to a finish harder than any of the special attack-team secret services Bert had run into over the years.

He carefully opened his eyes a fraction of an inch. Daylight was beginning to show him the room he was in, the small, cramped reception room of Khefte's own safe house here in Little Missenden.

Daylight also showed him the two men guarding him. One was resting, or asleep, his Armalite attack rifle cradled in his arms as he lolled back in a wooden chair. The other, blond like Bert, was smoking a cigarette and working out a game of patience on the small wooden table. Both wore masks of summer-weight cloth, not wool.

Bert shut his eyes as he caught a slight movement in the man's head. But pain had caused him to react too sluggishly.

A sharp blast of new pain knocked him sideways. Bert's eyes sprang open. The sleeping man had leaped up and swung the metal butt of his Armalite in a savage arc against Bert's jaw. He could taste blood welling up in his mouth.

"*Achtung! Wie heissen Sie?*"

Bert could feel the blood drooling down over his chin. He gagged, trying to speak.

"*Laut sprechen!*" the man snarled. It was going to be a long Thursday.

Showered, re-dressed but sleepless, Ned French arrived at the chancery by 8:15 and immediately headed for Royce Connell's office. As he expected, the embassy's number-two was already at his desk, trying to get through the first batch of papers in his in box.

"Yes, but five minutes only, Ned." Connell surveyed his deputy military attaché with some distaste. "That tie," he pointed out.

"Tell me about my tie."

"It might go with some other suit," Connell observed. "As for that patch of shaving soap behind your ear . . ." He smiled pleasantly. "Bad night?"

"Yes, and it's going to take more than five lousy minutes to explain."

Ned sat down with a thump across the desk from his civilian superior. Both men waited while Royce's secretary served coffee. Sensing the atmosphere, she escaped from there at once, not even stopping to offer orange juice.

"Begin," Connell commanded.

"We begin with the name Anthony X. Riordan," Ned said.

"Mother of God."

As a matter of fact it took Ned four minutes to explain what had happened to Riordan and one minute for Royce to recall that warning three days ago from Gillian Lamb. The two men then wasted a minute in absolute silence, sipping coffee and frowning into their cups. It was the chargé d'affaires who broke the silence.

"What did Forensic report?"

Ned checked his watch. "It should be coming through about now. Parkins will get onto me immediately, have no fear."

"That's another thing," Connell complained. "We can't have Special Branch spies wandering all over the chancery."

"You can't avoid it," Ned counseled him. "If we sack Parkins we'll get another just like him."

"Not if we hire an American."

"All right. But let's wait till this Riordan thing is sorted out. Otherwise it'll look like we're doing a whitewash."

"Why?" Connell demanded. "We have nothing to hide." He paused and thought for a long time, his handsome face tight with concentration. "You're in the clear, aren't you, Ned?"

"As a suspect?" It was Ned's turn to sit and think. "It depends what you mean. Did I kill Riordan? No."

"Any chance they'd nail you for attacking that driver?"

"No way."

"Then there's only one other thing."

"What other thing?"

Connell sat forward in his desk chair and sipped the last of his coffee. "The . . . you know. The business of where you actually were when Riordan was killed. I mean, if it was murder."

Ned sat back and gave him a fixed, steady smile devoid of mirth. "Funny. The only person to ask me that question is my own boss."

"Sorry. It's bound to come up."

"It hasn't so far. Even Laverne hasn't asked."

Connell looked suddenly ill at ease, a state of mind that contrasted so sharply with his normally calm, in-charge demeanor that it almost destroyed his statuesque façade, but not quite. "Ned, you know I have every faith in you. Would I put this awful Sunday mess in your lap otherwise?" He paused and stared down into his empty cup as if reading his fortune in coffee grounds.

"Who else do you have, with Follett gone?"

"That's not the point." The number-two seemed to pull himself together almost visibly. Not for the first time Ned was reminded how graphically Royce could project a mood, quite like a highly trained actor. "You have made an enemy of Mrs. F. I don't suppose that's news to you. But it may surprise you to know that she demanded you be removed from the security arrangements for Sunday."

"That's not nice."

"And I told her to forget it," Connell continued smoothly. "I told her you were an experienced, highly valued intelligence officer—"

"And besides, you didn't have anyone else," Ned finished for him.

"So what happens after Sunday? Pandora and I meet behind the cathedral with our seconds? Pistols or rapiers?"

"It's a feud, not a duel," Royce pointed out. "But, in either form of combat, you'd lose."

"She's that highly connected?"

Connell's face went bland. "This is the humiliating sort of thing we professionals have to put up with time and time again, Ned. I've balked her this time and it's possible after Sunday that she'll forget all about you. But somehow I don't think so. Therefore."

No further words were forthcoming for another of Connell's long pauses. "Therefore," he went on, "if there's to be a murder inquiry someone will be very interested in every tiny bit of your connection with it, even a link as silly as where you were last night, when Riordan was —well, whatever happened to the silly bugger."

"You're not unhappy he's snuffed it."

The second in command considered this for a while. "Has that idiot Max Grieves been bothering you?"

"It's no bother. And, to be fair to Max, he didn't mention any instructions he had from you, by name."

A long, sad sigh escaped Royce's finely chiseled lips. "Now that Riordan's a corpse, under the heavy hand of the Met with an assist from Special Branch, we can expect the Riordan Scandal, as I hereby dub it, to keep the London press in shock headlines for several weeks. Damn it."

Ned finished his coffee and found that he was rethinking Pandora Fulmer's sudden hatred. In either form of combat, Royce had said, he'd lose. Any form of combat?

"Have they routed those presidential videos into your in basket, Royce?"

"Presidential whats?"

"Mrs. F. plans to screen White House videos at the lawn party. They'll plead the presidential viewpoint on a number of controversies he's stuck with back home."

The clear, direct glance, suitable for a male model in a spectacles advertisement, focused so sharply on Ned's face that there was an almost physical impact, as if Royce had turned on twin arc lights. Then the strangest thing happened. Beneath the glare a broad toothpaste-ad grin broke out.

"You bastard," Connell said in an admiring voice. "You don't play softball, do you?" He rubbed his hands together gleefully. "Dear me," he chortled. "Dear me. I'm afraid I'm going to have to relay the whole question to Dan Anspacher in Political, don't you think? And by the time he gets guidance from Foggy Bottom back home . . ."

"She'll know I snitched on her," Ned pointed out. "In fact, she predicted I'd do it."

"You don't think I'm going to touch this controversial issue with a bargepole of any length whatsoever? Anspacher will have to initiate the inquiry on his own. But he's young. How else is he going to learn, except the hard way?"

Maurice Chamoun was sitting in his office, matching photostats of Winfield House floor plans with electrical charts. There were several layers of defense being planned for Sunday, some obvious and some rather exotic, some widely known and some known only to him and to Ned French. He toiled away quite readily at this rather fussy desk work, not because he liked it much, but because he did it better than anyone else and it needed letter-perfect execution. To delve any deeper into his motivation would be to uncover layers in himself he would rather have left untouched.

Most painful to possible prodding was that part of him that felt his whole adventure with Mossad was an act of grand disloyalty, not to the U.S. but to the man who had been his friend and mentor, Ned French. Serving two masters this way, one in secret while wearing the uniform of the other, bothered Chamoun very little because of the way it had all come about.

If he hadn't been recruited by Bricktop in Tel Aviv, he would never have joined the U.S. Army. It had been her idea that he could best serve Mossad as a permanent mole inside the American intelligence community. This being the history of his duplicitous position, the whole thing seemed natural and quite above guilt.

There was a knock at his door. He jumped up, turned the charts on his desk face down, and went to the door. "Yes?"

"Maurice, it's me."

He winced. Nancy Lee had never come to his office before. He unlocked the door and opened it. Past her face he could look down a row of desks where enlisted men in his section were at work. Two of them had looked up—simply because Nancy Lee had long legs?

Fortunately she had something in her hand, a piece of paper which she handed to Maurice. It was blank, a pretext for her coming to him.

"I can't phone Mrs. Henderson," she murmured. Bricktop had endless aliases, all of them prefaced by Mrs. "And I have to tell her something. She said you—"

"She was wrong," he cut in savagely.

"Please, Maurice. It's urgent."

He looked her over, rapidly but minutely. Brick had been right: this addlebrained daughter of the oil rich had somehow matured almost overnight. As an intelligence agent of some experience, Maurice mistrusted overnight conversions, but he knew Brick's policy: never mind how good they are or how long they'll stay good, use them anyway. She probably felt that way about him, too.

"I can't promise . . ."

"There's some kind of panic. Three of their best people have disappeared just before something very big. That's all I know." She gave him a small smile and walked off, making sure to give big smiles to the two enlisted men who had been eyeing her.

Chamoun pretended to glance over the blank sheet of paper. Then he closed and locked his door and sat down at his desk again. He couldn't talk to Brick except face-to-face and he didn't have time today for a meet. But what Nancy Lee had told him sounded important, if you added to it what he had already developed, that her Arab lover was hooked up with Bert Heinemann. That lifted him out of the rank and file of Arab activists and into the category of prime suspect.

Just before something very big?

Chamoun sat back in his chair and stared out the window at the square below, thinking: If I hand Ned the name and location of the leadership that will try to pull off an assault on Winfield House this Sunday, does that make me a triple agent?

He had heard of the breed before. In World War II any number of spooks triple-crossed their way to fame or death. It was supposed to be a harrowing experience, hard to live with. Chamoun smiled slightly. Times changed, didn't they? It now seemed the easiest thing in the world.

16

Leilah Hakkad, in her mid-thirties, was beginning to experience that chilling change in metabolism that sounds an early warning of obesity. Her body's changed use of food was beginning to produce useless pads of fat where fat had no business being, a stocky look to her figure, a certain thickening of the neck and wrists and ankles and . . .

Allah was not good, Leilah thought. He gave life but took away youth. Much better to depart life early. What was it the old Greeks said? "Those whom the gods love die young."

She had finished serving her brother his breakfast, organized his departure on another of his hegiras of money-making, and now, at nine o'clock in the morning, was enjoying her own breakfast. Except that it was no longer a joy when every flaky croissant, or chewy crumpet, every rich dab of butter or marmalade, the thick double cream in her coffee and certainly the brown crystals of Demerera sugar, all were her enemies.

Having disposed of the daily newspapers, she turned to her real passion, the European scandal magazines. Since she read French, Italian, and German, Leilah could enjoy titillating nonsense in many varieties of four-color trash with its endless round of adultery, illegitimate babies, rumored homosexuality and the rest of the simple vices of the famous.

Leilah was easily as intelligent as her brother. She knew most of these magazines dealt in half-truths and bold lies about people who didn't care what was printed as long as their names were spelled right. Even so, leading the terribly sheltered life of the Arab female in a well-to-do family, she doted on this secondhand excitement.

She had finished *Stern* and *Paris-Match* and began to plow through a long cover story in *Oggi* about an adenoidal Italian pop singer whose third wife was suing him for divorce, citing as grounds his incestuous relationship with his retarded fourteen-year-old daughter by his first wife. The daughter and father had been photographed in a Rome nightclub. As table companions the photo included the noted film producer Aldo Sgroi and his constant companion, Aida Battipaglia.

Leilah smiled in a slightly preening way. She was not a social climber but she did enjoy mingling with true celebrities, and hadn't these two been guests at her brother's party Tuesday night, right here at Number 12? And hadn't Leilah ferried all the ladies home, including Miss Battipaglia, dropping them one by one all over the West End?

Leilah had gorgeous eyes, dark and fully enhanced by much liner, shadow, and mascara. It was only natural, carrying that much added adornment, that she might blink occasionally. But this now was a squint. She had narrowed her eyes to make sure she was seeing what she was seeing.

Aldo Sgroi, here in her house Tuesday last, had been a fat young man with a wiry head of hair and pop eyes. Aida Battipaglia had been a petite brunette with wild cascades of curls. But in *Oggi* Aldo was stringy and bald while Aida was a large blond.

She placed a call to her brother's Rolls. He was a very excitable man. She would have to explain this to him in such a way that he did not start screaming then and there.

At about nine thirty, Ned French's telephone rang. He let it ring while he and Chamoun finished examining the captain's new set of Winfield sketches. Since most of the calls that came to Ned were, strictly speaking, not part of the Defense Section's official duties, he had set down a policy that no civilian secretary, nor American enlisted man, could answer his phone. Only Chamoun. On the eleventh ring, Ned picked up. "Colonel French."

"Sorry to disturb you, Colonel," P. J. R. Parkins's voice had a nervous edge to it. A sleepless night had pretty well eroded his politely wooden attitude and he was now using fake politesse as the cutting edge of his temper. "Did you sleep well?"

"Not at all. Did the forensic report come through?"

"That's why I'm calling." The edge was going ragged with fatigue.

Something perverse got into French, perhaps his own reaction to a sleepless night. "I hope this isn't classified information," he told the Special Branch spy. "These chancery phone lines are definitely not secure."

"Is that a fact, Colonel?" There was a long pause which Ned interpreted as P. J. R. Parkins pulling himself together. "The bottom line, as you chaps put it, is that bloody Forensic gives us percentages rather than results. It's hard to detect a situation in which existing damage was perhaps tampered with to turn it lethal. So we're getting eighty percent it's murder, twenty it's not. Something, in'it?" he asked with some rhetorical tartness.

"But you can't operate on percentages."

"Spot on. So we're putting it down as murder, Colonel, and since we already have a statement from you, we won't require another until further notice."

"We?" Ned asked. The monosyllable echoed slightly down the—why *not* tapped?—line.

"That is to say the Bill. The Met. It's a case for the Yard now anyway. They've picked it up and Jampot is—Inspector Mulvey, that is—will get a chance to play games with the heavy squad."

"Lucky Jampot."

"Yes, well, indeed, rather," Parkins said, firing off the usual British salvo of nonlanguage. "There it is, then, eh?"

"Is there a possibility that you won't need me till after Sunday?"

"Sunday? Oh, yes, quite, Sunday." Parkins made some other kinds of throat-clearing noises. "I'm told you've been on to the Traffic Department about checkpoints at Hanover Gate and Macclesford Bridge?"

"I applied for them Monday when we realized we needed to control entrance traffic."

"Would you be requiring our people?"

Ned thought for a moment. "You mean we can get a few bobbies from you, uh, that is, from Traffic Department?"

"Anything up to a dozen per checkpoint. Say the word."

Ned raised his eyebrows twice, giving a rather Groucho-ish signal to Chamoun, accompanied by a grin. "That would be most helpful, Mr. Parkins."

"Not at all, Colonel French."

"Is there any way of getting another few to help with perimeter control?" Ned understood that the offer of bobbies was a sop for having ruined his night for him. No better time than now to ask for the limit.

"Let's say fifty men in all?" Parkins said.

"Yes, that would be lovely."

"Leave it with me, Colonel."

Ned's grin widened. "Then I know it's in good hands."

He hung up and turned his grin directly on Chamoun. "Perfect! Fifty big unmistakable bobbies crawling all over the place, focusing everybody's attention on themselves. Who could ask for anything more?" he quoted on a rising note.

Chamoun responded, deadpan, with the Gershwin answer on a descending note: "Who could ask for anything more?"

By nine thirty Ambassador Adolf Fulmer III was normally well launched on his official day. New to the job, Bud Fulmer still relied completely on Royce Connell's staff for his daily diary of events. Thursday, he saw as he leafed through the large, leather-bound daybook, was not particularly taxing. He was due at the chancery at eleven to meet with a group of visiting American business executives Bill Voss had gathered. At noon they would adjourn for drinks and an early lunch in the chancery. Nothing else had been entered in the afternoon daybook except some TV sessions with Gillian Lamb. A reception was scheduled at six P.M. here at Winfield for a New York ballet troupe recently arrived in London. At eight thirty, Bud saw, he and Pandora were due for a small informal dinner at the Dutch embassy to meet Holland's current ambassador.

In other words, Bud noted, a day whose highlights were mostly occasions for drinking.

He looked grim at the thought of perpetually being surrounded by booze and boozing when he had given Pandora his word that he wouldn't drink. When Bud Fulmer looked grim there was almost no change of expression on his big, flat face. But his eyes did widen slightly when his telephone rang.

His telephone rang so rarely in these first weeks of his ambassadorship that the novelty of it was almost exciting. He grunted as he examined the call director on his desk, a small box in ebony and brushed aluminum with six small lights and six small buttons. Light number one glowed green. Light number two glowed red. The rest were not lit up.

"Good morning, sir. Are you taking calls?"

"Who is it?"

"A Mr. Weems, sir."

Bud Fulmer's face grew grimmer, signaled by the fact that his small, rather pleasant mouth flattened out slightly into a straight line. "Put him on."

Light number one went out. Light number two changed from red to green. The ambassador pushed the button beneath it. "Fulmer here."

"Jim Weems, Your Excellency. How y'doing?"

"Fine. What's the problem?"

"No problem whatsoever at all, sir, just to let you know the duke has hung that buck of yours and you're the proud possessor of some very, very fine venison whenever you want it sent down to London."

"Venison?"

"Oh, and the head. Can't forget that, can we? A very elegant stand of antlers and not a mark on him, thanks to your very, very sharp shooting."

Bud Fulmer tried to picture Pandora's face if he suggested they find room among their possessions for a stuffed buck.

"Hello?" Weems asked. "You still there, sir?"

Bud's face showed remote signs of a frown. All that shooting weekend with the drunken duke, Weems had been on a deescalating basis of address, starting with Your Excellency and moving down to Mr. Fulmer. After trying out a few Buds and finding them hard to manage, he had adopted the duke's mode of address, which was to call everybody by their last name. Now Weems had called him "sir" not once but twice. Bud knew he projected an image of slow moving and slow thinking, but hanging out with a pixie like Pandora had sharpened his powers of observation quite a bit. In other words, Weems wanted something.

"I'll have to let you know, Weems."

"Soon, though. I mean we're talking very fresh meat. I'll tell you what," Weems went on more slowly now, "why don't I send you the photos and an address where you can leave a message for me?"

"You won't be at the Fulmer Stores office?"

"On the move. On the move."

"What photos?" Bud wanted to know.

"Why, they took an awful lot of photos. You remember. Must be fifty or more. It's a very, very thorough record of what happened."

A silence fell on both sides of the conversation. Bud was still not clear what Weems wanted or why he was proving so hard to pin down, even as to his whereabouts. "Okay," he said at last. "Nice talking to you."

"About the photos." Another long pause. "This isn't very important, but when the weekend was over the duke took me aside and mentioned that we weren't in deer season."

"We were shooting out of season?"

"Can you imagine? He's a crafty old bastard, isn't he?"

"And you're offering fifty photos of me breaking the law?" Bud asked, his voice as calm as before but perhaps slightly lower in tone. "Now tell me about the negatives."

"Hey, listen, wait now, Your Excellency. You've got this very, very wrong. No ulterior motives, no tricks. I mean this is a gift, sir, very pure and very simple."

"Like the venison and the antlers?"

"Exactly."

"Well, I'll put the girl on the line and you can give her a number or something. My regards to all the old-timers at Fulmer Stores. Bye now."

He hung up before Weems could say anything more. It was only then that Bud Fulmer realized he was breathing hard and his hand, as he put down the phone, was trembling. God, a drink would help right now. He stared at the number-two light, which remained green for a long moment before winking out.

Exit Weems. The nerve of the nasty little bastard. Assuming on no acquaintance at all . . . And if that photo offer wasn't blackmail, what was? He'd have to tell somebody at chancery about it. Royce Connell, but he couldn't really trust him. There was really nobody he could tell about it except Pandora.

And this close to the party he sure as hell wasn't going to distract her with anything as stupid as this.

There had been a burst of activity a little while ago, Bert knew. He had no idea what time it was except that it was daylight. They had stopped hurting him. They had gagged his bloody mouth and carried him, chair and all, into the back of a large Army-type vehicle. It was actually an open-backed lorry with canvas covering.

Nothing was too clear after that. He had been moved from Khefte's safe house out into the woods, in the dark center of a stand of trees where sunlight rarely penetrated. There the elite troops had unwired him from the chair, roughly pulled some of his own clothes back on his tortured body, and rewired him to a large cherry or apple tree, Bert couldn't tell which. The gag in his mouth remained, choking him because they had smashed his nose and it was very hard to breath through. If only he could gasp air through his mouth.

Schrecklich, being in the hands of professionals. They understood the limits of the human body all too well. The fact that they addressed him in German was also disturbing. But perhaps it only meant that they knew his nationality and were well enough trained to use several European languages. His idea of responding to their questions hadn't brought him many results. They now knew his name and something of his background. But for some reason the elite troops had lost interest in him.

He tried to pull in more oxygen but his ravaged nose only let a faint trickle of air through. Yet certain things, he kept telling himself, were obvious. They were holding him for someone else, someone who couldn't get up here to Little Missenden just yet. Once he arrived, and reaped what he could from Bert, the harvest would be over. Death would come quickly.

Bert found it impossible to shut off thoughts of the past. He had had great dreams. They all had. They were to be the spear-sharp vanguard of a world revolution, lancing their way to victory. He would slice the Muenster cheese very thin so that his grandmother didn't know he'd helped himself. The Muenster would sink into the toasting bread and secretly become one with it.

Which was worse? he asked himself, his lungs working hard against the odds: to die without having had a dream at all, or to die knowing the dream had died long before you?

Good question. The trees around him swirled sideways. All was going black.

The day outside the conference room was sunny, Jane saw as she arrived at the ten-o'clock and took a seat. The rather dismal room was, thus, a bit cheerier. The cast of characters never remained the same at these morning briefings, but she saw that Mary Constantine was on hand to give a brief press summary, Max Grieves to put in an appearance, Anspacher to represent Political, but a less familiar face was standing in for the vacationing Karl Follett. Maurice Chamoun represented Defense and two men she didn't recognize sat together at one end of the room with Bill Voss of Economic and Commercial.

Royce entered, as always, with the hurried air of absentmindedness that no one had ever, in Jane's memory, challenged. In his actorlike way, Royce would have them believe he was carrying so many threads in his hands he had forgotten half of them. Only the first part of the proposition was true.

"Mary, sorry, we won't have time for your roundup this morning except headlines. Save them for the end, shall we? Kevin, please introduce yourself."

"Kevin Schultheiss, Administrative, standing in for Karl Follett."

"And Maurice?"

"Chamoun, standing in for Colonel French."

"Right. Gus, will you do Administrative announcements, or Kevin?"

"Sir," Schultheiss said, "I'm here only for the Sunday business."

"Right. Gus? Please?"

"They're still asking us to keep the surrounding streets free of parked cars this week," Gus Heflin said. "I've been told to advise anybody who wants to keep driving to work every day that arrangements must be made for private garaging. We're in a crisis situation over this. There just isn't any more parking."

"Yes, Gus. Next item."

Heflin's face reddened slightly but he plowed on. "The cafeteria will be closed on Friday for some redecoration and—"

"And a new chef?" Voss asked.

"Hear, hear," one of his assistants chimed in.

"All right. Gus?"

"Littering ordinances. People have gotten all kinds of warnings from police officers about dropping sandwich wrappings and—"

"Anything else, Gus?"

"That's it. The Red Cross blood bank will be collecting all afternoon Friday. Anybody who—"

"Thanks, Gus. Maurice? Security plans for Sunday. Just the overall picture, please."

Chamoun shuffled some papers in a folder but when he began to speak, Jane saw, he didn't refer once to his notes. "We are restricting entrance traffic in both directions. The south gate, which is boarded up, will be opened. Traffic from below Winfield will enter that way, through a checkpoint. Traffic from the north will enter by the main gate. Also through a checkpoint. The Metropolitan Police have offered to man the roadblocks. Some of us will be on hand to check credentials. All other traffic through the Outer Circle will be sent on its way along the appropriate part of the ring road that surrounds Regent's Park. None will be allowed to park. No breakdowns, either. They'll simply deposit guests and move on. The cabs won't mind. Limos may object, but that's life."

He paused and Royce said: "That's it for now?"

"Helicopter surveillance. Perimeter surveillance. The usual."

"What about these credentials?" Schultheiss asked.

"Mm?"

"Will you have time to get them to the guests?" Royce asked.

"Today's only Thursday. Technically we have until, say, noon Sunday to deliver."

"Right. Kevin? Max? Anything else?"

Everyone could sense, Jane felt, that Royce was pushing this ten-o'clock along at a breakneck pace, without scanting any necessary points. When none of the other security people said anything, Royce started to move on.

"Isn't this awfully informal?" Schultheiss asked then.

Royce's eyebrows went up. "Is it?"

Chamoun nodded. "That's valid, Kevin. But we don't want our response to get set in concrete this early in the day. We have to remain fluid."

"Yeah," Schultheiss agreed, "but too much fluid and you've got a washout. Does everybody know what everybody's supposed to do? That isn't asking too much this close to Sunday."

Royce turned to Chamoun. "What Kevin's saying is the old army motto: Simple plans for simple minds. Nothing too fancy and everything all spelled out. Am I right, Kevin?"

"Exactly, sir."

"The way it looks now," Chamoun told them, his grave face showing no emotion of any kind, his dark eyes almost without depth, as if dropped onto a drawing of his face in two blobs of India ink, "is that you'll get a detailed checklist Saturday but no earlier."

"Is that a promise?" Schultheiss demanded.

Chamoun laid his right hand over his heart and, with no apparent trace of sarcasm, intoned: "Kevin, that is a promise."

"Bill," Royce picked up immediately, "please brief us on this meeting His Excellency is having with business people today."

"Straight backscratcher," Voss said in his gruff voice.

Jane had spotted him long ago as an AA and, from what she had heard, so was the ambassador, which made for an uneasy match. Voss was the kind of administrator who seemed perpetually impatient with the red tape and advance planning his job demanded. He got through a brief description of the meeting with such ill grace that no one could guess he was describing a brilliant opening for government and business to stroke each other and groom out all the nits. Jane wondered what Voss was really sore about, but she didn't have long to wait.

". . . and for a windup, we take these various and assorted multi-millionaires and global-type hotshots to the ambassador's private dining room and feed them goddamned K-rations from the goddamned cafeteria."

Royce looked startled, not to the casual eye but certainly to Jane, who knew him and loved him well. Lately he had taken to blinking when surprised, surely a bad habit that might develop into a tic given the amount of startling stuff shoved under his gorgeous nose these days.

"You'd rather pay about a hundred dollars a head of taxpayer's money to feed these moguls at Gavroche?" Royce asked.

"More what they expect, isn't it?"

"Until they stop to think about it, yes. Then we get attacked for squandering taxes on frills."

Voss's face went through several quick changes. Jane could read the discourteous retort forming on his lips, but quickly dying. "Well, I guess that illustrates the difference between a real chargé d'affaires and a lowly civil servant like me."

"You guess correctly," Royce snapped. "Jane? Anything for us?"

"Not at the moment." The minute I get you in private, she added silently, but not in front of people like Schultheiss. She found herself wondering whether, all over the world where American embassies and consulates operated, there was always someone in these meetings who provided an ear for the CIA?

"Dan?"

Anspacher cleared his throat. His name, Jane knew, was not Daniel but, for some reason, friends called him Dan, a fact Royce would have made it his business to find out. Anspacher's hand went protectively to the outside pocket of his tweed jacket, to feel the pipe hidden there. Royce had banned smoking of any kind at any embassy meeting larger than two or three people. If anyone smoked at their desks, that was a matter for them to settle with their office neighbors.

"Nothing today, Royce."

"What about those videos?"

Panic jumped into Anspacher's eyes. They shot left and right as if trying to spot which videos Royce meant. "Videos?"

"Presidential videos on a variety of political topics. You've heard of them, of course."

"Of course," Anspacher said, and was obviously sorry the moment he'd said it. "Back home. Very professional, I hear."

"They're planning to screen some at the Sunday garden party, as you know."

Jane could read Anspacher like a thin and not very interesting book. What he spent his time doing was keeping out of trouble, although his own ignorance could get him in the worst binds of all.

"Yes, of course." Anspacher agreed, not smoothly but with a certain amateur show of ease. His hand groped wildly in his pocket for the reassuring feel of his pipe.

"Can you fill the rest of us in on them?" Royce prompted.

"Yes, of course." Even across the room Jane could hear poor Anspacher's throat click shut. They were about to get a display of bluffing, based on whatever Anspacher had read in the *Herald Tribune*.

"We're not sure," he began, instantly shifting from the personal to the collective pronoun to spread guilt, "how many there are. But there is one on the need for military incursion in the Caribbean. Another one on the Mediterranean, we believe. There are rumors, they say, of a video on cutting social services and another on liberalizing authorization for covert activity at home. They say the other videos would be of too specialized a nature for a gathering like Sunday's."

Bravo, Jane told him silently. Despite his barrages of wes and theys, Anspacher had done his homework.

"Find which ones are scheduled for screening," Royce suggested then. "And you'll of course need a preliminary sounding from D.C. about the suitability of politicizing a traditional date of historic value like the Fourth of July?"

"I'm sure—" Again Anspacher's throat snapped shut audibly.

"You're joking," Voss cut in in his thick voice.

"Pardon?"

"This'll go down in Foggy Bottom like a load of dead rats," Voss pointed out. "We've never politicized any Embassy social event, and especially not the Indepen—"

"Good point, Bill," Jane chimed in. She turned on Anspacher. "You don't have too much time to run this past the brass back home, do you?"

To save himself from a quick answer, Anspacher checked his watch. "It's too early to call D.C. I can't talk to anybody there till this afternoon, London time."

"You've got home phone numbers," Royce told him. "We've always resorted to night calls in an emergency. Dan, would you say this was an emergency?"

"N—well, I mean, yes, of course. Because of the time lag, that is." His mouth worked for a moment without getting out any words. Then:

"Everybody's asleep in D.C. I couldn't wake anybody up till noon our time, could I?"

"You're absolutely right, Dan. You do it then." Royce glanced at his watch and turned with a beautiful but sad smile to Mary Constantine. "I'm awfully sorry, Mary. We've run out of time." He stood up and headed out the door.

Voss got slowly to his feet, a vaguely evil smile on his lips. "Gee, Dan, you do get the beauts."

"What?"

"Mrs. F. is going to love being told she can't promote her dear, close, personal friend in the White House."

"Who told her that?" Anspacher wanted to know.

"It's future tense, Dan. She will be told. By you."

Anspacher's eyes widened slightly. He had been so busy deftly bluffing his way through that he hadn't foreseen what lay down the road for him. He brought the pipe out of his pocket. His fingers stroked it slowly for solace. "Surely," he said, "it's not for me to communicate that to Mrs. Fulmer. That's the job of our deputy ambassador."

"If you think that," Voss said, winking at one of his own people standing beside him, "then you don't know Royce Connell."

17

Lunch had been delivered hot by an extremely good Lebanese restaurant in Knightsbridge. Leilah had served the two men herself, taking special care to make sure the best bits of kebab lamb went to Elias Lateef, the Emperor of Water. But she had expected him to be a younger, healthier-looking man instead of this desiccated old stick. Whenever her brother brought home a bachelor why was he either hopelessly too young, or as ancient as this one? And that horse's grin!

Mahmet, her brother, had still not been told of the fake guests of Tuesday night. Leilah had not been able to contact him by telephone. It was just as well. She could tell by the way he treated Lateef that this was a lunch of great importance and profit for which her brother had to be tranquil. As a tribute to his guest, Mahmet had caused several different bottles of mineral water to be served, some French, some Italian, one Belgian, two British. The small bottles formed an impressive array on the low cocktail table in the great living room.

"The best does not come here to England," Lateef said, spearing several chickpeas on his fork and eating them slowly, one by one. "It is an Italian water from the far south, Mangiatorella. Italy is on my mind because since we met yesterday, I have had contact with that friend of yours, the film producer."

Mahmet's face was blank for a long time. Then: "Aldo Sgroi? But he is no friend."

"But you must admit his offer was a great improvement," the water merchant went on then.

"My dear Lateef," Hakkad said with some asperity. "Sgroi tendered a new offer from me? That is impossible."

"Indeed. This *baba gannouj* is delicious."

"I'm glad you find it acceptable." The doctor seemed lost in thought for a moment. "You must save space for the dessert, dear Lateef. It's *mubalbiah* with *laban*." He paused again. "You see, any protection is negative in approach. As a bad example, in the Republic of Ireland, the government is alleged to pay illegal IRA terrorists a regular bribe of millions per year to avoid kidnapings, bombings, shoot-outs, and other civilian disasters. The French have a similar secret agreement with the PLO. This is simply not a businesslike way to make money. Lending, my dear Lateef, lending alone makes sense." He paused even longer this time.

"A proper bank loan only requires that the banker recognize collateral in whatever form it appears. One banker looks for property, drugs, accounts receivable, illegal gold. That is the conventional approach. But Pan-Eurasian Credit Trust has always kept an open mind about collateral. We have been particularly successful, for example, in lending money to rising political movements. One day the borrower is merely in rebellion against an established regime. Often, in a matter of months, the borrower becomes the ruler, the investment has been a success, and our money comes back to us with dividends."

"But how can your friend Sgroi," Lateef complained with a slight whine, "propose a similar arrangement at better rates?"

"Better? My dear Lateef," the doctor said in a tone of such hauteur that it bordered on insult, "you are to invest half a million in this enterprise, which proposes to pay its sponsor in excess of five million pounds. It is a tenfold profit. And within a week."

The skinny man sopped up the last of the spicy kebab gravy with a scrap of pita. "But look here, Sgroi estimates the payback at ten million pounds on the same original investment. A twentyfold profit, my dear Hakkad." He munched away for a long time, his dauntingly equine teeth destroying the soft bread in a matter of seconds.

Then he swallowed and, for the first time, Dr. Mahmet Hakkad saw that there was a very greedy throb to this man's throat.

*   *   *

Jane knocked at the closed door of Ned French's office. She knew without having been told that the work Ned and Maurice Chamoun did was not what the rest of the Defense Section handled. They therefore kept to themselves, no secretaries, no file clerks. "Who is it?" Ned asked from inside his office.

"Western Union."

She heard the door unlock. As it swung open she saw Chamoun's basilisk eyes fixed on her, a tentative smile hanging below like an expression borrowed from someone else's face. Ned frowned, hand on the doorknob.

"Western Union hasn't delivered telegrams in years. Even then they rarely employed willowy brunettes."

Months of careful lying, of avoiding each other, of small social nods and brusque, impersonal conversation in public. And now Ned seemed to be going public with their affair. She could see deep lines etched below his eyes. Tension?

"Moe, give me five minutes with this lady."

But Chamoun was already deftly moving out of the office toward his own. "Take ten," he said as he disappeared from view.

"He knows," Jane murmured.

Ned shook his head negatively. He closed the door behind her as she sat in a chair. "What's up?"

"Up? Just wanted to dote upon your beloved physiognomy."

"Spare my blushes." Ned sighed. "Bad night."

"Laverne?"

His tired eyes widened as he looked at her. She saw that he hadn't slept. "After I left you I spent the night with the fuzz," he grumbled. "An American citizen got himself iced. He turned out to be the jogger I told you about on Monday, when I committed vehicular mayhem on a Mini? This Riordan was—"

"Anthony Riordan?"

"But his friends call him Tony." He stared at her. "You knew him?"

"Only by reputation." She told him what her young lawyer, Paul Vincent, had brought to her earlier in the week. "Apparently," she finished, "Riordan and Weems are able to get away with anything as long as the Company's great hand protects them."

"Weems?" Ned began pawing through papers on his desk. "You're too young to remember a dance band leader called Ted Weems? Chicago. Instead of a vocalist he had a whistler called Elmo Tanner?"

"I was doing better as Western Union."

"Honest, a whistler. Weems. Here." Ned lifted up a thick packet of papers stapled together and flipped toward the last pages. "This is Pandora's guest list, my little chickadee. And, lo, Weems's name trails all the rest. James F. Weems?"

"That's him. He's invited on Sunday?"

"One of Larry Rand's hardy houseplants." Ned found another sheaf of papers and checked it. "No, not carried as a Company man. Rand is exceeding himself, the little rodent." He saw her glance at her watch. "Stay a while."

"With all the goodwill in the world, Chamoun isn't stupid enough to believe we're still in a business conference."

"He's okay. I don't mean we can tell him. What I mean is even if he found out, he'd behave. He's a friend."

"Isn't that why one joins the army? To form lifelong friendships?" She was on her feet opening the office door. "So that's the latest guest count, as of eleven this morning. Two hundred and seven." Her voice had a strong, carrying quality without sounding too fake. "Mrs. F. seems to be losing ground. And, you understand, these are voluntary cancellations. There will be many guests who simply don't show up."

Ned mimed a silent kiss as she closed his door. He reached for his phone, punched up Rand's private number, and, when he heard the man answer, shifted to scrambler.

"Ned French here, Larry."

"Just the cookie I want. What's all this crap about new credentials?"

Since Chamoun had already told him what had happened at the ten-o'clock, Ned could snap back in a casual tone: "Schultheiss reports that fast?"

Silence at the other end. Followed by: "Well?"

"All guests must have proper credentials," Ned told him.

"They got an invitation. Why not just show it at the gate?"

"That your idea of security, Larry? I'm talking space-age, high-tech, state-of-the-art, holographic, laser-readable credentials."

"Don't shit me, French."

"Who is Ted—sorry, who is Jim Weems?"

"Come again?"

"James F. Weems. One of two clowns involved in some kind of investment scam. He's supposed to be yours, Larry, or if not yours, then Langley's."

"Up yours, French. You'll get just as much answer from me as I'm getting from you on the credentials. Whadya mean laser-readable?"

"That was meant to be funny, Larry. But Weems is no joke, now that they've killed Riordan."

"And let's not forget Cock Robin," Rand grated. "What're you smoking, French?"

"You can't stonewall this one, Larry. Special Branch is on it. The Yard has taken over the murder side."

"And at this very moment Sherlock Holmes is sucking my dick. Get lost." The line went dead.

The third time he tapped out the numbers on the keypad of the red telephone, Larry Rand's call finally went through and began to ring in the United States. He squirmed in his specially built-up desk chair which gave him the appearance of being taller by lifting his body an extra six inches so that his tiny toes dangled in the air.

"Hello?" An early-morning voice. It was noon in London but barely seven in Langley, Virginia.

"Who's this?" Rand grunted.

"Who's *this*?" came the annoyed response.

"Can the comedy. Rand, Station London."

"Larry? It's Durlacher."

"Then why not say so?" Rand asked peevishly. "Give me what you have on James F. Weems."

"The archives people won't stir for another hour. Somebody will fax it to you around two P.M. your time on Looney Toons scramble, okay?"

"Also run a trace on a Riordan, in connection with Weems."

"Give me a clue."

"Securities fraud maybe?" Rand guessed.

"That's FBI territory."

"Fuck that, Durlacher. I want 'em both. Call it an international crime ring that affects—"

"—national security," Darlacher finished for him.

"Smartass!" Rand slammed down the red phone and caused his special chair to creak unhappily as he leaned back in it with a violent shove. The fiery point of his anger focused on Ned French. He'd been right about the bastard all along, a maverick, a loner, definitely a security risk, definitely in need of weeding.

But he had to hand it to the bastard. Holding off on issuing credentials till the last minute was a smart move, the kind he, Larry Rand, would have thought of. It meant your opposition couldn't get its act together until almost too late. Trust a wise guy like French to understand this.

That was what made him so dangerous. He wasn't your ordinary linthead military, serving his time, making his points, building up his pension. Not French. He was a dedicated apple, wasn't he? In a way it was too bad he had to be wasted to teach Connell and the other embassy turkeys a lesson. But it couldn't be helped.

Never mind. You were always better off without the dedicated ones. In the long run the lintheads were better to work with. They didn't give themselves airs. They listened to you and followed your lead. Not French. Too goddamned bright to live.

Although Bud Fulmer had never actually headed up a business enterprise, he had often visited his father at his office. He had even been assigned an office of his own when he was a younger man, before he began to understand that this was a sham and that he would never be allowed to play a real role in the management of Fulmer Stores. It became, at last, one of the many places where he was made to feel useless.

Whatever Bud knew about life, however, he had learned as a hunter learns, by mimicry. Slipping stealthily through woods on the trail of an animal, the hunter imitates the technique of the prey, using the same covers and stratagems. So it was with Bud as he moved about his office in the chancery after bidding good-bye to the men Bill Voss had invited for lunch. He produced a replica of managerial behavior.

Younger fellows, most of them, not many older than forty, Bud mused. And in their carefully honed performances as business leaders they reminded him strongly of Jim Weems. Even their jargon was the same, a sort of partly kidding, highly ironic, heavily distanced language in which nothing was called by its real name and everything was stated in reverse. He recalled two of his guests today becoming involved in what was, for this new breed, an argument. Normally no one took a stand on anything. They reminded Bud of spectators at a ball game, all rooting for the same team.

"That'd be nice," one of the guests had said, apropos of a remark by Bill Voss that the British government, like any other, would if pressed impose further trade restrictions on imports. "That'd be nice," meaning not nice. "That wouldn't stir up the White House, not too much," meaning it would, and a lot.

One of the other guests had called the first man a free trader, as if this were a form of AIDS, adding: "Try selling American electronics hardware these days," meaning, don't try. "Try touting our quality control against Little Yellow Brother's," meaning you'd lose. "So tell me all about free trade, okay?" meaning I don't want to hear it.

"Time On My Hands," Bud recalled, was the name of an old song, wasn't it? Wasn't that the theme song of life itself? Certainly his own life. When you've always understood, having had it firsthand from your father, that you're a useless supernumerary, time was meant to waste, get rid of, destroy. Nothing really big in his book from now till six P.M. and no place here in the chancery to take a nap.

He picked up his telephone and asked to be connected with Royce Connell. "Bud Fulmer here," he began, with counterfeit managerial briskness. "Can I see you about a problem?"

"I'll be right in."

"No, I'll come to you," Bud countered commandingly. "It'll be the only exercise I've had today, basically."

Without booze things were even duller than Bud had imagined. Without booze a simple meeting with a bunch of upward-shoving managers became one long groan of boredom. And without booze he didn't even get sleepy enough for a good, long nap.

He stalked out of his office, causing his secretary, a big-boned girl from Oregon, to jump to her feet so quickly she upset her out basket onto the floor. "Miss Patch, sorry about that. Can you tell me how to get to Mr. Connell's office?"

It was obvious that Miss Patch couldn't make up her mind whether to remain standing or get down on her knees and retrieve the spilled paperwork. Her eyes flicked back and forth with a certain mute desperation. "It's just down the—awfully sorry about this. Down the hall to the—look at this mess. I'm terribly sorry, Your Excellency."

"Down the hall to the right or left?"

"Left, sir. The other corner office."

Bud Fulmer entered Royce's outer office in time to see him come to his own inner door, as if to greet him. It crossed his mind that Royce had come out to warn his own secretary about the approach of the great man.

Bud smiled, well aware that it was a secret smile, at the idea that he, useless Bud Fulmer, could stir up frenzied activity just by setting his big-boned frame in motion. It was a new sensation, carrying weight. His smile broadened at the double meaning of the phrase. He'd been sure that an ambassador's job would be simply a new and more boring pain in the neck. Now he could see that it had its advantages, the chief one being that for the first time in his life Bud Fulmer seemed to carry real weight in the world. He found himself wondering if this hadn't been what Pandora was seeking for him.

After being ushered most ceremoniously into Royce's warmly wood-paneled room and offered a choice of chairs, a cup of coffee or what Royce referred to as a "postprandial libation," Bud finally settled into a big walnut armchair with an upholstered back.

"Just some advice," he explained. "I know you've got a lot on your mind, Royce, and this isn't even embassy business, but it could be and then we might all be sorry."

"Oops. I'm all ears."

Bud surveyed his number-two with rather melancholy attention to detail. If anyone was perfectly formed, no part of him beyond those Grecian proportions the white man thought of as handsome, it was Royce Connell. That narrow, aristocratic head, that firm chin, that flat belly, those long legs. Jesus, Bud thought, how does he keep the gals from eating him alive?

"International manager for Fulmer Stores," the ambassador began, "fellow I'd basically never met before named Jim Weems, called me up two weeks ago and . . ."

By the time he'd finished the Weems story, complete with photographs of a law-breaking weekend shooting deer, Royce's classic lively features had hardened into the chiseled look of cold white alabaster. "It's plain ordinary blackmail," he brooded. "But he's got no case. Or, rather, we have a perfect case to bring to the police. Except . . ."

The two men watched each other for a moment. "I was about to say that our position is a good one. You're only recently arrived here. You naturally assume the Duke of Buchan is a law-abiding subject. You have no idea you're breaking the law. You're deeply apologetic. Except that it makes your staff look like a collection of idiots. Why didn't they stop you? That's what people will ask. What sort of scofflaw idiots are running the American embassy that they let their new leader walk into a clanger like this?"

"I can just explain that I didn't basically see the need to consult with . . ."

"That's even worse, Your Excellency, if you'll excuse me being blunt. An ambassador who acts without consultation is either a liability or, in your case, simply new to the job. That's an excuse I readily understand. But the public won't."

Bud Fulmer's stomach turned over. Was he doomed for the rest of his life to this sort of thing? To always and forever being told he was not to be trusted? Not to be allowed to make his own decisions? For a moment there, just before he'd told Connell the news, he'd basked in a new dawn of personal power. People *jumped* when he appeared. Then the bucket of ice water in the face.

"In fact, while we're on the subject, Your Excellency," Connell was saying, "there's a moral here for you and Mrs. Fulmer. I can't tell you what this Fourth of July party is costing us in manpower and energy diverted from other things. The security provisions alone . . ." Connell's handsome head shook slowly from side to side.

Oddly, Bud perked up. "I was afraid of that. Too much exposure."

"Too many prominent people. Chance of attack, kidnaping, your guess is as good as mine." Seeing Fulmer's constructive reaction to this, Connell pressed on. "After it's over and, God willing, a success, perhaps you could have a private chat with Mrs. Fulmer? You two are an example to the rest of us, you know. And to the British people, need I point out? By your example, we can all improve our own performance."

"And what about Weems?"

"I'm afraid it will have to wait till after Sunday, don't you think?"

Bud Fulmer nodded somberly and got to his feet. Although Royce Connell was nearly six feet tall, he looked stunted next to the ambassador. "You say he works for Fulmer Stores?" Connell asked. "But aren't you a major stockholder?"

"It's basically in escrow till I'm no longer an ambassador."

"Yes, but surely you can apply pressure."

"To have Weems canned?"

"Something like that. It makes for a counterthreat."

"It's nonvoting stock," Fulmer admitted.

"But does Weems know that?"

"Royce," Bud said in a heavy voice, "everybody knows that."

On his lunch hour, Chamoun strolled over to South Molton Street and did his usual perusal of the windows at Bricktop's boutique. The procedure was dated and had to be changed for a new one, but since he also felt distinctly uncomfortable working for Mossad, that, too, might have to be changed.

Why worry now, he asked himself as he moved on to the coffee shop to wait for the fat woman. The whole reason he had joined the American army and volunteered for intelligence work was that Mossad thought it a good idea—in fact brilliant—to use a native-born American who had been raised a Christian to infiltrate the U.S. establishment. That had been years ago, but this London assignment was the first in which Mossad seemed about to call the debt due. Until now no one from the Israeli intelligence network had even contacted Chamoun, except for occasional social visits by Bricktop. But just in this last year she had put Chamoun on active double-agent status. He was finding it awkward.

Why awkward? he asked himself as he sat down and ordered a coffee. It fit perfectly being an outsider, didn't it? The classic role, doubly so. But he'd counted without Ned's friendship.

The fact was that neither he nor Ned French made friends easily, if at all. He knew that something had sprung up between Ned and Jane Weil, had known it almost as soon as it began, and deemed it none of his business. But it did start him thinking about the nature of friendship. Between Ned and Jane there was an obvious physical attraction. You could almost taste it. But what accounted for the bond between Ned and him?

He wasn't jealous of Jane. He and Ned didn't have a homosexual relationship. There'd never been any of that fatherly come-on from Ned that a good-looking young officer like Chamoun would occasionally get from a senior man, that queasy protector-mentor thing, arm around the shoulder, squeeze-squeeze, help with your career, influential people, small party my place tomorrow night . . . None of that.

What had drawn him and Ned together was that both were too intelligent for U.S. Army Intelligence. Misfits, the pair of them, too broadly knowledgeable for the very narrow job of protecting America's welfare.

Still, Chamoun reflected as he saw the swollen shape of Bricktop silhouetted in the coffee shop doorway, if I triple up on old Brick I can do Ned a good turn. Worth trying.

Hubris.

The red-haired woman stood for a long moment at the order counter and then said, "Gino, I'm sick of snacks. I'm going up the street for a real sit-down lunch."

"Brickie, *bambina, mangia bene.*"

"Mangia, mangia. You sound like my mother." She waddled out of the shop. Chamoun got up to watch her enter a crowded, noisy hamburger place. He followed within five minutes and sat down at her small table without greeting or comment. *"Nu, Moishe, wus noch?"*

"Your little Arab-lover is onto something."

"Tell me."

"She says they're all in a panic. Three of their top people are missing for some time on the eve of a big caper. For which read that damned Sunday garden party of Mrs. Fulmer's."

"That's it?"

"No, Brick, that's not it. The rest of the message is I resent like hell having your airhead agents use me as a messenger boy."

"Sorry. It's an emergency."

"With you everything is an emergency. You get me *mishegas* with your emergencies."

The fat woman smiled, showing dimples so deep she could, if she wished, hide her thumbs in them. "When you do Yiddish, it's to laugh, Moishe. The word is *meshuge*. I'm driving you *meshuge*. *Mishegas* is a collective noun for any kind of craziness."

"No, the word for that is Mossad."

Her face darkened. "You got a big mouth, boychik." She glanced around her casually. "Having trouble with that Sunday clambake?"

"We're okay."

"I have faith in you, kiddo. You and Ned French are moderately bright for goyim." She winked at him. "Let me suggest the Danish blue cheeseburger. It's *meshuge*."

When Bert became conscious this time he could feel his body shaking, although it was no longer chilly in this deepest part of the woods. Yet a hard, steady tremor swept through him as if he were riding some vehicle speeding over a rutted road. The train of history, Lenin said. It may take a sharp turn. Those who cannot hang on will be thrown off.

Those with no base, Bert thought. He opened his eyes against the steady shaking of his head on its neck. The dark woods danced madly in his gaze as the shivering whipped his head backward. He closed his eyes. The bright blue image of the *Glockenblumen* vibrated painfully on his retinas, the colors reversed to a hideous brown-red.

Crackling of twigs. He took a breath through his smashed nose. They had loosened his gag enough for him to force a thin air channel through the blood-soaked cloth. His lungs heaved with effort, but the fresh air seemed to steady him against the buffeting beneath his feet. The train of history rounded a sharp, sharp turn.

Twigs. A hard slap across the face.

Bert's eyes opened as his head whipped sideways. Someone new, with big pop-eyes, pudgy, older. No one in the movement was fat. Class traitor.

Bert knew him now, from Hakkad's party. His accent was bad. His grammar was wrong. He was no German. *Verdammter italienischer Dreck.* Movie producer. Name Alzo. Also. Aldo.

"The combination of the lock, yes?" the Italian demanded in his scratch German. His wooly hair looked unwashed.

The Italian wanted the combination of the lock to the storage room? Bert's storage room? With perhaps a hundred thousand pounds worth of weapons and ammunition? *"Scheissdreck!"* he screamed inside his head.

"He can't speak," Khefte said softly.

Khefte?

Bert's eyes moved slowly. There stood his comrade, his brother, looking only faintly ashamed, not too much so. His eyes, the color of baby seal pelt, looked sideways at Bert. They hadn't tied him up, nor gagged him. Nor beat him. Nor was anyone holding a gun on his beloved brother.

Khefte's fingers plucked at the bloody rags. "Bert, they will kill you," he said in a small, cold voice. "I am buying our lives with the armaments, oh my brother. Give them the lock combination and we are free."

Liar, Bert thought. You are free at this very moment, trusted comrade. No one has brutalized your body. His lips ached as the gag was slowly pulled out.

He worked his jaw for a moment, then his tongue. His mouth was as dry as a grave dug in the sands of the desert. He was hot now. This place roared with heat like the entrance to hell. The Muenster cheese was melting down into the pores of the bread. Thin slices because he didn't want *Grossmutti* to know he had been stealing cheese.

He could gasp in breaths of damp forest air now, tasting of the funk of humus and decay. He let the oxygen soothe his battered lungs for a moment. Then he filled them with a great gasp of air.

"Traitor!" he screamed at the top of his voice.

Khefte stepped back as if slapped. The Italian, his protuberant eyes bulging, struck Bert across the face again, flogging his head to the side.

Bert could see waves of heat coming up from the forest floor as if it were on fire. We will do that one day, he promised himself. "We will set the world aflame," he shouted.

The Italian glanced back at Khefte and shook his head with a certain air of sadness. "You are the last person he'll talk to. We should have expected this, yes?"

"No, wait," Khefte begged. "I'll get the combination."

"This is what comes of dealing with amateurs," the film producer remarked to no one in particular. His pop eyes widened. He took another step back and pulled a small .25 Beretta automatic from his jacket pocket. "Stand aside while I finish him," he ordered Khefte.

"No, I can get him to talk."

Khefte removed a small pocketknife from his side pocket and flicked the long, thin blade open. It clicked into place. The blade was a scalpel, thin and honed like a razor, the point long, a weapon to puncture or slash or . . . or anything a man had a mind to, Bert thought. He's one of them, Khefte.

"Never!" he shouted at his beloved brother.

"No, no," Khefte said almost soothingly. "Never say that. Please." He advanced on Bert with the knife.

18

"I'm so glad it's this simple," Pandora Fulmer was telling Gillian Lamb. The two women stood in the center hallway at Winfield House watching the camera crew set up for an interview with His Excellency. They had just finished one with Pandora in another room.

"This modern equipment, you know," Gillian was explaining.

"Yes, of course. My experience with television has all been bad. Miles of thick heavy cables snaking all over the house. Those immense old cameras on their dollies, each as huge as a Volkswagen. And the lights! My dear, the lights!"

"Much more natural now, less intrusive." Gillian watched her director checking angles. "With these minicams we're mobile and not dependent on strong lights. I think we're ready, Mrs. Fulmer."

"I'll get His Excellency," the tiny woman said. She tripped off to somewhere, Gillian thought, some hideaway den or lair where H.E. carried on affairs of state in the midst of the turmoil created by her "Lamb to Slaughter" crew. Or perhaps, like a bull, snorted behind the *barrera* before meeting the matador.

Odd. The name of the program instantly disclosed its chief strength, the adversary posture it assumed. But no one, in Gillian's memory, had ever refused to let her come in with a crew.

People deserted a lifetime of behavior patterns when the cameras lighted up. They switched into a mode learned from watching TV. "I don't bear him any malice," a mother droned on about the evil psychopath who killed her child. "I just feel sorry for his mother."

TV created behavior, Gillian knew, as it filmed it. "Well, what did you feel when you found the body, Mrs. Catsmeat?" Sigh, pause. "Were you shocked, Mrs. Catsmeat?" Nod. "Oo, shocked beyond belief."

In the distance Pandora Fulmer, tilting along on five-inch heels like some scrubber parading Shepherd Market, was leading her gigantic bull into the ring. He looked, to Gillian, a bit dazed. Had he been drinking? Napping?

"Good afternoon, Your Excellency," she said, coming toward him.

"You remember Miss Lamb, honey?"

"Afternoon, Miss Lambhoney."

Gillian resolved to find out, sub rosa from Royce, just exactly how H.E. spent his private time when not officiating at the opening of cruise missile sites or whatever an American ambassador did. As if she could ever get anything confidential out of Royce.

She supposed she was a figure of fun, chasing Royce when he was so obviously one of those gentlemen of nature, the neuter. Not a eunuch and not a poofter, just simply not interested. Britain was full of them. It was, in fact, most accurately described as the English disease, neuterhood. Disinterest in sex, or a faint distaste for it or whatever it was that held men like Royce back from that ultimate commitment to the body.

Now, this specimen here, she thought, looking Bud Fulmer up and down, was clearly no neuter. No part of his fifteen or sixteen stone had disengaged from the opposite sex, as magnificently portrayed by his little hummingbird lady. Gillian found herself wondering how they managed it, other than the obvious arrangement of Pandora always on top. Big men weren't necessarily better endowed, of course. She'd have to have a long, sisterly talk about it with dear Pandora.

"We thought you'd be more at ease in this armchair by the hearth," Gillian was telling Fulmer. "I'm told it's your favorite chair?"

His Excellency looked blank and Gillian realized this was simply the little mythmaker, Pandora, churning out copy. "But then you haven't been here long enough to have a favorite, have you?" she persisted.

H.E. sat down in the indicated chair. "Not really," he agreed.

Gillian began to realize her problem. Well, two problems, really.

The first was that this face showed nothing. It had no expression whatsoever. And behind the face—problem number two—was a mind that bounced back your overtures like a brick wall did a rubber ball. This man was simply not ever, ever going to show you anything, anything.

"Comfortable?"

He nodded, his eyes roving about the large study with its walls of books. Although it was July, someone—the little mythmaker hard at work?—had started a small log fire which probably didn't show too well in the camera. Gillian seated herself on a short divan, a kind of love seat, at right angles to the ambassador's armchair. She crossed her legs, adjusted her skirt, and folded her hands in her lap.

"This is how we'll be," she explained. "This is my pose, so to speak. You see, however long we shoot, this will end up as only a few minutes of the final cut, so every frame of it has to match. If I forgot my pose and crossed my legs the other way"—swish of dress, hiss of nylons, flicker of H.E.'s glance—"in the final cut the result would look ludicrous. So find a posture that suits you and remember to keep the same pose?"

He nodded again. Nice, Gillian thought: no talking head he. How do I get these zombies?

"Did you have a chance to look over that list of questions?" she asked.

He nodded a third time.

"Anything else you'd like to talk about that isn't on the list?"

Something very vague shifted in his face. He did have expressions, Gillian saw, but they were microexpressions. She got up and went to her director. "Harry, can you get him in very tight CU? I mean so close up you cut off the top of the frame just above his eyebrows and the bottom just below the middle of his chin?"

"That tight?"

"Please?"

"Suit yourself, luv."

She sat down again. H.E. was looking nauseated, or whatever passed for nausea on that great flat slab of beef suet he used for a face. "Ah, well, Your Excellency?"

"Where's . . . is Pandora around?"

"Right here, honey."

"Okay." He managed something less nauseated as an expression, his glance settling on a long view of his wife, who stood in the doorway of the room about thirty feet away.

"Mrs. Fulmer," Gillian said, getting a brainstorm, "you're still in makeup from your interview, aren't you?"

"Why, yes."

"Please sit down here next to me. You'll be out of the frame more often than not, but I think His Excellency will feel more at ease this way."

"Why . . . certainly."

Tinkerbell twinkled over to the love seat and planted her minuscule butt beside Gillian's generous one. With her eyes, Gillian signaled the cameraman to include Pandora in the frame. He nodded slowly several times.

"Ready, luv?" the director asked.

"Ready."

"Roll sound."

"Sound rolling."

"Roll tape."

"Tape rolling."

"Slaughter, take seventeen." He pointed a finger at Gillian.

"Your Excellency, we're talking in the shadow, so to speak, of your American Independence Day, the Fourth of July, at a time when a lot of Britons feel we should be winning our independence from America. Mindful of all the controversy over American air and nuclear bases in Britain, American ownership of British industry, and, on the cultural level, American films, television, and the like tending to swamp our little island, how do you feel about your job right at the workface of this confrontation?"

Her director turned away to hide the grin on his face.

As Thursday drew to a close, Ned French tried as best he could to review his position with regard to the Fourth of July affair. He rubbed his eyes, gritty from lack of sleep, and got to his feet to look out at Grosvenor Square. Offices were emptying all over Mayfair. People were strolling home or to a pub. And there, in the lengthening shadows, stood Ambrose Everett Burnside III.

Ned stared down at him. Another sign? The silly old man was encased in the same sandwich boards, splintered and broken, but patched up again and repainted.

Ned had to smile in spite of himself. The old guy couldn't bother to shave or shower or comb his hair but he could find the time to repaint his loony sign.

True jUStice lies in
the dUSt, its
lUSter dimmed
by a thoUSand
meretricioUS
hUStles and
fUSses!
LudicroUS to
discUSs, as
USeless as
a bUSted
trUSs!

Ned's smile broadened to a grin. Attaboy, Ambrose! That'll show the world! He had to admire the old coot, after all. There he stood, defiant. Take me as I am, he seemed to say: The truth is never pretty. In fact, phrased the Burnside way, the truth can't even be discerned.

Ned picked up his phone and called Max Grieves. "It's Ned French. Got five minutes?"

"Gee, Ned, I—"

"But you are on your way out of the building?"

"Matter of fact, yes."

"Meet you in the lobby. Right now." Ned hung up.

He found Grieves waiting near the entrance. "You can keep the lady waiting five minutes, Max."

"It's my brother-in-law Jack on his way through London."

Ned hustled him out of the building and across the greensward of Grosvenor Square. "Oh, no," Grieves moaned. "Not Ambrose."

"Good evening, Mr. Burnside," Ned said. "I'd like you to meet Mr. Grieves. We thought we had an appointment with you the other day."

Burnside's pale eyes looked vague. He seemed, if anything, even grubbier than when Ned had seen him last. "You the comb fella?" he asked.

Ned's mind clicked through that question rapidly and came up with the right reference. "Yes. But you're not. You haven't even seen a comb in weeks. Or a razor. That's no way for a soldier to look."

It took the old man some time to complete the proper connections in his head, but when he did, his scowl was magnificent. "Get away from me, you two. You're trouble. You gave me a police record. I'm not allowed to buy a comb any more. I'm not allowed in Boots, either."

Giving up on this farrago, Ned stepped back and surveyed the new sign. "Very impressive, Mr. Burnside. I like the new lettering."

The FBI man kept looking from Ned to Burnside with a confused but eager-to-understand glance. "I don't believe I'm hearing all this," he said at last.

"Nothing out of line. My Dad back in Wisconsin is Mr. Burnside's age. And if Mr. Burnside and his wife, Vickie, had ever had kids, why, I suppose he might have one my age by now."

"No, thanks," the old man grunted.

"I've got four myself," Ned told him. "Four girls."

"That a fact." Burnside's fierce look seemed to drain off his ravaged, dirty face. "They say it's the father's genes, you know, decides the sex of the kids. That true?"

"Ned," Max Grieves complained, "by the time I get to Jack he'll be half in the bag and I promised my sister to keep him sober in London."

"This won't take long, Max. Mr. Burnside, is there any way I can get you all spruced up and over here tomorrow morning for an interview? Because after tomorrow it's the weekend and we're going to get very busy."

Burnside's eyes went crafty. "That so? Why?"

"Sunday's the Fourth of July."

The old man seemed to agree that this was a valid reason. "If I can dodge the coppers," he said. "But they don't want me to have a comb or a shampoo or a shave. So how can I be interviewed looking like some kind of goofball?"

Max broke out in a guffaw. "My sentiments exactly, old-timer."

"Never mind, Max. Let's say I'll have Mr. Burnside in your office at nine thirty. You know, Mr. Burnside's grandfather was not only a Union general, he was a governor and a senator."

"No kidding. I'm impressed. Look, my brother-in-law Jack is—"

"From the great state of Rhode Island," Ned added.

"Some people think Old Rhody's a joke, seeing how small she is," Burnside pointed out, "but you don't judge quality by size, do you, Mr. Grieves?"

"He'd be better off," Ned suggested, "asking that question of Larry Rand."

The Gethsemane of Adolf Fulmer III continued. Although the lights were miniature halogens that gave off very little heat, Bud's face had begun to look moist across the forehead. During a break, his petite wife

hopped across to him and daintily blotted that great slab of face. Gillian
Lamb had dragged him bleeding through half a dozen barbed wire fences
involving missile bases, trade with Russia, U.S. F-111s based in England,
political freedom, affirmative action programs for minorities, equal jobs
for equal pay, the political influence of organized crime, and anything
else guaranteed to act like a field of broken glass bottles as he crawled
gamely onward.

While Pandora sponged off her boy, much as a trainer does his fighter
in the ring, Gillian spoke sotto voce with her director. "How's he looking,
Harry? Getting much expression from that face?"

"Just grievous pain."

"You're stealing reaction shots from Twinkletoes as well?"

"Good ones. Her face shows everything."

"Soldier on, then." She turned to Fulmer. "We're ready for your
next take, Your Excellency. These will all be personal questions, nothing
political any more."

"Will I get to answer one from that list you submitted?"

Gillian scanned his face for signs of sarcasm, since she hadn't asked
even one of the announced questions yet. "I'm sorry, sir. Did we give
you the impression that we'd limit ourselves to that list?"

Bud Fulmer failed to answer. He merely shrugged. It was the proper
moment for Pandora to complain if she was going to. But she sat in
silence, almost as if pretending she hadn't heard. Gillian realized that,
after a lifetime of mediocrity, albeit of the wealthy kind, Pandora was
simply not going to ruin her chance at the brass ring.

"Slaughter. Take twenty-six."

"Your Excellency, the personal background of leading public figures
is of great interest to everyone. In your own life, could you say what
person had the greatest influence on you?"

Bud prepared to answer this question as he did the others—but this
could be edited out of the tape later—by nodding twice, shooting his
chin forward, and glancing at Pandora for support.

"Basically, my father," he said then.

Gillian's sixth sense picked up something special in the word, not
the usual stereotyped TV reaction, conditioned by overexposure to sit-
coms, disaster news, and old films. "Your father? But of course a boy's
father is always a great influence, isn't he?"

A faint look of confusion crossed Fulmer's flat face, as if having said
what he said he now felt stuck with it. "He . . ." He stopped and mois-
tened his lips. "Basically, he was a giant."

"Do you get your size from him?"

"I was referring to his mind, his stature in industry . . ." The ambassador's thoughts slipped down a side road. "I get my size from my mother. Her whole family was well over six feet, even her sisters, my aunts, who . . ." The side road ended in a clump of bushes. "But my father was a giant, too, in his own way. As a leader of men. A pioneer in chain-store operation. Basically, he never looked back. He just plowed ahead."

"If you had to, could you summarize his business philosophy?"

"Buy volume, sell at specialty prices."

"I beg your pardon?"

"You buy, let's say, a thousand of an item, cheap. But you've got five hundred stores to sell through. In each town, basically, that item is an exclusive and you can charge high specialty prices for it. You see . . ." He must have picked up a signal from Pandora that no one else saw because he stopped. "My father," he began again, slowly, "my father was a giant of intellect and of energy. You often find that in very small people."

Pained silence. Gillian was about to call for a break when His Excellency came to life again, slowly as always, shot his chin forward and nodded twice.

"We never did get along."

"Honey?"

"Basically wouldn't trust me to handle one damned thing."

"Honey?"

"Blighted my goddamned life, basically."

"Miss Lamb, can we have a break?"

"Sure, money. Tons of money. But, basically, what's money? Once you have enough to live on, what you want is something useful to do, something . . ."

Pandora was on her feet, crossing over and pretending to daub his forehead again. "Miss Lamb, did I understand that the embassy has the right to review this footage before it's aired?"

"Mr. Connell insisted on it."

"Then that's all right."

"Oh," Gillian said on that rising then falling note the British use to indicate disbelief. "Is it?"

Mahmet Hakkad had enjoyed a very busy day. His chauffeured Rolls had crisscrossed the city several times as a bee crisscrosses a flowerbed, and the results, Hakkad felt, would be similarly beneficial. Now he was proceeding toward Belgravia at the leisurely pace that rush-hour traffic enforces even on Rollses. It was that moment of the day when, if he had not been a devout Muslim, he would have opened the bar-refrigerator installed in the Rolls to pour himself something alcoholic.

His last appointment, while it could never have produced a profit, had possibly been his most important of the day. It was with a man who knew Aldo Sgroi, the mysterious film producer who, Leilah had informed him, was an imposter. So, indirectly, was the man with whom he'd had his last appointment, a man called Mustapha, who traveled in the darker back alleys of international finance.

"Aldo Sgroi," he had explained, "is simply an identity he chose for whatever he's planning this month. I have no idea what his real name is, or even if he is Italian."

"I assumed Sicilian," Hakkad had responded, making with his thumbnail the universal sign of a scarred face to indicate Mafia origins.

"I honestly do not know, esteemed friend," Mustapha had confessed. "A real Sgroi exists and perhaps he owes the mystery man something, which allows Mr. X to use his name. But when I ran into the man in Malta—this would be a dozen years ago—his name was Yussuf Drago and he owned all the houses of prostitution along Strait Street."

Hakkad had nodded sagely. "The principle is identical, the linking of financial services to an illegal source of cash. But he seems to have come a long way since his days as a superpimp."

"He was the one a madam went to when she wanted to open a new house. He would provide financing." Mustapha had leaned forward and dropped his voice to a low tone. "The last time I saw Mr. X he had a French name and was based in Geneva, doing business with representatives of various small governments who needed financing."

"So he's considered responsible?"

"He's respected, my friend. His information is always accurate. He runs, here in London, an amazing intelligence operation of his own. And his people are recruited from all over. They are not of our faith, and find it much easier to operate here in the west. There is also an iron-bound discipline that reminds me of the death's-head Waffen SS. It's an attractive combination for someone in need of funds."

At Number 12 the Rolls surged to a halt. The doorman welcomed Dr. Hakkad with a sweeping gesture, passing him along to the elevator operator. At the penthouse door, Dr. Hakkad brought out his keys and opened the apartment door. The elevator operator, smiling, closed the doors of his car and sent it downward. Hakkad walked into his apartment.

He took three paces and then stopped cold. He stared with such intensity that his eyes began to water. Even when they were children he had never in his life seen his sister Leilah stark naked.

Eyes streaming, Hakkad began to moan. The plump little man called Sgroi pointed a small-caliber Beretta automatic at him. Its tiny black eye had a baleful squint, but Hakkad's own glance remained riveted on his naked sister.

Leilah's pale skin was squeezed by copper wire like a trussed bird in the oven. She bulged moist flesh. Hakkad's moan seemed to choke in his throat.

"Easy, yes?" Sgroi suggested. "Move slowly, yes?"

Hakkad rubbed the tears from his eyes and sniffed very hard to clear his nose. The expression on his face changed from sheer terror to a fair imitation of outraged male protector. "I must prot—"

"Would you believe it?" Sgroi asked. "She's still a virgin? At her age?"

The rest of the room seemed to come into focus. His sister, naked and in agony from the wires, her plump mouth crammed with a nylon stocking, was the centerpiece of the tableau. Two young men with large-caliber silenced automatics stood near the windows, almost in silhouette. Khefte sat in an upholstered chair, smoking a cigarette. His American woman sat beside him, looking worried.

"Sit next to Khefte, yes? Easy, now."

After the first shock, Hakkad's mind began to function again. How had so many people gotten past the doorman and the elevator operator? Were his employees so easily corrupted? So quick to betray him?

"What do you want?" he asked the man with the Beretta.

"Tomorrow morning, when the banks open at nine thirty, cash."

"Oh, come now."

The man called Sgroi gave him an odd look. "Tomorrow morning at nine thirty there is cash, yes? Or there are a dozen of my men . . . and your virgin sister."

Hakkad's mind clicked shut at the image. He tried to restart his process of thinking and the first thing that came to mind was sitting calmly there on the sofa with him. "Khefte," the doctor said. "Why are you so silent, my hawk?"

"I am very sad, Doctor. My comrade Bert . . ." He placed his hand upon his heart as he carefully stubbed out his cigarette. "The same will happen to us all, Doctor, unless we cooperate with this gentleman."

"I do not see wires biting into your bare body!" Hakkad shouted. "Or your American whore!"

"You see?" Khefte asked of the man called Sgroi. "Emotional outbursts! It's as you say, the difference between an amateur and a professional."

Dinner at the Dutch embassy always began with this fashion show of gin, although Bud Fulmer had no way of knowing that it was not staged as a special temptation just for him. Pandora was locked in conversation with her hostess, leaving H.E. to first glance, then stare, at the array of bottles. They shared the same general shape: tall, straight-sided, coming to a narrow mouth somewhat like a chemical bottle.

Some were made of a deep green glass, some of a pale straw color that transmitted light, but quite a few seemed baked of a brown-glazed ceramic. "Ah, Your Excellency," a man said in an upper-class British accent, "one actually needs a guide with such a display of genever."

"That's all right," Fulmer assured him. "I'm not drinking."

The man looked familiar to him, but whether from one of these diplomatic parties or in another connection, H.E. couldn't tell. "That one there," the man was saying, stroking his full, wide mustache, "that looks as if it was plucked from some cobwebby cellar, is called Corenwyn, and it must be at least twenty-five years old. Or *oude*, as the Dutch say."

"Are you Dutch?" Bud asked. "Your face is very . . . familiar."

When the man smiled, twin parentheses surrounding his mouth and nose angled out sideways into dimpled slashes. "Permit me to introduce myself, Your Excellency. Gleb Ponamarenko, of Tass."

His hand went out and Fulmer shook it before the name and the word "Tass" registered. "You're Russian?" Bud inquired.

"Indeed. Now the ceramic bottle marked "O.G." is also heavily aged. You wouldn't think it of an artificial spirit like gin, but aging does smooth its flavor."

Although H.E. wasn't drinking, this was not exactly unfamiliar territory for him. "But you people don't age your vodka," Bud pointed out.

"Indeed not. We drink it too fast ever to have any surplus available for aging."

"Ha! I'm afraid I'm on the wagon," H.E. told him morosely. "My drinking days are over. My father would be happy as a clam now."

"He's, ah, no longer with us?"

"Died some years ago."

"He was a small man," Gleb observed mysteriously.

"Not even five-three. A real shrimp."

"My father also, very short," the Russian admitted.

"They're the worst, you know. Real tyrants."

Gleb sighed. "Alas, he died before I was born."

Bud Fulmer looked at him with real interest. "You're lucky," he grunted.

It was only later, after dinner, on the way home to Winfield House, that the ambassador found himself wondering how the Russian knew his father was a short man. But by then, of course, it was too late to ask him.

At this time of year, and for the rest of summer, the night sky remained bright over London until quite late. Lou Ann, their eldest, had often asked Ned and Laverne about this when they first arrived in England. He would refer her to a map, which showed that, in terms of latitude, London was on a level with Newfoundland.

"Does that explain anything?" Laverne had asked, requiring Ned to find a globe of the world and, using a desk lamp as the sun, explain about summer and winter solstices.

Tonight, even at nine o'clock, there was still a strong glow in the sky, not enough to see by, but it was not yet true night. Laverne stood at the living room window and watched two birds on their small lawn. "Long past bedtime, birdies," she called in a crisp voice.

"What?"

In the study Ned was watching the nine-o'clock BBC news on television. "What, Laverne?"

"Nothing."

These were funny little fellows, these birds, black with orange beaks and tremendous musical ability. Some kind of blackbird, Laverne knew, that her next-door neighbor, a Belgian woman, called a merle. Nearby Regent's Park was filled with their song this time of year. They seemed to be able to imitate anything, trumpets, steam whistles, violins, tambourines. Their agility put Laverne in mind of one of these jazz wizards Ned liked to listen to, quick jabs of sound, long sweeping loops of melody. And all from an ordinary little bird.

"No more worms, birdies," she told the two on her lawn. "Home to bed, now. Bye-bye, blackbird."

She could hear her voice slipping into the mode she had used when her girls were small. It had been wonderful talking to them on the phone this morning. It had made up for Ned's overlong absence from home. She had no accurate idea what he was up to except that it had to do with the Sunday party, one of the official ways Ned could shut her out of his life.

"Ned?"

"Come in here."

She waited a moment at the window. "Fly home, blackbirds. Bye-bye!" Then she turned and went into the study. On the TV screen a White House cabinet minister was telling a press conference that the United States would never negotiate with terrorists, be they "so-called holy men or plain ordinary criminals."

"Hey, that's the stuff," Ned called sarcastically.

". . . interests of self-defense," the secretary was telling reporters, "we are maintaining a combat-ready presence in both the eastern Mediterranean and the upper reaches of the Indian Ocean. This is in line with—"

"Our well-known desire for peace!" Ned told him.

". . . ready to teach them another unforgettable lesson couched in the only terms terrorists understand, which—"

"Nukes!" Ned suggested. "The only good gook is a nuked gook."

"Ned, will you shut up?"

He turned to her. "Don't worry, Verne, he can't hear me."

"But the neighbors can. And I want to listen."

He folded his arms across his chest and stared balefully at the TV until the cabinet spokesman was replaced by a large elephant, lying tranquilized on its side as three veterinary dentists attempted to fill one of its molars.

"Bite 'em, Jumbo!"

"Ned."

"Why can't we have a computer input that lets us change what's happening on our TV screen?" Ned demanded. "What an idea! The elephant crunches off their right arms and walks away, chewing thoughtfully. The Secretary of Nukeration presses a panic button and we all blow up."

She stared hard at him for a long moment. "Elephants," she said at last, "are vegetarians."

"Laugh if you want, I'm onto something. Every few years the new wave of historians rewrites history. They change everything around. Why can't we do it *as it happens?* The ultimate computer game."

"The first thing I'd do is send you off to the booby hatch."

"No, no, no. This is not meant as an instrument of personal revenge. Besides, what did I ever do to deserve such a fate?"

She had sat down beside him on the small couch. Both of them were watching the television without actually taking it in. Some pickets were marching in front of a store or office bearing signs that could not be read. Police in British helmets began to batter them with truncheons. Three bobbies knocked one small man over and began kicking him. Someone in the background threw a brick that ripped off part of one bobby's face. The TV camera jiggled wildly. Then a series of cars were racing around a long oval track. Laverne gave up trying to follow the pictures.

"Ned," she began then, "how long are we posted to London? Another year?"

"Mm?"

"I said how long?"

"Two years to go. You bored with it already?"

He was holding the TV remote control in his hand. He gave a button a sharp jab with his thumb and the set went dark. Then he put it down on the couch between them. He looked at her in silence for a while.

"This is a plum assignment, you know."

"Better than Stateside?" she asked.

"Ah." He made a "that's what I thought" face. "You're singing your theme song again. Nowhere is as good as the good old U.S. of A. Despite the fact that you haven't lived in the States for—what is it?—a dozen years now? My information may not be much better than yours, but I know there have been a lot of changes back home, Laverne. Your family tells you everything's fine, but they're talking about a controlled environment, with their hand on the controls."

"Don't start that." She got up from the couch. "My family's got nothing to do with it."

She could remember her mother's voice, calm and loving, over the phone this morning. She could remember the girls' yips of excitement. She could remember all of them begging her to visit them soon. Perhaps that was the reason she hadn't told Ned about the phone call yet. Well, turnabout was fair play. He hadn't told her what he was up to, either.

"Hey," she said, "are we missing 'Treachery'?"

He glanced at his watch and snapped on the TV again. "Treachery" was one of the popular nighttime soap operas imported from America. Its ratings here were as high as back home. With its complex overlay of betrayals and meannesses, lies and sins, nasty deeds and nastier characters, it was taken as perfectly typical of life in the U.S., but only, of course, at its higher levels.

"You watch," he said.

"I thought you liked it too."

"Verne, I brought home the entire contents of my in basket. I had no time today to push papers around."

She nodded. On the screen one of the "Treachery" actresses, dressed in a gold slash that started just above her nipples and ended, in back, where her buttocks came together, had just slapped another actress who promptly lunged for her eyes, fingernails clawing.

"Now what?" Laverne asked, turning up the sound.

". . . two-timing little witch! I'll teach you."

"Verne?"

". . . think I don't know what you're doing behind my back!"

"Verne."

The two actresses were rolling on the floor, pulling hair and kicking each other viciously.

Ned got up, took his briefcase from the study desk, and went quietly into the kitchen.

". . . choke the life out of you, you rotten . . ."

He closed the door and sat down at the kitchen table.

Part 5

FRIDAY
JULY 2

19

When Laverne awoke, the sky outside their bedroom window was bright. The clock radio showed the time to be a quarter to nine. She extended her arm and felt to make sure Ned had left their bed. Instead, she found he was still asleep.

She patted his bare shoulder and, when this didn't waken him, began to stroke his back, pressing down hard like a masseuse. "Ned," she murmured. "It's nearly nine. Ned?" He came to slowly, unwillingly. "I sh'be'n' Goodge Street."

"Did I forget to tell you, I talked to the girls yesterday."

"Girls." He rolled over on his stomach. "How are they?"

"Lou Ann is fine, although that boy she was writing to has stopped writing. Gloria was at a movie. De Cartha just got finished with her summer makeup session, all A's. Sally . . . you remember she started menstruating late. She's still irregular. Drives her crazy once a month."

"Not an uncommon complaint."

"Yes, but most women have a different reason. I'm happy to say there's no chance at all of any of our girls being pregnant."

"Very few pregnancies in a prison camp." Ned levered himself up from the bed and stood naked beside it, rubbing his eyes.

"Is that what you call Camp Liberty?"

"That's what I call any place surrounded by high Cyclone fencing, razor wire, machine-gun emplacements, electronic surveillance, and Doberman attack dogs, with monitored telephone traffic, and schools, stores, churches, libraries, and other public services under the control of one body. If prison is too weak a term, what about concentration camp?"

"God, Ned. You're totally wrong!"

"If a stranger was running this prison, not your own father, you'd think twice about committing four young girls to that grisly life."

"They're having a ball."

"Are they? When school starts in the fall, I want them back here with us."

For a long moment she was silent. Then: "In this godforsaken place? A banana republic welfare state? You want your daughters to grow up on handouts, talking like characters in 'Upstairs, Downstairs'?"

"I don't want them to grow up in some cracked general's idea of a perfect fascist state."

"Hold it!" She was out of bed, squared off for battle. "You want them at the mercy of every mugger and rapist? Of every do-good, corrupt political faker? Living with people who haven't earned a living in their whole lives? Who don't know right from wrong? Or American from Russian? Is that your hope for them?"

He stared grimly, not at her but out the window at the morning sunlight. "You and your father are living in the nineteenth century, surrounded by Comanches. Your one idea is to pull the wagons into a circle and load the guns. But if you'd ever looked out there," he indicated the sunlight, "you'd see that life is not a Western movie. We're more than a century away from all that single-minded frontier right and wrong. If you don't understand the world now, or refuse to, it's going to drown you, Laverne, and our girls, too. You, I've given up on. But I'm not cutting those girls loose to sink or swim."

"Given up on *me?*" She swung back. Her breasts were surging up and down now with the ferocity of her breathing. Her face looked drawn and white. "Who would you ever find to take my place? Who could ever live with you and suffer your fits and moods?"

"I can always count on you to make my day." He stamped off and, a moment later, she could hear the shower going full force.

Laverne was left standing there, ready for a fight but deprived of it. Since she was raised with four brothers, a fight was nothing new to her. But Ned didn't work that way, did he? Hit and run was Colonel French's style.

She hadn't started this one, he had, flaring up that way about Camp

Liberty. So she was not about to feel contrite, nor run downstairs and make the colonel his breakfast nor any other penance, thank you. Perfect fascist state, indeed. All her poor father was trying to do was bring some order, some sense, into the permissive mess that was America today, everybody with *rights*, rights they hadn't earned and didn't deserve but if you dared tell them so you were a fascist or an elitist or . . .

Never mind. The future belonged to sanctuaries like Camp Liberty and the brave handful of other places like it. That was the future her girls would have.

The soppy, rights-for-all future Ned had been infected with from being too long outside America, that future was already dead. They'd tried it. They had two generations now of welfare families who'd never held a job. The world was full of commie failures, not just Russia, but Sweden and Italy and England. It didn't work. There was a natural order to life, leaders and followers. You only had to look at nature, at the animals, to see that. Rights-for-all was perverse, unnatural, doomed to failure. Why couldn't Ned see that?

She marched into the bathroom and caught him drying himself. "Why can't you see it, Ned? They've tried your idea of the future and it doesn't work. They've never tried my father's idea be—"

"What were Hitler and Mussolini and Franco and half the dictatorships in Latin America all about? Testing your saintly father's idea. He's not the first to discover the obscene delights of fascism. Let's hope he's the last."

"You . . . are . . . insane!"

She turned and strode off, then checked herself and turned back to the door of the bathroom. "And if you think I'm bringing up the girls in this pesthole of freeloading you're even more insane than I thought."

A few minutes later, fully dressed, he passed her on his way downstairs. "Where do you think you're going?"

"To work," he snapped. "Trying to keep my little part of things going. I'm sorry I criticized your dad, Verne. But he's a dinosaur and a dangerous one and I won't have my kids trampled by him the way you were."

"Nobody's trampling me!"

He was outside the front door. "Take it easy, Verne."

"Hit and run, is that it?"

He watched her in her light cotton dressing gown, tied at the waist but with the knot sliding loose, revealing her nakedness in the morning sunlight as she stood on the front steps. "Verne, the robe."

"I don't want to live in this two-bit excuse for a country!" she told

him. "I don't want my girls living a second-rate life among people who
don't know right from wrong."

"Verne, tie up your robe, please?"

"Oh, is that what bothers you?" She flung the robe open. Her breasts
seemed to explode in the sunlight like two magnificent grenades, shooting
brilliant bursts of brightness, pale ivories, hot pinks, rose-brown centers
of her broad areolas, the bitten-strawberry thrust of her nipples. "Give
me the wide open spaces!" she shouted. "Give me liberty, Ned! I hate
this place!"

He retreated down the steps and onto the sidewalk. In the back of his
mind he could recall that he'd planned to take the tube to Goodge Street.
Make sure old Burnside was presentable. Bring him to the chancery.
Now he hesitated, confused by Laverne in her present state of disarray.
He took a step toward her.

"Back off, Colonel," she said, pulling her robe together and knotting
the belt. "On your way. You're late now. Late for saving this corrupt
handout world they have over here. It's not worth saving, it's worth
sinking, but you just go ahead and waste your time on it, Colonel."

She turned, marched back into the house, and slammed the door
hard. He stood there, wondering what to do. Only Laverne could get
him this mixed up. Then, far away and muffled, as if originating in some
deep underground cave, he heard her empty five .38 rounds into the
target of the basement practice range. Her way of letting off steam? Was
it the only way she could find?

He wasn't used to being confused. Shaking his head, he walked toward
the tube station, the muted sound of her gun still echoing in his ears.
Then he glanced at his watch and realized he and Burnside would be
late. He then did something he never did. Standing on a corner of
Wellington Road, he hailed a taxi.

The first one to come along.

In the communications center off Curzon Street Larry Rand sat at
the desk he used on his visits here, next door to Henning's office. Late
yesterday he'd received what was called in Company parlance a Looney
Toons facsimile, a message enciphered in an old-fashioned one-time-use
code to which only Rand had the key.

The problem would have been simple for the normal desk jockeys
who held down station head posts in other places. But Larry Rand had
been a field man long enough to have developed contempt for codes,
fail-safe signals, all the so-called agentcraft developed by sedentary ass-

holes who'd be lost if they ever had to operate away from their beloved desks.

Looney Toons had been developed before World War II as a cheap but very reliable code system. Nowadays, with computers handling most cipher traffic, it was used mainly to save money. It offered excellent security at a hundredth the price of electronic systems. Looney Toons required that Rand find his one-time pad, try to recall the last time it had been used, and locate the proper new sheet. Normally an agent with a pad used the top sheet, then tore it up and got rid of it, leaving the next sheet ready for the next message. That was how it was worked at the Langley end of things. But since Larry Rand hated writing and preferred telephone, he could neither remember the last time he'd used his pad, nor which the new sheet was.

He sat at his desk, feet dangling off the floor, glowering at the encoded message and trying blind starts, using each sheet of his pad. Each produced gibberish as he substituted letters. He had been at it all last evening at home and had finally worked his way down to the seventh sheet when, finally, he got a break.

NOKNO.

He grimaced at this and kept going. NOKNOWNRECO. He scratched his head and kept at it.   NOKNOWNRECORDRIORDANSTOP-WEEMSONCONTRACTSTATIONHONOLULUSTOPINACTIVE-STATUS. Larry Rand sat back in his chair and put in penciled strokes to break the message into words. Once he did he remembered that Station Honolulu had been involved in an investment scam years before.

They had followed the policy, as many CIA stations did, of enlisting cooperation from businessmen and journalists, whose normal routine involved a lot of traveling and transfers of funds in and out of many areas. These contract men, not really members of the Company but more like civilian employees, would shift or launder illegal cash for the CIA, carry packages, handle payoffs and drugs to suborned politicians, anything that a Company agent would find too sensitive to do himself. In this, the contract men closely resembled the Mafia *cosce* of business people, politicians, and police affiliated to a particular family without being official members of it.

It had often been argued by eggheads high up in the Company that to the public at large there was no difference between a staff agent and one of these contract men. Some of them really got into the thick of things and ended up permanently on two payrolls, their own and the CIA's. This was especially true in places like Latin America or Southeast

Asia where local governments were corrupt or unstable and a contract man could produce results.

But for Station Honolulu there had been a bad result to one of these contracts. The man had scammed everybody, even his control at Station Honolulu. Everybody had invested in his genuine, guaranteed, foolproof mutual funds. Later, when one of his suckers sued him, the whole ball of wax came unraveled and Company people felt like a pack of fools, having trusted a con man with their own hard-earned personal savings —but they still stubbornly stonewalled any admission that they ran him. One CIA man had even invested his parents' savings. In court, tearfully, he'd described how convincing the con man had been. "I really believed him. I still do, almost."

Rand knew the feeling. You set up a contract and you gave the man what he needed to function: genuine fake passports and ID, unaccountable funds, classified information, clandestine contacts. In return he gave an illegal CIA action the cover of his own business name. And pretty soon, like Station Honolulu, you began to believe, like Dr. Frankenstein believed in Boris Karloff.

The Looney Toons fax didn't actually tie Weems to that particular Honolulu scam, but hinted at it. Hadn't that damned Ned French mentioned some investment fraud of some kind? And a dead man? Special Branch, Scotland Yard . . .

Another Honolulu, right here in Station London!

Larry Rand sat back aghast. He spent a full five minutes sorting out fact from fear. He would first have to make sure nobody here had been in contact with Weems or Riordan. If he could prove that, he could protect himself. But if he found that someone here had been working Weems, he'd have to switch to an alternate strategy. He'd have to find out who besides French knew of the Company connection. And he'd have to shut them up before protecting Weems.

Rattling down the ruts and potholes of Cherry Lane on his way into Amersham, Bazzard saw the body only an instant before he would have run over it. This was a single-lane road. By stopping, Bazzard closed it. So he hurriedly got out of his Land Rover and squatted by the body.

A young man, cut up badly, even his clothes in rags, nose broken, mouth bloody. Bazzard wondered whether he could be moved, then realized he might be dead. Rare thing in Amersham, corpses blocking country lanes. Bazzard tried to remember what one did, felt for a pulse? None. There was some trick with a mirror next to the mouth but he wasn't about to take a mirror off his Land Rover, was he? Throat. Right. No pulse. No, wait. Something? Hard to tell.

Bazzard's hands were a peculiar mixture of farm and town. He lived up the road and farmed a few hundred acres but, in order to afford it, he was a solicitor in town. Solicitors weren't supposed to know how to suss out signs of life, were they? Still . . . best to treat the poor chap as if he were alive.

At Amersham Hospital the receiving intern looked shocked at the extent of the wounds. He, too, found it difficult to get a pulse. "We're going to have to take him to Stoke Mandeville," he said. "They've got a proper intensive care unit there."

From bits of bark and leaves, Bazzard and the intern realized that the man had crawled to Cherry Lane from nearby Second Wood or the one above Shardeloes.

"Which is mad," the intern pointed out. "There is no way a dying man could do that unless . . ."

"Unless?" Bazzard asked.

"Well, I was about to say, you know," the intern gabbled. "Well, some sort of mission or urge or almost superhuman desire to . . . well, one isn't certain of course. But there seems to have been something the poor chap wanted to *do*, if I make myself clear, and in his case it was clearly mind over matter."

As he strapped the body into a canvas sling, the intern kept making *tk-tk* noises and shaking his head. "Superhuman effort," he muttered.

"I suppose I'd better stay with him," Bazzard suggested. "They'll want my statement anyway."

"Who?"

"The police," Bazzard explained. "You don't think he got that way falling into a cultivator, do you?"

The taxi let Ned French off in front of the One Tun pub on Goodge Street. At this hour, almost nine fifteen, it was closed. Asking the cab to wait, Ned bolted up the stairs and pounded on old Burnside's door. "It's me, French," he called. "Open up, soldier."

After a long time he heard shuffling and then the sound of locks being opened, one after another. Finally the door swung open. "Jesus Christ!" Ned exclaimed.

Ambrose Everett Burnside III had not only taken a shower somewhere—a nearby public bath, he later confessed—but had washed his hair and combed it wet so that now, barely dry, he had the sleek look of a lounge lizard out of the 1920s. He had shaved, which dropped ten years from his face, and he had put on a shirt and tie.

"Is it really you?"

"Watch your tongue, young man."

"I've got the cab waiting downstairs. Let's go."

"All in good time. I'm collecting my, uh, documents," the old man said with a certain touch of asperity. "My honorable discharge, my pension papers, my Social Security card, my passport, that sort of stuff."

"Not necessary. I'll vouch for you."

"And who'll vouch for you?" Burnside snapped.

By the time they reached Grosvenor Square the cab's meter had gone well over seven pounds and the time was a quarter to ten, but Ned felt sure Max Grieves would be waiting. Burnside looked greedily around him. "I never saw this place from a cab," he announced. "I always walk here. I can't afford a cab anyway. And anyway the sign wouldn't fit in a cab, would it? Naw. So, you see?"

Ned could see that his elderly father-substitute was bubbling over this morning. In a way, Ned thought as he ushered the old man past the lobby guards, it really didn't matter what he contributed to the Riordan case. The main thing was to show him he wasn't alone, even though he'd lost Vickie. He's still got us. Or, as his sign put it, US.

"She will need a doctor's care," Dr. Hakkad said. "Those wires have permanently—"

"She will only get your care, Doctor, yes? Surely you understand the rudiments of first aid?" The plump, bug-eyed man he thought of still as Aldo Sgroi watched him closely while his two associates continued to count fifty-pound notes packed in three Swissair flight bags.

The bank run had been quite successful. Mr. X was sure he had only skimmed the surface of what Pan-Eurasian Credit Trust could cough up. But time was running short and, after all, this whole scheme was something of a windfall anyway, extra seed money for the Fourth of July operation, which might take weeks to conclude properly, ransom capers being what they were, a war of nerves. He had counted on taking perhaps two or three hundred thousand from Hakkad and was, all things considered, pleasantly surprised to have gotten nearer half a million instead. More than enough to do without Elias Lateef.

"Bravo, Doctor. You will stand as sponsor for us. It's ironic, yes?"

"Please, Leilah's arms, her legs."

Mr. X turned to Nancy Lee Miller. "You understand what is to be done? Rub her to restore circulation, yes? Put something on the cuts, nothing too harsh or the scars will be permanent. Perhaps merely hydrogen peroxide, yes?"

Nancy Lee nodded. Her glance swung to Khefte. "Can he—?"

"No, he cannot," the man called Sgroi said. "I need this handsome young man by my side, yes?"

Nancy Lee threw a robe over the naked woman and helped her, stumbling, into a large bathroom off the bedroom corridor. Leilah was moaning softly in Arabic. Her brother's glance followed them until the bathroom door closed. Then he turned to Mr. X.

Quite an ordinary man, Hakkad saw. Undistinguished physically. Unhealthily plump with a complexion like the underside of a flounder and an unruly head of thick black steel wool, the industrial grade, coarse and scratchy. Surely of such unprepossessing material an international figure could not be made.

"It's called the bottom line, Hakkad," Mr. X said. Hakkad became uncomfortably aware that his thoughts had been read.

"It's called a track record, quite like a Thoroughbred horse, yes? Those with whom I deal have heard of me. They choose me because I have a record of success. My intelligence network is superb, unique. I locate opportunities where no one else can, yes? Thus the bottom line is profitable. I make sure of that."

These were precisely the sort of things Hakkad knew his own investors felt about him, but he was not in a position at the moment to point this out to his upstart rival. The two young men with automatics had counted the cash twice now. One collected all three Swissair flight bags and left, handing his automatic with its long silencer to the other young man on his way out of the penthouse apartment.

"You place a great deal of trust in your people," Hakkad sighed.

"He will be in Geneva by three o'clock, with half an hour before the banks close, yes?"

The telephone rang. No one moved for three more of the double rings. Then the young man with the two silenced pistols picked it up. "Hello?" He nodded. He nodded again. "Good-bye."

His boss eyed him. "They have collected all the weapons from the lockup? Then proceed."

The young man nodded solemnly. He leveled one of the automatics at Khefte. Its heavy-duty silencer was as long as its barrel. Using it as a prod, he guided the young Arab into a cloakroom off the entrance hall.

The man called Sgroi raised his woolly eyebrows twice at Hakkad.

The two of them waited only a moment before they heard, through the closed door of the cloakroom, the two vivid coughs that even a heavily silenced automatic makes.

"Khefte I needed only for two things. Access to you and access to your cache of arms. I have them both, yes? Exit Khefte."

"But there are so many more things I can offer you," Hakkad suggested rather smoothly, considering the state of his emotions. "In Pan-Eurasian Credit Trust you are dealing with an entity of considerable mass, my good . . . Dear me, it is difficult not knowing your true name, sir."

"Yes? Truly?"

"If we are to negotiate, it would be most helpful to call you by your name, good sir."

"Very well." The unhealthy-looking man scratched vigorously at his matted tangle of tight curls. "Very well. You can call me, ah, Fownes. An English name. Yes?"

20

⚔◆⚔

"Okay. No lunchtime appointments? Right. Lock the door. Spread out the maps and charts. Loosen your tie, Moe. This is the big one. One of our last chances to find what we forgot, improve what we neglected, come up with some new and startling flashes, all that stuff. Okay, team?"

Chamoun sighed. "What's got into you this morning?"

Ned sat back in his chair and surveyed his assistant across a mulch of loose papers, lists, reports, photos, wiring charts, and position maps. "Just the fact that Friday is only one day away from Sunday. You don't even need to be paranoid to have a premonition."

Chamoun turned on a clown's grin and began shuffling a packet of three-by-five note cards. "I have here an ordinary deck," he began, "such as you might buy at any drugstore."

Ned took the cards out of his hand and placed them, like a deck, on the desk face down. "All week," he said, "we've been kicking around ideas, some good, some bad. Some old and obvious, some slick and tricky. I assume they're what's on those cards?"

"Glad you asked," Chamoun responded in a pitchman's voice. He spread the deck like a fan. "Pick a card, any card."

"Moe, the minute we finish this session, I want you to recast all our ideas as a timed sequence. Step by step. Like a checklist for a complicated piece of machinery just out of its carton. Got it? Then we'll go over the draft checklist to make sure nothing's been lost or put in a place where it shouldn't be. By noon I want to lock it up, Moe. I mean literally, too. One copy in your safe, one in mine."

He picked up the deck of notecards, split them into two decks, and fanned their corners together, casino-style, to shuffle them. Then he shoved them back across the desk to Chamoun. Their eyes met. Ned felt the need to say more, utter cautions, repeat advice, emphasize the absolutely primary importance of getting the sequence right. Hell, he thought, Moe knows all that. Moe is like a second me, he told himself. Words were almost unnecessary.

The thought seemed suddenly to rob him of words. This morning's scene with Laverne, and the raw power of the insight he had felt in the dark corners of her American soul, had shaken him deeply. He glanced up to find himself staring into those ripe-olive eyes that let you in but didn't give you any clues as to depth. "Moe," he said then, "when was the last time you were back home?"

"Christmas."

"Sandusky put on a big parade for its homecoming hero?"

"Naturally. They hung colored lights on all the main streets. Fake snow in the store windows. People put up evergreen trees in my honor. Didn't you know that?"

"Evergreens in your honor?"

"You never heard of the cedars of Lebanon?"

"How'd they look to you back home? I mean, you've been stationed overseas for, what, four years? How were the contrasts?"

Chamoun shrugged. His normally expressionless face took on a slight look of pain. "It's the same story every home leave. Pop wants me to resign my commission and come back into the business. It used to be that he didn't even want me to show up in my uniform he was so ashamed. But things have changed in Sandusky. He sort of likes to show me off in a my class-A's."

"I know." Ned pushed the papers aside and lifted his feet to his crowded desk. "They hate us or they love us. It's a pendulum." He stared at the burnished tips of his black loafers. "The whole country's on a swing now. You can feel the change in attitude. They're starting to put up barriers again."

"We always have barriers. Two oceans? We'll always be isolated."

"Yeah, there's that. Isolationism. It's a grand old American creed. Let Europe stew in its own juice. Let the Third World rot. We have the grain, the steel, the beef, the fuel if we're careful. Who needs the world?"

"That's Sandusky," Moe Chamoun agreed. "Is it like that in Fond du Lac?"

"And Chicago and New Orleans and Denver and . . ." He groaned softly. "Is this getting our work done? Protecting Winfield?"

"Let me start with what I didn't tell them yesterday at the ten-o'clock." He fanned through his card file. "First of all, I got permission from the Signals guys to set up that covert TV surveillance system of theirs at the two gates. There's a remote on all the cameras that leads to a van with computer terminals that can access almost any photo file in the world, ours, Special Branch's, Interpol, you name it. Within seconds we can ID any doubtful arrival." He put the card down and picked up another.

"I'm thrilled. Go on."

"Snipers on the rooftops of Winfield House."

"Mixed blessing. More?"

"I've got a dozen of our own enlisted men on electronic sweeps of the grounds around Winfield every fifteen minutes. They're divided in squads. At any given moment one squad will be out there, day and night, with night binocs, proximity sensors, parabolics, the works. Yeah, mine-detection equipment, too."

"Dogs?"

"No dogs. They start sweeping at sundown Saturday and don't quit till the last guest goes home Sunday."

"Why no dogs?"

"Ned, what do we program the dogs to look for? Shove a turban under their noses? Dogs won't work." He picked up another card.

"You're right. Go on."

"Outside the perimeter fencing we've got those bobbies you promoted for us. I've got infantry volunteers in civilian dress, just ordinary Joes out for a Sunday walk. They'll be mingling beyond the fence with whatever normal strollers there are."

"Armed?"

"Couldn't get permits for concealed firearms. They've got whatever they've got: lengths of pipe, knucks. They volunteered because a lot of them have hand-to-hand training. Karate. I don't want to know."

"Yes, go on."

"That's about it. The special passes are being printed tomorrow afternoon on an Army multilith in Woking. We'll deliver them Sunday midmorning." He shoved the deck of cards to one side.

"More?"

"You tell me, Ned."

He swung his feet off the desk and sat up straight. "We're not fully gripped to this, Moe. Literally. We're at arm's length. It's in the nature of this that we can't show our hand or we spoil the party. But I don't like the distances between us and possible trouble."

"Don't you like my civilian infantry sluggers?"

He laughed. "I'd like 'em better inside the perimeter fence, but that can't be helped. No . . ." He thought. "You've got a surveillance van there for the entrance TV?"

"I know what you're thinking. It's not very big, though."

"But what about the 'Lamb to Slaughter' crew? Haven't they got vans?"

"Just two. They're only using minicams, each with an operator and a sound man."

"But when you walk down a street and see BBC or one of the in-dependents doing a remote from inside some place, you see vans, big mothers, vans galore. Nobody complains because there are those two lovely letters on each van, a T and a V."

"You want a big TV van?"

"I want two vans. Empty inside except for twenty guys with twenty Armalites. It's the old Trojan Horse ploy."

"Jesus, Ned, forty GIs sweating it out inside? We'll have a mutiny on our hands."

"Air-condition the vans."

"You're serious."

"I'm serious. Station the vans here"—his finger stabbed the map—"or here. We've got the place surrounded now and not from half a mile away, but more like fifty feet. Anybody starts anything, the air is thick with GIs." He watched Chamoun make a note on a new card.

Chamoun let out a chortle of glee. "I think you've got it."

Ned nodded but said nothing. An image came back to him: Laverne naked on their front doorstep for all the world to see. He blinked. What things were boiling up in them? Between them? Why did everything arrive together, never separately but heaped one thing on top of another with a cruel, indiscriminate carelessness?

"Laverne."

Chamoun looked up at him and, when he didn't go on, looked down at his cards again, saying nothing. "None of this is real to her," Ned heard himself saying. He loathed people who unburdened their private lives on others. It was such a cheap bid for sympathy, such an insincere form of flattery, as if any advice anyone could give you had any validity at all.

"Europe isn't real to her. It's just a collection of banana republics. It's a theme park by Disney. The people are corrupt and on the dole and don't know right from wrong or America from Russia and besides they speak funny."

Chamoun looked up again. "And, anyway, we don't need them. We're the big time and they're midgets."

Ned smiled, relieved that Chamoun took it as a political instead of a personal conversation. "Have you been talking to her?"

"No, my brother-in-law in Sandusky."

"Americans really feel that way?"

"Come on, Ned. When I tell them I work in an American embassy they ask me 'What the hell do we need embassies for?' They think it's just some stupid way to waste taxpayers' money. They want to know why we have to be represented to a bunch of third-rate, tin-pot fakers. The real world's right here in Sandusky. I mean Fond du Lac."

"Yeah. Didn't our forefathers escape from Europe? What do we owe them any more? Loafers. Welfare families."

Both men fell silent for a while. They turned in tandem to look out the window at the lunchtime scene, people eating sandwiches on benches or strolling two by two.

"Isn't that . . . ?"

"Yeah," Ned replied. "Ambrose Everett Burnside III. He's got quite a spring in his step."

"What's the story?"

"After Sunday I'll fill you in. Right now I'm bothered. It's my usual foreboding, like a girl having her period. Indulge me."

"Two Trojan horses of GIs hidden in reserve? Stop worrying."

"It's not enough. We're missing something."

Silence reigned again. Slowly their glances turned back to the mess on the desk. Ned fished out a stapled sheaf of paper. "Here's the staff list," he said. "In addition to the normal compliment for Winthrop, we've got twelve musicians, twenty waiters, ten chefs, ten busboys, six bartenders . . ." He stopped himself. "Who hired them? Who vetted them?"

"It's a catering outfit the embassy has used for years, Hodgkins and Daughter."

"Who vets this bunch? We're looking at nearly sixty people, most of them men."

Chamoun picked up Ned's telephone and tapped out a number. "We'll let Harry Ortega tell us," he whispered. "Harry? Chamoun at chancery. Does Hodgkins and Daughter submit a personnel list to us for clearance?"

Ned punched up the same line on his other phone and picked it up in time to hear Ortega say ". . . of them are regulars, Moe. Familiar faces. We see them ten, twenty times a year."

"All sixty of them?"

"Off and on, probably."

"And that's the clearance procedure?"

"More or less."

Chamoun hung up in the middle of Ortega asking: ". . . you got any complaints, please don't—"

The two intelligence officers stared at each other. "Never a dull moment in the service of Uncle Sam," Ned intoned. "And it nearly got past us."

"Check them as they arrive. It'd be a good way to test that TV surveillance system, interfaced with the computer files."

"Moe, listen. Let me spin a scenario."

"Lights. Camera."

"What does your average catering worker look like? I mean he's either Filipino or Turkish or Cypriot or . . . you get the idea?"

"Looks something like me."

"But what does your everyday neighborhood Arab terrorist look like?"

"Like me, but nowhere near as handsome."

"See the problem?"

"Tell me, Ned, what does your normal friendly IRA bomber look like? Or your down-home good old Red Brigade kneecapper? Or the boy next door who belongs to the Rote Armee Faktion?"

Silence dropped down over them once again. Ned shifted in his chair but said nothing. Chamoun began shuffling the papers into some semblance of order, but also kept silent. Time passed.

"Okay," Ned announced. "No more premonition. I've exorcized it."

"Just take two aspirin and let me know if it crops up again."

"Hodgkins and Daughter are going to be hopping mad. But we have at our disposal the greatest employment agency in the world, handling musicians and cooks and bartenders and brain surgeons and you name it. We call it the United States Army, soldier."

"And?"

"And that's who's supplying sixty caterers on Sunday!"

                    *   *   *

The Scot with whom P. J. R. Parkins often spoke on a secure telephone line turned out to be as large a man as Parkins himself.

The two of them went back a long time in Her Majesty's service, the one in MI5, a secret service which spied on domestic affairs but whose very existence was denied, and the Special Branch, a police facility openly acknowledged. In practice there was so much confidential traffic between the two services, and so much interchangeable staff, that the average Briton who knew of both would be hard put to separate the responsibility of one from that of the other.

On the inside, where Parkins and the man he called Jock obviously stood, the basic difference between the two services was as clear as glass: Special Branch had to account for some of its funds; MI5, since it didn't exist, could spend all it wanted without fear of accountability.

The same was true, of course, of the equally nonexistent MI6, which looked after affairs outside Britain. Its relationship to MI5 was analogous to the CIA's relationship to the FBI in America, with just as little love between them. It was a matter of funding. There were only so many dollars, or pounds, the taxpayers of each nation could be bludgeoned into providing for covert services.

Sitting across from each other in Jock's small wood-paneled office with its bow window looking out over a tiny mews in Mayfair, the two men seemed not rivals but colleagues of long standing. Parkins had served in the army during the Suez troubles in '56 as a training officer in Cairo while Jock had been with the embassy there. They had first met in Teheran when Western powers were busy toppling the Mossadegh regime at the request of the oil companies and putting the Shah on the Peacock Throne. Both had kept a secret eye on EEC bureaucracies in Brussels and Strasbourg and both had supervised various covert activities in Cyprus and, earlier, in Greece.

Between them there existed nothing as warm as a friendship. They hadn't the vaguest idea of each other's private lives except, perhaps, that Parkins was single and Jock was, by now, a grandfather several times over. But from long rubbing against each other they had developed a shared background of common experience, some of it quite bitter, and a general get-on-with-it attitude that differed a lot from the younger officers in their services, who tended to be political.

". . . some point in pulling him in," Jock was saying. "After all, Riordan's tellyphone record shows he called th' Weems bugger four times."

Parkins scribbled something in a small cop's notebook. "We'll look after that, Jock, never fear. What bothers me is that we're not yet to the bottom of the Yanks' involvement in this at their embassy level. I take it French is still lying to me, although nothing he won't cough later, once he's through his Sunday problem."

"That's forever the trouble with the Yanks," Jock responded testily. He had a normally reddish complexion. Now his considerable expanse of freckles seemed to stand out in sharp relief as his skin grew more inflamed. "There's always fifty-three cards in their decks. Didna we find them snooping around British companies looking for socialists?"

"Ah, well." Parkins gestured softly. "We've pulled that one ourselves, often enough, Jock. Goes down well at budget time when you have to tell a bunch of MPs what you spent money on. It's the same for the Yanks. If they didn't sweep Reds out from under their beds regularly God only knows how many men they'd have to let go."

Both men fell silent for a while. The Scot's small office seemed to have been adapted from the front parlor of a flat, with its wood paneling and its broad views of the quiet street below, a place for contemplation. Jock sighed luxuriously. "T'will all come out," he said in an almost smug tone. "We'll learn the Yanks' game, never fear." He yawned as he glanced out at the road.

Past the bow window two very attractive women moved briskly along the cobbled mews toward a posh eating place that lay beyond the MI5 office. "Will you look at that?" Jock asked. "Th' way th' cobbles cause th' hips t' waggle?"

"It's the high heels, Jock."

"Aye, leave it to a bachelor t' spot th' reason."

Both men watched in silence for a while. Then Parkins spoke up: "Do you find as you grow older that women of that age get more and more attractive? I mean they've both seen forty, Jock, but I'm damned if I'd say no to either."

The Scot's glance swung back to consider Parkins as a candidate for middle-aged randiness. The gaze was unswerving, unblinking, and gave away nothing of what Jock was thinking about a fifty-year-old bachelor who still lived with his mother. Instead he nodded very sagely. "We're finished here, surely," he said. "Go get 'em, Peter."

Parkins laughed in an embarrassed way. "I'm due back at the embassy to try and pump the whole lot of them. There's something they're hiding, but I'll lay hands on it soon enough."

"Lay hands on th' Weems bugger, too, laddie."

                    *   *   *

Nancy Lee Miller came to the door of the bedroom and addressed herself to Dr. Mahmet Hakkad. "She's, like, resting now. I think she'll be okay. She wants to talk to you."

Hakkad was on his feet, but turned to the plump man. "Mr. Fownes?" he began, trying out the new name. "May I?"

"Certainly, Dr. Hakkad."

The self-styled Fownes, with his protuberant eyes, watched him go into the bedroom. He waited a moment, then moved to the cloakroom off the entrance hall. He murmured softly: "It is I. Open up."

The door opened and the blond young man with the silenced automatic stood at attention. This was not easy to do in the small room because beyond him Khefte stood, unharmed. Two bullet holes defaced the tiled wall behind him.

"That was well done," the man called Fownes told his lieutenant. "Take Khefte down to the floor below, yes? You can put away your weapon. Khefte is one of us."

"Unlike Dr. Hakkad," Khefte complained. "He would sell his own father for the hairs in his beard."

"He was about to sell you to this Lateef person."

"When I tell my men of Hakkad's treachery, they will be hard to control. They will want his blood."

The man now called Fownes smiled softly. He had a very engaging smile despite his protuberant eyes. "Leave Hakkad to my men, yes?" he said. "I have plans for him, even after Sunday. In fact, especially after Sunday."

"Then the attack *will* be made?"

"Did you ever doubt it, my hawk?" Fownes gave him a very Italianate pat on the cheek. "Speak with your warriors. You," he focused on his blond lieutenant, "show them the plans of the mosque, yes?"

Khefte frowned. "Mosque?"

"The Great London Mosque, yes? It is barely across the road from Winfield House. But who am I to tell you these things when you have already so thoroughly laid your plans?"

Mindful that it had been Bert who'd laid the plans, Khefte could only nod wisely. "Why do we need a plan of the Great Mosque?"

"It is from there," Fownes explained, "that the assault will begin. Symbolic, yes? To show the world the power of Islam. Think of it as a battle cry, yes? As the lion roars before he throws himself upon his foe. Yes?"

Khefte was silent for a while, thinking. Then his eyes lit up from within with that peculiar sheen that Bert had often noticed. "A symbol!"

he enthused. "A symbol for all the world to see! Yes! The Lion! Oh, yes!"

Laverne was not used to being crazy. She thought of herself as an essentially calm, low-pressure person. How could you raise four kids and not keep your cool? She was used to everything around her going wrong, but when it got inside her and upset her equilibrium, she was venturing into new and hostile territory.

Out of the blue, she thought. Ned just wakes up, lobs a grenade at me, and runs off.

How was she to know that Ned hated her father that much? Sure, he'd poked fun at Camp Liberty. A lot of people did. Her mother would sometimes send her clippings from the papers in the States and there would be cartoons satirizing Camp Liberty and General Krikowski. But that was to be expected. It was just part of the pinko-liberal press campaign in the States. The liberals' days were numbered anyway so why get upset? But when one of them was your own husband and he was charged with protecting his nation's security, what then? The enemy within, Laverne thought.

So what did a good American do, when faced with that problem? Turn in her husband? The father of her children? First she had to solve it as a wife, then as an American. None of it would be easy, not when, deep inside, she was going crazy.

She'd never before had the symptoms so obviously. First there was a kind of inner rage that spoiled her aim at the target range. She'd let off five rounds and not one of them had connected with the bull's-eye. She, with her medals for sharpshooting. Because you didn't win medals when inside you were trembling.

It was a sign of craziness. It was a sign of loneliness. It was a sign of anger that you were married to someone who had lost his way and would drag you down with him. It was a sign of despair, of fear that there was no way to make it come out right.

She wished she had someone to talk to about it. Ned sneered at unbuttoning your troubles to a friend, but that was his damned pride in his own intelligence. She'd only rarely had a confidante, which was not surprising the way the army moved them around from base to base. And when she did have a next-door neighbor or another woman to confide in, the traffic usually went the other way.

That was the trouble with being General Krikowski's only daughter. You gave off an air of infallibility. Toughness. Efficiency. You had a stance that told the world: This is some stainless-steel cookie who can handle anything life throws at her. Which showed how wrong the world could be.

Usually her confidantes unburdened themselves to Laverne, not the other way around. Well, hold it, she thought. Hold it. When was I ever in the bind I'm in now? What would I have had to confide to somebody?

There was a chaplain in London, in fact the army had quite a few in the area that people could go to for counseling. But this was not something you told a man. And, anyway, she'd have to pick a Catholic chaplain, wouldn't she? And a fat lot of good he'd be.

Somewhere in this big rotten-from-inside city there had to be what amounted to a woman chaplain or marriage advisor or whatever. There had to be a woman who, for money if need be, would listen and give advice. After all, Laverne didn't have to take the advice, so what could she lose except the money?

Only one trouble. How did you find such a woman?

Who could she ask? Laverne wondered. Who did she know who could keep her mouth shut about it and still have the resources to come up with a few good names? There was a WAC detachment north of London, but she didn't know a soul there and, anyway, a WAC detachment was like a nunnery. Secrets became public property inside of ten seconds.

Outside the kitchen, a small blackbird with an orange beak erupted in song, an endless ripple of music. Laverne waved at him. "Hello, blackbird."

She fixed herself a cup of coffee and sat down in the kitchen to run through her address book. No help there. Most of the people were back in the States. She knew almost no one overseas and, certainly, no one here in London. The blackbird trilled and chirped.

She sat staring at the little pots of herbs she was keeping for Lou Ann. Inside the tremor seemed to mount slightly in fervor. The caffeine was doing that, Laverne told herself. Then she put her head in her hands and wept silently for a long time.

The man who now called himself Fownes felt that, at least for the moment, all his plans were going well. He considered the idea Hakkad had presented him while he smoked a cigarette of grand dimensions, very thin and very long, made for him by a tobacconist in Monte Carlo, where he kept his headquarters. He liked everyone to think he was based in Geneva, but only his money was there.

To kill Hakkad and the women. Or to become his partner.

For what Hakkad had offered him was half of Pan-Eurasian Credit Trust. This was no minor concession. Overnight he would become one of the richest men in Europe or the Middle East. He would have the solid, prestigious name of Pan-Eurasian behind him and the benefit of its—largely imaginary—impeccable reputation. In banking, impeccability meant only that a bank had not yet been caught in a crime or conspicuous mistake. But time would change that. Meanwhile, he could milk what goodness was left in Hakkad's cow.

He tapped cigarette ash over the railing and onto the sidewalk below. There was more mileage to be gotten out of the American woman and the sister, he reminded himself. One was a key to Khefte, the other to Hakkad. So, all of them lived a while longer.

Khefte, only until Sunday afternoon. He was even now exhorting his brethren on the floor below—and there were nearly fifty of them—to the new and more glorious Islamic symbolism devised for Sunday. Imagine, a full commando of dedicated Arab warriors consecrating their jihad in the great mosque before marching on Winfield with a lion's roar.

Fownes's small smile came and went, hardly disturbing the slender cigarette in his mouth. Dear Khefte. Without his easy treacheries where would this project be now? On Sunday the traitor would learn the military value of the feint. Minutes before his freedom fighters occupied the Great Mosque, a telephone call would alert the police.

The pleasant smile stayed put for a moment. The eyes seemed to protrude less violently. Once Khefte's diversion had attracted the full attention of the Winfield security forces, the real cadre would strike.

By the time the gunfire had died down and hostages were secured in the Winfield basement and the Americans realized how they had been tricked, it would all be too late for them. The rest would be negotiation, slow, agonizing, and filled with the casual brutalities of the kidnap principle, severed ears, agonized pleas, calculated rapes, highly selective murders . . . the usual.

Until he played his unwitting role as decoy, then, Khefte and his American woman would have to be let run free. As security, Hakkad and his sister would remain under guard. A nice balance of forces. There was plenty of time to deal with Hakkad later.

He drew in another lungful of smoke and offhandedly flicked the cigarette itself in a wide arc out into the streets and sidewalks of London. As a gauntlet thrown down, it was a superb gesture.

*   *   *

The meeting in Royce's office was brief, barely ten minutes, during which Max Grieves and Ned French told the deputy ambassador what they knew about Riordan, Weems, and company, while Jane Weil added her story of CIA protection and Royce produced a really thrilling scowl.

Grim it was, without being in any way deformed by anger or hatred. It consisted partly of a firming up of that great chin, a tightening of those chiseled lips, and the introduction of two vertical lines between his clear, wide-set eyes, lines that bit gently into the well-cared-for skin without threatening to produce a new set of wrinkles there.

"Amazing, isn't it?" he asked no one in particular, "the way we can be sitting here, tending to business, keeping an eye on things and helping them along and all of a sudden, out of the sweet blue sky, somebody casually chucks a monkeywrench into things. This Weems. The story's not complete without H.E.'s contribution."

He quickly reviewed the hunting-weekend blackmail ploy. "You see why I'm upset," Royce went on in his least upset tones. "This Weems is virtually all over the map and out of control. He isn't one of the Russkis' menaces. He's one of ours."

"Special Branch may pick him up," Ned observed. "If so, this can blow into headlines overnight."

"Can we delay that till after Sunday?"

"Let me talk to my favorite secret agent."

Connell's face reflected his displeasure at being reminded that he was harboring a Special Branch spy in the midst of the chancery. "Better yet," he said, "why don't I have a chat with a few pals at FO.?"

"But why," Jane asked, "should the Foreign Office take responsibility?"

"Because I have no pals in the Home Office," Royce confessed with a charming smile. "Do you?"

"Nothing special."

"Can you try it?"

She nodded. "But don't get up your hopes." Her glance moved sideways to Ned. "I think your two-faced Mr. Parkins is the key to this."

"Right." Connell's glance swept around the room. "Anything else? Then that's it." He stood up. His eyes followed Ned and Jane as they left his office together, but he drew no conclusion from this. Instead he found himself worrying about a call he'd had this morning from Mrs. F. She was expecting them to monitor and censor Gillian Lamb's footage.

Knowing Gillian, Royce realized he was, to employ an American phrase of his youth, between a rock and a hard place.

Ned walked with Jane to the door of her office, but remained out of sight of her secretary, that lady having had more than enough opportunities to see the two of them together. "This work," Ned complained.

"What work?"

"This stuff they pay us to do," he explained. "It sure gets in the way of a fellow's love life."

She broke into a charmed smile, touched his cheek, and then, without saying anything else, disappeared inside her office. He left for his.

"Miss Weil?" her secretary called as she went past.

Jane sat down at her desk before replying. "Yes, Amanda?"

"This person has called twice already. I'm holding the call on line four. Do you want to take it?"

"Who is it?"

"It's Mrs. French."

21

"Dris, Khefte baby, I just don't get it. The central mosque? It's, like, too far out."

Nancy Lee Miller was window-shopping with Khefte. Since she had come to Number 12 with just the clothes she was wearing, she stood in need of a few basic purchases. With six of Pan-Eurasian Credit Trust's fifty-pound bills in his pocket, courtesy of the man he now called Fownes, Khefte was in a mood to buy her the moon. Something Fownes had counted on when he'd released him.

"What is confusing?" he asked. They were looking in windows along Oxford Street and he had to raise his voice against the noise.

"The names for one thing. I mean, like you're not Dris, you're Khefte? And, like this Mister Big is now calling himself Fownes? It's crazy. I'm not supposed to tell Hakkad or Leilah you're alive because they think you're dead and they're next? But we're free to go shopping? It's wild."

He pointed to a set of lingerie in sheer black lace. Neither of them was old enough to remember when that kind of waist-cinching intimate wear, with its garter belts and push-up bra cups, was considered the ultimate in Viennese boudoir sexiness. But, for some reason, it still carried a kind of transcultural shock value that excited something deep in Khefte. "Let us buy one of those for you."

Nancy Lee wrinkled her nose. "How do you like your new boss, Fownes?"

Khefte's handsome face darkened slightly. "I have no boss. I am my own master." The traffic noise was deafening.

"That's cool, Dris. So this mosque thing you were planning, it's still like *on?*"

"On? It was never off."

"Terrific. Where are we? South Molton Street? Look, no cars. It's like a walking street." She led him, not directly, but rather quickly, to the boutique called Bricktop and spent several minutes praising the contents of its windows.

Inside, one of the sales girls began to listen to Nancy Lee's requests, some briefs, tights, and she did need either a dress or some skirts and blouses.

"I have a brand new shipment," the owner cut in.

Khefte had grown bored with the proceedings by now and was staring out the window at the passing throng. Bricktop, looking grim, gathered a few articles of clothing at random, dismissed the sales girl with a brisk sweep of her glance. "Would you like to try these on, miss?" she asked Nancy Lee.

"Yes. Won't be a sec, Dris."

He turned in time to see Nancy Lee tag along behind an extremely fat woman with orange hair. Khefte couldn't see her face. After a moment he forgot all about her. He had spotted a men's shoe store across the street. That would be their next stop. For too long he had, under Bert's political guidance, led a monastic life. He would give the girl her heart's desire and then he would buy himself a pair of those snakeskin shoes he could see across the street.

Inside the changing booth, Bricktop kept her voice very low but there was no mistaking the anger in it. "This was completely irresponsible, Nancy. I expect better judgment. Nobody comes here. Especially with the goddamned PLO in tow."

"It was the only way, believe me." She sounded contrite enough. "You don't know what I've been through, Brickie. I had to get to you because I know exactly what they're up to. I even know where."

The fat woman stripped off all of Nancy Lee's clothing. "Look at this," she said, pointing to love bites all over the girl's buttocks. "He really digs ass, huh?"

"Every way. Let's try that orange thingie."

"Never mind, it'll fit. Poor baby." She began kissing Nancy Lee's neck. "The things women have to put up with. What was so important you had to break security?"

"It's the central mosque."

Bricktop was licking her ear. "What?"

"He and his people are going to occupy the mosque on Sunday at exactly one P.M."

"For God's sake why?"

"It's the time of one of their midday prayers. They'll all enter, face Mecca, kneel, and, when the prayer's over, take command of the mosque."

The fat woman took a step back from Nancy Lee and broke contact with her body. "You're sure?"

"After that they'll attack Winfield." She sounded authoritative. "Brickie, you remember that way you showed me?"

"The raccoon?"

"The raccoon! Please?"

"The raccoon uses his paws and his tongue," Bricktop said. "This booth is too damned small," she added as she sank to her knees.

"Royce, I am a bit surprised at this." Gillian's voice sounded cool over the phone.

"It pains me more than it does you," Royce assured her. He sat at his desk, looking absolutely unruffled, only his voice carrying angst. "And rather than break it to you at the party this evening, I felt I had to give you some kind of early warning."

"My agreement is with you, Royce, not with Mrs. Fulmer."

"Precisely why I'm doing the talking. And, mind you, I'm only suggesting in my masterfully diplomatic way, that perhaps you don't do your program any good showing—"

"Oh, dear," Gillian cut in. "Whenever someone wants to censor me it's always for my own good."

"I am not for a moment trying to cens—"

"Has Mrs. Fulmer ever tried this with an American TV program?"

"No idea." Royce's tone had become slightly edgy. It bored him to tears to pull chestnuts out of the fire for ambassadors with no diplomatic training. He seemed to have spent his whole life doing little else, with nothing more to show for it than a magnificent wardrobe and a flat bank balance.

"And what's more," Gillian was saying, "I've seen the tapes and your precious ambassador doesn't come off half badly. He knows when to say nothing, and when to say he doesn't know. For a public figure, that's nine-tenths of the battle."

"Somehow Mrs. F. got the idea you were making a fool of him, or so she led me to believe in, um, almost exactly those words."

There was a long pause at Gillian's end of the line. "Royce, are you as uncomfortable about this as I am?" she asked at last. "Is this the price we have to pay because we're trying for a personal note amidst a roar of background noise?"

Royce's face went totally blank, as it usually did when Gillian seemed headed for a personal conversation. "My dear, you know I adore you. I don't exactly adore Mrs. F., but it's my job and let this be engraved on tablets of stone: Connell does his job."

"Why, Royce, that happens to be the *Lamb* family motto."

"Think about it, will you? See if there isn't an inch of tape here and an inch there that you can snip off and I can let Mrs. F. hang on her belt like a scalp."

"Will I see you tonight?"

"What time am I expected?"

"It's more of an open house drinks party than anything else. The Beeb's unveiling these new studios in Hammersmith and every possible personality they can muster will be there. So long as you arrive by seven you're guaranteed at least a head shot in the promo they're running later tonight."

"No head shots for me, my dear."

"With a face like yours you can't avoid it. I'll be between the entrance and the cameras. Look for me first."

"Is it likely to run on very long?"

"We don't guarantee the kind of world-class celebs Mrs. Fulmer is billboarding for Sunday. But I just wanted you to see what stars we Brits can muster at short notice. Should be out of there by eight and into a dry martini at my place by eight thirty."

This was the first Royce had heard that they had a date after the open house. He began to realize that this telephone call had merged several different requests into a network of interlocking favors. If he wanted Gillian to make token cuts that mollified Pandora Fulmer, how could he refuse a drink at her apartment?

"Lovely," he said, not a quaver audible in his voice. "Remember our family motto."

*   *   *

Between five and five thirty, as she cleared up what was left in her
in basket, Jane Weil kept asking herself the same question: Should she
tell Ned that she was meeting Laverne for a drink? What if he suddenly
appeared at her office door, as he sometimes did? How could she not
tell him?

It occurred to Jane that over the past year she had talked to Laverne
perhaps a dozen times, nearly always at quasi-official social gatherings.
She knew little about her except what Ned had let drop. But she rather
liked the woman, even though it was impossible to talk politics with her.
That, of course, was true of most of the embassy people, as if politics
were in the same category syphilis had been in at the turn of the century,
a social taboo one didn't discuss in front of the ladies.

Even the embassy's political officers, people like Anspacher for instance, refrained from talking politics. In their case they relied on the
impossibility of discussing such an arcane and abstruse subject with a
mere layperson. But in Laverne's case, it was simply that she and Jane
differed on so many points there was no place to make a start since the
only ending possible was a painful one.

Laverne seemed to have sensed this early in the game, which was
why, when they met, they painstakingly selected subjects far from politics.
Jane had heard about Laverne's children (Ned's children!) often enough,
and about her brothers who had all neatly escaped the army as a career
and were getting fat on government defense contracts for their companies.

She and Jane had compared mothers at least once and Jane had even
discussed her sister Emily, if only because in a peculiar way, Laverne
reminded her of her sister. Emily, too, was buxom and pretty and blond.
Oh, perhaps the beauty had gone a little haggard now. Institutional living
did that.

But there was something more to it than that, a kind of self-assurance
in both Laverne and Emily that came from the fact that they had been
adored as babies. How could one keep from adoring little Emmy? And
Laverne, as the only girl, what great gobs of devotion had been slathered
all over her? While angular, awkward scarecrow Jane, whose skin didn't
clear up until she was seventeen, at about the same time as she reached
five feet ten inches in height and finally stopped growing . . . this was
not a little girl you could cuddle, like Emily.

At five thirty she left the building quickly, praying that she wouldn't
run into Ned, and made for a big, impersonal hotel a few streets away

on Park Lane where she had arranged to meet Miss Blond Bombshell in the bar. She really had to stop comparing her to Emily. She had to stop being so damned nervous about meeting her lover's wife. As long as only she knew, there was no cause for alarm.

Still, her breath was coming in panicky spurts now as she entered the lobby and made for the bar. She was a few minutes early, another obvious sign of guilt; Laverne, living at some distance, would certainly be late in the rush hour traffic. But no, she was there.

"Yes," Jane said as she sat down, "what a good idea, planter's punch."

"Thank you for coming," Laverne said, getting right to the point. "And this drink's on me. Ten minutes, I promise."

She waited impatiently for Jane's drink to arrive. They touched glasses. "Cheers."

They sipped their long rum drinks. "Let me just say . . ." Laverne stopped herself. "I mean I owe you an . . ." She took another sip that brought the level of her drink halfway down. She had, Jane saw, got herself thoroughly dressed for this occasion in a very attractive beige suit whose jacket, hanging open, tended to camouflage her bosom. Never a problem of mine, Jane noted. She could see that tables of men nearby were already watching Laverne, the way men had always watched Emily.

"Here's the thing," Laverne began again, "here in London I don't seem to have any close woman friends. This is the sort of thing you could discuss with a friend. But I really don't know . . . I said that already. But I know there are women whose profession is listening and advising. That's why this is only going to take ten minutes, Jane. I figured you might be able to steer me to one of these, uh, women."

"Therapist?"

Laverne winced openly. "Is that what I mean?"

"Analyst?" Jane considered for a moment. "Actually I've got a list of qualified people back in my office. You'd be surprised how many requests like this we get."

Laverne, who had been sitting hunched miserably forward over her drink with a very tight look on her face, seemed suddenly to relax. She sat back, glanced around the room, looked instantly more at ease. Somehow Jane had said exactly the right thing to put Laverne's mind at rest. She was one of those women who judged herself by others. If enough of them did it, Jane supposed, then Laverne would feel at ease doing it too.

"But they do tend to specialize," she went on. "I mean the problem may be medical or emotional or it may be an economic problem or something to do with the . . ." Jane could hear her voice break on the word "marriage." She hoped Laverne wouldn't take too keen a note of it.

"But that's exactly it," Laverne responded.

"What is?"

"My marriage." Laverne gave her drink a little push away from herself, as if she no longer needed such props. "If you told me, even two years ago when we were in Bonn, that people could grow so far apart so quickly, I'd have sent *you* to the shrink, not me."

Jane looked at her, unable to speak.

"It's reached the point where I'm going crazy," Laverne said in her matter-of-fact voice, almost as if talking about someone else. "Split personality? I don't even want to *be* here. I want to be in California with my family. And the worst of it is that Ned . . ." She stopped herself. "I promised you ten minutes, Jane." She gave her a small, pained smile. "Why don't I call you at the office tomorrow and get those names from you then?"

Jane nodded. "Yes, of course."

Both of them were shocked when Laverne began to sob. She made only small sounds. No one else in the bar noticed. Just Jane.

The big-windowed dayroom had been set aside as control center for the lawn party on Sunday. It was here in Winfield that Belle Crustaker, or Pandora, answered the special RSVP line, although it seldom rang now. It was here that last-minute details of the catering were decided with the man from Hodgkins and Daughter. And it was here, at sundown, that Pandora sat by herself gazing out through the great expanse of windows onto lawns and gardens that, this time Sunday, would be filled with torches, music, and celebrated guests.

She knew a little about the way offices functioned, enough to know that as the clock neared six P.M. on Friday, she would hear no more out of the chancery crowd. She had passed beyond their carping and niggling now and it was almost a bobsled run, all downhill under her own power from here till the Fourth of July. Which reminded her . . .

They had originally told her there could be no private fireworks. But, of course, if she had consulted the authorities, the experts, especially her own at the chancery, she would have been told there could be no garden party. It was in the nature, Pandora knew, of essentially small, small, small people to say no, no, no.

But, as to the fireworks, she had finally got someone in the protocol section to arrange for a permit and now there remained only the selection of a company to produce the display. Apparently there were three, all out of London, none answering her urgent messages. "Not the right time of year," one helpful girl had explained over the phone. "We don't really come to life till fall. Guy Fawkes Day."

The phrase meant nothing to Pandora and she persisted. Accordingly, she reached for her address list, selected a number, and turned to the phone. It rang.

Pandora glanced at her watch: 5:55 of a Friday night. If this were one more guest canceling, she would burst into tears. "Winfield House."

"Is Mrs. Fulmer there, please?" An American voice, male, diffident. If this were someone from the chancery, she would absolutely burst into tears.

"This is she. May I help you?"

"Mrs. Fulmer, Pendennis Anspacher here, from Political."

"Dennis, I'm terribly busy at the moment."

"Th-this won't take but a moment, Mrs. Fulmer. It's about those videos?"

Pandora put down the phone, turned away, and squeezed both her tiny fists as hard as she could, making them vibrate up and down in the air. She could hear him talking on the phone. After a moment she picked it up.

She had a vision of Pendennis Anspacher, defrocked academic by his prissy voice, East Coast Ivy League snob eunuch sadist baboon monster! "Yes, Mr. Dennis."

"Pendennis Anspacher, Mrs. Fulmer. I just wanted to say we've had a reading from State back home. I don't think you're aware of the controversy those videos have been causing in Congress, Mrs. Fulmer. I mean there is even a move under way in the House to investigate their origin, cost, authorization, et cetera. So the advice from State is that we can't possibly involve ourselves or the diplomatic service in this sort of brawl."

There was a long pause at his end of the line. "Mr. Dennis, am I being told that I cannot screen the president's own videos at my party?"

"I haven't made myself clear, Mrs. Fulmer. Let me try to expl—"

"You've made it abundantly clear, Mr. Dennis."

"Pendennis Anspacher."

"I am asking if this is a direct order from State."

"Well, in theory, Mrs. Fulmer, in th—" A loud glottal click. "In th-theory, an ambassador plenipotentiary is free to do what he wishes in matters of protocol. But that is an ambassador of long experience, or of career provenance. For ambassadors new to the service, we must stick pretty much to the book, Mrs. Fulmer. And the book says—"

"Thank you, Mr. Dennis." She slammed down the phone, whirled so quickly that her pleated skirt billowed out like a ballerina's, and rushed to the window. The day was dying and so was she. So was she.

The telephone rang again. She let it.

Although the Amersham hospital was a fairly modern place, the facility at Stoke Mandeville was far more extensive. The size of a town, the hospital was made up of individual buildings separated by grassy plots and parking lots. Near the Department of Genital Medicine stood the Accidents Building, spread out like an H with an extra leg. In this place they handled critical emergency cases from all over Buckinghamshire with an array of space-age equipment that all television viewers of medical dramas were familiar with, tall glass things, rubber whats-its that pumped and moaned like a *calamaro* in heat, oscilloscopes that displayed jagged lines of heartbeat or, with a dying *breeeee*, a single flat line of death.

Bazzard had been here before, never as a patient, thank God. He'd had brothers splinted up here after hideous ski accidents, farm hands after putting their elbow in a running cultivator, the usual round of country misfortunes. But never one who lay as still as the young chap he'd found in Cherry Lane.

"Dead, is he?"

The attending physician in Intensive Care made a face, as of a baby rejecting a nipple. "It's very hard with these hypo cases."

"Hypo?"

"Hypo everything: no blood sugar, no white cells, no red cells, no bloody blood," the doctor complained. "If you examine his injuries they are serious but superficial if you get my drift. There are a lot of 'em but no piercing of vital organs. So what we have is a chappie who's lost too much blood. We're doing what we can." He indicated tubes attached to plastic bags of whole blood and saline. "But it may be too late."

"Then you do have signs of life?"

With a twist of his head the doctor indicated an oscilloscope hanging at eye level near the bed. "You've seen those thingees on TV, eh?"

Bazzard could follow as the instrument traced a low, jagged line of peaks, an ancient range of hills, not the vigorous up-and-down of a Himalayan massif. This sort of thing was always happening to him in hospitals. Because everyone in the area knew him as a lawyer, it was assumed that his professional qualifications more or less overlapped those of a doctor. "But does this mean he can actually recover?"

"Too soon to tell."

A call came over the loudspeaker and the doctor perked up his ears. "That's me. Back in a jiff."

Either mistaken for a doctor, Bazzard saw, or for the next of kin. In this case they didn't even know the poor chap's name. Nothing had been found in his ragged trousers to make any sort of identification.

"*Vater.*" A faint sigh from the man with all the tubes and wires attached to him.

"I say," Bazzard got to his feet.

"*Küss mir, Vater.*"

"I say, old man!" Bazzard shouted. "You're going to be just fine!"

By six fifteen they had finished their second Planter's Punch. A woman pianist had come in and was working out small, tinkling melodies that could barely be heard across the room as it filled up with cocktail-hour customers. Laverne had stopped talking for the moment, having told Jane just about what she would have told a counselor. The pianist rattled on.

She was just now concluding a set of songs relating to climate. She had done "Isn't It a Lovely Day to Be Caught in the Rain?" and also "Rain on the Roof." Having polished off "Stormy Weather" she was now whanging away at "Singin' in the Rain" in an up-tempo beat that would provide a smash finish to the medley.

"It's deceptive," Jane said at last.

"What?" Laverne's hurt glance swung on her. "I don't understand."

Jane could see that she'd overshot the boundaries of Laverne's view of things. There was an odd, mulish set of Laverne's jaw, as if she were rejecting something because she didn't want it to be so. Jane had seen Emily do the same thing often enough, memorialized in the folk saying: "Don't confuse me with facts; my mind's made up."

"But that's so much worse," Laverne cried out suddenly. "What the hell, Jane. Politics is just a game men play, isn't it? So a woman can just ignore it, can't she? But if the dividing point is something emotional, what chance have I got?"

"I don't really—"

"I remember my Dad and my brothers arguing politics. It's a time waster, Jane. It's like the sports pages. The batting averages, the forward passes and end runs and overtime penalty shots and, what the hell, it's the way men pass their time here on earth while the women have babies and help them grow up. If you tell me the difference between Ned and me isn't political, then there really is no hope. I'll just pack my bags and hop that transpolar to San Francisco. I swear it. I don't have to suffer this way."

Something bright and hot seemed to flare up inside Jane. Ned, alone in London! Dear God, what a selfish joy! This woman miserable, this one in ecstasy. Who ever said life was fair? Fly, Laverne! Take wings and fly!

At the piano, by one of those meaningless coincidences nobody ever pays any attention to, the woman entertainer had just finished playing "I Left My Heart in San Francisco." It was metropolis medley time.

"Hey, you two, cheer *up!*" someone shouted.

Jane glanced up to see Mrs. Kathryn Hearns coming toward her, with her counterweight-cum-deadly enemy, Chuck Gretz, in tow. "Ladies, what a pleasant surprise," he hollered.

He sat down next to Laverne and moved her over a foot or two by bumping hips. "We're off to Frankfurt in an hour."

"He is flying," Mrs. Hearns explained, "but the plane don't take off till later."

At the piano, the woman began a perky version of "New York, New York." If one weren't watching closely, it was possible to miss the tears that formed in Laverne's eyes. But Katy Hearns always watched everything closely. "Oooh," she said. "That's my song, Mrs. French." She reached across and chucked Laverne under the chin, very gently. "Come on. Smile."

"Hey, look, we all need a drink," the South Dakota congressman said. "Miss?" Gretz called to the pianist. "Do you know 'Sioux City Sue'?"

"Do you?" she called back.

He went over to the piano. "No good'll come of that," Katy Hearns commented. "Anything I can help with?" she asked Laverne. A brief, negative shake of the head.

"Sioux City Sue," Chuck Gretz was singing. "Sioux City Sue. I sold mah horse and gun fer yew. They's nothin' that I wouldn't do fer . . . Sioux City Sue, Sioux City . . ."

"I think I'll just freshen my makeup," Mrs. Hearns said then. "How about you?" she asked Jane.

In the ladies room they stood facing the mirror, watching each other as reflections. Even behind a closed door they could hear the Gretz baritone bawling, "I left my heart in Pierre, South Dakota."

"She's gonna figure it out," Mrs. Hearns said then. "It's only a matter of time."

"Yes?" Jane felt breathless, as if running.

"She's too miserable at the moment. Once she calms down, she's gonna get the message about hubby. Hell, missie, I got it Tuesday night at Mr. Connell's house."

"Everything's up to date," Gretz yodeled, "in Rapid City."

22

Hargreaves stood in the foyer of the Lyric Hammersmith theater, once the site of a noted theater at the turn of the century, now reborn as part of an immense shopping-living-office block here in this western section of London usually described as "on the way to Heathrow."

He was staring across the street at a new building in which the BBC was tonight opening its latest television studio with a bang-up riproarer, the kind that would supply Hargreaves with material for his next two weeks of gossip columns and also get him laid. *Quel ennui*, he thought.

Still, one shouldn't knock the old gossip column. It was the only earner an ancient sod like him could find in journalism these days. Nobody wanted antiquated crocks who still typed on yellow sheets of copy paper with two fingers by the hunt-and-peck system. Nobody wanted a drinker in his sixties who couldn't chase down a real job of investigative reporting by trapping a prince of the royal blood in a ski chalet with a pornoflick actress. That took not only energy but the feckless gift of youth.

Whereas here, observing the gorgeous people and chronicling their gambols and didoes, was the only game in town for geriatric war horses too fond of their booze. Hargreaves winced. He had what was for him a not unusual condition known as P.M. hangover, the result of lunching in the style to which Hargreaves was accustomed, that is, on someone else's expense account.

Freeloader, dirt-peddler, womanizer (when he had the cash), friend
of the great and the lowly, Hargreaves saw himself in his more hung-
over moments as a kind of catalytic agent or enzyme in the bloodstream
of London society. Oh, not that constipated prewar society with its dukes
and countesses giggling over farting jokes. No, today's society, scruffy,
dynamic, compounded mostly of gall, conceit, dodgy deals, and a lot of
help from drugs.

Hargreaves blessed whatever benign spirit had charge of his life, who,
amid decades of temptation and easy access, had kept him from becoming
a drug addict. Dear God, yes. And dear God, the bar was finally open
across the street, was it not? Hurry over, Hargreaves, and stanch that
heroic, hung-over thirst.

He nearly collided with a Mini as he hastened across the street and
marched in past the guards without showing his invitation card. There
were damned few perks for the working hack these days, Hargreaves
mused, but crashing parties was one of them. Any nobody could try it,
but only a journalist could get away with it. He had a perfectly legal
invitation in his desk at the office but he hadn't actually been to his office
in more than forty-eight hours. In the distance, Noonan the bartender
waved at him now.

Terribly gauche, arriving on time. But the crush at the bar got to be
virtually inhuman at these Beeb thrashes. Hargreaves waylaid a passing
waiter and relieved him of two flute glasses of champagne. Terribly gauche
to gulp champagne, Hargreaves told himself as he did so, but the need,
dear God, the need was pressing.

Well! Now, then! Wasn't this a gay scene, after all? Not to brood,
Hargreaves advised himself. Not to moan on about getting old. In this
great gray city, wreathed round with ambiguities, the only place to be
was where someone had paid for gaiety. Yes, not a bad idea for an opening
to the column. "As a purveyor of gaiety, the Beeb is second to none."
No. " 'Since everything else is for sale,' thought the Beeb, 'why not
gaiety?' " No. "In case you're wondering where all of London's fabled
gaiety has gone, it was sold off to the Beeb for their Friday night stampede
celebrating the opening of the Ham—"

Waiter. Yes, take these, thanks. I'll take those.

Much better! Gayer! One has to worry these days about that word.

He found himself wondering what it had been like in previous periods
of artificial gaiety. Rome under Nero came to mind. The last days of the
Weimar Republic for another. Desperately rouged young fellows, tuxedoed

gals, George Grosz bankers, and ex-generals. Hideous cripples. Gaiety galore.

Not that bad here, Hargreaves noted. The early comers were always the young hopefuls, the would-be starlets and juveniles in their absolutely tattiest casual wear, sweaters with mothholes, punk hair, ankle warmers without socks, livid makeup, cross-sexual behavior, epicene but not quite transvestite. Weimar Night in Hammersmith.

And the music. That bray of stapes-smashing noise, mumbled words, with a rhythm section that consisted of several silicon chips and a large loudspeaker which could mimic everything about a live drummer but the sweat. And, of course, the air already thicker by half with grass smoke. By selectively moving here and there Hargreaves knew he could easily acquire a contact high.

Ah! But no laser! Thank you, dear Beeb. Thank you, Auntie. Mine ears have you not spared, but mine eyes flourish under your tender ministrations. 'Ello, 'ello, 'ello?

"Is it you, dear, this early?" he inquired.

"I invited my next victim, Royce Connell," Gillian explained. "Have you seen him?"

" 'S only quarter to seven. Waiter. Oh. I see." Hargreaves gave the waiter a sour face. With a live companion by his side he could no longer take on two glasses at a time without giving one to her. "Are you really after that fellow?" he asked her.

"Call it Lamb's death wish."

"But, I mean, Gillian, dearest, it should be obvious." Hargreaves stopped cold, knowing that if he pushed the thought too far he would be minus his lovely "Lamb to Slaughter" free-lance work. And he hadn't drunk enough for that yet, thank you. There were secrets he knew about La Lamb that it would be folly to reveal, such as her family origins. She could, if pressed, be ruthless.

"I know all about it," Gillian confessed. "I'm afraid that's what attracts me. A challenge."

"Good God, why couldn't I have been the one?"

"You, a challenge? There isn't anything in this place under eighty that you wouldn't fuck if they held it down."

Her tawny eyes sparkled at the picture. Then they focused on Hargreaves and he wished suddenly that the Beeb had, after all, provided a laser. It would have been much kinder to face than her glance. "What do they say about Royce?" she asked him.

"Tables Turned," he quoted an imaginary headline. "Columnist Quizzed by TV Reporter. No Comment, Fleet Street Cries."

"Hargreaves, it's me asking, the darling of millions."

He looked her over in the very tight white sheath she had worn tonight, the kind of fabric that, while it enhanced the shape of what was underneath, also had the effect of dazzling the camera lens like a major conflagration. Her straw-colored hair, long and parted in the middle, curved down around her face in two sheltering arms. A shame to waste all that by bouncing it off Royce Connell till it broke in two.

"They say almost nothing, luv," Hargreaves assured her. "That's because he's got no proper private life whatsoever."

"Not even boys?"

Hargreaves puffed his cheeks. "Leave it out, luv."

"Tell me."

"Nothing to tell. No rumors among the gay young blades, and I know 'em all. Never a whisper."

"You're being evasive."

"I'm being honest, and you're not likely to see that in Hargreaves so early in the drinking."

Down front near the street curb flashbulbs were going off. "There he is. I warned him."

"Doesn't he like to be photographed?"

"When you're the number-two, Hargreaves, you must make sure all the photographs are of number one." She strode off toward the entrance. Hargreaves watched her rear end every stride of the way. To think that something that luscious was also talented. And wasted on Boy Connell.

"Mr. Hargreaves?"

An American voice, rhyming his name with "grieves," or perhaps "thieves," issued from the tall man beside him in one of those American tuxedoes of a royal blue set off by a very, very large yellow bow tie and a fuchsia dress shirt. "Have we met?" Hargreaves asked.

"No, but that's very, very easy to repair," the man said. He had a most appealing face, open and boyish, a sort of cross between Anthony Perkins and Jimmy Stewart, Hargreaves judged, which meant that he was some kind of con man. He'd have to ask Noonan about this new face.

"Ah, but should we chance it?" the columnist asked.

"It could be to your advantage," the American promised.

"Really?" Hargreaves privately complimented himself on spotting a con man almost solely on the basis of appearance, even before he opened his wicked little mouth. "We are speaking monetarily, are we?"

"Yes, that too. In the sense that information, to someone like you, is very, very bankable."

"I am dying to know your name, young man."

The American thrust out his hand. "Jim Weems, sir. Happy to know you."

It was a new experience for Royce Connell, and he wasn't sure he liked it. Putting to one side the universal look in people's eyes that clearly enunciated the cliché "Don't they make a handsome couple?" Connell wasn't absolutely thrilled at playing second fiddle to a television personality so accessible that everybody came up and chatted with her like some long-lost cousin.

Much of Connell's rise within the ranks of diplomacy could be attributed to the astute way he was able to edge the spotlight of publicity over one notch to shine down upon whomever was his immediate superior. The photos were almost always the same, someone with a title like ambassador or general in the foreground, grinning fatuously, and, just at the very rim of the flashbulb's circle of light, the good-looking old-young man with the slight but knowing smile. If Royce kept photo albums of his life, that picture would have been duplicated dozens of times over, only the man in the limelight changing identity.

But Royce did not work for Gillian Lamb, he reminded himself. In fact, his relationship to her was possibly a mystery to the world and certainly a dilemma to him. Well, perhaps the world, with its careless way of painting scenes in broad strokes, was not as confused as he was. Perhaps the gossip that was making the rounds during this extremely star-studded BBC party was the usual cynical tittle-tattle.

"Who's the pretty boy with Gillie? Oh, on second look, her dad?"

"Been having it off with her for months."

"Does make for an even match: nympho vs. homo."

How unfair the public tongue could be, and how well oiled. He knew, for example, that she was not widely regarded as an easy lay, far from it. And he himself, Royce also knew, had managed to keep the gossips guessing about his preference in partners, male or female. That guessing game had followed him throughout his years of service. Now and then he got angry about it but, as with any game, there was a certain fun in continuing to mystify the world. God knew there weren't many other joys in a career increasingly devoted to making political appointees look good.

"Rather blows her credibility as a reporter, doesn't it, being escorted about town by a U.S. dip?"

"I give 'em six months and she'll eat him alive."

"I give 'em six weeks and he'll break her heart."

Tonight's event was created for gossip, every variety from the calculated leaked item of a PR flack to the nasty whisper of a jilted lover. The big Fourth of July garden party on Sunday was, in its own way, merely an upward variation on this one tonight. It would cost the embassy infinitely more than this was costing BBC, and it would tax the embassy's security forces and expertise to the limit, whereas the BBC probably had put on, if they'd even bothered, two extra private cops just to keep out gate crashers.

That was the difference between being a government which made itself a worldwide target for every hopped-up terrorist or ambitious politico and a beloved national institution that came into everyone's home around the clock with news and music and excitement and information and only charged them something like fifty pounds a year license fee.

"You don't look too damned thrilled, do you?"

Royce blinked. He knew this was a recent, and bad, habit of his, and he hated people for startling him, but this was that alcoholic Hargreaves, wasn't it, and he supposed he had to be "nice."

"Why, how thoughtful of you," Connell said, relieving Hargreaves of his spare glass of champagne. "Did you bring it over just for me?"

"Not noticeably, no." Hargreaves looked grieved as the champagne began to disappear down the Connell throat. "But you looked a bit dour."

"Not sure I'm made for flashbulbs."

"I'm not mad-keen on them myself," Hargreaves admitted, "but it's been yonks since anybody took a snap of me. While you, on the other hand, are hot copy."

"Only as an object discerned in the shadow of La Lamb."

"You two are very much an item," the columnist said, with no hint of a question in his voice.

"One of yours?"

"Damn me for a fellow of breeding, no," Hargreaves complained. "I have been known to break a story like that in advance, but only if the principals agree."

"Story like what?"

Hargreaves puffed out his cheeks. "Hot water. Hot water. I seem to swim in it. Never mind, old boy. Damned cheeky of me."

Connell grinned at him. "On the other hand, you do have a real purpose here tonight and one that will earn you my undying gratitude."

"What may that be?"

"Aside from you and Gillian, I don't know a soul and . . ."

"And don't want to," the reporter finished for him, "but you wouldn't mind a few captions under the snapshots. Hargreaves will finger the celebs for you by name, occupation, and bank balance. Ask away."

As Connell looked about him, Hargreaves deftly stole his half-full champagne glass, drained it, and handed the two empties to a passing waiter, who replaced them with full glasses. "I know that one over there," Connell said. "He's the chap who interviews everyone."

"Absolutely everyone. The term 'bottom of the barrel' takes on new meaning when you read his guest list."

"And she's got a comedy hit in the West End?"

"Lucinda? I'm not sure what you call her new play," Hargreaves muttered. His voice had started to get a bit unsteady. "Apart from two topless scenes and some bare bottom in the second act, about all it has going for it is that if you've temporarily lost any American friends you're sure to find them in the lobby during the interval."

"Very popular with tourists?"

"Wot, tits and ass? Bloody amazing," the columnist said. "Oh, quick, turn away. There."

"Who am I hiding from?"

"Not you, me."

Instead of turning away, Connell tried to spot whom it might be that had driven Hargreaves into drunken retreat. "There's a fellow looks like your younger brother."

"He's the one. Mind walking me to the bar?"

"I'm supposed to be available to Gillian," Connell explained, indicating his lady, with her back to the wall a yard away from them, facing off a handful of young people with cameras and small notepads. "She does seem to be able to handle it herself." He waved at her and indicated the direction of the bar. She blew him a kiss and held up an empty glass to indicate what his motivation should become.

"I do admire that girl," Connell said. "She can keep several tracks running in that lovely head of hers."

"Make the perfect diplomat's wife," Hargreaves said as he dived through the throng toward the bar.

"Your brother is following us."

"Damn all. I suppose he wants to meet you."

"Seems to me you're the one he wants."

"Not my brother." Hargreaves belched softly but at length, delicately covering his mouth. "Dear me, no. Bloody hell." He stopped in his tracks and turned with a faintly sheepish look as the man who looked like him caught up with them.

"Oh, there you are."

"Comrade journalist," Gleb Ponamarenko said, "introduce me to your friend."

"Darling, will I see you on Sunday, then?" Gillian Lamb asked the other woman, small and busy, with short dark hair cut in a severe bob and bangs, emphasized by a pair of thick-rimmed glasses of the same color, a deep sable. The woman had a faintly simian quality to her face. She was attractive in a boyish way, almost clownlike, one of those people who are forever being accused of joking, of not being serious, of swinging about by her tail when she should be solidly planted on her feet.

"I suppose so, luv," she responded. "Isn't everyone here tonight going to be at the Fourth of July do?"

"I suppose the Beeb is running this as a kind of dress rehearsal," Gillian mused. "Tina, can I get you a drink?"

The bobbed-haired woman shook her head so vigorously that her hair flew out centrifugally like a dark brown halo. "I wouldn't dream of disturbing you, darling."

"I've got a, um, a chevalier at the bar," Gillian confessed. "He could bring it you."

"Champagne, mum?" a waiter asked.

He had been hovering in the area for some time, Gillian noted. A plump man with protruding eyes, he was dressed differently from the other men with trays in that the rest wore very short black tuxedo dinner jackets with black ties, while this one had a longer jacket, white tie, and pale gray trousers, as well as a rather lovely cornflower-blue buttonhole flower.

The waiter bowed slightly as he presented his tray. His face was an unhealthy paste color, emphasized by a messy mustache and an even messier head of dark woolly hair. "Will we have the pleasure of serving mum on Sunday as well?" he asked.

Gillian listened to the accent. It was not English nor quite American. "Oh, is your firm catering the embassy garden party?"

"Yes, mum." His pop eyes swiveled slightly to Tina. "You, mum?"

"That's fascinating," she said, taking her glass from him. "You mean it's always the same caterers? What's your name?"

The waiter looked at a loss for a moment. "I mean the name of your firm," Tina amended.

"Hodgkins and Daughter, mum," he responded briskly. "At your service."

European, Gillian decided, but has worked a lot in America. "It's nice to know one will keep meeting one's waiter party after party."

"Oh, no, mum, I'm not a waiter." His bulging eyes widened and his steel-wool hair seemed to bristle slightly. "I'm the supervisor."

"Which accounts for the buttonhole," Tina pointed out.

"Thanking you so much," he signed off, backing away with his empty tray.

"Do you think it's true?" Gillian asked thoughtfully, "that all these big dos are catered by Whats-it and his Daughter? You would know, Teen, of all people."

"I have heard of them," she admitted.

"Yes, but if so, have you ever run into Gollywog before?"

"Who, my plump, smitten domestic? Never."

"Nor have I."

Tina gave forth a dramatic sigh. "Just ships that pass in the night," she murmured.

From approximately the moment they had been introduced, Royce Connell had been trying to find a polite way of leaving Ponamarenko. He had introduced the idea that his lady was thirsty and he was tardy in delivering a drink, but the waiter with the buttonhole flower had put an end to that excuse.

It wasn't that Connell objected to fraternizing with Russians. He had had to do it often enough in his diplomatic career. But those had been carefully deloused Russians with vouched-for pedigrees, ranks, titles, and dossiers supplied by State Department Intelligence. The scenes of such conversations had been carefully controlled diplomatic events, dinners, receptions, anniversaries, and the like at which everyone was on his best behavior and conversation was kept to the crushingly boring one of "Yes, indeed, that was an exceptional year for Pouilly-Fuissé, was it not?" and the like.

But Gleb Ponamarenko was dangerous, a known maverick, Soviet agent to the core but practically his own boss in London, charged with the kind of activity that could hardly be spoken of in public. And tonight was an unbuttoned, unstructured event in which large doses of show-biz people acted somewhat like raw cloves of garlic in a stew. They gave off an inimitable aura without ever blending into invisibility.

This party was an occasion for seeing and being seen, Royce knew, for gossiping and being gossiped about. And the one thing he didn't need was to have been seen chatting endlessly with a Soviet agent as high-ranking as this one. Of course there were extenuating circumstances, but the art of rising in the diplomatic service was never to have to stop and sit down and explain extenuating circumstances.

". . . lovely extra earner for old Hargreaves," the Russian was saying. "He's getting on in years and the cash is welcome."

"He's a sort of bird dog for Gillian, is he?" Connell asked.

"Very apt description. That plump fellow who was serving them champagne a moment ago," Ponamarenko went on, "the one who preempted your gallant gesture?"

"Yes, rather overdressed for a waiter." Drink in hand, Connell began to edge in the direction of Gillian.

"But he's not a waiter."

"Do you know him?"

"Dear Connell, I have seen him before, in another connection. He was pointed out to me, one might say. No, I learned he was a supervisor because that is what he told your charming lady. And I read lips."

"Saints preserve us," Connell intoned. "That's a nasty little surprise to spring on a new acquaintance."

"May I suggest you learn the art yourself, dear Connell. It's absolutely invaluable at these noisy receptions."

The deputy ambassador stopped edging away from him. He looked the Russian over very carefully. "That is a damned useful suggestion," he said then. "Did you go to school to learn?"

Gleb shook his head. "One watches TV and slowly turns down the sound. Week by week one gets better at it. Of course, you realize, dear Connell, I only lip-read in English."

Connell burst out laughing and, a split second later, so did the Russian. "But you do know that fellow," Connell persisted. "The one with the wild hair and banjo eyes?"

Ponamarenko nodded. "Yes." His glance had been moving slowly sideways. Now his face lightened up. "Connell! My dear friend, this is a rare opportunity. You are going to meet the most brilliant woman in London."

"I was under the impression I'd brought her here tonight."

"Ah, yes, to be sure, a thousand pardons, naturally, of course," Gleb pattered on like a Victorian translation of Tolstoi. "My dearest Miriam," he called.

An immense woman with bright orange hair and a glowing cerise gown swung around. The cerise was a sort of sari or wrap that revealed great expanses of pink flesh here and there in a random pattern that dazzled the eye much as a camouflage pattern did, an elbow here, a fat shoulder there, the creamy curving top of a breast, the broad pillar of a throat, the tiny hand, as delicate as a raccoon's paw, the thick calf and narrow ankle, the brilliant high-heeled orange pumps. Connell found himself wondering how someone this overweight could still manage to exude such an aura of sexual desirability. Auto-hypnosis?

"Watch yourself," Bricktop called, "you're with the most dangerous man in London."

"My dear Miriam, to whom was that warning addressed?" the Russian asked. "You are looking, as always, absolutely . . . edible."

"If you dig carbohydrates," Bricktop said. "Mr. Connell, this *dshlub* has no manners." She extended her hand. "Miriam Shannon."

"Cultural attaché," Gleb added.

"Of the Israeli government," Connell finished. "My we're all a proper bunch of pros, aren't we?" He took her hand. "Shannon's an Irish name, like Connell."

"Sure, but me ould mither spelled it C-H-A-N-I-N. Do you realize," she went on, fixing him with eyes outlined in kohl and spattered with sparkle, "that a grenade rolled neatly at our feet would start World War III?"

"Or prevent it forever," the Russian sighed. "Ah, there's my esteemed countrywoman, the devil's her name, dancer defectee? God, my memory!" He headed toward a painfully slender brunette surrounded by young men wearing crew-cropped hair and neat mustaches.

"She's frightened to death of him," Bricktop murmured. "His sideline is reprogramming defectees. People who left Russia ten years ago. He convinces them it's all different back home now. And they believe it."

"You said his sideline?"

"Well, his card says he's a correspondent for Tass."

"And yours says you're a cultural attaché."

"Wrong. Mine says I run a boutique on South Molton Street. And I do."

"So Ponamarenko was just stirring up trouble?"

"Isn't that what correspondents do?"

"Do you always answer a question with a question?"

"Was Moses Jewish?" She had been touching him here and there,
on the arm, the back of his hand. Now she took his wrist and held it
tightly. "My God, it's her, Gillian Lamb. I am totally in love with Gillian
Lamb."

"Yes, well for that you must stand in line."

"You know her?"

"She's my, um, date tonight."

Her grip tightened. "Introduce me, you sweet man."

Hargreaves, who had never moved on from champagne to harder
stuff, was now congratulating himself for his abstemiousness. He reckoned, in his fuzzy way, that he had destroyed at least two bottles of
the Beeb's best bubbly but he was still on his feet and quite *compos
mentis*, thank you, and still waylaying any passing waiter for his ritual
two glasses.

Left to his own devices, and with a corner of his brain still functioning
over the rising tide of bubbles, Hargreaves brooded on his self-assigned
role as enzyme in the social blood of London. The beneficiary of a good
education before the war—he could still handle a Greek or Latin tag
with aplomb, plus a dictionary—Hargreaves dimly remembered the enzyme as a catalyst, one of those chemicals that caused reactions without
participating in them. Nifty way of describing his own role in functions
such as this one. The enzyme, still holding both glasses of champagne,
began to circulate through the bloodstream once again.

". . . having hell's own job getting financing. No British money
available, needless to say."

"Try shooting the film in Yugoslavia? They do one a neat subsidy."

"How boring. Yugoslavia?"

Hargreaves, having finished possibly his twentieth glass, set it down
empty and began on his twenty-first. In the distance he could see his
own ravishing Lamb in eye-to-eye consultation with a gigantically fat
redheaded woman while Royce Connell was being chatted up by someone
else.

". . . they take a tuck here and here and sew it up behind your ears
where the hair covers it completely and, hey, presto, you're ten years
younger."

"And so's your arthritis, eh?"

Hargreaves veered left and managed by an amazing feat of juggling to keep from knocking down one of the young actresses dressed in rags to advertise her talent. "Sorry," he muttered.

"You're Hargreaves."

"Is that an accusation, my dear girl?"

"I'm called Nicola Strong."

"Hargreaves the Weak. I seem to have this single solitary glass of champers. It's yours, sweet one, because I have always adored you."

"Even though I have only just arrived in London?"

"From Capetown?" Hargreaves asked.

"Does the accent still show?"

"But even in Capetown I adored you," the columnist insisted doggedly. "Even when you were an infant we were fated."

"So," she said, looking him over. She seemed under twenty, but not inside her head, a finely drawn young woman with one of those faces that had edges and clean-cut points, like a minted coin, golden under a mop of golden hair. Despite her rather grave look, she seemed jolly enough to Hargreaves, something in the eyes that said: You take care of me and I'll take damned fine care of you.

"It must be marvelous to know all these glitterati," she was saying. "I'm invited only because I've landed a tiny speaking line in the next BBC Dickens extravaganza and my producer wants me to 'be seen.' "

"And now you have," Hargreaves said, folding her hand and arm in his. "Shall we go walkies?"

Drunk or sober, an enzyme continues to function. In the next quarter of an hour Hargreaves had introduced Nicola to five film producers, three directors, and two other gossip columnists. It made a change, he thought to himself, from the diplo-espio circuit he'd been in before. A waiter arrived with six brimming glasses of champagne. "Courtesy of Mr. Noonan, sir," he murmured. Hargreaves gravely distributed one glass to Nicola, four to himself and one to an animated director now talking.

"It's a sort of Roman Western," he explained. "Not one of those spaghetti ones like the old Clint Eastwoods, but what I mean is a kind of outdoors action film on horseback but the characters are ancient Romans in togas and such sent to quell an uprising of the aborigine Etruscans in the year, oh, say, one thousand B.C. and there's a lot of chase and sword fights and several sort of gorgeous setups in grottoes around Florence and a magnificent battle in which the Romans sort of pull all the wagons into a circle whilst the Etruscans on ponies cruise around the perimeter sort of shooting off fiery arrows and sending spears through Roman chests and uttering their savage Etruscan war cries whilst sort of scalping Roman babies and abducting Roman matrons and . . ."

The enzyme's attention faltered. In a corner of the great foyer in which the reception was being held, that American chappie Weems was talking to the plump supervisor of waiters, the one with a blue buttonhole flower.

Wait! Hargreaves's brain seethed. He knew that plump, doughy face. But from where?

". . . the most intelligent producer on the Italian side," the young director was saying, "who's called Aldo Sgroi, quite a sort of name in film circles there although quite unknown here in London but don't you find that's always too true, that London is actually so sort of provincial after all and at the end of the day entirely unnecessary and actually rather sort of redundant?"

Hargreaves's yawn was neatly stifled but Nicola saw it. She piloted him in the general direction of the entrance. "Can I give you a lift home?" she asked.

"You've got a car?"

"It's a Mini I borrowed from a mate. I'm not used to driving on the left yet. Nearly ran over some chap when I arrived."

"Out in front? That was me, dear girl. Did I not say it? We are fated."

Silly business, Ponamarenko thought as he prepared to leave. The grind of gathering tiny details and fitting them together like bits of a jigsaw puzzle was one he steadfastly refused to do on a regular basis. He had more than once had to explain this to his superiors but they remained unconvinced that his chief value was to be left to do the work he had chosen for himself, not the routine drudgery of the low-level intelligence clerk.

And yet nights like this were made for collecting bits of the puzzle. An intelligent man, Gleb told himself, cannot simply ignore the common details of such a scene, shimmering with chance meetings and faces in the crowd that carry extremely private histories. He had, for example, spotted the clever dog who fleeced the Hungarian equestrian team last year. Back in circulation, bold as brass, posing as a supervisor of waiters for the omnipresent Hodgkins and Daughter catering firm.

If there was one thing the Russian knew with total certainty it was that the plump man with what Connell had called "banjo eyes" was no more in the catering business than Ponamarenko himself. Somewhere

in the Hodgkins and Daughter organization there existed opportunities
for . . .

The Tass correspondent stopped in his tracks. The plump man would
be at the Sunday garden party given by the new American ambassador,
to which Ponamarenko was not invited. The plump man would be at
every big party in London, or certainly his fair share of them.

And, of course, all parties represented opportunities, for the plump
man as for Gleb, as for Hargreaves, as for the charming young thing who
was taking him home now.

And, of them all, Ponamarenko reflected, perhaps the lushest opportunity of recent history would be Sunday's. Whatever one was interested in, sex, blackmail, espionage, career advancement, or sheer bloody-
minded chaos, kidnap, and ransom, the Sunday garden party represented
a nearly perfect opportunity.

Gleb smiled softly and slyly. Perhaps that was why they called America
the land of opportunity?

At that moment, a man he knew appeared in the entrance to the
lobby. He was tall, dressed in dinner clothes and a long black raincoat,
its collar turned up as if it were snowing outside on this fine night in late
June. Partially bald, what hair he had was a thinnish blond red. His face,
too, was choleric red in febrile spots and spatters of freckles.

Gleb glanced quickly around the great room. More than half of the
guests had gone on to other Friday night appointments, lubricated nicely
on BBC booze. Gleb's new friend, the chargé d'affaires of the American
embassy, had already left with his precious cargo of not one but two
effervescent women, each fizzing sparks like catherine wheels. And who
said life was fair, Gleb Sergeyevich? Tonight that man will taste heaven.

So. Nicely timed. The choleric man in the doorway was John Pringle,
something rather high up in MI5 and known to his peers as Jock. The
Russian again surveyed the room, more slowly this time, looking for some
of Jock's men. What do you suppose, he asked himself, was the idea of
Jock in formal attire, as if having been summoned hurriedly from a Royal
presence? It smacked of Boy's Own adventures, or the hoary spy tales of
E. Phillips Oppenheim.

And who was the stalwart beside him, smelling even at this distance
of cop? P. J. R. Parkins still wore his regular business suit, having just
come, the Russian surmised, from his hidey-hole in the U.S. embassy,
where he lived the life of a termite, feeding off bits of the house in which
he lived. Gleb's mind sorted through what else he knew of Parkins, who

still carried the regular army rank of major though he was, by now, something on the order of deputy chief inspector of Special Branch.

The Tass correspondent knew by now that these two members of the heavy squad were not looking for him, a possibility that always existed. Jock's pale gray stare, like the twin afterburners of some terribly efficient jet fighter, had raked twice across Gleb's face, scorching him somewhat but moving on without any overt recognition. No, they were looking for . . .

Ah. The Russian's trained eye spotted the plump supervisor of waiters, with his banjo eyes and blue buttonhole. He looked ill at ease, his steel-wool hair more disarranged than usual. He gesticulated, his eyes protruding with an anxiety that Gleb could feel even across the large room.

Jock Pringle rubbed his chin, one of those unsubtle secret signs that police devise for clandestine communication. Instantly three husky young men in business suits, white shirts, and out-of-date narrow ties sprang forward at the general space occupied by Popeye the Waiter. Somewhere a woman gasped. Even Ponamarenko was startled, but nothing showed on his face.

Their burly arms encircled a tall man with an honest, if juvenile, face, dressed in an American tuxedo with a fuchsia dress shirt.

Gleb invoked several antique and officially forbidden Russian saints. They hadn't collared Popeye after all, but some total stranger who was now protesting vehemently as the three sluggers escorted him out the entrance. They passed Jock Pringle and P. J. R. Parkins, who seemed not to have noticed.

But, Gleb told himself. But.

He was absolutely certain that the waiter with the buttonhole had fingered the tall, probably American, guest. Gleb, who had himself often employed such informers to point out a wanted person, knew as sure as he was standing here in his handmade Locke shoes that between them Pringle and Parkins operated Popeye as a stoolie and perhaps a general provocateur as well.

Which was, in itself, nothing special. Waiters, bartenders, chambermaids, and other domestics were regularly suborned by intelligence networks to spy on people. What made it a bit special, almost kinky one might say, is that the man with the cornflower in his buttonhole was also the financial pirate who had ripped off the Hungarian equestrian team.

And who knew, Ponamarenko asked himself, what else?

Part 6

SATURDAY
JULY 3

23

Saturday, the third of July, dawned as days often did in London, with bright sunlight from the east coming in almost horizontally under leaden skies. A contradictory day, as so many were now.

They had slept badly, both of them. Laverne had had something on her mind when she went to bed. On the few occasions when that happened she would toss all night, waking Ned from time to time but never saying anything. People who had slept together for a long time, Ned mused, occupied the bed under an unwritten set of rules having to do with letting the other person sleep no matter what tormenting thoughts kept one awake.

At breakfast, which he made for himself, Ned surveyed the morning newspapers glumly. He was looking for what Hamlet called a "cue for passion," something that had happened overnight which might stir someone out there—the leader of a country or of some underground cell— to violence. With or without a cue, in thirty hours or less, people of that kind would have a maximum window into violence at Winfield House.

The news was indecisive. Nobody in Washington had called down any thunder, no preemptive bomb strikes in the night, no inflammatory speeches, no lobbed insults. As if by mutual agreement, no one in Europe had complained of anything America was doing at the moment, contenting themselves with the usual Common Market infighting about farm prices and overproduction of wine in Italy.

Ned looked up and let his eyes unfocus. He and Chamoun had been at it for a long time yesterday, getting the checklist in shape. Not that a list ever solved anything, even one as long as this, four pages of typing.

In a universe ruled by Murphy's Law, Ned mused, checklists were really just a form of amulet to guard against devils. Still, with an operation as complex as Sunday's, he and Chamoun had to have some clear idea of what they were supposed to do next. He let his glance drop to the newspaper again and scanned it for a few more pages, trying to outguess Murphy.

In the Third World, Ned saw, no dramatic new massacres or famines were making headlines. No refugee camps, overcrowded and underfed, were being machine-gunned. For a change nothing new and sickening was being reported about the murderous normality of lives lived under famine and repression.

Perhaps no new messiah would rise up on Sunday in the name of such crimes and claim his place in the headlines by staging an assault on Winfield. Perhaps . . .

A short reprieve. Ned looked up to see Laverne in her housecoat, watching him. He wondered how long she had been standing there and how silently she had padded downstairs on bare feet. She looked drawn and unrested.

"Rotten night, huh?"

She nodded and made her way to the coffeepot. "Thanks for keeping it hot," she said, pouring some and dropping bread into the toaster.

"Something on your mind?" Ned asked. They both knew he had to be at the office today, of all days, but life would be a little easier for both of them if they got this out in the open with the breakfast coffee and not at the front door.

He shoved the butter and marmalade in her direction. "What's up?"

"Thinking about the girls."

"Miss 'em, huh?"

"Don't you?"

He hesitated a moment. "Naturally. But you know damned well if they were here I wouldn't be seeing them more than ten minutes a day."

"Are you bragging or complaining?"

He smiled, but it disappeared quickly. "One of these days," he said then, "when I'm eligible for a full pension . . ." He let the thought die.

"But until then, wherever the girls are, you don't have time for them," she pointed out. "Listen, Ned, I have to talk about me, not you."

"Sorry. Shoot."

"I want to fly back home and—"

"This is home," he cut in.

"California, I mean. I want to take off for a month or two with them."

"Behind barbed wire."

"We don't have to stay at Camp Liberty. We might visit one of my brothers. Phil has been asking us for a long time. So has Pete."

"How long would you be away?"

"Till school starts. I'd have them back here by Labor Day."

"How long have you been thinking about this, Verne?"

"Not very long, in one sense. But in another, it's been bothering me ever since we came to London. Ever since you . . ."

It seemed as if both of them were waiting for her to finish the thought, but she let it go. "Since I what? You were telling me, weren't you, that I'd changed and you felt left behind? Wasn't that it?"

"Nothing wrong with your memory, Ned."

"And you've been telephoning the girls." He nodded to himself. "I get the picture. And you see your prime responsibility with them, because you feel I'm shutting you out of anything else. Got it. Just one thing. How do I know you'll bring them back?"

"Because I say so."

They stared at each other, his very dark blue eyes leveled at her pale ones, neither of them wanting to drop their glance. "Okay, Verne. That's good enough for me." He shook his head as he finished his coffee. "What decided you?" he asked then, getting to his feet.

"Ha. That's a story all by itself. I had help."

"Oh? Some sort of professional?"

"A friend."

"Betsy Voss?"

"She's not a friend." Laverne looked pityingly at him. "What would you know about having a friend, Ned? You don't have a single one, unless you count that Lebanese flunky of yours."

"I thought we were talking about you, not me."

"Yes. I was going crazy, real schizo. I knew they had people in London, women, you know, counselors or marriage guidance people. Therapists. But who could I ask to recommend someone?"

"Who did you ask?"

"Jane Weil." Laverne smiled rather proudly. "And it's funny about the two of us. After I talked to her, really talked to her, I didn't need to see a professional. All I needed was to let my hair down with a friend."

The toaster clicked, whirred and shot up two underdone pieces. Laverne buttered them in silence.

Ned stood motionless for a long moment, not knowing whether to sit down and get all the news in one blow, or pretend to be disinterested and get it later from Jane.

"She told you to go to California?"

"Not at all. She didn't give me any advice except one thing: not to do anything permanent. Whatever I did, think of it as only temporary. Something I could revoke. Not cast in concrete. Do you understand?"

"Perfectly. The two of you gabbing away about our marriage. It's a terrific scene, Verne. How do you know she won't talk about it at the chancery?"

"Because Jane's not like that. You know her, Ned. How can you think she'd do something like that?"

"Accidentally?"

Laverne shrugged. "I'm sure the great intelligence plumber, Colonel French, can handle something as simple as a household leak."

He felt rooted to the floor, wanting to know the whole conversation, every word, yet afraid to seem too interested in it. But he was due at Winfield House to meet Chamoun and Mrs. Fulmer for a last-minute session.

"When were you thinking of leaving?"

"Well, Monday or Tuesday."

"That soon?"

"Ned." She looked up at him and when she spoke her voice was pitched at a very gentle level. "Don't take this wrong, but I would leave this morning if it wasn't for that rotten garden party. After that, I'm packing."

"And I'm left with the wreckage."

"If you're in trouble, ask Jane. She has lists of experts for things like that."

"That's your advice? Ask Jane?"

The lovely Art Deco building called Number 12 seemed unusually quiet to those of its Belgravia neighbors who occasionally looked out at activities there. The usual slouch in and out of scruffy youths had stopped. The man who delivered newspapers said neither the elevator operator nor the doorman were there; they had been replaced by a much younger, tougher man who wouldn't let either the news vendor or the postman inside the building. Trash men collecting garbage found the rear trades-men's entrances to Number 12 bolted and locked. There was only one way in or out and the new guard was not the welcoming type.

In the penthouse, although this third of July had dawned cloudy and humid, all the windows were locked shut. No one stood on the terraces, scanning the city below. Within the top floor life moved very quietly indeed. Leilah and Nancy Lee Miller slept in Leilah's bedroom, the door locked from the outside, the key in the keeping of one of the pop-eyed man's young henchmen. But at least the women were released now and then to cook meals for the household. They were forbidden any con-versation with Hakkad. He remained a prisoner in his bedroom, his meals brought to him by an armed keeper.

Since yesterday noon no one had come or gone. The man with the woolly hair who commanded the guards had not seen fit to visit them. He had taken Khefte away with him and wouldn't let him off the leash long enough for even one telephone call to Nancy Lee.

In the course of such incarceration, Hakkad felt he would go mad. He was given his meals, his television set, and nothing else. They had taken away his razor and unjacked his telephone. Even the food Leilah prepared was carefully searched for a possible note hidden under the boiled rice.

Nancy Lee was not going mad . . . yet. She had delivered her in-formation about the Sunday attack to Bricktop yesterday morning, think-ing that when she and Khefte returned from their shopping trip to Number 12 there would be subsequent chances to report again. Instead the gates had clanged shut and she had access neither to information nor Khefte nor Bricktop.

One of the two guards with the silenced automatic pistols played patience endlessly. The other listened to classical music on Radio 3, turning it off only when poems were read or an extremely learned astro-physicist discussed thermonuclear fusion. Occasionally the telephone would ring and be answered so monosyllabically that Nancy could make nothing of the news from outside.

"They will regret this," Leilah fumed. "Never fear. My brother is a very powerful man. These dogs will regret the way they have mistreated us."

It didn't occur to Nancy Lee to ask Leilah for more details. As a result, she had not yet understood that the original attack plan had been hijacked by the man with the wiry hair and bent to his own purposes. She only knew about one thing—the occupation of the central mosque—and since she had reported it to Bricktop, her mind remained empty. She did her nails, leafed through Leilah's fashion magazines, drank Cokes, remembered now and then to do her floor exercises, and tried not to complain.

From time to time she fantasized about Brickie, wondering whether she would arrive to rescue her so they could be lovers again. She had never met anyone like her, not ever. It had changed her life. She had thought Dris—Khefte—had changed her life, but that was nothing to what Brickie had done for her. Liberation was the word. She owed Brickie everything.

Royce Connell emerged from Gillian Lamb's bedroom as slowly and with the same stunned stealth as a German expressionist actor in a Dracula film, holding to doorways, feeling walls, glance darting this way and that, a bruised look to his eyes and the wordless plea of "Where am I?" streaming silently from his handsome face.

Behind him as he carefully closed her door, he could hear Gillian's deep, regular, healthy breathing, wrapped in sleep, her arms embracing his pillow as they had embraced him earlier in the night.

Morning? Royce moved stealthily on stockinged feet through the small annex attached to a huge mansion called Aubrey Gate, atop Aubrey Walk. This was one of London's high places where one could look out in every direction and see not only neighboring Kensington, but, far away as in a dream, the spires of the Victoria and Albert Museum, pushing up through early morning fog like the sharp breasts of a mermaid.

He found his way to her tiny kitchen and stood in a daze, wondering how, or where, or even if he ought, or would be able, to make himself a coffee. He hadn't made his own in many years. An embassy employee like Fishlock had always done it for him. Still, old skills never really deserted one, did they? Carefully he set a kettle boiling. On a shelf, a small orange plastic quartz clock showed the time to be early for a Saturday morning, not yet seven A.M. Royce took firm hold of the stainless steel sink and rocked back on his heels, trying hard to fit together what had happened last night.

He thought: There were three of us, right? Gillian, the amazing Miriam, and the fellow I once was. A night of ambiguities, of secrets kept and secrets revealed. A watershed night. He put too much instant coffee powder in a mug and poured boiling water over it.

He wandered now into Gillian's small living room, enjoying for the first time the look of fine furniture and interesting paintings on the walls. Such a bachelor's place, barely big enough for one woman. Wait! Was that a Corot? And, on the other wall, a small landscape sketch . . . Cézanne? Not possible. Reproductions. He spotted his shoes under a small sofa, next to Gillian's high-heeled strap sandals. But last night Miriam's orange pumps had been there too.

Bisexual, that one, he told himself, frowning down at his shoes while he tried to step into them. He sipped his coffee. Mad about Gillian, she was, till Gillian indicated she wasn't mad about women. Then Miriam had turned the whole evening into a kind of scout jamboree, singing songs and practically toasting marshmallows. And the matchmaker had come out in her, that deadly genetic defect in Jewish women that drives them to get everyone married off, preferably to a nice professional person, a diplomat, say, or a TV reporter.

There had, Royce vaguely recalled, been a spirited defense on his part of blessed singleness, a kind of polemic against people "owning" each other, the transaction that characterized most love affairs. They had sung songs over that, hadn't they? "You Belong to Me." Ownership songs. He could very clearly recall Miriam in her hoarse baritone belting out those immortal lines from "Sleepytime Gal" in which the love object is flatly told: "You'll learn to cook and to sew; what's more, you'll love it, I know." The coffee was awful.

That sketch was definitely a Cézanne, and those penciled acrobat cartoons were Klee. Before he lost his mind.

Royce moved back into the kitchen, where he neatly dumped all of his coffee, rinsed out his mug and placed it upside down on Gillian's little wooden dishrack. Everything about this place was small in scale, befitting a hard-working young TV journalist. Royce couldn't help but contrast it with the immensities of housing at Corinth House showered on him by his government. And yet, if you could believe Miriam, there was more to this than met the eye. Like the art on the walls.

Gillian had been out of the room getting snacks to go with the much too much they'd already had to drink. "Lovely girl," Miriam had murmured. "Lovely little bijou house. Gatehouse for the big mansion."

"Who lives there?" Royce asked.

"Nobody. When Gillian cut off from her family, she made sure none of them could get their hands on Aubrey Gate."

"You mean she owns that immense pile?"

"My dear."

Miriam had shifted her titanic bulk into more intimate conjunction with Royce. Matchmaking turned her overly amorous. "My dear," she went on, "I seem to know a hell of a lot more about your girlfriend than you do."

"She's not my g—"

"She's Lady Stoke-Monckton." Miriam's plump mouth opened and closed like an oracle's. "She'd die if you knew. She loathes her family."

"Name's not familiar to me."

"Great-grandpa made millions in opium during the last century," Miriam hissed in a low, sharp whisper. "When Papa dies, she and her brother inherit megafarms in the north, dark, satanic mills in the Midlands, and property in London, my dear Royce, property that beggars the imagination. But it wouldn't surprise me if she gave it all to charity. She—*sh!*"

Royce could hear their hostess on her way back to them. "But how do you know all this?" he asked Bricktop.

"My business, sweetie."

"The boutique business?"

"What're you two whispering about?" Gillian demanded.

That entire chunk of information had now floated back verbatim to Royce as he stood in the kitchen. Half-dressed, he really should continue to get ready and slip out of the house. It was actually only a brisk walk to Corinth and the exercise would do him good. A small but persistent pain nagged his lower back region, the result of Miriam's spirited matchmaking, he supposed. She'd left some time after midnight, he dimly recalled, the better to let her work proceed unhindered by a third party.

But, in a way, it was the implied presence of a third party that had made the whole thing possible for Royce. His encounters with the opposite sex had, by his own choice, been few and far between. His fornications had always ended with him tiptoeing out of an apartment by midnight, shoes in hand like the protagonist of a porno comic book. The reason he'd never stay the night was the reason he so rarely got involved in even a one-night stand. It wasn't the sex that bothered him, it was the enforced intimacy thereafter.

Things were expected of one, words, enduring phrases of endearment to barter with. Breakfasts to live through. All of it was distasteful to Royce. He supposed if one had a powerfully obsessive sex drive one simply *put up with* the bruising intimacies of conversation. But his own urge to copulate burned lower than that. It might, he admitted to himself can-

didly, have to do with something unresolved in him that having sex with
a man might clarify. But this late in life he wasn't about to try that, thank
you.

Yet last night, or this morning, whenever it had happened, it was
the lingering whirlwind of someone as over the top as Miriam that made
it unnecessary to trot out any expected conversation. He and Gillian had
been the mute survivors of a hurricane that hits and moves on.

He turned to stare out the kitchen window at London below him.
Another work day, picking up other people's broken pieces, snipping off
other people's loose ends, making other people look great and glorious
or, in Bud Fulmer's case, moderately acceptable. This high up in the
foreign service, Royce told himself, one should have learned that one
remained not much more than a nanny to the rich. He'd had almost
thirty years in which to learn that. He had lived well, spending every
penny he earned and never regretting it. But early retirement, for which
he would soon be eligible, was not financially possible.

His attention shifted to the electric kettle. He frowned slightly and,
as he did so, he slipped out of his shoes. Admittedly, the coffee had been
abominable, but if he had used less powder . . .? Moving quietly on
stockinged feet, he made two mugs of coffee, found some shortbread
biscuits, and made up a small breakfast tray.

Padding across polished floors, he let himself into Gillian's bedroom,
put the tray down on her bedside table, and bent over her sleeping face.
He kissed her cheek, lightly but slowly.

"Breakfast, darling. Wake-up time!"

Outside London lie a series of large and small towns devoted mostly
to providing space for businesses too large to be fitted into the expensive
space of London itself. Such a place—the British use the word "con-
urbation" to describe it—is the unpronounceable town of Slough.

Along one of Slough's wide thoroughfares, custom-designed for vehicular traffic, sandwiched between the service facility of a large computer
firm and a depot that readies French automobiles for use in Britain,
stands a two-story building that had once, in the 1930s, been the home
of a manufacturer of kitchen equipment. Fittingly enough, it now bore
the sign: HODGKINS AND DAUGHTER—CUSTOM CATERING.

The place looked surprisingly modern for being one of the few local
structures left over from an earlier era. Its Art Deco lines, meant to mimic
a contemporary kitchen of the 1930s, were very much in style now that

the rest of today's trendy house closely resembled the kitchen. Its walls were, in fact, glass brick, flooding the interior with light whenever the sun cooperated.

The pudgy man with the unhealthy complexion and pop eyes had a small desk in the center of the open office area. It was distinguished from other desks by having several extension lines on its telephone and a private phone as well. This morning the man sat quietly, staring down at some notes he had written on a pad. He was alone until noon, when this place would come to life both for parties given tonight and in advance mobilization for the grandiose garden event Mrs. Fulmer was giving tomorrow.

The private line rang but the man showed no sign he had heard. The tip of his pencil traced several notes on his pad. Finally he reached for the private phone. "Yes?"

"He has escaped."

The man's bulging eyes widened abruptly. "Who?"

"The German."

"Fool! Escaped how?"

"He is nowhere to be found, sir. I could have sworn he was d—"

"Enough. Find him."

The phone slammed down. The man with the wiry hair vented a deep sigh of anger. Were there no more professionals in this world?

He had spent time and money and blood—none of it his—assembling an elite commando from among several nations of the world. They obeyed him like automatons. In so doing he had squeezed the creative juice out of them. He had to do all their thinking for them. Much better that way. People attributed his successes to ruthlessness, or inside contacts, or secret political protection. It was all these.

He began with his own private intelligence network of those who served at parties and receptions. They produced an amazing amount of information. He was constantly surprised at the carelessness of people speaking in front of domestic help with not a notion in the world that what was overheard could be offered for sale. Waiters, chauffeurs, maids, bartenders, cleaners, butlers, secretaries . . . none of them earned so much that they could afford to turn up their noses at extra cash.

The starting advantage produced a second one. His network of informants often gathered intelligence that wouldn't lead to profit for him but was of use to the Bill. Never mind which part of what was laughingly called the law-enforcement establishment—and he did business with all of it, including the secret services—modern police work was based almost entirely on purchased information, usually from stoolies, which the Brits called "grasses." As one of London's most reliable brokers of information, he could count on protection from those who earned a living by harassing criminals.

An opportunity like Winfield House tomorrow came rarely. By contrast, a thrash like last night's at the Beeb might offer similar opportunities but almost no promise of success. The new studios were located on a crowded street often clogged with traffic, while Winfield House, with its vast hostage-holding cellar, stood on its own parklike grounds where helicopter escapes would be easy.

Of course, luck also played a major role. He smiled coldly as he thought of the stroke of good fortune that had dropped an entire gaggle of ignorant Arab geese into his lap, perfect fodder to throw the police, divert attention, and ensure his own triumph. When he had first heard rumors of the Hakkad-financed coup, he had made it his business to get an invitation to the noted doctor's home and learn for himself whether these Muslim amateurs were actually considering something so far beyond their capacities.

Nothing had convinced him they would succeed. Not until, at Hakkad's party, he had seen the German boy called Bert. Such lads had dossiers as thick as telephone directories, dossiers to which he had access. Bert was a political who had to be removed. An ideologue committed from childhood on, Bert was so purely political that he couldn't be manipulated the way a peacock like Khefte could.

But instead of staying safely dead he was now missing. He would simply have to be killed properly this time, none of this fancy "death of a thousand cuts." Something plain and sure like a handful of slugs.

The private line rang again. So occupied was he that he continued to review his situation while he picked up the phone. After a moment, he realized someone was speaking. A tinny little voice came through, belonging to a woman. An excited one.

"Mr. Fownes?"

"Ah, Mrs. Fulmer. Such a pleasant surprise. Is all well?"

"All is *not* well!" Silence on the line. She seemed to have placed her hand over the phone in order to speak to someone else. Then: "All is quite out of hand, Mr. Fownes. I am being asked to . . . But this is impossible!"

"Hello? Mrs. Fulmer?"

"Totally unacceptable. Isn't this typical army? Isn't this just the sort of idiocy for which they're famed? These are soldiers, mind you, not caterers. And I'm supposed to accept them as accomplished cooks and waiters and even musicians? It's entirely unacceptable."

She seemed to be addressing this to someone else, not him. But the man with the protuberant eyes sat staring at the blank glass-brick wall nearby, thinking: This is not possible.

Not possible that one of the Americans—that Colonel French, probably—had out-thought him. That his own substitution of commandos for waiters had been foreseen. A stroke of bad luck, but still salvageable.

"Mrs. Fulmer," he said. "Please, dear madam."

"What? Speak up, Mr. Fownes."

"Listen to me, madam. I have an idea."

It had begun to rain outside the big windowed room where Pandora Fulmer kept track of her garden party plans. The three men sat looking at the downpour: Ortega, who normally supervised Winfield security, and the two intelligence officers, Chamoun and French. They seemed secretly to have agreed to concentrate on watching the rain rather than listening to Mrs. Fulmer on the telephone with her caterer.

Chamoun found himself worrying about Ned French. He'd arrived in a fairly incoherent state, saying little, seemingly turned in on himself to avoid giving clues to his inner weather. Another shoot-out at the breakfast table, Chamoun surmised, between Ned and Laverne, possibly without bloodshed but not without internal injuries.

This inward turn of Ned's had grown even more noticeable after Pandora Fulmer had exploded in their faces over the issue of catering staff. No matter how Ned explained the expertise and vast experience of army Quartermaster personnel, Pandora was not about to give up her commitment to Hodgkins and Daughter.

"Do you understand the meaning of the word contract, Colonel French?" she had almost shouted at him. "I have contracted with the caterer. There is an agreement in writing. To an army officer, used to Pentagon cost overruns and influence peddling, the concept of honoring a contract falls on deaf ears. But in the world of honest people, we do put faith in contracts, Colonel French. We require a caterer to live up to his side of it and we certainly intend to live up to ours."

The loud voice had moderated, eventually, to a choked murmur, the kind a python would use, Chamoun supposed, while beginning to wind itself around your neck. Now the three of them, like chastised schoolboys, were made to sit and listen while Mrs. Fulmer, in effect, bypassed them completely.

"Yes, Mr. Fownes. That's most thoughtful of you . . . Oh, would you, Mr. Fownes. You're being a perfect gentleman about this . . . I can't thank you enough, Mr. Fownes, for helping me out of this embarrassing position."

Chamoun glanced at Ned out of the corner of his eye. No reaction. Just sitting there watching the rain. Finally Chamoun could stand it no longer. "Ned? Do we need this?"

Slowly French's face turned toward him without making eye contact. Then, in a faraway voice: "Perfect timing. With this much rain the garden will look beautiful tomorrow."

Ortega grimaced and said, in an undertone: "Thank God it rains today and not tomorrow, huh?"

Ned French's face turned to him, again without eye contact. "Is that how it works, Harry? You're telling me weather has a memory?"

"You think it might rain tomorrow?"

French finally glanced at Chamoun. "Only if we're lucky." He got to his feet. "Mrs. Fulmer, may I interrupt a moment."

She put her hand over the phone. "You . . . may . . . not."

"What have I done to deserve this unbroken succession of strong-minded women?" French asked the world at large.

"I beg your pardon?" Pandora Fulmer's voice had crusted over with ice.

"Hang up, Mrs. Fulmer. Tell him you'll call him back with his instructions. Who is employing whom? He seems to be making all your decisions for you, whoever he is."

"Mr. Fownes, I apologize. I am dealing with some extremely rude public servants here. I'll phone you in half an hour. Yes. How sweet. Thank you. Yes. Good-bye."

The look in her eyes had suddenly calmed. No internal storms shook Pandora. She seemed to have congealed into a small but perfectly formed block of ice. "Colonel French," she began, "I intend to have you transferred if not court-martialed. You have exceeded your responsibilities in a completely unacceptable manner. You will have to learn that ours is a civilian government in which the decisions are made by civilians, not time-servers in olive drab."

Ned smiled slightly at what was, Chamoun had to admit, a neatly controlled attack. "To get right to the immediate point," Pandora went on coldly, "you will not be allowed to introduce any of your clodhopping

Quartermaster Corps hash-slingers into Winfield House. Not tomorrow. Not ever."

Ned glanced at his watch. "I beg your pardon, Mrs. Fulmer. Is His Excellency on the premises? Is he seeing visitors this morning?"

"You are not to bother His Excellency with this."

"I'm afraid you leave me no choice."

"And I'm afraid you don't understand the position you're in, Colonel French. You carry no weight here. And as soon as I can, I intend to see that you carry no weight anywhere else. People like you can't be allowed to dictate civilian policy on behalf of our president."

Watching them as dispassionately as he could, Chamoun tried to size them up as boxers, one bantamweight, physically out of her class, but as game as a bantam hen nevertheless. She had risen to her full height and was glaring up at Ned with such a chilly, fixed stare that Chamoun had a sudden vision of a medusa and Ned frozen in stone. He cleared his throat; any sound would have done to break the force of that tight, gut-wrenching standoff.

"Isn't it possible that we can use both?" Chamoun suggested. "I mean, some of ours and some from Hodgkins and Daughter?"

"At last! Sanity!" Pandora's voice had dropped to a serpentine hiss. "Precisely what Mr. Fownes so obligingly suggested. He's not stonewalling me, Colonel French, only you are. He's willing to compromise. And now your own able attaché follows suit. Does that register in that military brain of yours?"

"I think we'll ask His Excellency what he thinks," Ned said.

"No!"

"I'm afraid I'll have to."

"No!"

"I have no ch—"

"No!" She sank into a tiny ballroom chair and suddenly burst into tears. Almost immediately two black lines of mascara coursed down her cheeks, one from each eye. She had assumed an appealing, clownlike pathos in a mere second or two.

"Wh-why do you h-hate me?" she asked Ned.

Chamoun took a step back. The aura around this little woman had the force of some immense electromagnetic field. She was like a judo expert, using her opponent's greater mass to do him in.

Ned dropped to one knee and extended his white handkerchief. Through tears Pandora saw what was being offered and struck it from his hand. It flew across the room, weightless, bewitched, like one of those laboratory demonstrations of great electrical power.

Keening very softly at the thin edge of audibility, Pandora burrowed like a helpless kitten in the pale fawn sleeve of her sweater. She came up with a tiny wisp of something which she pressed first to her petite nose and then to her cheeks.

This woman, Chamoun found himself thinking, with all the titanic power of the White House behind her, with all the innate maneuvering ability that the president's Directive 103 had given her, power that had stymied even Royce Connell and had given Chamoun and Ned French a week of anguish, this woman still was able to see that she could win more battles helpless than by wielding power.

There was a pitiful catch in her throat as she drew in one small, shuddering breath and stared in reproach, in dismay, in deep disappointment, at Colonel French.

"You have set yourself to frustrate me at every turn, sir," she quavered. "You have used all your powers to trample me down and make me look ridiculous and . . . and extravagant . . . and silly. You must have felt marvelous when I was informed by the State Department that I couldn't screen my presidential videos. You must have smiled cruelly, sir, when guests began to cancel in droves. You must have felt quite proud of yourself when I failed to locate any fireworks. And now you strike at the very heart of the affair, sir, the catering, leaving me at the mercy of hired assassins from the Quartermaster Corps who wouldn't know one end of a chicken from the other unless it had labels tattooed on it."

She stopped to gulp in air and Ned struck quickly. "You're absolutely right, Mrs. Fulmer. I didn't do any of those things, but you're absolutely right to blame *somebody* for them. But, Mrs. Fulmer, we're teetering on the very edge. It's Saturday. Let's pretend for one moment that we're both on the same side and let's make some decisions fast."

She stared up at him, blotting the mascara lines that had dropped from her eyes. Chamoun, with his outsider's cold view of things, realized that she knew all about those lines without recourse to a mirror. So their existence was nothing new, then. She'd caused them to run appealingly on other occasions. Part of her ammo kit, eh?

"Wh-what did you say?"

"I said let's trust each other for twenty-four hours. Then you can try to get me transferred. But until then let's behave like adults with a common problem that has to be solved."

Ortega, who had been acutely uncomfortable through all this, now chose the moment to jump in as peacemaker. "But you have to stop needling us, Colonel French. We've been protecting Winfield for a long time now. I know Mrs. Fulmer has Winfield's best interest at heart."

Listening to this gibberish, Chamoun was afraid it would send Ned off into a tantrum of his own. He had never seen French that angry, except in the privacy of his own office with no other witness but his deputy, Chamoun.

Ned rose from his knees, picked up his spurned handkerchief and thoughtfully tucked it away, like Pandora, in his sleeve. He looked from her to Ortega, glanced sideways at Chamoun, and said:

"I accept the compromise."

"Which compromise?" Ortega asked, thoroughly confused.

"The suggestion that we only augment the professional caterers with some of our own people. Instead of replacing them, that is."

Without another word, Pandora reached for the telephone. Her rather distraught eyes remained fixed on Ned for a long moment. Then she dialed a number. "Mr. Fownes? Yes, hello. Listen, the problem's solved."

That part of Pimlico surrounding the Tate Gallery, which stands at the River Thames, should by rights be quite fashionable. One day, Hargreaves hoped, it would prove so. It was not for that reason that he had, in a flush period some decades back, bought a tiny basement flat which faced out on a tinier garden. It suited him, always had, as a combination of centaur's cave and recovery room. This morning, with Nicola Strong in attendance, it suited him even more.

He had very few illusions, old Hargreaves, least of all that a girl who could easily have been his granddaughter would stick around any longer than it took him to get her well known and safely planted on some higher rung of the British theatrical scene. Over the years there had been perhaps a dozen Nicolas who had hitched a ride on the Hargreaves publicity bandwagon, some being talentless ninnies or gross opportunists. But Nicola Strong seemed to him an improvement, certainly in looks and, as far as could be told this early on, in brain power as well. Maybe, with age, he was finally learning to pick winners.

He sat in a ratty bathrobe at his small round oak table in the kitchen, which faced out onto the garden. There, clad only in one of his long and shapeless sweatshirts, she knelt in the grass and picked flowers. Whatever else the neighbors would say about all this, they certainly couldn't complain of the beauty of the scene, especially when the sweatshirt rode up higher than it should have.

Nicola came back into the kitchen and ran cold water for a moment, filling a tall glass and arranging her small bunch of flowers in it. "You never take care of that garden," she accused him.

"No time."

"Yes, well, as you've no one living with you, I'm moving in, trowel and all."

Hargreaves sat up in his chair. "How nice!"

"I mean, just because the neighborhood's a bit tatty doesn't mean your garden can't look spiffing. It's a matter of ambition and work."

"Not tatty, my dear," Hargreaves said, reaching for a pencil and pad, "Tatey."

He watched her pawing through a net bag to find the opening through which she could get an orange. She looked terribly young to him, but somehow not at all vulnerable. Not with dreams as ambitious as hers.

"You sound like a firm believer in ambition," Hargreaves suggested.

"All the proper virtues. Hard work. The primacy of talent."

"Those British with talent and ambition have a choice," he said. "We can leave England for a society where our gifts are appreciated and rewarded. Or we can stay and tailor our expectations to ever more modest, shrinking patterns."

She bent over the orange and was slowly peeling it in one long strip that she dangled over the paper bag in which Hargreaves kept his trash. Slowly the strip lengthened and the orange grew smaller and whiter. Clever little monkey.

"I'm not saying this will happen to you," Hargreaves told her. "You may be luckier than the rest. Show biz is often the exception. It's like black boxers. Boxing is often the only way blacks can make a career. And acting may be the only lucrative profession left to the British."

She rapped her chest, Tarzan-style. "Me Strong."

"You'll need to be. Because this shrinking pattern of expectations affects even show biz. It's not always going to be Dickens or Shakespeare. Often the only way you'll be able to pay the rent is some hideous trash act. Are you old enough to know?"

"Trash act?" Her thin fingers pried the orange into segments. "I'm old enough to know trash."

"It's the verb form I'm after. A trash act is an act that trashes everything good that came before it. It even trashes the trash of a former era."

She sat back down on his lap and began feeding him segments of fruit. "And TV," he managed to say past the orange in his mouth. "Still in the car-chase stage, most of it, these tiny autos careening around a tiny screen in your bookcase. Or housewives of great wealth insulting each other in Texas steak houses. And what about books?"

"Trash," she said in a hollow, tragic voice, "all trash."

"Self-help books like *Recycling Personal Waste for Fun and Profit*. Thick doorstops of nonfiction on creative masturbation." He swallowed an orange segment almost unchewed. "You do bring out the ranter in me."

But he was scribbling on his pad again, a few more book titles: *100 Things to Do with Maggots*. He kissed her ear.

"What do you think they'll say when they see us together?" he asked.

"I hope something like lucky Hargreaves."

"It's not luck. I told you. We were fated."

"The fact is, I'm the lucky one," she said in a rather casual tone, throwing the line away. "You know what the greatest enemy of a young actress is?"

"An old lecher."

"Never. My greatest enemy is a young actor. A straight one who digs girls. More careers go up in smoke that way."

"Whereas an elderly crock with a taste for booze . . . he's safe."

She gave him a hug. "He's safe."

He wrapped his arms around her and joined in the squeezing, thinking to himself how old the young were these days.

When they arrived at the chancery, the place had its usual weekend look, not deserted but underpopulated. If Ned French stood in the silent corridor and listened for the sound of the building, that inanimate blend of machinery, telephones, and other vibrations, it was very faint. The chancery wasn't open to the public today but many staff people were at work.

He sat down at his desk and set Chamoun to some task that would keep him in his own office for a while. Ned didn't really want to talk to anyone. He felt bruised without knowing whether he'd won or lost a fight.

The one with Laverne he'd surely lost. Perhaps the one with Mrs. F. Time would tell. But there was another way to look at it. When fighting with a woman, there was always another way. And from this viewpoint, perhaps he'd won. God only knew. He reached for the phone and called Jane Weil's office. No one answered. He switched to his private line and phoned her home. No one answered.

He sat back and reviewed the various reasons why she was temporarily away from one or the other of her telephones. Nothing was going right this morning. He called her home again. Twenty rings.

Imagine it, she and Laverne, probably in a pub somewhere. His wife and his mistress discussing his marriage. Something had to be really bad before it required a repair job like that. He called her home again and again no one answered. This was becoming ludicrous, Ned decided. He had to stop behaving like a moonstruck calf, or whatever you called someone whose girlfriend wasn't coming on to him.

Still, it bothered him. Perfectly good explanation somewhere. But his intuition told him it was something more serious. He congratulated himself on having completed the defenses of Winfield before being hit by one of Cupid's more poisonous darts. Duty first. Everything else second. No reason she couldn't be out, not home.

His private line rang.

"Ned," Jane began, "please stop calling me."

"How the hell did y—"

"Just stop, please."

"But I want to see you today."

"No."

"Look, Laverne has—"

"I'll see you tomorrow at Winfield," she said. "But I don't want to see you today."

"Winfield?"

"I'm handling protocol for Royce at the party. At least I think I am. I haven't been able to get him at home or office."

"Maybe he's not answering his phone either. Look, Jane—"

"Good-bye."

The line went dead.

24

On the map, Slough is two-thirds of the way between central London and the Buckinghamshire village of Amersham. As he drove rapidly north into Amersham, the man with the pop eyes and bushy hair congratulated himself on still running very much in luck. He had managed to keep Mrs. Fulmer on his side.

Now for the problem of the missing German. Would Bert talk? Lads like him grew up in a strict code of silence. It loomed over them with the same awesome authority as Marx's theories on excess profits.

Nevertheless there were no guarantees that, having been betrayed, tortured, and left for dead, Bert would still feel a lively sense of solidarity with his former comrades. Ideological links were dependable up to a point. But they could dissolve in the need for revenge.

So wasn't he lucky, the man who called himself Fownes asked himself, that Slough was only a few minutes drive from Amersham and Little Missenden? Or wasn't it simply good planning, phenomenal planning, sensational planning?

Hubris.

He slowed down as he turned left off Highway A355 into the old town of Amersham. The blond lad he had ordered to wait for him was supposed to be standing under the old market building that served as the town's center. This was an ancient brick structure of two stories enclosing an open-sided gallery or trading area on the ground level where farmers once brought their produce and where today leather belts, ceramic-bead necklaces, and burned-wood souvenirs were for sale. There stood his man, fingering a kapiz-shell box whose decal flatly proclaimed: SOUVENIR OF AMERSHAM.

He didn't know the blond lad's real name. In his organization everyone was free, following his own example, to choose whatever name he pleased. At Hodgkins and Daughter, which he'd bought last year, there was a regular payroll because those employees were not part of his elite strike force. For his warriors, however, there were no real records, no duty rosters or payrolls. Once a week he distributed cash. After a particularly profitable venture—tomorrow's for example—he would hand out bonuses, again in cash, to his elite troops.

He pulled his unobstrusive car to the curb and waited for the lad to join him. Yes, tomorrow would be immensely profitable. Thanks to his recent looting of Hakkad's London cash accounts, he had eliminated sponsors. He would share with no one, unless Hakkad's Pan-Eurasian Credit Trust. One did need a bank somewhere in one's organization, if only to launder ransom.

The blond lad got in beside him. "Nowhere," he said, sounding out of breath. He had been trained to cut conversation to a minimum.

"Then someone must have removed him," the man with the unhealthy complexion said. "He could not have escaped under his own power."

"We are checking the hospital here."

"But carefully, yes?"

The lad nodded. "That's what takes time, sir."

"We have time." Fownes backed the car out of its parking place slowly. "But for the German, time is running out." Pausing to enter the flow of traffic, he saw something a few cars along the curb. "What is that?"

"What, sir?"

The man's hand moved so quickly that the blond lad didn't see it in time to avoid knuckles raked across his cheek, hard, stinging. "The Fiorino van, fool!"

It took the lad some effort to keep from touching his slapped cheek, but he sat without moving. "It belongs to the Arab, sir."

"Who relettered it 'Hodgkins and Daughter'?"

"Khefte suggested it."

This time he was anticipating the backhand slap. When the knuckles crashed into his cheek he could feel the pain all across his eye and face. He winced, but still refrained from touching it.

"Drive the van to Little Missenden, fool. I'll be right behind you. Park it in the safe house garage, do you understand? Spray out the lettering this afternoon, do you hear? And replace that window with the bullet hole. Fool!"

Fownes gave the lad a rough shove. Still not touching his face, the blond young man got out of the Metro and, with some dignity, made his way to the gray Fiorino and led the way out of Amersham.

One of the good lads, the man with the protuberant eyes reflected. He nursed his knuckles as he drove. One of the ones who likes pain, he thought. My kind.

At eleven o'clock two telephone calls came into that part of Defense Section under Ned French's authority. He answered one and Chamoun the other. Then both men left their desks and conferred in the hall outside their offices.

"Parkins," Ned told his deputy. "They have Weems in the Savile Row station and they want me for no more than half-hour."

Chamoun nodded. "I'll mind the store."

"What was your call?"

"A breather," Chamoun said.

But Ned was on his way out and didn't stop to pursue the question. The call had, in fact, been a breather, but Chamoun had neglected to add that it was one of Bricktop's bits of emergency agentcraft, to be used only in dire necessity. The first breather was the alert signal. If not followed by a second, it meant a rendezvous at the usual place, near the boutique. If a second call came through, Chamoun was to get to a secure phone and try a series of numbers until he located her.

As he stood there, with Ned barely out of earshot, the telephone rang and, when he answered it, clicked off. Second call. Chamoun stared out his window at Grosvenor Square, empty of people at the moment since Saturday shoppers weren't likely to enjoy the rather threatening weather. The rain had stopped, but high leaden clouds were piling up again in the west.

Ned's departure had given him at least a half-hour. He hated to leave the office unmanned since, if neither of them were at their desks, calls went unanswered. But the second breather was too urgent to ignore.

He left the building almost on Ned's heels but turned north toward

Oxford Street and found a telephone on Duke Street near one of the clothing stores whose basement levels formed shopping arcades for the Bond Street tube station.

He tried the boutique number, just to be on the safe side, but the girl in charge said Bricktop wasn't expected till later. Then he tried her safe house in Chelsea, with no answer. Finally, he had her "Mrs. Henderson" number, which was a desk she rented, with its own telephone line, from a company in the Shepherd Market section of Mayfair, a slightly seedy outfit which sold a good address for something like fifty quid a week. This desk telephone had a message recorder attached to it.

"Mrs. Henderson is away from her desk. Please leave a message or telephone the following number."

Chamoun listened to the number, hung up, and called it. Brick's voice, fat with pleasure, came on the line. "Mersh? Sorry about this. And the line's not all that great."

"Then why the hell—"

"Shuddup and listen, *bubeleh*. Tomorrow, your visitors will occupy the mosque first. It's a symbolic act. Timed for the noonday prayer."

"What?"

The line went dead. Cursing, Chamoun put in another ten-p piece and punched up the number again. But this time no one answered. Ten rings. Twenty. Goddamn the woman!

He stared accusingly at the telephone itself, then turned and made his way upstairs and back to the chancery. As he walked he regained his temper and began to realize that Bricktop had done him a favor.

A terrific favor, in fact, a gift of information that could save the day. But it was a poisoned gift. How could he produce this key piece of information without explaining to Ned how it came his way?

"Oh, say, Ned, we had an anonymous call. Must've been that breather I mentioned? Some guff about the big central mosque tomorrow. Probably nothing to it, but still . . ."

It smelled. Not only that but, presented in such an offhand, over-the-transom manner, it didn't have enough authority to galvanize real response. Because if Brick was right—and he knew her informant was centrally close to the action—this half-crazed symbolic gesture had to be contained by planning that would begin now, as soon as Ned was told of it.

Back at his desk, Chamoun studied map blowups of the area. The mosque was practically across the street from Winfield. But it was singularly unsuited as a base for a ground assault. One came into the mosque from the direction opposite Winfield, thus doubling the distance between the two structures.

To try to think with the mind of the German agent who served as Khefte's political commissar—for Chamoun assumed that Khefte alone would never be able to design a workable battle plan—the occupation of the mosque had to be staged without gunfire or any act that could be deemed a desecration. Once having raised a defiant shout within the holy place, the attack force would then have to swing around in almost a complete circle before storming the gates of Winfield. It didn't make much sense. But as a symbolic act, of course, it rang a rich and mighty bell.

He sat back in his chair and stared at Grosvenor Square again, remembering when he had first spotted Nancy Lee Miller out there with her little notebook. That such a dumb-dumb was making notes had sounded the first alarm for Chamoun. Then, spotting Khefte and the German, he had been able to identify Nancy Lee's allegiances. But here she was, nestled in the very armpit of Khefte's cadre, working for Brick.

The power of love.

He smiled a bit, a Chamoun smile, very controlled but worried. He had reason to be. His duty to Ned—call it love if you wanted, Ned was his only friend in the world—demanded that he report Brick's information. And identify its source; otherwise it had no authority.

If the information was accurate, it would mean the difference between a noisy, publicity-grabbing assault that would cost many lives and a soft implosion, the strike force blotted up so silently it need never even make a headline. True, there were camera crews at Winfield. But none at the mosque.

Then how was he going to tell Ned? Was it Brick's way of kissing him off? Mossad had spent too much time getting him in place to blow it over a piece of intelligence that, after all, meant very little to the Israelis. The only road open to him was the well-crafted lie and then outright denial of guilt.

Not far from the art galleries on Cork Street stands a pale gray building that runs between Old Burlington Street and Savile Row, where the custom tailors are. In this part of London tourists frequently get lost turning into cul-de-sacs like Coach and Horses Yard because nobody has told them that "cul-de-sac" means "dead end." Few of them enter the pale gray building in sedate 1930s Gothic unless they are in need of a policeman.

The room P. J. R. Parkins had taken over was a small one, normally a place where one plod and one villain talked quiet-like until one steno was summoned. There were three men in it when Ned arrived, none of whom seemed all that pleased to see him. Perhaps they had exhausted the room's available oxygen and didn't welcome an additional pair of lungs.

"Right," Parkins said in lieu of hello or how are you or so glad you could come over. "Mr. Weems, Colonel Edward French of the American embassy. Colonel French, this is James F. Weems, U.S. citizen. He's been squealing for somebody from the embassy and I thought it ought to be you."

"Did you?" Ned turned to face a red-haired man with an angry splatter of freckles. "And this gentleman?"

"Is just leaving," Parkins said. Without a further word the man called Jock left them.

"Was it something I said?" Ned asked.

"All right, Weems. You asked for him."

The tall American with the honest face looked very tired. He'd slept off and on in a cell here at Savile Row and his royal blue dinner jacket showed it. So did his face, drawn and worried.

"I asked for a Mr. Rand," Weems said.

"You'll get your Mr. Rand," Parkins promised him in a no-nonsense tone. "It's just that he's taking his bloody fucking time about it, isn't he?"

Ned made a face. "Language, Mr. Parkins."

"No offense, Colonel French."

"Well then, if Mr. Weems didn't ask for me, I suppose we'll just call this a false alarm and I'll be on my way. I do have a lot to finish off before Sunday's, um, matter."

"Colonel." Parkins stopped uneasily and Ned realized he was trying to find a way of telling him that he was wanted here not on Weems's behalf but in connection with the Riordan side of the case.

"Is there anything you want to tell me, Mr. Weems?" Ned said then. "Or ask me?"

The tall American looked away, as if in thought, but said nothing.

"P'raps," Parkins suggested, "he could begin by telling you why he had no passport. Claims it was stolen. Claims he applied for a new one but the embassy hasn't come up with it yet."

"Is that true, Mr. Weems?"

"Yes and no."

"Could you find time to assign each of those words to its proper place in Mr. Parkins's statement?"

"And who the hell is Mr. Parkins?" Weems demanded. "Nobody shows me anything in the way of ID except cards they pocket before you can read them. Where's your card? Who was Jock?"

"Jock?"

"The guy who hightailed it out of here when you showed up."

Ned turned to Parkins. "We're all speaking English, Mr. Parkins. Perhaps you could relieve me of the role of interpreter?"

"Yes, well, of course." Parkins got to his feet and began to pace an extremely small area near the door, hardly more than a yard by half a yard. "As you both know, the death of Riordan leaves a tremendous number of questions unanswered. We are trying to start at the beginning, which, in this case, means the four phone calls the dead man made to Mr. Weems over the last week."

"Before he was dead, that is," Ned added for the information of Weems.

But Parkins was in no mood for jokes. His oaken face seemed to harden and grow entirely immobile. "Yes, we do watch those American TV films about your funny detectives, Colonel French. We know all about smart dialogue. Over here we usually save that for the pub, after we've nailed our villain."

"Meaning me," Weems supplied. "These idiots think I'm involved in Tony's death."

"One might say the same about me," Ned told him. "Why don't you tell Mr. Parkins why you're not a suspect? If you can account for your whereabouts recently, that would help, too."

"Is this the kind of protection I can expect from my embassy?" Weems flared up. "Whose side are you on, French?"

"Yours, as long as you've been paying your taxes."

The nuttiness of this answer stopped Weems with his mouth open. "What do you mean? You mean the IRS is . . .? You're kidding, right?"

"Wouldn't that be a terrific efficiency move?" Ned asked them both. "You don't get any benefits of government unless you pay your taxes. If you're delinquent, or fraudulent, we retract all benefits, even retroactively. We take back Vietnam, Chile, Grenada, Nicaragua, Libya. We withdraw covert surveillance by the FBI and the CIA and any other team of government spooks. We stop going through your garbage cans. We no longer intimidate your kids' schoolteachers or your neighbors. We don't use your taxes any more to subsidize filthy-rich political TV con men-preachers or gigantic agribusinesses or oil companies. We even withdraw any outstanding IRS audits. It's a complete withholding of all the benefits of American citizenhood that your taxes had previously bought. Then, when you're broken, sobbing for mercy, we *allow* you, in our generosity, to pay your taxes and you once again join the happy throng."

Parkins, whose mouth had dropped open early in this outburst, now closed it, with an audible snap. "That'll be the day," he muttered. Then, returning to his pursuit: "If you two would like to be left alone for ten minutes? But I expect some good to come of it." He let himself out and closed the door behind him.

"Well," Ned said then, "this is odd. I'm not your lawyer."

"You're not my anything, Colonel. I asked for Larry Rand."

"What if Rand doesn't want to acknowledge you?"

"Oh, you've heard about me?"

"I know you think you're navigating under the protection of the Company."

Weems seemed to think twice about answering. "Then we don't have anything to talk about, do we?"

Ned shrugged. "It isn't a total waste. I think Old Parkins wanted a pee break anyway."

He sat down across from Weems and let his face go dead. Either Rand protected this nasty specimen or he didn't. It mattered not. Ned was heartily sick and tired of this whole thing. He was unhappy at Jane's not wanting to see him or even talk to him. He was uneasy, as well, about Laverne's ultimatum, no, decision. And he was furious at having to compromise with Pandora Fulmer. All in all it had been a lousy day so far, and this cell-like interrogation room with its unwilling suspect— or was it suspects?—only promised more grief.

He wondered what kind of day Chamoun was having.

Stoke Mandeville hospital employed only two security men on a regular basis in its Accidents Building. Both of them had once been military police and were now past fifty years of age. Between them they managed to handle virtually any security problem Accidents had, whether it be unwelcome visitors like the press, or patients who suddenly went violent beyond the restraint capability of nurses. In other words, as Trevor Butt had often confided to Will Nightwater, "It's a fair doddle, this, compared to the old days."

They had been in the same detachment of military police. To Trev and Will, the old days included night duty in Germany and Cyprus getting British servicemen out of trouble with irate publicans, pregnant ladies, and shopkeepers whose premises had been boyishly wrecked.

"And dead dull," Will responded to Trev.

"Any doddle's dull," Trev explained. He was two years older than Will and often played the role of man of the world. They met only once a day, right before dinner, when Trev went off the day shift and Will went on night duty, but they had worked it out so that they were able to spend the better part of a half hour sipping tea and reminiscing. Trev was a man of parts, in addition to being a man of the world. He had illegally managed to keep hold of his Browning Parabellum 9-millimeter service automatic. Still unregistered, it was kept in the security office, locked in a desk drawer. For this Will was thankful since, if there were to be any serious trouble, it would be on the night watch, wouldn't it?

"Stands to reason, Trev. I see you've bought us a few extra clips. How'd y' manage that without the weapon being registered?"

Trev seldom responded to searching questions like that. A man of parts didn't have to explain to an old mate, did he? "Just don't you give the game away, you dozey old fart."

Will looked hurt. "You know me, Trev. If it's a really bad night I might stow it in my jacket pocket, but no one could see it."

"There won't be any excitement tonight. We've nothing but auto crashes at the moment."

"And what about that German lad?"

Trev frowned. "The one that got himself punched up good and proper down in Little Missenden?"

"He came to when Sister Prewitt was on duty and fair pestered the life out of her. '*Wasser, bitte. Entschuldig mir, Wasser zu trinken.*' And Sister Prewitt hadn't any idea what he wanted. So I explained."

"He's lucky he can hold water, that one," Trev said in his ominous man-of-the-world tone. "There's enough knife cuts in him to sink a cruiser."

The two men finished their tea in absorbed silence, remembering old knife fights they had stopped, or helped cover up so the British soldiers involved could escape the local law. Nothing quite like a good knife fight. Nobody in England fought that way any more, of course. Pity.

". . . want you to know this is voluntary on my part. You have no jurisdiction over . . ."

Larry Rand's voice, low and tough, could be heard outside the small interrogation room long before his sawed-off body appeared in the doorway. He sounded mad as hell, but Ned French could never remember a time when he didn't sound mad as hell. It was part of the Rand persona.

"You!" the station head said when he laid eyes on Ned. "I might have known some dingbat asshole like you was mixed up in this."

French stood up. "Would you like to repeat that outside, Larry? I have been dying to turn you into a short pail of pigshit. It shouldn't take more than a minute or two."

Rand backed up several inches. His irate glance swept the small room. "What the fuck *is* this? You guys taking buggery lessons?"

French gently laid his right hand on Rand's left shoulder. "Apologize, you little turd."

The Mickey Rooney face went through half a dozen contortions, blinks, grimaces, half-smiles. "Can't take a joke, huh, French?"

"Not from you, short stuff."

Wince. Growl. Chuckle. "No sense of humor." His glance moved to Weems. "Who's this?"

"Apologize." Ned let his hand weigh heavier on the Rand shoulder.

"Okay, okay. No hard feelings. Who's this guy?"

Ned took his hand away. "James F. Weems. He asked for you. Can't imagine why."

"Weems?" The very word seemed to sprout horns in Rand's mouth. "Weems? Whadya want, Weems?"

The tall American cleared his throat. "Do I have to tell you?"

Rand swung on French, as if to an ally. "What is this guy? Some kind of joker?"

"No sense of humor, huh, Larry? He thinks he's got a right to Company cover. What do you think?"

The station head put together several steaming responses but none got beyond his lips. He closed his mouth very firmly and puffed out his goblin cheeks several times. "Do you have any idea how many violations of security procedure you just committed, French?"

"Oh, Christ, not that again. He asked for you *by name,* numbskull. And Parkins knew damned well who he was talking about. So take off the false beard and let's start dealing."

After a pause, Rand sat down in a chair and immediately looked larger, more on the same scale as French although never as tall as Weems. Ned began to see that Weems couldn't expect much of a break from a

shrimp like Rand. It just wasn't in his shriveled little genes. No one spoke
for the longest time.

"Since you ask," Ned began then, wondering if P. J. R. Parkins's
tape recorder was secretly getting this unlovely scene, "let me review the
case of James F. Weems. To begin with, and my memory may be rusty
on this, the IRS is after his ass. That's just for openers. I also understand
that he's wanted for questioning by the fraud squad of the Met Police,
acting on orders from the Department of Trade and Industry and the
Securities and Investment Board. That's here in London. In New York,
the SEC had a reader out on him but when they asked Justice to im-
plement matters they hit a brick wall. Weems and a lad called Tony
Riordan have Company cover. Did you know that? Which brings us to
Mr. Riordan, who—"

"Hold it, for Christ's sake." Rand's right hand started to cover his
face, as if to help him concentrate, or hide tears. But instead the hand
returned to its position flat on the table in front of him. "You expect me
to follow all that rigmarole?"

"I expect most of it's familiar to you already."

"Like shit it is, French."

"First you've heard of it?"

"Mm." Again the hand almost got to his squashed-out elf's face but
was held down by sheer willpower. Oh, Ned thought, does he want not
to be here now.

"If you're rejecting Mr. Weems," Ned said then, "he comes under
my jurisdiction, at least until I can unload him back on the Bill." Ned
turned to the tall American. "I presume you have a lawyer?"

"Probably."

"Then the only thing I'll do for you now is make sure you get the
chance to phone him. The rest lies with Parkins and his crew."

"Parkins?" Rand wanted to know. "The old guy in the chancery?"

"If I'm any judge, he's your age, Larry."

"Okay, French. You got the upper hand. I walked into this without
knowing it was booby-trapped. Next time it'll be on my terms. Remember
that." He got to his feet and instantly dropped to boy size again. The
visual effect was so strong one expected his voice to shoot up into soprano
range, too.

"Any time, Larry." Ned let him open the door. "When I make my
report I'll simply say you denied any knowledge of or connection with
the accused. Right?"

"Go fuck yourself." The little man disappeared.

Neither of them spoke for a while. Then Weems said, "You really fixed me up with him."

"You think I queered your chances of cover?"

"I know you did." Weems sighed in a tired, unhappy way. "It was up to him to get you out of here so we could make our deal."

"So why didn't he?"

Weems laughed mirthlessly. "How well do you know your Company history?"

"It's never been a favorite subject of mine."

"Ever heard what happened in Honolulu?"

"Anybody who reads the newspapers remembers that."

"Well, when the chips go down here, Rand can see himself singing aloha to Station London and dropping into early retirement with prejudice. So he chickens out on me. That's all."

"You're saying you really have a contract with the Company?"

Weems shrugged. "What difference does it make? Whoever put out that hit on Tony did me in, too."

"Who paid for that auto collision?"

"Somebody Tony must've taken big."

Ned looked him over for signs that he was up to his usual con again. "You don't know his name?"

"Christ, French, it could be anybody. Riordan was my best salesman. He was racking up three, four hundred thousand a week in fund share sales."

"So, whoever was mad at him might be just as mad at you."

"I'm not going to let it spook me. I've got a few more cards to play." Weems sat up straighter, and his look of utter honesty grew more intense.

"What's that supposed to mean?" Ned demanded. "You had one ace left and your pal Larry just trumped it."

"That won't be the first mistake he's made. But maybe he'll remember it better than some of his others."

"Weems, I don't think you understand where you're sitting. They don't fry people in the electric chair in England, but they can sure as hell lock you up for a couple of dozen years if they can hang Riordan's death on you."

"Only you're not going to let them." Weems glanced almost triumphantly at Ned French. "I was in Scotland with the Duke of Buchan shooting deer."

"Is that your alibi?"

"And so was His Excellency Bud Fulmer."

Ned eyed him sourly and yearned to wipe off the self-righteous as-
surance that showed on Weems's open, choirboy face. "So, Mr. Fulmer
has bad taste in friends."

"Very bad. It isn't the deer season, French. He was breaking the law
of the land. You know how the Brits are about killing deer?"

Ned's face went bland. Weems had now maneuvered himself into
an interesting position. If Ned wanted to keep H.E.'s name out of the
papers, he had to shield Weems's alibi from Parkins. "What kind of proof
are you selling?"

"Photos?"

"You do realize this could be a murder case? I'm not sure what I can
do for you even if I wanted to."

"Oh, you'll think of something, you and Royce Connell."

"What makes you so sure of that?"

"Let's not kid around, French. You two are going to cover me all
over nice and cozy with the American flag. Rand wouldn't, but you have
no choice. I don't expect you to do it at a moment's notice. I'm a
reasonable man. I'll stay dummied up with the Bill till you figure out a
way."

He put out his right hand in the most sincere and casual way, one
American to another. Ned frowned unpleasantly. "Put it back in your
pocket, Weems. And let's change the subject. Parkins has probably heard
the whole thing."

"Deal?"

"You'd better worry more about your own health, Weems," Ned told
him. "If you didn't kill Riordan, whoever did will go after you next."

Parkins opened the door. "Too true, Mr. Weems," he said. "The
next thing you know you could be tangling with a Mini in a street
accident."

The sky overhead still maintained a seamless gray cover above London, but now, in midafternoon, the sun was beginning to move lower
in the west. In a while, Ned thought as he walked slowly back from
Savile Row to the chancery, the sun would make its mendacious little
bow again, coming in under the cover for a quick curtain call and round
of applause.

He walked slowly because he was troubled. Everything today troubled
him, and nowhere could he find a ray of relief, not even a fake one of
the kind the evening sun would soon manufacture. Betrayal seemed all

around him. He felt as if he could almost breathe it in the air. Unlike his usual premonitions, this one had a name.

It didn't do to brood too much on the subject of betrayal. Inevitably, it would lead him back to his own life and times, his own betrayals. For some reason, the sight of a con artist like Weems, who had never given a sucker an even break in his whole life of crime, twisting in the wind as Larry Rand left him to hang high and dry, gave the whole unhappy day an even more melancholy feel.

Even more depressing was Ned's feeling that Rand had been putting on a performance in front of him and would later, privately, bail Weems out of his predicament. More betrayal.

It *was* in the air. Perhaps not just the air of London. Perhaps betrayal was everywhere these days. But he was in London and his lungs were full of the stench. Not even the dead Riordan could escape it. When Ned had finally left the police station, Weems had been busy pinning every scam, every cock-and-bull mutual fund, every surreptitious cash shipment to Switzerland, on dear dead Tony. An excellent maxim: The absent are always to blame.

He moved from Berkeley Square to the bottom of Grosvenor and stared across it at the rather unprepossessing façade of the chancery. No, he thought, you'll never be just another pretty face.

What had gotten into Saarinen when he designed this combination of stone and glitz? The eagle . . . well, you couldn't very well find fault with an eagle as big as the Ritz, modeled after one of those New England weathervane eagles. It added a note of class to an otherwise dull experience.

He nodded to the security men at the door and, as was his custom, walked up the inner stairway to his office. As he sat down at his desk he could hear, through their common wall, the thin lisp of sound from Chamoun's small transistor radio. He had a habit of tuning it to the news broadcasts now and then throughout the day.

Ned knew he was lucky to have an aide as bright as Moe. It certainly made his job much easier to work with someone who could read his mind and pick up his verbal shorthand without a moment of doubt. Laverne . . .

Oh, yes, Laverne. Yes, she had gone on about Ned not having any friends unless you counted his "flunky." It just wasn't in Laverne to see that Moe was quite unusual, a superior type of person the army was lucky to have. Bit of jealousy there? It didn't matter, Moe *was* his friend as well as his deputy. What had Jane said, kidding him? Wasn't that why people joined the army, to form lifetime friendships? Yes, as long as a lifetime lasted. Wyckoff's, for instance, hadn't really lasted too long before he ended up a cold cut in French's fridge.

But neither of them, Laverne nor Jane, could understand that in the kind of work he did friendships were liabilities. In a normal life one made friends, one lost friends. But not by decapitation, or 9-millimeter slugs, or what the boys in G-2 had taken to calling "quotesuicideunquote." This was a new form of suicide in which you had help. Something like what they had in Latin American police states, called "quotedisappearanceunquote."

He leaned back in his chair and looked at his desk. For the first time he saw a note stuck in his phone. He picked it up: "Before you leave the office tonight, be sure to see me."

Since it was in Moe's handwriting, it had no signature. Typical Chamoun caution. Beyond the wall the radio had gone off. Ned got to his feet and knocked on Chamoun's door. "Open up."

After a pause the door opened. Chamoun stood there, his dark eyes looking forlorn. "Saw my note?"

"What's up?"

"Come on in." He locked the door behind Ned and sat down at his desk. There was something different about his face, Ned saw, something was there that had never been there before, a kind of added dimension, not fat, not a wrinkle or a bulge, a psychic dimension that was new.

"Okay," Ned said sitting down. "You have something to tell me? Tell me."

"Don't look at me that way. It's good news."

"Good news I can use. Lay it on me."

"How would you like to know where the opposition is going to kick off the festivities tomorrow?"

"What opposition, Mrs. F.?"

Chamoun laughed softly. "I mean the Arab contingent, under the leadership of Bert Heinemann and that fellow called Khefte."

Ned had been sitting back, simulating relaxation. Now he sat forward. "What are you saying? You intercepted something?"

"Ned, these clowns will start by occupying the inner court of the central mosque. During the noonday prayer. Having made a whatever, political statement or symbolic outcry or benediction or whatever Arabs do when they face Mecca, they will then launch an assault against Winfield."

The skin between Ned's dark blue eyes creased so deeply that the wrinkle created its own shadow. He seemed frozen in his forward-leaning posture. Nothing moved for a long moment. Then he sat back and tried to regain the fake look of relaxation.

"Who's been smoking kif?"

"No joke, Ned. This is pukka gen."

"You're telling me this little commando of freedom fighters, whatever their number. Say fifty. Say a hundred. Say they have everything portable that the armaments manufacturers of the world can concoct, including two-man teams with bipod launchers. Name it, they have it, with ammo coming out of their ears. Now follow me, Moe."

"Yes?"

"They hump all this crap into the mosque, hit the prayer rug, shout a few *Inshallahs* and hump this ton of equipment *out* again? Nobody is that insane. Let's even say they truck in the stuff under tarps. Tell me how many trucks roll up to the central mosque at prayer time? It's to laugh, Moe. It makes no sense."

"If you tell it that way, sure."

"I'm not finished telling. Let's assume these lads have not read their Clausewitz or their Machiavelli. Let's assume they never learned that in warfare, surprise is the major element of victory. But you and I know that a hotshot like Bert Heinemann has read his Clausewitz as religiously as he's read his Marx. So that's another nonstarter."

"Listen, Ned, if you . . ."

"Still not finished. When they raise a shout at the mosque, do we simply go on at Winfield sipping champagne from ladies' slippers? When we hear the pit-a-pat of combat boots hammering down the road to Winfield and we see this band of dedicated assault troops yelling and firing and just having a hell of a good time, what do we do? These cats don't have invitations, Moe. So we are not about to let them in."

"You're assuming they know we'll have Winfield heavily guarded. But maybe their intelligence isn't that good."

"Maybe they're babes in the wood. They'd have to be to try such an amateurish stunt. It doesn't sound like old Bert, not to me."

"Finished?"

"Go on."

"Where is it written that guerrilla troops operate by the principles of Clausewitz? The thing that makes them hard to beat is that they *don't* fight conventionally. Tell me I'm wrong."

"Go ahead."

"The other thing is that you never know whether they're in it for the propaganda or the money. If you were a dedicated Muslim striking a blow for Islam, what better publicity-grabber could you dream up than to consecrate your jihad first. Get Allah's blessing. Then massacre whitey."

Ned's fingers had been flicking back and forth across his lips, lightly, as if impatient to talk. But when Chamoun finished, he said nothing. The fingers continued to twiddle for a long time. "You have a point," he said in a distracted voice. "Moe?"

"What?"

"Where'd this bumf come from?"

Chamoun gestured vaguely, a kind of look-all-around-you movement of his right hand, as if casting seed upon furrows. "Does that matter?"

"Does that m—? Are you kidding me?"

"You remember that breather I had just before you left for the police station?"

"Continue."

"The guy called back. Slight Iranian accent. Half in English, half in Arabic. Half the time I could barely understand him. He might have been calling from overseas. Asked for me by name."

"Oh?"

"Because I speak Arabic, I suppose." Chamoun sighed, a truly unhappy sound. "He rattled off a lot of rhetoric about jihad and the duty of Islam to battle the great Satan. You don't want all that. It was a PR news release, Ned. I kid you not. The guy was giving me his battle plan in advance to guarantee we'd hold space for him on the front page and the evening TV news."

Chamoun's voice seemed to give out. He sat looking down at his desk, where a blown-up section of the central mosque lay. Ned watched him for a while, then turned to gaze out at the square. "Okay, Moe."

"Okay what?"

"You're bullshitting me."

"Ned, it's the truth."

"You know as well as I do: information is worthless unless we know where it comes from. And don't give me any more telephone calls, will you? You thought enough of this information to make sure you told me. Later on I might even thank you for it. But right now it's useless, Moe, unless you stop covering up and start telling me where it really came from." He could feel his head swelling with anguish.

"Isn't it enough to know what the battle plan is?"

"No!" Like migraine, the feeling put an eerie aura around everything.

Ned jumped to his feet and faced furiously away from his colleague, staring blindly out the window without seeing the square at all. "God damn it, Moe. The truth!" His temples felt as if they were being crushed.

"Does the name Bricktop mean anything to you?"

"Miriam Shannon. Something in Mossad here in London."

"Station head," Chamoun told him.

"Really? Good to know. Wait a second, you mean you got this from Mossad?"

Chamoun nodded slowly. He wanted to get up but he had the horrible suspicion that Ned was wound so tight he'd throw a punch at him. "From Bricktop."

"And because it's from her you call it pukka gen?"

"Yes."

Ned's face looked incandescent. People in ecstasies of love or rage looked that way, Chamoun thought, but there were usually words to go with the look, words that told you what they were feeling.

Slowly, by sheer power of will, Ned French seemed to loosen a bit. The hellish inner glow started to fade from his face. His dark eyes hooded slightly. He sat back down in a very straight, alert posture, his glance moving here and there about the desk, from the phone to the transistor radio, from the computer screen to the blowup of the central mosque floor plan. Everywhere. Anywhere but Chamoun's face.

"Okay," he said then in a very low voice. He cleared his throat, exactly as if someone had been punching him there. "Okay. It may be pukka. I'd kind of agree with you there. Mossad doesn't play disinformation games with us. Not yet."

"I've been studying this ground plan, Ned. What I . . ."

"Moe, there's only one more thing you have to tell me. Okay?"

Chamoun nodded.

"Why Mossad gave you this. Tell me that."

Chamoun took a long time answering. "Do I have to?"

"Oh, yes, Moe. Your whole career hangs on it. Would that be too exaggerated a thing to say? No, I don't think it would. Your whole career and maybe a court-martial and a prison term."

"Ned!"

"The court-martial would take your record into account. Four years or more of exemplary service. Your dossier is full of good stuff, Moe. Some of it I put there myself, so I know what they'll find there. And, after all, Mossad isn't an enemy agency at the moment. But our G-2 will dig back, won't they? Eventually they'll come to something. If I had to guess I'd say when you were in college you might have taken a trip to Israel. Sometimes they recruit a kid that way, but he'd be Jewish. You can see how it'd work. But you're not—"

"Ned," Chamoun cut in. "It was 1980." He shoved across a pencil and a pad of paper. "You want to make notes? I graduated Western Reserve and went to visit Lebanon. Then Israel. That's where I met Bricktop, only she wasn't called that then because she hadn't dyed her hair orange."

"And was it her idea for you to join the U.S. Army?"

"Yes."

"And work for Mossad?"

Chamoun saw that Ned was now staring directly at him, no longer avoiding his eyes. "I was raised a Christian, Ned. But in Lebanon I found out my family there were Jews. It was something of a shock."

"Yeah. Perennial outsider. Nothing wrong with my memory, as Laverne told me this morning." He shoved the pad of paper aside. "I can't imagine you were too useful to Mossad in your previous assignments. What do they pay you?"

"Nothing. They never went near me till London."

"What've you been giving her?"

"Nothing yet."

"How were you supposed to explain this to me?"

"She doesn't know you that well, Ned. She probably thought you'd be happy to get the information. It is valuable."

"Um-hm." Suddenly Ned sat back and looked at ease for the first time. "So this makes you a triple agent now, doesn't it? On only one salary. Cheap."

Chamoun nodded.

"I must say you're not as slimy as most of them." Chamoun looked up to find Ned's unsmiling face squared off, his eyes focused at a point between Chamoun's own eyes, as if sighting a firing-squad rifle.

"As such, you're going to be useful, Captain. No question about it."

Chamoun tried to relax, but couldn't. "That's good to hear."

"Is it? How do you think I feel, finding out I've been nursing a double agent? How do you think that makes me feel about you?"

"But you said—"

"I said you'd be useful. I'll make damned sure of it. That's all you are to me any more, Captain, useful. I'm not turning you in because of that and also, let's face it, because it makes me look like a horse's ass not having spotted you long ago."

He stood up. "But if it gets back to me that you've wised up this Bricktop lady, you can count on me revoking your license to live, Captain."

"I . . . I guess . . ."

"Why guess? Let me tell you. I'm making the best of a lousy mess. Don't expect me to like it. Or you."

He slammed the door on his way out.

25

Will Nightwater was making his first round of the evening. He had finished his cuppa with Trev, bid him good night, and started off in the North Wing, the northeast corner where the operating theater was located.

Trev was right, of course, the job was a doddle. Nothing really to do but patrol the halls, check with the sisters on duty, try the doors to the outside that were meant to be kept locked, and keep the eye open for anything unusual.

If there were to be special things, patients leaving late at night, for instance, Will got advance notice from the head sister. Even if something like an emergency operation was called for he usually had at least half an hour's notice. He liked it that way. He hated surprises. Well, who didn't?

He had just finished the north wing and was heading down the central corridor that led into the reception area in the South Wing, when he heard a nurse scream. But nurses never screamed, did they? His pace quickened to a trot because the scream had come from the reception area.

Will Nightwater could hear someone shouting up ahead. Like a big dog barking. *Rowf! Row-rowf!* And another scream. Far ahead a pool of light lay over the reception area, which led out under a portico to the parking lot. Four people stood there under the downdropping light like actors on a stage.

Will sidestepped into a doorway and peered around the corner. Two sisters, Jacobson and Prewitt. Two fellas, young ones. They were wearing Balaclava face masks.

He peered out again. Christ, they were carrying M-10s, nasty little machinepistols, all silencer and magazine. Will Nightwater had never handled an M-10, but he'd seen it often enough in the movies. Usually Max von Sydow mowed people down with it, but he remembered a movie where John Wayne was a cop in San Francisco and—

Fi-di-dit.

Nurse Jacobson screamed. Three red holes opened up across Nurse Prewitt like a bird shitting on her. Will Nightwater glanced around the corridor. The security room was directly across from him but they'd see him crossing, wouldn't they? God, what would Trev do in a spot like this?

Nurse Prewitt had sunk to her knees. Her hands covered her breasts as if to shield them from any more silenced bullets. Then she fell forward on her face with a thud like a felled tree.

Will dashed across the hall and into the security office. He wished Trev hadn't left. The bastards had waited till there was one man on duty, hadn't they? Where the Christ was the key to the desk? Key! Key!

In the darkness he unlocked the drawer and pulled out the grim Parabellum, a heavy gun with a terrifying kick if you weren't used to it. No accuracy, but if a slug caught you, it dropped you, dropped you the way they'd dropped Nurse Prewitt.

His fingers were shaking badly. He scooped up a heavy thirteen-round loaded magazine and crammed it into the Parabellum, then cocked the hammer. He pocketed another magazine and cautiously peered around the edge of the doorway.

They had turned off the lights in the reception area.

Along the corridor little oases of light shone down a few yards apart, islands of light in a fearful corridor of darkness. They could be anywhere, Will Nightwater thought. But he hadn't switched on a light so perhaps, with any luck, they were all even, all blind. But two against one?

If only he knew what they were up to! Trev would've figured it out by now. There was no cash kept in the safe at night, damned little in the daytime. Drugs. Maybe that was it.

Will slid around the doorjamb, trying to keep his squat, middle-aged frame glued to the wall and out of the brilliant spill of ceiling light just down the corridor. Could he be silhouetted in such a light? Only one way to find out. He dropped to a low infantry crouch and, hugging the wall, inched forward toward the reception area, heavy Parabellum in both hands.

Ahead someone moaned. Nurse Prewitt, still alive?

"Nobody's out there," a man's voice said.

"I saw something."

"Come on. Keep this one as a shield."

"I told you," Nurse Jacobson stammered. "I have no idea who you're t-talking about."

"Young fellow. German."

Will Nightwater knew exactly where the German was sleeping. It was in the central corridor, the east end where Intensive Care was located not a hundred yards around the corner from where they were. What to do?

If Trev were here, he'd know. Trev had that kind of mind, the sort who could figure the odds in a jiff. Would they hurt Nurse Jacobson before getting the room number from her? Not likely. But if he let off a round at them, and missed, they'd spray the corridor and be sure to get him. Tossup, wasn't it?

The thing to do was hold his breath and wait for them to get so close to him that he couldn't miss. But if he got one, would the other shoot the nurse as retaliation? What kind of villains were they, cool or hot?

"You're w-wasting your time with me," Nurse Jacobson said. Their voices were much nearer now. "I don't know the man you want."

"Then we'll find someone who does."

"There is no one else on duty this time of night," she lied.

"Leave it out, sister."

"I mean it."

They were only two or three yards away now. Will Nightwater should be able to see them, but, like him, they were hugging the wall.

"Sister Prewitt is still alive," the other nurse was saying. "She needs help. Do you want to be hunted down for a murder?"

"Do I wot?" One of the men started laughing.

Will saw him suddenly, a silhouette, inching along next to a bigger silhouette that had to be the other man and Nurse Jacobson. "Hunted down for a murder, did you say?" For some reason he found this hilarious. The other man produced a noise somewhere between a grunt and a chuckle.

Will Nightwater shot the first man through the head.

A great sheaf of blood and brains burst like a bright cerise fountain under the downdropping light. The nurse screamed loudly and Will Nightwater shot the other man in the stomach, punching out a hole the size of a grapefruit.

Then he keeled over and began throwing up.

Grosvenor Square was empty now. The sun had done its little act, striking in horizontally under cloud cover. The Saturday shoppers had long vanished. Only a few pedestrians moved quietly through the area as streetlamps came on. The square belonged to auto traffic now, an endless intertwining chain of blue-white headlights and orange-red taillights, plaiting itself into strands, raveling, parting, contrary flows of traffic crossing and blending with each other.

Ned French was sitting on his windowledge. Not so long a time had passed since he had got the full brunt of Chamoun's betrayal, possibly half an hour, no more. As far as he could tell, the younger officer was still at his desk, no doubt brooding over being caught or, more likely, laughing at the way he'd maneuvered Ned into keeping his secret for him.

So, Ned thought, this day of betrayals has finally wound itself up into one ball of treachery.

For what else could you call the bombshell Laverne had dropped in his lap at breakfast. Was "betrayal" too strong a word? How about disloyalty? And what word could you find to describe Jane's behavior toward him? First her coddling of Laverne, her . . . *complicity!* And then her cowardice in not wanting to talk about it after the harm had been done.

Beside these two women, Pandora Fulmer stood as a rank amateur. She was merely pigheaded, merely self-aggrandizing. What a grand day Saturday had been.

In this business you grew a hard shell. You had to. But even a hard shell can be split apart if you hammer away at it hard enough. That's what he felt like now, split apart and very vulnerable. He didn't take kindly to betrayal, destruction, cowardly silence, straight ordinary military treachery, nor the idea that what he had decided was best for Winfield security had been compromised by that peanut-sized idiot.

This was the way molluscs and bivalves felt, wasn't it, when they were forcibly deprived of their shells and eaten? The mammalian version of the bivalve was someone like him, who had secreted a protective shell reinforced by laminations of army discipline and skills. You couldn't get at Ned French with any ordinary pickaxe. You had to hit him simultaneously with his wife, his lover, and his only friend, hit him in such a manner as to expose all three as shams, and all three relationships as meaningless.

That had now been done.

He heard his telephone ring and, being the fool he was, had the sudden hope that Jane was calling him to apologize and invite him over. He picked up the phone. "Deputy Defense."

"This," said a British voice with a slight giggle in it, "is the Art Hodes Fan Club. The London branch is holding a Saturday meeting at the usual place."

"What?"

But the speaker had hung up. Ned replaced the phone and smiled grimly. When your friends and loved ones betray you, that's the precise moment your enemy befriends you.

Gleb Ponamarenko always held court in a Knightsbridge pub or bar on weeknights. Evidently he also did on Saturday. But was that any reason for calling on him?

"Phil," Laverne French asked into the phone, "is this a bad time to call you?"

"Verne! My God," her oldest brother responded. "It's lunchtime at the old homestead and guess who's tending the barbecue."

"Have you got a second?"

"Talk to me. How's my baby sister? How's Ned? How are the girls? Well, I know how the girls are because Mom calls me once a week."

"Everybody's fine. And Cathleen and the baby?"

"Terrific. What's on your mind?"

"I'm coming home."

There was a pause at the other end. Then: "What do you mean, to Camp Liberty?"

Laverne realized he'd had precisely the same reaction as Ned. For men home was where *they* were. "Just a visit and then I'll bring the girls back here."

"Can you stop by and see us?"

"That's what I called about. I'd like to bring the girls and spend a week or so."

"You're on. Just don't come the first two weeks of August because I've got sales meetings in Baja and Maui."

"Where?"

"Never mind. The rest is wide open. When you know your plans, give Cathleen a call and fix up the dates."

"I called you first," Laverne went on hesitantly. "I'll be calling Patrick and Pete and Paul later."

"And scrounging free weeks with them?" he laughed.

"Yeah, well, sort of. I mean my girls don't really know their uncles and cousins all that well, us living in Europe."

"So." Phil sounded hesitant too, something he never was. Something, Laverne reminded herself, that no offspring of General Krikowski ever was. "So you won't be spending much time at Camp Liberty?"

"A week. I mean the girls have been there two weeks now. Mom and Dad'll understand."

"Yeah. Yeah." Silence.

"To tell the truth, Phil," she went on more slowly, "Ned isn't all that happy with them staying there."

"That so. I'll be right there!" he yelled at someone. "I'm talking to Verne! Long-distance! From London! So shut up!"

"Go tend your barbecue."

"What do you mean he's not happy about it? Laurie and Linda spend all their vacations there. It's making real persons out of them."

"Ned calls it a prison camp."

"Verne! I thought you married an American."

"He's still an American. He's got a higher security clearance than anybody else in the family."

She paused, trying to make her brother understand what was happening. But first she had to understand it herself. "He and I used to think alike, Phil. I mean we all did. But Ned says the world's changed and the way we think—let's be honest, the way Dad raised us to think—what did he say? He called Dad a dinosaur. He . . ." She gave up. "We'll talk about it when I see you."

"We sure as hell will. I don't like the idea of my baby sister—" He yelled something unintelligible at someone. Phil had married late, in his forties, and now, at fifty, didn't have the resilience to handle young children any more.

"What kind of creep has he turned into?" he asked then.

"Phil, he's not a creep. He's a responsible American intelligence officer who's been at it so long he's lost track of what's right and what's wrong. That happens. Not always in combat either."

"Sounds like he's lost his guts," her brother said in a disgusted voice. "Okay! Okay! I'm coming!" Then, to her: "Gotta run, Verne. See you."

Laverne hung up the phone and looked in her address book for the number of her brother Pete. Then she let the book close. She'd call later. Right now she didn't have the heart to explain it all over again.

Of the two Knightsbridge places where Gleb Ponamarenko met people in the early evening hours, he had installed himself at the rather grand bar of an American-style hotel built at the head of Lowndes Square. It was a huge cylinder of windows known locally as the Gasometer.

When Ned French arrived, the Russian was listening very intently to something a young fellow was telling him, one of those anonymous young city fellows in his three-piece pencil-striped suit, his tightly furled umbrella and bowler hat poised on a nearby barstool. It took the young broker or banker another ten minutes to finish his tale, during which Ned ordered and drank a whisky and soda and ordered a second one. He didn't have to be on his guard with dear old Gleb. All he had to remember to do was tell him nothing and say no to everything.

Finally, when the young financial type left, Gleb sat hunched over his own whisky, shaking his head sadly. "*Kak stranya, gospodin, kak stranya.*" He glanced at Ned to see if he had heard, picked up his drink, and sat down next to the American.

"That boy is in what your fellow countrymen call deep shit, if I am not mistaken."

"That's what they used to call it," Ned agreed. "I've been out of the country so long they could be calling it deep borshch by now." He eyed the Russian. "If you have another Art Hodes album for me, produce it at once."

"Nothing that good." Ponamarenko sounded genuinely depressed.

"But over the phone you said—"

"I know what I said. It's not true that we Russians are a deeply depressed people, like all those who live in the land of long nights and deep winters. No, we Russians can be gay, in the old sense of the word, also the new, and when we are gay, we pay for it later. The name of the syndrome is manic-depressive. I was gay on the phone because I thought I could do you a good turn, old friend. But now I realize that nobody can help you in such deep borshch."

"Just how old a pair of friends are we?"

"Take that back," Gleb told the bartender, "and change it to a double.

And one for me, as well." He sighed heavily. "For as long as you have been in London. A year? Before that I was virtually unaware of your existence, as you of mine. But in the past year I have studied you closely, as well as your operation. That is why I am sad."

"Cheer up, Gleb Sergeyevich. My condition is fatal, but not serious." The double drinks arrived and both men touched glasses ceremoniously.

"I am talking about tomorrow," the Russian explained. "You are about to be ambushed, sandbagged, and left for dead."

"Sending up great cheers of joy in the Kremlin." Ned smiled crookedly. "What's actually on your mind, old pal?"

"As stated previously, I am concerned at the state of your operation." He held up a finger in a teacherlike gesture, calling for attention. "Look, French, in the normal course of events this garden party would have been Karl Follett's baby. Since he is infiltrated that means it would be the responsibility of E. Lawrence Rand. I need hardly tell you how that gentleman, with his well-known finesse and sensitivity, would have handled it. So, you were on the spot and you improvised brilliantly. But you are no match for your opposition, Colonel. Your operation is not meant for that kind of civilian work, anyway. That's supposed to be handled by Rand's bunch but they are an incompetent lot. Am I boring you? Or have these thoughts crossed your mind, too?"

"And if they have?"

"Then it comes as no surprise that, viewed as a national effort, across the board, so to speak, the American intelligence community is in a sorry state. If it is a conversation or a message that can be combed out of the air, ah, there you excel! You have the latest hardware to find and record and decode the merest whisper in Vladivostok or Antofagasta. But in the dirty, person-to-person side of the business, you are totally out of touch. I mean, look at Rand. How can you expect first-class people to work for a dyspeptic midget?"

Ned suppressed a giggle. "Rand's side of the business isn't our only effort."

"It's the side that's supposed to run circuits of agents and collect something with a bit more flesh on it than astral murmurs from the troposphere. The only people who will work with a type like Rand are those exactly like him, clones, so to speak, or mindless slaves who don't really care who cracks the whip over them as long as it stings."

Ned stared down into his half-finished drink. With old friends like Ponamarenko, who needed enemies?

"But coming back to you, old friend," the Russian persisted, "the only reason you are still in the running is that you can count on the help of friends in Mossad and the advice of yours truly, of Tass."

"Of Tass," Ned repeated. Something beneath his diaphragm seemed to spasm upward at the casual way Ponamarenko alluded to Maurice Chamoun's treachery. Christ, did everybody in town know?

"First I'm in deep trouble," Ned told him, "now I'm still in the running. Make up your mind, honored correspondent-worker."

"I just wanted to whistle something in your ear. If your mind is closed, I can withstand the urge to whistle."

"Don't get huffy. You know me. I take advice from anybody."

Gleb glanced around them, then murmured close into Ned's ear: "This Hodgkins and Daughter, you know the firm I mean?" Ned nodded. "They, too, have been infiltrated. There is a fellow there, a sort of supervisor who peddles backstairs gossip he collects from his staff. He bought the firm last year with money he stole from the Hungarians. At the moment he's calling himself Fownes. Does that ring a bell?" Ned nodded again. "He is one of the new breed. Not political. He serves only one master, his own towering greed. I don't need to explain how dangerous that could make him?"

Ned nodded a third time but the Russian had stopped talking. "That's it?" Ned asked. "Nothing more specific?"

"What is it you Americans say? Does a house have to fall on you?"

Ned chuckled softly. "Okay. Thanks for the tip. Here's another thing we Americans say: What's in it for you?"

"In essence, I don't ask for anything big. I may produce a contract and ask you to prick your finger and sign it in blood. Nothing special. Your immortal soul."

"You think I think you're kidding," Ned told him.

"You think I think you think it's impossible?" Gleb countered. "It's not impossible. Considering everything that has happened to your character, your dedication, your whole outlook on life since that night you found poor Wyckoff's head in your refrigerator?"

Ned sat in silence for a long moment, then downed the rest of his drink in one gulp. "That does it, old pal. You only opened the file on me when I arrived in London?"

Gleb shrugged. "I do my homework." He finished off his drink almost as rapidly. "Time to move on. A chill has developed in this vicinity."

"A barometric low," Ned agreed. "Listen, you tried."

"And will again."

"And thanks for the tip about Franz."

"Fownes." The Russian spelled it. Then he walked off, leaving Ned to stare into his empty glass.

"Bartender, another double."

"Yes, sir. This will be a new bill, sir. The other gentleman has paid for your previous drinks."

"Oh, has he? God Almighty but I am rich in friends."

Outside Chamoun's office window, Grosvenor Square loomed peculiarly in the dusk light. It was not entirely green any more but a kind of memory of green on his retinas, being gradually replaced by a pearly aura of grays as darkness leached the color out of everything.

Depressed and angry at his own bungling, Chamoun turned away from the window and switched on his transistor radio for the news. He pushed papers around aimlessly on his desk, managed to arrange them in a kind of pile.

". . . in Geneva without coming to any decision on multilateral arms control. Meanwhile, reports are just coming in to us of a terrorist attack a few minutes ago at the Stoke Mandeville hospital in Buckinghamshire. Two masked men shot and killed a nurse, according to preliminary reports. Here, on the scene, is Caroline Carr."

A woman's high voice, which its owner was trying to keep low, persisted in rising to peaks at the end of each sentence. ". . . name of the murdered sister has not yet been released, pending notification of her next of *kin!* Meanwhile, we talked to the hero of the day who stopped the assault by shooting both intruders at almost pointblank *range!* Mr. Will Nightwater, security man here at Stoke Mandeville: Did either of them say what they were *after?*"

"What they were after," a local voice repeated, broad and drawling. "They were asking for one of the patients, a German chap with multiple stab wounds."

"And both intruders are now dead, Mr. Nightwater?"

"Both intruders are now dead. And they left their van."

"In the parking lot, Mr. Nightwater?"

"In the parking lot. Caterers they were. Or they stole it."

"Thank you, Mr. Nightwater, and thank you for your heroic defense of the *hospital!* This is Caroline Carr for Independent Radio News here in Stoke *Mandeville!*"

"Meanwhile, football hooligans struck again in the Scottish—"

Chamoun snapped off the radio. Caterer's van. Wounded German.

He called an information number and got Stoke Mandeville hospital's number. The call rang endlessly. Someone picked up at last, without identifying the hospital. As soon as Chamoun established what he wanted the phone clicked off. He went to Ned French's office door, knocked, listened, went back to his own desk and called an air base near Stoke Mandeville, where a small U.S. Air Force photo unit was operating. On the third try he reached someone in the S-2 and identified himself.

"You guys monitoring that assault at Stoke Mandeville?"

"We heard about it. Why?"

"Can you find out something for me?"

"If it means going over to the hospital, Captain, forget it. I'm duty officer till midnight."

"Do you know anybody at the hospital? Could you phone them?"

"Not a soul, Captain."

"Shit! How far is it from London?"

"That's the spirit, Captain! Geronimo!"

Ned was not drunk. He had readily found his way from Knightsbridge into Chelsea, on foot, without a false move or missed turn. Now he stood at the beginning of Mossop Street, looking at Number 37.

Because of the cloud cover, night had fallen earlier than usual. The sky already had that strange salmon-rose sheen it took on at night, against a black background. The streetlamp near Jane's house was lit. So was a lamp inside her house, in the front room, Ned decided. But nowhere else. Perhaps she wasn't home. Perhaps she was, but not to him.

He rang the bell. Nothing happened for a long time so he rang it again. He could hear it sound inside the house. Then he could hear very faint footsteps, as if someone in slippers had come to the other side of the door but had not yet touched it.

"Ned?" Jane asked from inside. "Go away."

"Please open up. I have to talk to you." His voice was low and as desperate as Colonel Edward J. French's voice ever got.

"What?"

"I have to talk to you," he repeated in a louder voice. Across the street two young women stared at him as they walked by.

"Go away. Please."

"Not till you talk to me."

The two girls giggled. Ned squared his shoulders. "Jane, give me as much time as you gave Laverne?"

There was an awesomely long silence at the other side of the door. Dumb, Ned corrected himself. Sure to anger her.

But he heard the locks unfastened. The door swung wide. He could see the moment he walked in that she had been crying. Or something. Reading fine print? Peeling onions? Sneezing? He tried to take her in his arms and she backed away from him.

Standing in the center of her living room, looking almost haggard, her thick black hair falling unadorned, her eyes red, she stared at him as at a stranger, and one who brought woe. She wore a long dark green velvet robe that came to the ground. "That was unfair," she said then. "I *had* to talk to Laverne. She's your wife. But I don't owe you anything, Ned."

"She's leaving me."

"Oh?"

"Going to that prison camp in California. Says she'll bring the girls back in the fall. I don't believe her. Is that what you advised her to do?"

"No. Did she say that?"

"No. She said you told her not to do anything permanent. What do you call leaving your husband and settling six thousand miles away?"

"If she said she'd be back, she will," Jane told him.

"I call it goddamned permanent."

"And you're angry," Jane finished for him. "You want her by your side throughout your entire affair with me. Right?" She stared at him in a devastated way. "You've been drinking."

"I've been a lot of things. Including betrayed."

He sat down in a chair and stared at the fireplace. No gas flames danced merrily there now. "Not by me, Ned," she responded.

"No? Why not you? Join the gang."

He stretched out his long legs as if he were freezing and the imaginary fire would warm him. "It's in the air. Nobody's what they seem. Everybody knows everything about Ned French except Ned French."

"I don't un—"

"I just had drinks with a man who told me what was wrong with me and my operation. He hit the nail on the head every single time. Mind you, he was KGB. So, by now, it's easy to see that Ned French is a bit of a public scandal. And it couldn't have come at a better moment. Laverne winging off to sunny California. Winfield House in the hands of the enemy. Chamoun . . ." He stopped talking. "And then there's Jane Weil, everybody's advice to the lovelorn."

"Ned, if you came here to insult—"

"Dear Jane Weil. My husband doesn't understand me. As you happen to know him far better than I do, please tell me what to do? Signed, Heartsick but Not on Welfare."

"Ned."

"Have you got any Scotch?"

"Tons of it. You're not getting any till you shut up."

"Um. Mm. Mmm."

"Ned, she was unhappy. She thought it was political. I told her it was emotional and physical. That upset her even more. If it had been political, she could have rolled with it. She told me politics was just a time-wasting game men played. Women paid very little attention to it. She was prepared to ignore the differences between you till I told her what they really were."

"I love the way women do any outrageous thing that enters their head and it's ohhh-*kay!* It's ohhh-*kay* because a *woman* is doing it. Women have a license because they are women. All is allowed. Betrayals that would get a man shot in the head and hung out for the crows to peck are allowed to women. She is going *home.* Home is wherever she designates. Everything is allowed the mama bird winging home to stuff worms down the throats of her young."

For a moment he thought she was sobbing. He glanced up at her and saw she was laughing. At him. "Very revealing," Jane said. "You want her here, not somewhere else. You're saying her presence is soothing. Her absence is appalling, unheard of, outrageous."

"No." He understood she had backed him out on some kind of logical parapet. "Why did I think, after the worst day of my life, that barging in on you would be soothing or resolving or healing?" He was batting zero today, striking out so often it would certainly make the Baseball Hall of Ill Fame.

"No," he repeated. "As a matter of fact it's just as well Laverne's leaving. But I don't need it now. Or tomorrow. As for coming back in the fall—"

"She will."

"Oh, she promised you, too?"

"Laverne doesn't lie, Ned. She is without guile. She was raised that way, whatever you think of her politics. That's why she's capable of what you call an outrageous act. Because it's done openly and without guile. I'm not saying women are always like that. But I've run into a lot more devious men in my day than devious women."

"So what?" He stared belligerently at the ceiling. "Who cares?" he demanded. "Women are always giving themselves airs. I speak as a father of four of them. Always arrogating advantages they don't merit."

"If I give you a drink will you shut up? You've turned into the worst kind of chauvinist pig."

When he looked at her he saw that she was still slightly teary-eyed. "On-Demand Weeping Our Specialty," he muttered. "Save the drink. I'm getting out of here." He scraped to his feet, tottering slightly but standing erect. "G'bye, Jane. Many happy returns." He started for the door.

"Bye, Ned."

"You're not going to let me go? In this condition?"

"I'm not going to let you blackmail me into holding your head."

"Look." He was standing in her narrow doorway. "We have to talk."

"You and Laverne had to talk. I don't know what you were doing for twenty years but you weren't talking. So, finally, she reached out to talk to a stranger, me, not knowing I was her betrayer. You complain about betrayals, Ned. Ask yourself where they start."

He walked back into the room. "Can I have that drink, please?"

They stood there for a while, staring at each other, two people, the masts of two passing ships, rocking slightly in Ned's case, but still upright, still rigged with signal flags crying out disaster.

"How do you think I felt, talking to Laverne?" she asked then.

"Yeah. I do see that."

"Yeah," she mimicked. She turned away from him and went to a bookcase. On a clear plastic tray stood a few bottles and glasses. She poured two whiskys and added some ice, gave him one glass and sat down by the cold fireplace. "You think this was the worst day of your life?" she challenged him then.

"Bit of melodrama. That title is reserved for tomorrow."

"Can we discuss this without bringing in the defense of Winfield House at every turn? One thing at a time, or nothing gets solved."

"And what makes you think anything ever gets solved?"

"What indeed." She gestured with her glass and he with his. They sipped. "You know, Laverne . . ." She paused. "Talking to her was like talking to my sister Em. I don't understand that type of woman. I never have. They have everything I never had, looks, figure, sparkle. From an early age I was the librarian type."

"Come on, Jane. That's horseshit."

"Oh, I've learned to look better. It's a matter of how you do your hair and your makeup. I've got that solved. Nobody looks at me and outright vomits. In fact, neurotic intelligence types can fall for me, temporarily."

"Really? Have you had many?"

"Even one is too many."

"This really is feel-sorry-for-yourself day." He sat down opposite her. "And, somehow, I've let you take it away from me. It was *my* bad day."

She said nothing for a while, slowly sipping Scotch. Her pale complexion had grown very slightly warmer. "She's really leaving? We'll have the whole summer together? Or is that an impossible dream?"

"When you realize that we're probably already office gossip . . ."

"I don't think so," she said. "It's hard to tell. But, at least a few nights in a week you could spend here with me."

He nodded. "Or you with me. Except that stray types keep my place under surveillance."

"And not mine?"

"Who knows." He sounded disgusted. "I don't suppose Room 404 . . . ?"

"Never again. You know, we're like a pair of addicts. We can't even wait for Laverne to leave."

He was silent for a long time. "Would you turn on the gas fire?" He watched her light it and, suddenly, the room got much more friendly. "Do you suppose," he said then, "that Laverne has outfoxed us both?"

"No." Jane was kneeling beside the fireplace, regulating the gascock to lower the flames slightly. "Women don't do those things, Ned, not women like Laverne."

"No? Goes to see her deadly rival for a bit of advice?"

"Does it make it any easier for you if you think she's tricky?"

He shook his head. "Just trying it on for size. A scenario, nothing more."

"Games."

"What?" he asked.

"Games men play. And then whine about the outrageous acts of women. You'd think she was kidnaping her own girls." She stayed on her knees, now holding her glass and staring down into it, her big dark eyes looking mournful in a classic Grecian way.

"There's something in a book . . ." She stopped and frowned, trying to remember. "Somebody sent it to me last Christmas from the States." She stood up and went to her bookshelves, muttering until she finally found a large-format book of drawings with the title *Echoes from the Bottomless Well.* She started paging through it.

"He's Dutch," she said of the author, "an artist and also a philosopher. I'll just . . ." She kept paging. "Here." She handed the book to Ned. He saw that it was simple drawings in brush, pen, and ink, and this one was a charmer, a roly-poly woman on her back, legs spread.

"Ah, the gynecologist position," he said. "Lovely."

"Don't be stupid, Ned, it's the quotation from the Buddhist nun."

"From here," the quotation ran, "all the Buddhas, all the Christs entered the world." The artist had added the name of the nun, Myolei.

"I see," Ned said, handing back the book. "It's from this genital equipment that you all get your license to be outrageous."

"I don't know about Buddhist nuns," Jane mused. "They may have been celibate. But celibate or not, having had children or not, I can tell you that every woman knows the truth of what she's saying about us. We're fastened into the planet and the race this way, as no man is. I've never had any children and I'm not likely to over the years left to me, but I feel this connection just as strongly as Laverne. That's why she—"

"Hogwash."

"Oh, Ned."

"Listen, the father's connection to the race is just as clearly defined. He has a biological connection, although nowhere near as dramatic. And he has the same emotional connection as the mother. But when it comes to the transactional side of things, his role changes. The mother nurtures. But the father has to get out and hustle up the nurture. It isn't as dramatic as pregnancy and childbirth, but don't ever think we're not as intimately connected with the human race as the sex that has the babies."

"You're not going to allow Laverne even that?"

He puffed out his cheeks in a gesture of disgusted resignation. "You see what I mean? You women do whatever you want, share all sorts of intimate gossip. I wonder how long you'd last with official secrets."

"How many women are intelligence officers? Or agents?"

"In peacetime, damned few."

"How many are made members of the Mafia?"

"None."

"Even among the ranks of terrorists, women are scarce."

"Yes." He glanced warily at her. "You're preaching the gentler, more caring sex? Don't get me started on that."

"Oh, there must be horrible examples of heartless, murderous women," she admitted. "Just as there might be one or two murderous, evil soldiers." Her smile went askew. "Or intelligence agents."

"Until the modern era, the trade of soldier was indistinguishable from that of murderer," Ned told her. "But with the development of remote-control murder, especially by nuclear bombing of civilians and the use of chemical or bacteriological weapons, the trade of soldier has gone respectable. The moral blame has been passed to the politicians."

"Your favorite whipping boys."

"Somebody was talking about the difference between a terrorist and a soldier. The terrorist kills for what he believes in. The soldier kills for what politicians believe in."

"Sorry. I'm an American. I don't buy it."

"Jane?" He gave her a surprised look.

"I'm a citizen of a democracy. We get precisely the stupid, corrupt politicians we like and want. If you think we don't, just check the opinion polls by which we live."

"When everybody's to blame, nobody's to blame."

"Which is why sensitive military types keep trying to pass the buck along to the politicos."

"You're impossible," he snapped.

She stared for a long time at him. "Ned, I'm always going to be that way." She came over and stood in front of him, a tall figure in long folds of green velvet. She looked like a high priestess in her ceremonial robe, but a priestess given more to dire prophecy than to comforting reassurance.

"Is that some kind of Jewish thing?" he asked. "Is that why you were all placed here on earth?"

She finished her last sip of whisky. "Now that's what I call a very Christian thought." Her huge eyes never left his face. "We were not placed here on earth for anything special. We drink whisky. We do a day's work. We fall in love with completely inappropriate people."

He reached out for her and they embraced slowly, fitting into each other almost gingerly, as if wary of hidden spikes.

"That's not what old Chemnitz told me," Ned said then. "He said the curse of the Jews was that they had been ordained to keep the rest of the human race on course. And who can love a busybody?"

"Chemnitz is nutty as a fruitcake," Jane told him. They kissed then, softly but for a long time. "And so," she said with a sigh as her lips left his, "is his star pupil."

"That, I've been warned about. Earlier tonight. By a fellow spook."

"Takes one to know one. French, is this how we're going to spend our lives? Ships that pause in the night?"

"I don't know. I damn near panicked when you wouldn't talk to me on the phone. I got a completely cut-off feeling."

"You're sounding Jewish already."

He frowned down at her. "Is that a circumcision joke? You mustn't torment me, Weil. We have to keep access open to each other, even if we're pissed off. Even if all we communicate that day is 'Hello; I'm fine; how are you?' We have to remain accessible."

Her arms around him seemed to tighten until his ribs began to ache slightly. "You paint such an appealing picture of our future as a loving pair," she murmured in his ear. "Grow old with me, the best boredom is yet to come."

He lifted her slightly off her feet so that their eyes were on a perfect level with each other, dark brown staring deeply into dark blue. "What ever gave you the idea," he asked, "that our main strength together was conversation?"

She laughed in his ear. "I can't take too much flattery," she complained. "You think some of my sister Emily's genes rubbed off on me?"

"She's the physical one?"

"She sure isn't the mental one." She had placed her hands on his shoulders and levered herself upward until she could look down on him. "I guess that's love," Jane said then. "Being the only man on earth to think I'm physical."

"It's only that tall women turn me on. Nothing personal."

"Right." She slowly let go so that her body slid downward in a long, drawn-out occasion of total friction that left them both more excited than they were willing to admit.

Her dark eyes looked defiant and hurt and aroused, all at the same time. "Here's what I want you to do," she began then. "Call Laverne. Give her one of those marvelous monosyllabic excuses of yours and stay with me a few hours. I've had all the aggravation from you. I might as well have some of the good."

Ned's face went blank. "I'd like nothing better," he said, aware that the next word was always "but." He stared intently at her. "You do remember that tomorrow's the Fourth of July?"

"Tell me," Jane responded in a rather tart voice, "haven't you and Chamoun got everything in order by now?"

"Everything we can think of."

"Then . . .?"

He paused, thinking back over the past week's headlong flood of activity, culminating finally in a checklist that guaranteed absolutely nothing more than what a white cane guarantees a blind man. Still, everything that could be invented was ready to go: snipers, sluggers, spotters, waiters, Trojan Horse guards, and even a small combo that could segue neatly from bossa nova to funk while carrying concealed automatics. Add a platoon of Marine Corps guards. Add his own volunteer brigade of plainclothes "guests." What the hell was he worried about?

"Then," he echoed Jane, "let's test some fireworks in advance."

The mouse-colored Ford Fiesta rattled along Highway A355 southward from Amersham to Slough. Chamoun glanced at his watch. Ten P.M. and not a bad night's work. He'd have to phone Ned when he got back to London and give him a full report.

The police on the scene at Stoke Mandeville had been reluctant to show him any cooperation at first, but he'd worn them down with goodwill until they finally let him have a peek at the German lad. One glimpse was enough to know that Bertolt Heinemann was out of commission at present. His former comrades had twice failed to kill him. Tough cookies, these Kraut Marxists.

The mangled bodies of the dead men had been removed to a mortuary, but everyone agreed that they had definitely not been Arab in appearance.

The police had also let him look at the small Fiat Fiorino van. It had been lettered and recently resprayed to remove the Hodgkins and Daughter emblem. On one side of the van this showed through the gray paint, as if the owner couldn't quite make up his mind. Apart from a bullet hole in one window, nothing inside the van gave any clues. According to the fingerprints man, the dabs all belonged to the two dead men, plus others too numerous to check.

But the scenario Chamoun would bring back to Ned was clear enough. Their suspicions of the catering setup were now proved. People belonging to it had wanted the German very dead. That part was confusing, but squared with Nancy Lee Miller's report that some of Khefte's key men had gone missing.

Too bad the German hadn't been able to talk. He seemed to know he had been the target of another attack. His eyes had glittered feverishly, but when he spoke everything was disconnected and in German. It might be days before he made any sense and what they didn't have was days.

Behind the Fiesta, Chamoun could see in his mirror a pair of very bright lights closing the gap. He had often noted the eccentric way British

drivers used their bright lights, sometimes leaving them on without realizing they were blinding others. The British also used their brights
incorrectly as a warning in traffic situations. Elsewhere in the world when
a car flashed its brights it was meant to signal, Watch out, I'm coming.
In Britain it meant: Please go ahead of me. Confusing. Eccentric. British.

Chamoun reached up and flicked his rearview mirror down to avoid
the bright beam in his eyes. He wanted to reach out his open window
and tilt his outside mirror, too, but the car behind was closing the gap
so fast he didn't think it necessary.

Now it was pulling over to the right to pass him. It was abreast of
him and hung there for a long moment. Chamoun could see that it
wasn't a car at all but a white van, a larger one than the Fiorino, larger
than the Fiesta he was driving. He had just a faint glimpse of the driver's
face: big staring eyes, bulging almost. He clutched a small round micro-
phone in his hand.

The van swerved left. Its fender shoved hard into the Fiesta, sending
it off the road onto a narrow shoulder. They were crossing a bridge with
concrete railings. Chamoun fought his steering wheel back in line just
in time to avoid hitting the railing. He tramped on the brakes.

The van shot forward. Chamoun fell back deliberately, but he wasn't
prepared for the next move. The van, tires squealing, roared ahead to a
wider place in the road, did a hard U-turn, and came bearing down on
him, bright light blinding.

Chamoun pulled off to the right. The van swerved, clipped his front
fender a second time, roared past. In his mirror he saw it U-turn again.
Chamoun stamped on the accelerator pedal. He should be able to outrun
this madman. His car was lighter than the van.

The two vehicles roared down A355, cutting great flares of white out
of the night around them. Chamoun gritted his teeth and kept his foot
down on the gas pedal. He had a very clear idea of what was happening.
In its U-turns, the van had displayed its logo several times: HODGKINS
AND DAUGHTER—CUSTOM CATERING.

As long as he could keep ahead of the van, he'd be all right. This
was a deserted stretch of road but they'd soon be passing through built-
up areas like Beaconsfield, giving him a chance either to shake off the
van by dodging, or find the police station and take refuge. In any event,
Chamoun had no doubt, he would be able to get back to London with
his information.

That was before he saw, in the distance ahead of him, another van
with painfully bright lights, bearing down on him head-on.

Part 7

SUNDAY
JULY 4

26

A noise. Something stealthy, a dry, disturbing whisper that woke Ned French on the Fourth of July with the thud of foreboding.

He had fallen asleep with his arms around Jane. In the few hours of slumber they had shared, his body had worked its way down in her narrow bed—hardly a double by any standard; a true librarian's bed, consecrated to sleeping alone—so that his head nuzzled against her small breasts and her long legs surrounded him like great vines embracing a tree.

The noise again. A very private sound.

He lifted up on one elbow, wide awake, mouth dry, eyes wide. Then he saw what it was. Jane had one of those early digital electric clocks in which a thin flap of numbered metal turned over once each minute. It read 04:02 now but, as Ned watched, it made its infinitesimally small slap: 04:03.

D-day, he thought.

He eased himself off the bed, disentangling their limbs so deftly that although she made a sound she failed to awaken. They had drunk a lot of whisky last night, a lot for Jane, anyway. And they had made love endlessly. And he had not phoned Laverne.

04:04. The faint noise seemed to spell out his life like the tolling of a bell. Watch your life lisp away. Watch your castles crumble and your body wither and your brain—04:05.

Naked, he tiptoed downstairs into the tiny kitchen at the back of her small living room. Like her bed, the entire house had never anticipated double occupancy. He filled her electric kettle and plugged it in, then began searching for instant coffee. By the time he found it the water was boiling.

Was he in as much disarray as he felt? Had he alienated everybody he needed and a few he didn't? The coffee was too hot. It burned his tongue. That organ gets you in most of the trouble you're in, kiddo.

D-day. And what kind of commander could he be without his adjutant? A good way to find out was to wake Chamoun. They weren't pals any more. Wake the son-of-a-bitch triple traitor. He dialed Chamoun's home number. Twenty rings later he hung up, dialed again, hung up after ten rings. Okay. Chamoun, eve of battle, out getting laid. Okay.

Ned glanced around the room and saw that every single piece of his clothing was somewhere within sight, evenly distributed like seed corn on a furrowed field. One item was Jane's entire wardrobe of last evening, that is, one dark green velvet robe. She'd had nothing on under it. Simpler.

So, he thought, his eternal outsider wasn't home at four A.M. That was the trouble with outsiders, they didn't behave like insiders. He had also collected Ambrose Everett Burnside III, an outsider so far outside he was virtually on another planet.

He pulled out Jane's A-to-D telephone directory and found, not to his surprise, that Burnside had no telephone. Or else an unlisted number. Too many cranks calling up at all hours.

Ned had been dressing. Now he stepped into his black loafers and stared at himself in a small mirror as he knotted his tie. "What's the rush? Nothing's open," he told himself in a low voice. Then he remembered something that was.

A strange sensation, walking the silent streets of London. Not an auto. No cabs or trucks. No pedestrians. The traffic lights changed, held, shifted, with no traffic to obey them. He reached Hyde Park Corner about four fifteen, and found a few cabs swinging around the circle at murderous speeds. He got to Grosvenor Square at four thirty. The chancery at night had lost a lot of its raw look. Only the gold glitzy bits shone in the street lamps' illumination. The guards at the chancery took a long time examining his pass before letting him in.

The unshaven face, Ned remembered. The moment you skip a shave, your stubble turns you into a subversive character. You begin to fit all the guards' carefully studied profiles of terrorists, agitators, anarchists, and people who eat whole-grain bread and drink unpasteurized milk. Let the beard go another day and you are shot on sight. Damn right!

He unlocked his office door and found a note propped on his telephone. God, he thought, I should have left a note for Jane! What a boor, creep, pig! He unfolded the note:

"Left for Stoke Mandeville Hospital. Masked attackers driving a catering van were trying to get a young German patient. Worth a look."

Chamoun had closed without a signature, just the number of the hospital. Ned tapped out the number on his keypad. It rang for a long time. Finally a woman answered. "No," she said, "you'd have to ask the police about that, sir."

"Is there a policeman about?"

"Excuse me, sir," the woman said, not to him but to someone at her end. "There's a gentleman asking questions."

"Who's this?" a man asked.

"Colonel Edward J. French, U.S. Army. Who's this?"

"I was wondering how long it'd take you to call," P. J. R. Parkins told him. "How did you find out?"

"Parkins? Find out what?"

"Oh." A long pause. "Colonel, do you know the bridge over the Thames at Henley?"

"Not really. What's up?"

"A brown Ford Fiesta crashed into one of the iron structural members. This was ten or ten thirty last night. No one saw it. At that hour, you understand, everybody's in the pub squaring off for last drinks."

"The driver? What about the driver?"

"No driver. Presumed thrown clear into the river."

"Crap!" Ned burst out. "Chamoun is the best driver I know."

Parkins paused for a moment. Then: "There are dents and bangs on the car inconsistent with a supposed crash."

"What're you doing up there, anyway?"

"Helping a friend. Can you come up?"

"I don't have my car."

"Tell me where you are and I'll have you picked up in ten minutes."

Outsiders and insiders. A cruel game.

The board on which they played was an immense tract of old and new buildings, a hospital made up of buildings, red brick and precast concrete, parking lots, new grass, half-grown trees, a checkerboard of small units. Accidents were handled in this long, modern two-story structure which, from the air, looked like an H with an extra leg.

Ned watched Parkins and the tall man with sparse red hair and dense bursts of freckles. The man sat behind an entrance-area desk commandeered for the occasion. They conversed in low insider tones that failed to carry more than a foot or two, the confidential voices of two elder insiders who didn't want anyone else playing with them.

Evidently this very entrance had been the scene of the shoot-out. A large puddle of blood had sunk into the dotted beige carpeting near the desk Parkins and the redheaded man were using. Further down a hall, under a down-dropping flare of overhead light, more blood and nasty little chunks of brain and intestine had been spattered liberally on walls and carpet as though a giant hand had cast these grisly chunks like dice on a gaming table.

The entrance area itself had been sealed off. Little steel standards had been set up with orange plastic tapes running from one to the next to delineate areas of death and keep the casual visitor from stepping in them.

Of course there could *be* no casual visitors here. Ned found himself wondering when they would let him see Chamoun's car and the scene of his . . . call it "accident." "Pardon me, gentlemen."

The redheaded man looked up. "Yas?" he demanded. He had a way, Ned had seen, of using his Scots accent like a blunderbuss.

"How long before I can look at my aide's automobile?"

"Half hour."

"Is it possible to talk to the German?"

The redheaded man frowned intimidatingly. "For what pairpus?"

"I speak German. If he's conscious . . . ?"

The Scot glanced at Parkins. "To kill a half hour?" Parkins asked. "Why not?"

"All right, then," the Scot agreed. He jerked a thumb over his shoulder. " 'Tis that way, in Intensive Care."

It was getting lighter, Bert saw. He had opened his eyes just now and actually seen where he was. It came back to him. This clean hospital. The clean bandages. The clean, lovely nurses. The quiet. The peace.

As the grave. In the woods, decorated with *Glockenblumen*. Two boys and nearly one more, a boy from Stuttgart, where—

Who was this man?

The man who sat down beside him. Familiar face. Come to torture Bert. Knows that face. "*Morgen,*" the man said. "*Wie geht's?*"

"Are you my friend?" Bert burst forth in a flood of German. "Have you come to help me? Or are you one of them, the torturers, the traitors, the murderers? Because I cannot sustain myself against more torture. I have chosen the difficult path in life. I do not expect soft treatment any more than my class enemies expect it of me. But there is a limit to what a human body can withstand." He stopped abruptly and Ned could see that one tear of self-pity had slid out and was running down his cheek.

One only. Dear God, what control lay there.

"I am not your enemy," Ned told him in German. "I am someone who can help. I did not come here to hurt you more. It will take months for you to heal. But nothing serious is broken and nothing is infected."

Only Bert's face was free of bandages. Some of his teeth had been broken out of his mouth. Yet he talked, lived on sheer luck and terrifying toughness. "You are a lucky man, Bert."

"I am," Bert agreed eagerly. "But you have no idea the betrayals these class traitors are capable of. And all because I had no popular base. You understand. You are an intelligent man and a German. I seem to know you from the old life, do I not? So you will understand that when one's only base is ideological, one runs the risk of treachery."

"They betrayed you? Your comrades?"

"Khefte. And for what? You are an intelligent man. You understand that when you have the whole world in your grasp, when the future peace and well-being of humanity lie in your hands, there is no price large enough to buy away your dedication."

"He betrayed you for money. It is the old story, Bert." Ned poured some water from a carafe into a paper cup and held it to Bert's lips. He swallowed greedily, choked, coughed, and swallowed again. "And to whom were you betrayed? To mercenaries. Am I right?"

"I knew you were an intelligent man. To mercenaries, yes. We were so close to victory. A victory in every way, propaganda as well as financial. And these savage running dogs of Mammon, these—" He coughed again.

"These mercenaries smear filth over your ideals," Ned told him, getting at last to what he wanted to question him about. "What plans did they have that were any better than yours?"

"I have no idea. They sprang on me out of darkness and deceit. They—" In his excitement he had evidently moved too violently. Now pain seemed to shroud his face. His one unbandaged hand darted toward his groin. "I am permanently butchered down there, like a steer."

"No. No. Not so."

"And for this I can thank Khefte, who did it with his own knife."

"They say you will recover. You will have children, Bert. Do you believe me?"

A strange look came over the German's face. He stared at Ned, still trying to place him, but his glance had gone distant. "The children toast the bread," he said. "They put thin slices of Muenster on the bread and the Muenster disappears. Nobody knows the Muenster is there. It is a clever secret. Only the children know."

"Do you want children?"

"There is no place in my life for children." A second tear slowly welled up on Bert's lower lid and, just as slowly, rolled down his cheek. "You do understand? Once I escape from here I have much work . . . among my own kind. You are German?"

"I speak German."

"But with an American accent." Bert covered his groin now in a sudden burst of fear, cringing as if being attacked. "You will bury me beneath the *Glockenblumen*." He writhed away from Ned and the pain of his ill-considered movement caused him to groan and black out.

Ned watched him for a long moment. Not much but his face was left to see. He felt Bert's forehead. It seemed to be on fire. He went looking for a nurse.

The only thing crueler than the insider's game was the outsider's game.

On Sunday the entire Thames comes to life in small boats. By six A.M. a group of early risers heading upstream had reached the lock above Marlow at Temple, just below Henley.

That was how they found Chamoun.

In the night his body had drifted downstream like Ophelia's through reeds and islets. It caught in the upriver side of the lock. No one had passed through during the night. But the first time they did, Chamoun's battered face, blue-white and very grave, surfaced beside a small blue-white eighteen-foot fiberglass motorboat called "Unda Ovadraft." The man at the wheel didn't see Chamoun. His wife did. Her scream stopped everything on dead center.

There is a telephone in the lockmaster's house at Temple but the nearest a wheeled vehicle can get to the river at that point is a neighboring farm. Parkins had wheeled a police launch out of the local station at Henley. He and Ned French stood in the rear of the long, low-slung boat as it puttered downstream, threading its way through a thickening mass of private boats. With the Temple lock closed for investigation, traffic was building up.

"What's amiss?" one weekender called to the launch.

"Plenty, you sodding wanker," P. J. R. Parkins responded under his breath but through a beautific smile of calm, peace and plenty.

Ned could find nothing to say, neither abuse nor self-condolence, none of the ancient formulas of the mourner. He watched the small boats and hefty cruisers at impatient rest as the police launch passed by.

The PC at the helm muttered curses on the surrounding throng. "Call yourselves seafaring folk," he grinned at them. "Clogging up the waterways of Britain, you bleeding pack of wallies."

"We're a seafaring nation," Parkins told him with a slight wink. He turned to French. "Everything all right, Colonel?"

"Tremendous," Ned said. "How much farther?"

"Right here, if the silly prats'll let us through."

Ned hadn't bargained for finding everything untouched and guarded by one lone police constable. He'd assumed they would have hauled Chamoun from the water and spread him out somewhere private and peaceful, covered with a tarpaulin. The scene would be familiar to him from Vietnam: roll back the tarp, stare into the dead face, nod, cover the face again. In and out. Hit and run.

Oh, no. Chamoun's body bobbed up and down in the greasy riverine effluvia that usually collected overnight against a closed lock: detergent foam, yellowish and diseased looking, orange peels, cigarette butts, swan feathers, ancient condoms in white or a pale fluorescent chartreuse, and, amid this flotsam, Captain Maurice Chamoun, face up, eyes wide open, staring at his colonel on the start of a gorgeous sunny summer day.

Ned bent over the side of the launch and tried to fit his hands under Chamoun's shoulders. The body was icy, frigid, slimy with the sputum of the river. A huge weir nearby produced a steady, hissing roar. "Help him," Parkins ordered the Henley PC, a young lad and none too muscular.

The policeman took Chamoun's legs and he and Ned together slowly pulled him aboard the launch. To do this, Ned had to embrace the body, hold Chamoun's corpse close to his own breast. Somewhere in the distance he heard a child or a woman making a vomiting noise of disgust.

They settled the body on the duckboarded bottom of the launch. The weir thrummed endlessly. Chamoun stared directly up into Ned's eyes. The contact was intimate and as gelid as the inside of a refrigerator.

Ned felt his legs give at the knees. He sat down so abruptly on a side bench that the launch shipped sideways for a moment and some of the Thames mucus splashed over the gunwale. A swan glided toward them for a brief moment of curiosity, then swerved and paddled away in disdain.

"Yeh," Ned told Parkins in a breathless voice. "That's Captain Chamoun."

"Thought it might be, poor chap."

There was no need of resuscitation. Chamoun hadn't drowned. On the way back to Henley and the waiting ambulance, they decided the weapon could have been a large wrench, something whose wound would seem consistent with a car crash.

Moreover, Ned thought, a wrench belonging to a catering van with banged-up fenders of its own, but he said nothing about it to Parkins, who had probably reached the same conclusion. Ned felt very lonely as the launch slowly returned upstream past the stalled boats, bearing its funereal burden for everyone to see, if they bothered to look. Traffic was moving again.

He felt personally injured, as if it had been he at the wheel of the little mouse-brown car, he driving back to London with his small load of information, he whom they ran off the road and worked over so professionally, but in such a hurry, too rushed to do a thoroughly confusing job, much too callous to care about real agentcraft.

He knew Parkins wanted to talk about it, but he didn't. Cut and dried. Hit and run. Cause and effect. Another frozen pair of eyes to stare him down. Not as icy as Wyckoff's, but this bunch didn't have an imaginative butcher on their staff, did they? By the time meat reached a caterer's it had already been butchered.

"Right?" he asked no one.

Parkins waited a moment and then cleared his throat very softly. "I suppose," he began in a tone too solemn to use in discussing someone he hardly knew, like Chamoun, "you'll be the one to notify his family?"

"Yes."

"And you don't need a tip from me as to what bearing this has on your garden party today?

"No."

"I'd cancel the bugger, so I would. Divert the guests and send them home." A pause. "Was he a decent sort? I didn't know him well."

Ned nodded. "Yes. I mean. . ." He gestured vaguely. "We had our differences of opinion." He started shaking his head from side to side. He fell silent at last.

"If it's any consolation, Colonel, we will get the bastards who did it."

"Yes."

"And make sure they pay for it."

"Oh?" Ned's face went absolutely blank. "There I hope to be a step or two ahead of you."

The plainclothes Special Branch auto moved swiftly along the M4 into London, speeding past Slough and Heathrow along almost empty highways. In the rear seat of the unmarked black Rover, Ned closed his eyes for a moment. Although P. J. R. Parkins was sitting beside him, making notes in his small spiral-bound book, and both a driver and a guard sat in the front seat, Ned felt entirely alone.

I am, he told himself. A commander without an adjutant, going into battle. All the plans for which were sitting in Chamoun's office safe. It had been Chamoun who expedited the whole thing, arranged for the copter cover, the snipers, the electronic sweep team, the . . .

Ned almost groaned, but stopped himself in time. Better Parkins should think he was grabbing a nap. He had had fewer than four hours sleep, but that wasn't what was causing him to feel inadequate. It was the loss of Chamoun in such an unfinished, haunting way.

In a film, Ned reflected, where the audience was never as meanly buffeted about as in real life, there would have been hints. The last conversation with Chamoun would have held some verbal clues. But, try as he might, all Ned could remember of it was that he had been disgusted and angry. A selfish feeling of betrayal had blotted out everything else. No chance for a scenarist to drop in a few ominous hints. Not even a sort of yearning look in Chamoun's eyes: "Dear Boss, I will redeem myself." He had only looked as disgusted and angry as Ned, possibly disgusted with himself for having played the Mossad game.

But that didn't make sense, either, Ned reminded himself. If it hadn't been for Mossad, Chamoun would never have volunteered for the U.S. Army, never have met Ned. He'd been diverted—from the grueling boredom of the rug business and Sandusky, Ohio—by the simple fact of finding out he was a Jew. Not an outsider at all. Ned's smile went askew as he thought of how the Elegant Outsider's life had been rechanneled by the simple knowledge that he did, in fact, belong somewhere after all. Inside the oldest religion? Well, what did that buy him, besides grief?

"You tiptop, Colonel?" Parkins asked in a low voice not meant to be heard by the men in the front seat.

"Just a bit tired. And sorry about Chamoun."

"You're short one right-hand man today, then."

"I'll manage," Ned assured him, opening his eyes and finding that Parkins's own small, piercing eyes were fixed steadily upon him.

"Got a replacement?" the Special Branch officer persisted.

"Chamoun was very methodical. I've got the entire battle plan outlined in the smallest detail as a checklist."

"What is it you Yanks say?" Parkins continued boring in. " 'Don't be a hero'? Is that it?"

"As a matter of fact, that was something Chamoun used to say."

"Damned shame, that. I don't suppose it'd be on, my letting you have a temp number-two from my own people?"

"Definitely not on."

"Still."

"Not on, Mr. Parkins. Feeble giant though we may seem, we can still manage to defend our own embassy." He tapped the driver's shoulder. "Left here, please."

The heavy Rover saloon swung left into the street where French lived. "Fourth on the left. Black door," Ned told him. The car sighed to a halt.

"Have you time for a nap?" Parkins kept asking.

"No. Shower, shave, change of clothes, coffee."

"Your lady wife will see you right, then. Cheer-o. Take this." Parkins handed him a blank business card on which he had scribbled two telephone numbers. "I'll be at one or the other all day."

Ned glanced at him, with his Punch-like face in which a long down-curving nose seemed to want to meet a long, up-curving chin. "Thanks, Peter."

He left the car. As he mounted the stairs to his entrance, he realized he had never called the old buffer anything before but Mr. Parkins.

The shower restored some of his energy as he sluiced himself with hot, then cold water. As far as he knew, Laverne was still in bed, but only pretending to be asleep.

He knew, for example, that she had been at the window when the police Rover dropped him off. With the exception of his early years in military intelligence, when he was away from home quite often, this had been his first night in many years not actually spent in bed with Laverne. It was ironic, in a particularly nasty way, that he had a perfect alibi.

Once shaved, he came back into the bedroom. The tiny bedside clock said 7:32. It was the newer kind, silent as its neon-red numbers changed, no whisper of a hint, as Jane's clock gave, that life was slowly spinning on, passing, dying.

Poor bastard Chamoun. Sideswiped and dumped, only the crudest attempt to make it look anything at all like an accident, almost as if the craftsmen who had engineered his death had decided: enough finesse, what do we care if they know it's murder? Anyway, when a spook gets killed, some sort of plausible cover story is needed for the press. Auto accident would do.

Ned decided that, for the first part of today, at least until the moment when guests arrived, he would dress in class-A's. It would give everyone a sense of security seeing the olive drab, and would help him in ordering his own GIs around. Then, probably at one P.M., he'd shed the jacket and trousers for a dark gray suit. This he now folded carefully and fitted into an attaché case.

It was only then that he saw, in the dimly illuminated room, that Laverne had also been packing. Her two big suitcases lay open on racks in a far corner, half filled with what looked like every bit of summer clothing she owned. She'd even fitted her famous Webley twin set into one case, but Ned wasn't sure it would get past weapons check either at Heathrow or San Francisco.

Collector's item, the twin set. Webley had turned out only a hundred pairs of these extremely light, very flat .32 automatics for the use of SOE saboteurs dropped behind enemy lines in World War II. Their main advantage was their flatness, hardly wider than a .32 cartridge, which made them amazingly easy to hide on one's body. The set had been General Krikowski's wedding gift to his only daughter. But what a gift to send your daughter off on her honeymoon!

Thinking that she would need a sheaf of written authorizations if she wanted to get the twin set out of England, Ned turned to the bed and found Laverne sitting up, watching him. "Morning, Verne."

"Another pit stop?" she asked, her eyes as wary as if she actually hadn't slept at all. "Shower, shave, and off you go?"

"Verne. They killed Chamoun last night."

Her pale eyes widened. "Jesus! Who?"

"I think I know. I even think I have a name. Somebody warned me about him, but it wasn't a reliable source."

"Who warned you?"

"KGB."

"Is that why you let him get killed?" Her mouth opened wide, then shut down tight, clamped shut, pressure lines around her lips. In twenty years he hadn't shared that much information with her, it being strictly forbidden. Chamoun's death seemed to have shoved him off center badly.

"Look," he went on, "I have to function without Chamoun for the rest of the day. Will you be all right, getting yourself to Winfield?"

"Of course."

"Embassy people are supposed to show up around ten thirty to eleven, but that applies to employees, not spouses. So suit yourself. Guests are due at one on the nose."

"Yes. Ned?"

"What?" He was already moving out of the room. She was right, wasn't she, he asked himself, he really did deal with her on a hit-and-run basis. He stopped in his tracks and turned to her. "Yes?" he repeated.

"Don't forget to call his parents."

"I'll send a wire. Phone call later, after the party."

"Yes, that's better. What can you tell them?"

"Line of duty. Patriotic sacrifice. I don't know."

"But that only makes sense when we're at war," she pointed out.

"It would make life a lot simpler for you if we were."

"Then why not admit we are, you damned fool!"

"Because we're not, Verne. The only hope is to keep that in mind. The worst danger is when simple-minded patriots break down under the pressure and start calling for missiles."

She jumped off the bed and stood there in her fighting stance, legs slightly apart. "And suppose that happens, Ned?" she demanded. "What will *you* do then? Go over to your pals at KGB?"

"If that happens," he said in a falsely calm voice, "if the politicians really get us into a war, I'll just die along with everybody else. Now don't be so silly, Verne. You're starting to behave like your father and you haven't even got there yet. What the hell do you need that Webley twin-set for in the U.S. of A.?"

"If you have to ask you'd never understand the answer," she told him in a scornful voice. "The streets back home are running with scum. Winos, rapists, junkies, saboteurs, thieves, terrorists, fugitives, illegals, every kind of trash. And you have the nerve to ask me why I have to go armed?"

"But you don't go armed here, with all the welfare dropout loafers?"

"Oh . . . shut up."

"Have you got documentation and permits for the Webleys?"

"Plenty." They stood there watching each other, like karate fighters trying to anticipate a next move. Then Laverne relaxed and pushed her fingers through her head of fine blonde curls. "Ned, his parents," she called, "what can you tell them?"

He took a deep breath. "Lies," he said, and walked out.

At ten minutes to eight on Sunday morning, July the Fourth, the small white Renault 5-TS slowed as it entered the circular inner drive of Regent's Park. The uniformed U.S. Army colonel at the wheel of the car made note of the fact that roadblock checkpoints had not yet been set up to control traffic hoping to enter the grounds of Winfield House.

The American flag fluttered peacefully from poles inside the gate, partially obscured by greenery. The day had dawned bright and was staying that way. Ned braked his Renault and turned left into the main gate. He was immediately stopped, not by the crabby old gentleman who normally guarded the gate but by two big United States Marines, both sergeants.

"When did you guys come on?" Ned asked.

"Just a second, sir," one sergeant said. He was checking the name on Ned's AGO card with a long list clasped in a steel clipboard. "This takes a while, sir. We got here at seven."

Silently and with a deadpan expression, the other sergeant pulled the clipboard from him and substituted a second one with a much shorter list fastened to it. "Oh, here you are. Top of the list." The Marine's stolid expression dissolved in a wide grin. He handed Ned's pass back to him, swapped a salute, and stood aside.

Driving slowly into the grounds of Winfield, Ned noted the three covert TV cameras. They pivoted slightly as the small white car swung to the left. It meant the men in the control booth were already on duty. Once out of their view, Ned braked the car abruptly, killed the engine, and jumped out. Moving erratically this way and that, he plunged into a thick growth of rhododendrons and started toward the house, moving stealthily in deep cover. An instant later two young men in civilian anoraks seemed to rise up in front of him, holding guns.

"Freeze, Jack."

"Uh, sir," the other one added, eyeing the pass Ned was showing them. "Some kind of field test, sir?"

"Right. Keep patrolling."

"Nice," one of the men called as Ned left them. "Very smooth, Colonel."

Breaking into the sunlight, Ned stood on the forecourt of Winfield, staring up at the sky and swinging his glance slowly in a circle. Some snipers he could see; they had yet to take cover. There were to be eight hidden among the eaves and flat places of Winfield House itself, although the mansard construction didn't offer much cover. Two snipers controlled each side of the house.

Across the road, where an empty dormitory building stood, more snipers were supposed to be in position. Perhaps they hadn't arrived yet. Or perhaps they were having trouble gaining access to the roof.

Overhead, at precisely eight o'clock, a small, light copter of the brilliant scarlet Her Majesty's Government uses on everything it owns bobbed low across the sky like a nervous dragonfly, jouncing here and there in spasms as air currents from the park's greenery began to rise under the heat of the sun.

At the far end of the twelve-acre enclave a small loop of watery canal fed off from the ornamental rowing lake that partly surrounded the area called Queen Mary's Gardens. It was too early for strollers, but Ned could see several large young men in civvies moving here and there in pairs. The loop of water that invaded Winfield's grounds was fenced off and too shallow for a boat or swimmer. Nevertheless, one pair of these Sunday morning strollers had paused at that obvious entry point. Ned hoped they didn't look too suspicious to the ordinary passerby. To him they stuck out a mile.

He turned and went into the front entrance of the house.

"Yes, Colonel?"

A big, low, heavy voice with a dangerous purr to it, like a Mercedes truck engine. Ned turned to see an exceedingly tall black woman get up from an armchair where she had somehow contrived to hide herself. "Colonel French," he said, extending his AGO card again.

She took the card and held it at arm's length, obviously missing her reading glasses. "Oh, yes, the famous colonel. Did you want to see Mrs. Fulmer?"

"If she's up."

"Up? Oh my, yes. She's been up since about four."

"Odd coincidence. So have I. If you would . . ."

"Belle," said a man's voice. Ned turned to see His Excellency approaching in a rather chewed-up dressing gown. On closer view it wasn't a gown at all but a plain dark blue terry-cloth bathrobe. Ambassador Fulmer's hair was damp from his morning shower. "Belle, did I see somebody trying to get in? Oh. It was you?" he asked Ned.

"Colonel French, sir. We haven't met before. I'm the fellow who—"

"Who made such a big hit with Pandora," Fulmer said, with no expression whatsoever. "I have, as they say, heard a lot about you." He extended his hand. When Ned shook it he found it damp.

"They tell me you're quite a hunter," Ned went on in his best embassy manner. "From the way you spotted my entry, I guess we don't need as much security as I thought."

"Basically," Bud Fulmer began, then stopped, listening to the sound of heavy footsteps outside. "Basically the hunter is the aggressor, Colonel French. It's easy to be alert when you're incurring on someone else's turf. But today we're in the position of being the game. Somebody else is the hunter."

A Marine sergeant was rapping on one of the French doors. Ned opened it for him. "That your car, Colonel?"

"Yes. Sorry. I'll park it in back."

"Do that thing, will you, sir? Random cars tend to get us nervous." He saluted and disappeared.

Ned saw that, whatever else Chamoun had done, he had certainly revved up everyone to heightened-awareness levels. "You don't want to tangle with the Marines, Colonel," the ambassador was saying behind him.

Ned turned. "Not a good idea, eh?"

Bud Fulmer's big, slablike face showed absolutely nothing. "It'd be something," he said, "like tangling with Pandora."

The two men eyed each other for a moment. Then Fulmer turned away. "Will you excuse me, Colonel? I've got to dress," he said, and left.

The man who called himself Fownes had already dressed: clean white T-shirt, white duck canvas trousers and sneakers, thick white neck scarf, and a chef's pure white *toque blanche* hat neatly folded and tucked in a back pocket.

None of this could he see in the darkness where he sat. A good moment to practice meditation, yes? He was adept at the kind of meditation ascribed to spiders, private calculations of ominous complexity that always ended up with someone being eaten alive.

Sitting in utter darkness cleared the mind. Marvelous relaxation. He took a deep breath, but the air was not all that fresh. He sighed. The sacrifices one had to make on one's way to the top, to the very stars! Fownes composed himself and turned loose that spider's mind to think, to rethink and to taste in advance the mouth-watering juices of his prey.

At eight in the morning, Royce Connell's private telephone rang in Corinth House. Fishlock, the English butler-housekeeper, normally slept at his own home each night, but, for overtime pay, could be persuaded to use one of the multitude of untenanted bedrooms in the huge house. With this emergency procedure went emergency authority to answer the private line. Royce considered this a secure enough arrangement, meant for those nights he might spend out of London, since a top-priority telephone caller could not possibly mistake the butler's plummy British voice for Royce's.

"Mr. Connell's residence?" Fishlock responded on the twelfth ring.

"Who's this?" a suspicious American voice demanded.

"Fishlock speaking."

"And who the fuck is Fishlock?" Larry Rand inquired. "Put Connell on the line."

"I'm sorry," the butler sidestepped. "Mr. Connell is not available at the mo—"

"Bullshit. Put him on."

"May I take your name and number, sir? Mr. Connell will return your call in a quarter hour."

"Is that like fifteen minutes?" Rand bellowed mockingly. "Christ! Tell him it's Rand and snap it up!" Slam.

Fishlock called the number Royce had left and waited patiently until someone answered. It was a woman's voice, low-pitched, thickly creamy with sleep and very familiar. Where had he heard her before?

"Can I help you," Gillian asked.

It took another five minutes to get Connell on the line and pass along the irate message with an apology for "disturbing" Connell.

"Expect me there in ten minutes, Fishlock. Black coffee, please."

If his early Sunday-morning call had discommoded Royce Connell, there was no sign of it as a taxi deposited him on his own doorstep. He looked, to Fishlock's rather jaded eyes, very much the lad, about ten years younger and springy of step. The gammy back pain was gone. He went directly to his office-den and began making calls. On the third he connected with Rand, who rarely stayed in one place, even on a Sunday.

"Finally," the station head remarked, one of those semi-rude phrases for which he knew he couldn't be directly criticized.

In his dealings with Rand over the years Royce Connell had never been reminded of the usual animal analogs for such a short, hyperactive specimen. Terrier? Sheepdog? Not Rand. In Connell's mind there had long ago formed the image of a honey badger, that extremely nasty little creature which instantly goes for the genitals of whatever it singles out as its prey. The fact that Rand had never actually sunk his incisors in the Connell equipment simply meant that Royce was better buffered than most by layers of high-ranking dips and State Department officials whom he had befriended over the years.

"What's your problem, Rand?" Connell asked, putting the onus on the Company.

"More your problem than mine. Have you read your A.M. signals yet?"

Connell glanced at his watch. Eight fifteen. "As I'm not a mind reader and the signals haven't arrived, no. If you have something to report, Rand, will you please report it like a good little fellow?"

There was a shocked pause at the other end while Rand wondered if now was the time for a lightning killer snap at Connell's groin. Then, coldly: "Something on the overnight, I didn't get a clear message. Some sort of preemptive strike in the eastern Med or the Gulf of Hormuz."

"Whose? Ours?"

"Looks like."

"I don't know what telephone calls cost you, Rand, but this is my nickel so squeeze out a few more words of wisdom? Air strike? Landing assault? Missiles? Location? Statements if any from D.C.?"

"No use getting nasty, Connell. I only know it looks like ours and it could well be against one of those little sheep-buggering oil states. There isn't one of them wouldn't be a whole lot improved by nuking."

"Anything in the morning papers?"

"No, but early radio is reporting rumors."

"Of what? Same thing?" Connell asked.

"Riots. Civilian casualties. Who can believe journalists? They just pass along what the bedsheet-heads feed them."

"Where else could you dig out the news if not from the people who were bombed?" Connell stopped, angry with himself for arguing with a mind like Rand's. "Anything else?"

"How much more do you need? A red alert coming down the lines from D.C.? I'm surprised your ace, Colonel French, hasn't alerted you. But he's just never on the job when you need him, is he?"

Connell hung up and immediately called his press deputy, Mary Constantine. "Wake you up?" he apologized.

"Is this about that bombing?"

"You're onto it. What can you give me? Location?"

"Not yet."

"Keep bothering your press contacts."

Royce found a night number for someone on the duty desk at State, back home, but the night line failed to answer, a clear sign that something ugly was developing. Fishlock presented him with a steaming mug of black coffee. Royce called Gillian's number.

"Is this Miss Lamb's secretary?" he asked her when she answered.

"This is Miss Lamb's everything, and yours, too."

"Up and out of bed!" Connell said. "Some kind of U.S. bombing raid in the near east. Ask around. If you get anything, call—"

"What makes you think I'm in bed?" she cut in. "The second you moused out of here the phone started. Royce . . ." She paused. "It's bad."

"This bombing raid?" A sudden tension churned in the pit of his stomach, as if someone were aiming a punch at it.

"We don't know if it was a raid. It's Damascus. The casualties so far . . ." She faltered again. "It looks like an inside job. Bombs planted in a heavily populated area. A lot of children are dead, Royce."

"But, look here—"

"I've had three calls already, including my producer, who wonders . . ." She hesitated for the third time. "Who wonders if this is the best moment for a program about America and her Independence Day."

"Gillian, what makes you think—"

"There is a riot in Damascus now. The entire thrust is anti-American. They're storming the consulate. Burning American autos. They're—"

"Please," he interrupted. "Let's be sensible." He stopped and tried to sound coherent. "Is there an official accusation? Has anyone blamed the U.S. except street rioters?"

"Is that necessary?" she countered. "Royce, bombs over a sleeping city? Isn't that a . . ." Once more she paused. "A trademark?"

In silence, Royce stared down at the floor, feeling as if that stomach punch had landed. They had only been lovers for two nights, but his deepest fears about intimacy had blossomed with this new horror. Would it be easier to bear if she were an American? Would she be voicing such unthinkable thoughts?

"I'm sorry," he heard her say. "But you have to know how this is being seen by the outside world. Royce, I'm on *your* side."

He tried to smile. The tension began to go away. "Thank you," he managed in a low voice. "I do appreciate you, my dear." He actually smiled then. "Indeed I do."

After they said good-bye he phoned for his limo and got into the shower, automatically thinking as he always did about his clothes for the day. He was dressing now for the party at one P.M. Oyster-tan suit? Strong blue shirt, he thought, with a white knitted Dacron tie and a matching belt to—Damascus.

He winced, turned off the shower. Toweling himself, he thought: Independence Day around the world and murdered children in Damascus. What had Washington been thinking?

The telephone began to ring.

27

At nine on the morning of July Fourth, two small TV vans arrived at the north gate of Winfield House. They were preceded by a Metro driven by Gillian Lamb, ready to beam her incandescent smile upon the crusty old gatekeeper who already loved her.

"ID, Miss," a deadpan Marine sergeant said, holding out his hand.

"Oh, dear. I'm afr—I know it's here somewhere." Gillian pawed desperately through her handbag. She looked up and gave the Marine a thousand-watt smile, right to the heart. "But you know me, Sergeant, I'm sure?"

"Sure'd like to, ma'am. But I need your ID first."

This had the strange effect of causing Gillian to blush, increasing her appeal severalfold. She finally found her pass and handed it over. He scrutinized it in a way that clearly indicated he had never seen her before in his life.

"Thank you, Miss Lamb, ma'am." The Marine ticked off her name on the list that began with Ned French's name. "What about the vans behind you? Everybody got passes?"

"Why don't you ask?" she inquired acidly and zoomed off into the Winfield enclave.

At the same time, the south gate, which had been opened to traffic

390

only for today's events, was filled by two larger vans, also bearing the magic TV initials. The lead driver showed credentials to the Marine guard and then asked:

"I need a nice shady spot near the house."

"Shady? Why shady?"

"Lot of sensitive equipment inside. Has to stay cool."

"Try over there," the Marine pointed.

Standing on the terrace of Winfield, Ned watched both sets of vans maneuvering. It occurred to him—for the first time—that the crew of "Lamb to Slaughter" might wonder about the other vans. He was about to walk down to the driveway when Mrs. Crustaker, from inside the big room and without raising the pitch of her powerful voice, called to him: "Telephone, Colonel."

"Ned, Max Grieves. We're starting distribution of the official invitations. I tried not to bother you, but Moe Chamoun's not around yet, they said."

"How are you handling the distribution?"

"Normal London motorcycle courier. Each kid gets one. After he delivers it and gets a signature, he returns and gets another to deliver."

"Perfect. Do you have someone helping you?"

"Two of our guys."

"Good. Max, two favors. See if you have a dossier on a man called Fownes. Then drop what you're doing and fill in for Moe, will you?"

"Fill in for Moe?" The FBI man's voice went up half an octave at the strangeness of the request but he asked no further questions. "Be there in half an hour."

"No, I'll be back at the chancery. Wait for me."

Ned hung up and turned to find that the tall and impressively mature Mrs. Crustaker had been joined by a wan, childlike sprite: "I preferred working with Captain Chamoun," Pandora Fulmer announced coldly. "Where is he?"

"Oh, good morning, Mrs. Fulmer."

"Where is he?"

"Somewhere else," Ned explained. "But don't worry. When I return that nice Max Grieves will replace Captain Chamoun. You'll like him."

"That remains to be seen."

Pandora had put on only part of her makeup this early in the day, the base and some of the eye shadow. She hadn't—although Ned didn't know the precise details of it—put on lipstick, eyelashes, mascara, liner, blusher, or glitter, or added fine penciled grace notes to her eyebrows. Perhaps this accounted for the wan, hollow look of her face, a kind of hungry, questing expression, the orphan Oliver holding out an empty bowl for gruel.

"No, you will like Max," Ned assured her, smiling nicely. "He's not part of the corrupt military constraint you dislike so much. He's a civilian, Mrs. Fulmer. You two will hit it off." He started for the terrace.

"Colonel."

He stopped and slowly turned toward her. "Yes, Mrs. Fulmer?"

"It's pretty obvious that we two never will get along," she said briskly. "But for today we're going to have to. Can I have your word on that?"

Ned extended his right hand. "You have it."

Solemnly they shook hands and Ned thought he could see a faint flash of zany hilarity flare up in Mrs. Crustaker's elderly eyes before she turned away to hide a . . . smile? It couldn't be easy wet-nursing Pandora, Ned decided, but it probably paid well in laughs.

Outside, what he had feared would happen, had happened. One of Gillian's cameramen had aggressively walked up to the two big TV vans: "Wot's with you lot, then?"

The black driver, a disguised lieutenant, had started to respond, but saw Ned coming to rescue him. "This gentleman will 'splain," he said in a pure Georgia drawl.

"Please take me to Miss Lamb," Ned began. "This has nothing to do with British TV. I'll explain it to her."

"Damned Yanks coming over here taking our jobs?" the cameraman asked as he led Ned French away. "Bloody hell, the old story, innit? And nig-nogs, too!"

"I'll explain to Miss Lamb."

"Explain what?" Gillian asked. "Those two vans? Are they American? Are they union? What's going on?"

Ned took her behind some trees near the flagpole and waited to speak until her crew were out of earshot. "Do they trust you?" he asked. "Are they your usual crew?"

"Yes. But they think their jobs are being poached on."

Ned stared into the tawny eyes, framed by that cornsilk sweep of hair. It was a moment for honesty, not charm.

Without a smile, he said in a very low voice: "You remember the Trojan horse?"

"What did you say?"

He moved so close his lips brushed her ear. "The Trojan horse episode? You do remember?"

She glanced sideways at him, those tiger eyes flashing suspicion. "Is this a joke, Colonel?"

"The vans have armed men in them. I'm hoping they aren't needed. You must keep that entirely to yourself for the rest of the day. But give your crew a story they'll believe."

The sideways glance looked fearful now. "They'll be locked in there all day? And that's how you treat your own troops?"

"It's necessary. At least, we think so."

"Does Royce know about this?"

"Nobody. Only you."

Her rather daunting glance moved from his face to those of her crew, watching from a distance and then, farther away, to the offending vans. She pressed her lips into a flat line but still managed to look gorgeous. "You might have kept them out of sight."

"I need them close to the house. What's this?" Both of them watched two more vans come in slowly along the driveway from the main gate. On their sides was lettered HODGKINS AND DAUGHTER—CUSTOM CATERING.

"Work it out!" Ned called, sprinting for the lead van. He stopped the vehicle and ordered out the two men in the front seat. "ID, please."

"We just showed it to—."

"Show it again."

The two vans turned out to be crammed with food and heavy items of kitchen and catering equipment. The four men unloaded everything under Ned's eye, installing a huge assortment of platters, trays, glassware, alcohol-burning warmers and warming ovens, coatracks, and four magnificent portable toilet booths, already labeled LADIES and GENTLEMEN. Ned opened each booth and checked the interiors.

Harry Ortega, strolling past, saw him exit from a LADIES and gave him a lewd wiggle of the eyebrows. "Anybody stolen any shit, Colonel?"

"Passably funny. Harry, I'm leaving for a while. I'll surely be back by ten thirty. I want these four men and their vans off the premises now. Any people and vehicles from Hodgkins who arrive at the gates, I want held till I return."

"Listen, I know these guys."

"That's good. But hold them outside the gate till I arrive."

"I don't know," Ortega said, worried.

"Sure you know, Harry. I just told you."

The Winfield security man brightened. "Oh, well, okay. If it's an order, it's an order."

"Harry, you're improving all the time."

Ned moved off quickly in search of Gillian Lamb. He spotted her bright flag of blonde hair in the distance and, beyond her, saw that her crew was going about its business and seemed to have forgotten its grievance. Or put it in abeyance.

"What excuse did you give them?" he asked Gillian.

"What could I tell them? Anything your rival TV vans might be doing would be a threat to my lads."

"So?"

"So I just told them to trust me. And I smiled."

Ned placed his hand on his heart. "My dear, even I trust you."

By ten o'clock in the chancery Max Grieves and Ned had gone over all the many details of Chamoun's master plan set down as a four-page checklist. Although Grieves claimed to have it in hand, Ned realized with a hurtful pang that he would never again work with anyone as intelligent as Chamoun, who could anticipate him like a mind reader. Grieves was a poor substitute, but he was, at least, willing.

Whatever the Bureau had failed to teach him about crime fighting, they had at least instilled enough plain discipline to keep him from asking the one question Ned knew he was burning to ask. As they each pocketed their copy of the security checklist Chamoun had prepared, Ned decided he'd been right not to explain Chamoun's absence. It would upset Grieves too much. Later, if there were to be a later, he would get the truth, or what part of it French could swear was true.

"What did you come up with when you quizzed your computer about Fownes?"

"No record."

"That means we can't get a photo." Ned picked up his hat as he rose to his feet. "Let's go. We've left Winfield alone too long as it is."

His phone rang. "Deputy Defense."

"Ned," Royce Connell began at once, "I've been tracking you all over London. Come down to my office right now, please."

"I've got Max Grieves with me."

"Yes. The two of you." Royce hung up.

When Ned arrived with the FBI man in tow, Royce was paging through a thin sheaf of telexes. He sat in his shirtsleeves, unusual for him. Then Ned realized why: he wanted the jacket of his bone-colored suit to look pristine for the garden party. It hung carefully on a wooden hanger nearby.

"We still don't have a firm idea of what happened. It's Damascus and it's a series of explosions, planted on the ground or delivered by air. The body count is in the neighborhood of twenty-seven Syrians, including a lot of children."

"And who's accused? Us?"

"This happened in the middle of the night, so everyone's claiming it has the U.S. trademark, night bombing of open cities. Our way of standing tall," Royce added bitterly. "But it was followed by rioting, looting, burning of autos and buildings, all of them launched at Americans. With quite a few additional casualties, mostly Syrian."

"What does D.C. say?"

"It's five A.M. back there. I can't get anybody to answer the emergency phones except night duty clerks who tell me I know more about it than they do."

"May I?" Ned asked, reaching for one of Royce's phones. "Either we're innocent or we did it. The Pentagon or the Company has to know, depending on how the explosives were delivered." He was tapping out a long series of numbers that would connect him to his own head office back home. Ned listened to the rings until someone answered in a sleepy voice.

"Who's the duty officer? This is Colonel French, London embassy."

"Ned, it's Rafferty."

"Tom! What's the goods on this Damascus thing?"

"We think it was local. Nobody we know was scheduled for any kind of flying around there."

"You know they're blaming us."

"Don't they always? Say hello to Laverne."

"Bye." Ned turned to Royce Connell. "Delivered locally. You'd better talk to Rand. I always want to punch out his nasty little mouth for him."

"What makes you think the Company planted the bombs?"

"Did I say that?" Ned countered.

"Mm. All right. I imagine you're needed back at Winfield. I'll be there late. I've got to keep tracking this till I know what we're dealing with."

Outside in the corridor, Ned handed his car keys to Max Grieves. "Get the little white Renault 5-TS. Meet me at the phone booth on Duke Street off Oxford. I'm running back up to my office."

"What for?"

"Actually Moe's office. He's—On his desk he's got a little radio. I think before the day's out, we're going to need to hear what's really happened in Damascus.

"Why is that?" Max asked.

Ned stared at him for a long moment. "Go get the car, Max."

Only one person answered this private number, typed on a card in Ned's wallet. He had no idea where the phone was, in the man's office or home. In any event, it was not a line he could call from the chancery.

"Gleb," he began, "this man Fownes. Can you—"

"Should I even talk to you?" Ponamarenko cut in.

"What?"

"The news from Damascus."

"Fownes," Ned repeated.

A heavy sigh, speaking of storm-blasted tundra in the far wastes of Siberia. "Whether responsible or not, the blame falls on the big nations. You are now in our league, eh? Not a very useful reputation to have."

"Gleb, I promise to meet you next week for a hair-shirt lecture. Right now, describe Fownes for me."

"Medium height. Overweight. Bushy, wiry hair. Exophthalmic eyes. Pasty complexion. Sometimes a mustache, sometimes not."

"Accent?"

"Vaguely American, but not native-born."

Outside the phone booth, the small white Renault pulled up to the curb and a very curious Grieves peered out at Ned. "I owe you one, Gleb."

"You owe me ten."

"Some day."

"Some day your people will stop making problems for me. Do you realize I must now file ten thousand words on the horror and revulsion with which the average British man in the street views this barbaric act of terrorism unleashed by Uncle Sam?"

"Off you go, then."

Ned hung up and stared back at Max Grieves sitting at the wheel of Ned's old car, with its left-hand European steering. It was supposed to become Lou Ann's car when she celebrated her eighteenth birthday.

Had he run up such a heavy bill with Ponamarenko? What he'd asked for wasn't anything held dear. He'd have to downgrade his appreciation next time he talked to Tass's star correspondent. No sense letting him think he was owed anything more than a drink.

He turned on Chamoun's little radio, hardly much bigger than a ten-smoke cigarette pack. Holding it to his ear, he walked to the car and got in. ". . . angry backlash across the entire Islamic community as well as in nations with large Muslim minorities. Meanwhile, in Moscow, the . . ."

"Back to Winfield, Max. First things first."

A short cortege of vans and lorries labeled HODGKINS AND DAUGHTER—CUSTOM CATERING waited outside the main gate of the Winfield House enclave as Max Grieves steered the little Renault through Marine guard identification.

Ned got out of the car. "You park it around to the left, Max. Then search these trucks. Then take Chamoun's checklist and go over the premises with a fine-tooth comb. When you run into Harry Ortega, tell him I want him to meet me outside the north gate at once. Go."

He watched the bewildered FBI man drive away. It was too easy to compare him with Chamoun, to Grieves's detriment. But there would never again be anybody like Chamoun. *Christ!* His parents hadn't been informed!

Ned started for Winfield House to use a telephone, but Ortega waylaid him. "What's up, Colonel?"

"We're going to let the caterer's people enter one by one. Harry, you've been telling me you know them by sight? Here's your chance. I'm going to run them past you. If you know him, or her, give a hello. If you never saw him before, say nothing. Got it?"

"I'm the finger guy. Got it."

"Ah, Harry, when you signed up for government service, the private-eye business lost a really colorful master of the cliché."

With two Marine sergeants as ushers, the drivers and staff of the caterer's vehicles moved quickly along a tree-shaded path. "Wait over on this side, please," Ned told them as they walked past Ortega.

"Hiya," the Winfield security man would say. "Hi, there."

The first twenty men and women out of the vans turned out to be known to Ortega. But of the last twenty, all men, he recognized only four. Ned moved between the known catering workers and those who seemed new to Ortega. He signaled the two Marines to join him and waved Ortega in as well.

"We have an agreement with Mr. Fownes," Ned explained in a reasonable tone. "He was to supply thirty people but what we have here is a lot more. So we're going to have to wait till Mr. Fownes gets here."

He spoke slowly and very distinctly to project as friendly an atmosphere as possible. "You bunch," he said to the twenty-four "cleared" people, "drive your stuff inside and go to work. You bunch," he said in an even friendlier tone, "wait a while till Mr. Fownes arrives. Sergeant," he told the nearest Marine, "find a six-by-six or any appropriate vehicle and get these men out of the hot sun."

"Right, Colonel."

Ned watched while the unknown workers boarded the big olive drab truck. He tried to see, by their posture or faces, if they were any different from the rest, perhaps in better shape? But it was impossible. All he could do was move fast and present them with a fait accompli before they realized what was happening. "Sergeant, take whatever men you need and drive south on the Outer Circle, around Regent's Park to the east, then turn north to Chester Gate and you'll be looking at the Albany Street police station. Turn these men over to an Inspector Mulvey. They're to be detained on orders of Mr. Parkins. Is that clear?"

The men seated inside the truck began to grow restless. "Lock the doors, Sergeant. Fast!"

"Yes, sir. An Inspector Mulvey? A Mr. Parkins?"

"Off you go!"

Ned turned and made his way to Winfield House. He entered via the kitchen this time and found a telephone in an isolated corner near the freezer units. Taking Parkins's blank card, he dialed one of the numbers penciled on it and reached him almost at once. When he'd told him about the sixteen men, Parkins grew very quiet.

"Yes, we'll handle it," he said after a moment. "Did you take my advice? Are you canceling?"

"Not my decision."

"Is that prayer meeting still on for one P.M.?"

"No change, as far as I know," Ned told him.

"We're starting to get reports of mass demos being planned here in London."

"The Damascus business? But what's happened there? Does anybody know?"

"Nobody has to, Colonel. It's a matter of past performance. Something bad happens to Arabs sleeping away the night peaceful-like, the blame goes to your lot. Don't tell me, I know it's daft. But you have to live with it. Or rather, when it's demos, we do."

"Look, can I send more prisoners to Mulvey?"

"He's got almost no lock-up facilities. Send any new lads to the station, corner of Greenberry and Newcourt. It's quite near your house."

"Thanks. Bye."

"Colonel! You can still cancel."

"You'll be the first to know." Ned hung up and immediately took out his wallet. He removed the typed business card with a few dozen telephone numbers of special interest to him, like Gleb Ponamarenko's, a cousin who lived near his parents in Wisconsin, and Chamoun's family number in Sandusky. He dialed the number and waited. It would be five thirty in the morning there, if Ohio were in the Eastern time zone, otherwise four thirty. He hung up quickly. This sort of news could wait to be delivered until after an uninterrupted night of sleep.

He then dialed the number of the adjutant's office at a nearby Quartermaster Corps company.

"Captain, this is Colonel French. Are your food handlers ready?"

"And loaded into transport."

"All white clothing?"

"No insignia."

"Turn 'em loose!"

Ned hung up and studied the neatly typed checklist Chamoun had prepared. With a pencil he checked off most of the items on page one. As detailed as the checklist a co-pilot and pilot put an airliner through before takeoff, the compilation ran on for three more pages. At the top of page two was the item: "If temps above 75° check interiors of fake TV vans."

Ned left Winfield House and made his way through undergrowth to where the two Trojan horse vans were parked in the shade. He showed his AGO card to the black Georgia lieutenant pretending to be a driver. "Everybody breathing nicely?"

"No grunts yet, suh."

"How are they dressed?"

"Combat fatigues. Berets. Light field pack. No insignia."

"Have they got inside crappers?"

"Chemical toilets. That's asking a lot of the guys."

Ned nodded. "It's asking a lot of the toilets, too."

"Would there be some way of letting them out now and then, suh, to just sort of stretch their legs and get some air?"

"Lieutenant, if there is, I'll let you know. This may all be a false alarm, after all."

"Better not be," the lieutenant said darkly. "Otherwise these guys will tear each other's throats out. They're what you call combat-eager?"

"I would be too, locked up with a chemical toilet."

From the roof of the house in which Khefte had rented several bed-sits, he fancied he could actually see across the treetops to Winfield. Backed up against Primrose Hill, the neighborhood's buildings did have the advantage of long vistas to the south, but on this particular morning, Khefte felt it would have been unwise for him to attract attention by standing on the roof. Nor would he let any of the other men do it.

His entire cadre, now that Merak, Mamoud, and Bert had been lost, numbered precisely forty-five, all youngsters in their teens, with fire gnawing their bellies and the pure truth of Islam flowing through their veins.

A lot of them came from Iran, where the ayatollahs had recreated Islam in its most active form, as a jihad to wipe Satan off the face of the earth, with all his evil works. Those who hadn't died in the boy's battalions overrunning Iraq, now that they had been toughened by combat, were fed in small groups of four or five into the mainstream of the worldwide jihad, some further to disrupt Beirut and Cairo, some to go underground in Israel, some to stiffen the cadres of other Islamic groups, and some, like Khefte himself, to be the spearpoint pressed into the very ribs of Satan, the lance to slit the carbuncle of corrupt Judeo-Christian evil.

Khefte glanced at his watch. Eleven o'clock. He took four men with him and left the bed-sit. Outside, parked here and there on neighboring streets, were half a dozen cars his men had stolen during the small hours of Sunday morning. In these his entire cadre would arrive at the mosque in two relays or shifts. They would be dressed, as now, like ordinary London working men, but they would be carrying automatic weapons and extra magazines for them, with every fifth man carrying grenades and every tenth assigned to use a rocket launcher.

Even now, parked in the lot of the mosque, a locked van contained the larger of these weapons. Khefte and his squad spread out in several directions now as a patrol, checking the streets around them for signs that the cars might have attracted the attention of great Satan. The scene looked peaceful. A typical Sunday, with most families out in the country and the streets largely empty of traffic.

On Finchley Road, Khefte stepped into a telephone kiosk and dialed the number of Hakkad's apartment. "Yes?" A man's voice, terse, flat.

"Khefte here. Let me speak to the American woman."

"Not possible."

"I said this is Khefte."

"No phone calls. Orders."

"Then let me speak to Sgroi. The man called Fownes."

"Not possible." The line went dead.

Khefte could feel his cheeks burning. For a moment he was going to place the call again, but realized he would only be further humiliated. To be spoken to in that ignorant way! If only he could get to Fownes, he would demand the head of the dog who had just insulted him. He knew, because Fownes had told him, that only one man now guarded the Hakkad apartment. The blond bastard was needed for the taking of Winfield House.

In less than two hours the attack would begin. Isolated, completely on his own for the first time, Khefte looked about him at the small houses and neatly clipped gardens of this residential street.

At the head of the street, a white police Rover with a red and yellow stripe paused while its driver surveyed the corner. Khefte could feel his bowels liquefy. Horrible pains wracked his abdomen, a feeling of the outpour shoving to escape. Sweat drenched him. The Rover moved on and disappeared. Beads of sweat chilled Khefte's face. He swallowed hard twice. Surely Allah would not leave him alone in this hour. Comrades were at hand. The elite troops, Khefte reminded himself. Surely in hiding, but only waiting for the moment to attack. Surely.

He glanced about him and found that it had become hard to breathe. He took in a great lungful and sighed it slowly out. The elite troops were there, he told himself again and, still out of breath, slowly mounted the stairs to the bed-sit, moving carefully, like an elderly man with rotted insides.

"Am I glad to see you," Mrs. Crustaker murmured quietly in Jane Weil's ear. She had just arrived with Bill Voss, his wife, Betsy, and many other embassy people, all checking themselves in the anteroom's mirrors, touching their hair, tightening their ties, and freshening their lipstick. To Jane they resembled the company of an amateur small-town playhouse in some communal dressing room, readying themselves for the curtain. They were, in fact, mostly security people.

"Mrs. F. must be very nervous," Jane told the tall black woman. "I know I'd be frantic."

"She's already had her first run-in with that Colonel French—sweet man, isn't he?—and they've shaken hands on a truce. But that's only going to last till the first booboo." She eyed the others to make sure they couldn't hear her. "You're the only one she behaves herself for. The rest of the time she's just the real Pandora."

"You think I have any control over my boss's wife?"

Mrs. Crustaker chuckled. "Somebody better. I have known this little missy all her life. Today has got to be the peak climax of her career, Miss Weil. Do I get my message across?"

"If it flops, we're in for hurricane weather?"

"Washington won't be able to get the Fulmers out of England fast enough. So, please, do your bit?"

"Why should she listen to me?" Jane asked.

"Do I know?" Mrs. Crustaker's eyes went wide with wonder. "She respects you. You're a professional person, a lawyer, a diplomat. She thinks of herself that way, so, naturally . . ." She let the thought remain unfinished. "Also, you're tall, like me. Pandora Fulmer can stand up to any man, but she makes lots of room for tall women. Her Ma was tall. I 'spect she associates tall with spanking." Her eyes snapped with glee.

"So you figure, between the two of us—"

"No, if you handle the small one, I can devote myself to keeping Mr. F. and booze from meeting face to face."

She disappeared in the direction of the kitchen area just as Pandora Fulmer arrived, totally made up and dressed in a white fairy-light chiffon garden frock with exaggerated flower designs in blue and red. Her five-inch high-heeled pumps were white linen stenciled with the same floral/patriotic motif.

"People," she said in a low, urgent voice. "People, I thank you most kindly for coming today." Her voice had started to emphasize the dactyls and soften their edges into a lush Southern accent of the sort that cozens most Americans into believing its owner is charming.

"People, you are all such darlings. I don't know what I would do without your loyal support. I don't suppose any of us knows everyone who's coming. I'm depending on you, as you mix and mingle, to locate the truly important guests and make absolutely, positively certain, without fail, that they get to meet His Excellency and me. That isn't too hard, is it?"

"Not at all, Mrs. Fulmer," Betsy Voss told her with an equally sincere most-holy-acolyte voice, as if discussing the details of transubstantiation. "Believe me, it's an honor for all of us to do what we can, each in our small way, to help forward the great work you and His Excellency are even now—"

"Betsy means," her husband broke in rudely, "you can count on us. Period."

Pandora's large, thoroughly made-up eyes swung this way and that. She was holding in her left hand a wide-brimmed pale straw garden hat of the kind that flaps freely in even the lightest breeze and, at a touch of rain, folds up like an umbrella, trapping one's head in an iron embrace of fibrous shrink.

"Jane," she said at last. There followed a complicated movement of the eyes. The two women left the room and stood for a moment in a small area where the caterer's first delivery had stored four large, squat aluminum warming ovens. "Jane, tell me the truth, honey. Will even one guest show up?"

"Mrs. Fulmer!" Jane found herself stretching her neck as if to increase her already considerable height. "What makes you ask that question?" She had couched the question in a faintly hectoring voice, as if demanding an answer from a schoolgirl. "It's quite the event of the year."

"It would have been till the experts got hold of it. That Colonel French has been giving out all sorts of threats."

"Someone has, I agree, but not Colonel French. And, in any event, Mrs. Fulmer, in view of this morning's news, you can hardly blame guests for wondering about terrorist reprisals."

"For what? What news?"

"The Damascus bombing and riots last night?"

Pandora's great eyes widened for a moment, then slowly closed to a frowning squint. "I could kill the president," she said. "On the very night before my party!"

At eleven fifteen another traffic jam built up, this time at the south gate, the one normally chained shut. Here two anonymous open-backed trucks with oval canvas covering tried to enter the grounds of Winfield at almost the same time as two large refrigerator vans bearing the ubiquitous Hodgkins legend. Although the two Marine sergeants on guard could have admitted the vehicles by the usual slow process of checking identification, they had been warned by Ned French to call him instead and bring him directly to the gate. He arrived with two more Marines, Max Grieves, and Harry Ortega in tow.

"These two trucks," Ned ordered, "check ID and pass. These two . . ." He eyed the Hodgkins vans. "Harry, is your finger still working?"

In all, he chose six "innocents." The four marines, working in unison, hustled the remaining caterers aboard two lockable trucks and drove them off to the Greenberry Street station. Ned turned to Max Grieves. "If Harry's on the ball, we only have good caterers inside the enclave. Plus the QM boys who just arrived. Enough staff to prepare and serve. And no sign of Fownes. So, as of this moment, we're golden. But the only way we can stay that way is by not letting in any more caterers."

"These last two vans are loaded with food," Max reported. "The booze is already on hand. So we seem to be in the clear."

"For now." Ned turned to Ortega. "Why don't you get back to the house and make a double check on the people you passed through originally?"

Ortega nodded and jogged off toward the mansion. "Do you doubt his first count?" Max asked.

"No. I just want him out of earshot. At one o'clock"—he glanced at his watch—"ninety minutes—something is going off at the mosque across the road."

"What?"

"It's diversionary, but it's real. The way we figured it out—" He opened his copy of Chamoun's checklist. "Look at page three, item forty-one."

"It says: 'Twelve fifty, alert Special Branch.' To the mosque thing?"

"I took care of that. Special Branch already knows and is ready to swamp the thing like a blanket thrown over a fire."

"What is it? A demonstration?"

"A sort of religious rededication. Kind of inspirational and rabble-rousing. It's supposed to kick off the jihad of the day. But a blanket doesn't always get all the flames. Some of the lads may show up with rocketry and automatic weapons. The only way is through the south checkpoint and we're ready for them there."

"So we're still home free. Right?"

"No. I said this was diversionary." Ned stopped and thought about the ability of Max Grieves to absorb theory in the abstract. It was a question he had never needed to ask when working with Maurice Chamoun.

He had to stop making these comparisons. Moe Chamoun was dead. The Fourth of July was barely half over. He still had a long way to go, and, in a sense, he would go with Chamoun by his side as they worked their way through his heavily detailed battle plan. Time for real mourning later. Time to phone his folks.

"Ned?"

"Sorry. I . . ." He paused, at a loss to remember what he had been saying. Yes. "Diversionary. That means someone inside Winfield is expecting us to rouse to the mosque alarm, lower our vigilance at Winfield, and let him—let's call him Fownes—take over here by a surprise coup."

"Which he can't do," Max added enthusiastically, "since we have screened out his own people. We've even screened him out. So it's an abort, right, Ned?"

"I'll let you know after one o'clock. Right now, I'm trying to think like Fownes. Suppose he knows we've pinched off his troops and we'll stop him if he tries to enter. Does he have any other choice but to abort?"

"None."

"He's got ninety minutes to think of something else before he throws in his cards."

"He's outguessed and outmanned, Ned. Exit Fownes."

"You're thinking like Max Grieves," Ned said, trying not to make it sound like an accusation. "Say to yourself: I have spent a lot of time and effort on this and it's worth millions. Is there any way to save it at the last minute?"

"I suppose . . ." Agony distorted the FBI man's features. "I suppose if he *could* get into Winfield, he'd have no choice but to go for hostages. The highest-ranking he could find."

"Named Fulmer?"

"Yeah, like that. But how does he get into Winfield?"

"We aren't paid to figure that out so much as to figure what to do when he gets in. You get the distinction there?"

"Nothing's happened and nothing will," Grieves insisted doggedly.

"Max, stop being stupid!"

There was a hurt pause, as if he'd slapped the FBI man, who said in a mournful tone: "Ned, I'm not stupid. I'm *ordinary*. It isn't fair, having to fill in for him, Ned. Ned? Where is Moe?"

"He's dead." A rough patch turned his voice into a rasp. "They killed him last night."

"Ned!"

"Not possible, right? But the only law we have is Murphy's Law, Murphy's Law in overdrive: no matter how impossible something bad could be, it *will* happen."

"Ned, Jesus Christ. He was like a brother to you."

Ned French nodded. There was nobody near them. Just the two men, standing under tall trees. Overhead, blackbirds sang on and on, happy in the sunshine. He could have wept, with only Max Grieves as a witness. "The Germans," Ned said in that same rough rasp, "have a word for it. *Doppelgänger*, sort of a double image of yourself."

"That was Moe."

Ned nodded again. "That was Moe."

28

At twelve noon a small black Mini stopped in front of Number 12 in the Belgravia area and a slight, dark-haired young fellow almost as small as a child got out. When the burly new guard challenged him, he fired a single silenced slug into the guard's kneecap. As he doubled over in agony, the guard's hands were deftly bent behind him and handcuffed. The boy-sized invader began dragging the guard out of sight as Bricktop entered and made for the elevator.

"Neat," she told the small man. Standing side by side they resembled the old "penny-farthing" bicycles of the nineteenth century, one wheel huge, one tiny.

"Neat?" he demanded. "How about miraculous? You ever try to hit a kneecap on purpose?"

As the elevator car moved up to the penthouse, the little man removed the magazine of his automatic and popped in one new cartridge. "Brickie, what're you carrying?"

"What do I need a gun for with you around?"

"One-liners," the diminutive hit-man muttered. "You murder 'em with one-liners? What is so important about this Nancy Miller lady?"

"My business. But I can tell you this, you better straighten out that schlock tie of yours. You're about to meet the most grateful banker in all of Islam."

*   *   *

Where Hanover Gate enters Regent's Park from the west, a curious, octagonal stone gatehouse bisects traffic with a wedding-cake effect of scrolls and statues. Windows on all sides command a view of traffic moving into and out of Regent's Park. Located just around the corner from the entrance to the central London mosque, the gatehouse usually looks deserted of life, but not at half past noon this Sunday, the Fourth of July.

Inside the grimy windows, on the second floor for a better view, P. J. R. Parkins had just gotten off the telephone with Winfield House, where Colonel French had assured him that no one had made a hostile move within the enclave; they had been kept out by a vigilance at the gate.

"Or so he says," Parkins concluded as he reported his conversation to Jock Pringle. Both men were dressed casually in Sunday park-walking costumes of old trousers and patched sweaters. But to see them standing there, as erect as two stalks of asparagus, peering suspiciously out the perpetually dirty windows of the gatehouse, was to know that there was nothing casual about either of them, ever.

"I'm not sartin I trust his judgment," the redheaded man said. "But then, what does the wee mon have t'due annyway, with us blottin' up the Ayrab contingent."

"It's one of those self-starting cadres financed by Pan-Eurasian Credit Trust. You know what that means."

"Indeed. No rough stuff."

"That's the ticket, Jock," Parkins agreed. "It's all right for our lads to crunch a few black Caribbean skulls, always supposing they don't bust their batons on bone that hard. Or the odd kidney kick. Even a few gunshot deaths are in order for blacks because they've no strong nation to back them up."

"I'm no eejit, Peter. Ayrabs kneeling to Mecca and squads of prods working 'em over for the pure joy of it?" The redheaded man smiled slightly. "No, today we canna turn the lads loose for a bit of good clean fun. They must wait for the next football riot."

"The way I see it, this lot of faithful must arrive either on foot or by car. They're at their most vulnerable then, separated into groups."

"I had that van of theirs cleaned out and put back in the mosque parking lot." Jock laughed softly but for quite a while. "I do want to see their faces when we jump the lot of 'em and they reach inside the van for the dairty tricks and their tiny hands grasp nowt but air."

Both men were laughing now. The redheaded man asked quickly, "Are y'still holding that bugger Weems?"

"Yes."

"Let him go."

Inside the small gatehouse the dust lay heavy, permeating the air with a kind of grave silence between the two men. Parkins said nothing for a moment. "Let him go, is it?" he asked in a pinched, sniffy voice.

"Forensic got it wrong," Jock explained with terrifying blandness. "There's nae sign of anyone tamperin' with poor Riordan. He died of the injuries he got on Monday."

"Forensic . . .?" Parkins's voice trailed off. The two hard men eyed each other in silence for a long moment while the air seemed to vibrate with the hiss of new betrayals, new string pulling, new blackmail. Then Parkins produced a fake smile. "Yes, quite," he said then, very clipped. "So happy they finally got it right."

"Death by misadvanture, says I," the redheaded man suggested with a derisive smile.

"Look out, Jock, here come the bedouins!"

Both men, despite their size, were on the run now, clattering across the street and around the corner behind a small Datsun loaded with young, dark-complected men. Ahead of them, intercepting the car, three uniformed police brought it to a halt with upraised hands and ordered the passengers out.

One by one, five young men got peaceably out of the Datsun. They were frisked, handcuffed, and shoved firmly into a police van parked at the curb. Just then two young men of Arabic mien rounded the corner and strolled in the direction of the mosque. Another three bobbies halted them. Only one Arab struggled, a handsome devil with sharp cheekbones and eyes the color of pale caramel. He tried to pull a gun, thus making himself fair game. Complacently, two bobbies stomped up and down on his genitals and kidneys before handcuffing him and adding him to the load in the van. With this, Khefte's last work on behalf of jihad, any idea of resistance evaporated. Parkins glanced at his watch: twelve forty.

In the next fifteen minutes, on foot or in cars, more than a hundred young Arabs arrived for the noonday prayer and were hustled off in an endless procession of police vans. When Parkins went inside the mosque to inspect, the great marble prayer hall was empty.

Jock Pringle pulled a small black leather walkie-talkie from his hip pocket. "Jock to Bill One."

"Bill One to Jock. Over."

"Close both checkpoints into Winfield," he said. "Nothing moves in either direction till you get an all-clear from me."

"Bill One to Jock. Understood. Out."

The redheaded man turned to Parkins. "You never know, do you? No sense filling Winfield with on-time guests, eh? The Yanks'll scream at us later. Nae matter. Let's stall half an hour before we let guests through."

Parkins had wandered out into the road. "What guests? The road's empty both ways."

Overhead, mournful but strong, the quarter tones of the muezzin split the air, calling the faithful to prayer. But no one responded. They had all been arrested.

The short man and the tall man sat on a bench in Golden Square, a scruffy patch of greenery where London's theatrical district begins. No one else had any use for the place this Sunday, not even tourists. The men's eyes shifted this way and that and their words seemed addressed only to the deserted space before them.

". . . a Cathay Pacific flight to Hong Kong at five P.M. today. When you check in at Heathrow ask for Mr. Chen. He'll slide you past Customs onto the aircraft. Don't use the Weems passport."

The tall man frowned. "Look, Rand, I have business to attend to. It can't be done on a Sunday."

"Your ass, on the plane, five P.M."

"Look, I—"

"Shut up, shithead," the small man rasped. "You prefer rotting in London on a murder rap?"

Weems sighed. "Okay. Okay."

"You ever mess up the Company again, it won't be an air ticket we hand you."

"I said okay."

"You get terminated. With prejudice. Christ, as it is I got my hands full protecting the Company in this disaster area. When I think of that goddamned garden party today . . ." He shook his head sadly.

Weems glanced at his watch and stood up. "How's it going?"

Rand got to his feet and resolutely refused to glance skyward at the tall man. "Washed my hands of it. French is on his own."

"But you have people backing him up."

Rand's smile was a tiny, evil wrinkle, like the underside of a leech. "He thinks so," he muttered, almost to himself. "He thinks so."

*   *   *

Ned French had also gone to inspect the Outer Drive, where the cabs and autos of guests would be arriving, beginning at one o'clock. He heard the muezzin's call, thin and disembodied, rather like the cry of a strange bird, alone and far from its natural habitat. Dressed now in civilian clothes, he glanced up and down the outer drive and saw no traffic. Nor did he hear any noise from the direction of the mosque. He got out Chamoun's tiny radio and held it to his ear.

". . . now the one-o'clock news from BBC. Earlier rumors throughout the Middle East have now been confirmed by Syrian authorities after a raid on a villa outside Damascus and a running gun battle in which four Maronite Christian Lebanese, said to be in the employ of the CIA, were killed. Open speculation by high government officials in several Arab countries suggests that the American-funded saboteurs were responsible for detonating a series of more than a dozen high-explosive devices last night in central Damascus, leading to the direct and indirect deaths of more than sixty-five Syrians, including twenty children. Meanwhile, in Washington, D.C., official sources have yet to respond to the charge. Here in London, the foreign secretary discounted strongly any idea that—"

Ned switched off the radio and made his way back to Winfield. The silence in Regent's Park was strange, to say the least. Of course, he decided, without guests the whole place would be rather quiet. The small dance band from Quartermaster had not begun to play in a corner of the garden. There was no muted ping of glass or tinkle of ice.

No auto traffic, either. Ned turned back for a moment to watch the drive outside the ground of Winfield. Not a soul.

He found himself marveling at the degree of control Parkins and the MI5 man with the red hair seemed to exercise. As he turned back to the house, Ned could hear a blackbird high in one of the trees scolding another bird with a series of high, liquid warbles, like a coloratura in a mad scene.

Our muezzin, he thought, summoning the great, the good, the celebrated, and the well-heeled to pay homage to the great and good United States on the anniversary of its independence, a fledgling land struggling to bomb everybody else. Sing louder, muezzin.

Near Winfield itself he saw a few people moving back and forth, embassy and TV people, jockeying nervously before the curtain rose. To one side a tall, slender brunette with jet black hair talked to a shorter, buxom woman with a head of fine blond curls. Both had chosen a pale ivory color, Jane in a knee-length dress of crisp folds, Laverne in a longer skirt of a fabric so light it billowed. She wore a sleeveless bolero vest that left her arms bare and lush-looking in the dappled light.

Ned stopped in his tracks. He would have given anything for the power of invisibility and the chance to eavesdrop on the conversation between Jane and Laverne. He moved restlessly toward them and stood there as if daring them to continue talking. They did.

". . . can't always believe what the Syrians say," Laverne was counseling Jane. "They could have shot up just anybody and pinned the blame on them."

"I know." Jane glanced worriedly at Ned. "It's all over town," she told him. "Royce has heard that they're planning a protest demonstration at Grosvenor Square at sundown tonight. Candlelight vigil for the Damascus dead."

"Who is? Syrians here in London?"

"Peace groups. Disarmament people. Anti-nukers." She nodded in the direction of Anspacher, who was talking to someone and puffing pipe smoke in his face at the same time. "Anspacher's been saying it's a much broader coalition than usual. A lot of children were among the casualties in Damascus."

"But why does everyone assume we did it?" Laverne demanded.

Somewhere inside Winfield House the high, tearing noise of a woman's shriek seemed to rip through the trees and heavy foliage like an icy blast of wind. Ned started toward the house on the run. An instant later there was a shot.

He doubled speed, dodging in through the terrace doors. A gun roared. The mean whine of a 9-millimeter slug tore past his head.

He stopped in his tracks and raised his hands. Across the huge room the tableau was primitive, the cave scrawl of some Neanderthal tribe.

A man with wiry hair and huge, pop eyes was holding Pandora Fulmer's wrist, twisted behind her and pulled up to drain from her face the color beneath her makeup. She moaned more softly now.

In his right hand the man held a 9-millimeter Browning Parabellum. From across the room Ned could see that it was regular NATO issue, the kind GIs were always selling for drugs.

At Pandora's feet, Bill Voss lay doubled over in a widening puddle of his own blood, his hands trying to hold together his blown-apart stomach. His eyes stared at his blood staining Pandora's tiny pointed linen shoes another shade of red.

Behind the man Ned recognized as Fownes stood a young blond

fellow—one of the ones Ortega had called a regular—with another Parabellum. From the way he held it, in two hands, its muzzle unwinkingly aimed at Ned, he realized the blond had nearly hit him but had now paused, awaiting orders.

"Easy, Colonel French. Slow." Fownes's voice was high and tense.

As he spoke, his own automatic swiveled slightly until its muzzle obliterated Pandora's right ear. "One bad move," Fownes said then. "I'm a very jumpy man, Colonel French."

"I'm unarmed." Ned stood motionless. "May we give Bill Voss first aid, please?"

"We may not."

"He's dying."

"He won't be the only one, yes?" Fownes took a long breath. "Thought you had me boxed out?"

"Obviously not."

Max Grieves, standing off to one side, cleared his throat. "The warming ovens, Ned." His voice sounded like a croak. "They came this morning hidden in the warming ovens."

"Boxed in," Fownes snapped. "The guests'll be here any second. I want them welcomed, yes? The minute I have enough of them—I'll tell you when—you're going to close down Winfield. Got it?"

Ned let his glance move slowly, here and there around the room. Behind him, he knew, some of the people who had been outside were now inside. He hoped Jane and Laverne had been fast enough to see the trap and avoid it. But where was His Excellency?

Any second the guests would begin to arrive. It might take a while before some really expensive hostages could be assembled, but once that happened, Fownes had them totally under his command. Vanloads of assault troops did no good. All control rested against Pandora Fulmer's right ear. All the Marines and security people, the bobbies and Trojan troops . . . all of it meaningless. Anyone who might help was frozen in his tracks by one gun, held against one ear.

"Look," Ned said, not wanting to use the man's name for fear of alarming him, "if there's a political point to all this, you're not—"

Pandora's cry of agony cut him short. Fownes's unhealthy white face was splotched an angry red. "Mrs. Fulmer isn't too happy, Colonel French. You're causing her pain. Shut up and get over to that wall, next to the FBI bastard."

As he moved to the wall, Ned kept surveying the room. It was a huge area, originally meant as a ballroom and now cleared, except for a few chairs and end tables, for a large crowd of guests. One wall of French windows looked out to the terrace. He could see that Laverne and Jane had both inadvertently followed him into the room. Bad!

One man with an Ingram M-10 stood by the French doors. Another, similarly armed, held the passage back toward the kitchen area. A third, the blond one, stood beside Fownes.

Ned's glance fixed finally on Bill Voss, a big man with a lot of blood to lose. He had stopped moving now and his eyes, although open, seemed motionless.

An honorable end to a career in the foreign service. And his widow, Betsy? Where was she? Where was His Excellency? Where, for that matter, was Royce Connell?

Was there any possibility of help from the outside? Could Fownes be negotiated with to . . . to what? Give up a scheme, desperate but wildly lucrative? So that the U.S. Cavalry, pennons whipping in the desert wind, could thunder down on Fort Apache for a last-minute rescue? Or were they truly pinned down, help nearby but powerless to help?

Ned considered all of them in this huge room which now seemed as small as a prison cell. Of them all, Fownes had the best chance of surviving. Ned considered his own chances least promising. He had people to protect, all of them women: his ambassador's wife, his own wife, and Jane.

"I think they're coming," Fownes said then.

Outside the windowed doors to the terrace there was a noise, confusing, not the escorted steps of guests arriving but the muted scuffle of several waiters, peering into the room and then running away. Ned could see them perhaps better than Fownes, being nearer the doors. He couldn't tell if they were Hodgkins and Daughter people, or his own GIs from Quartermaster Corps. It didn't really matter. Not one of them was prepared to barge into that lethal ballroom and trigger off new deaths.

No, Fownes's position was for the moment impregnable. Nothing outside this room could affect him. Only mistakes made inside it could bring him down. But a man who can sit silently curled up for hours in an airless warming oven, cradling his dreams of glory, can be expected to have foreseen mistakes and avoided them.

But where were the guests?

The waiting was beginning to tell on Fownes. His huge, protuberant eyes darted here and there, sopping up visual information but without finding a sign of guests. Sweat dripped from his gray-white cheeks, the color of the fibrous kind of suet butchers peel off beef and throw away.

The effect of waiting seemed to have passed Pandora Fulmer by. She hung from Fownes like a small rag doll, only her highly arched insteps showing the effort she was making to lift up her slender body and keep its weight from increasing the agony in her back-twisted arm. The makeup on her face seemed to have lost contact with the flesh beneath. Pale sheet of cardboard, the layer of cosmetics stood firm while behind it her skin crawled in agony.

"Helmut," Fownes called to the man guarding the kitchen passage. "Pull this out of sight." He indicated the body of Bill Voss. "We don't want to alarm our guests."

Tucking the Ingram under his arm, the young man grabbed Voss by the leg and slid him through his own blood into the back corridor. He returned and carefully dropped a large tablecloth over the puddle. It instantly went red. He removed it and arranged a small Persian rug where the blood had been. He worked like a conscientious waiter.

Where were the guests?

Ned knew better than to make any move toward reading his own watch. But past Fownes, on a sideboard, stood a magnificent gold-cased carriage clock that showed the time to be almost twenty minutes after one.

Fownes turned and muttered something to the blond beside him. The young man nodded and, Browning automatic stretched in front of him, advanced toward Ned French.

"Come wid me," he ordered. "Be very careful."

Ned could hear a slight accent in the blond's voice, possibly Scandinavian? He allowed himself to be propelled toward the windowed doors that led to the terrace. As he passed Laverne and Jane, motionless in their ivory dresses, he let his eyes flick sideways toward them. He produced a meaningless smile to be reassuring.

Outside, the blond moved in behind Ned and kept the Parabellum muzzle pressed against his ribs. They advanced in the direction of the north gate, with its contingent of Marine guards.

"All we want to know about is kests," the blond breathed so close to Ned's ear that it was like a lover's murmur.

"Ask them about guests?" Ned suggested.

"Say nothing. We only look."

High overhead the blackbird muezzin summoned the faithful again and again, cheeping and trilling and bubbling with music like a bird orchestra. Come all ye celebrities! Honor the land of opportunity! Celebrate the independence of free enterprise!

"Stop."

The two men, close as lovers, bodies in contact, the penislike prod of the Browning a connective tissue linking them, paused under a tree rich with birdsong. Ned stared in each direction. To the north he could see the roadblock, but no cars waited there. In fact, no cars were moving at all, as far in either direction as he could see.

"Stranch," the blond murmured in Ned's ear. His sibilant breath tickled the fine hairs inside.

"Back to the house." The gun-prod jabbed hard. The two men wheeled about and returned at the same leisurely, strolling pace to the terrace, oceans of time to enjoy each other's dear proximity.

Out of the far corner of his eye—the French peripheral vision—Ned could see something move in the direction of the driveway that circled to the rear of Winfield House. The blond with him did not react.

In the second or less allowed him, Ned had spotted two men in the shadows of Winfield, heading out toward the gatehouse with its Marine guards. One was tall and bulky and looked like the ambassador. The other was pulling him along, as if hauling on a reluctant dog. This second man, resplendent in a pale suit and brilliant white tie, could only be Royce Connell.

Typical. Royce saving the embassy's bacon. Let the rest of us die. The first priority of number two is to make sure number one is safe.

Unfair, Ned told himself. In Royce's place he would have done the same thing, yank His Excellency out of there, then sort out the kidnap, or whatever you called it. For one insane moment he wanted, prayed to change places. But he knew his place was here. The blond stopped them in the doorway and, again like a lover, whispered: "Be very careful now. Don't make me hort you."

In the shrubbery near the gatehouse, a small group of men crouched in hiding. Royce Connell kept bending Ambassador Fulmer's head down and out of sight. A Marine lieutenant hunkered in the gravel with the black army lieutenant.

"Is that clear?" Connell demanded. "Nobody goes near the house. No heroics. No assaults. And, sir," he turned to Fulmer, "I do appreciate your concern, but if we can stay calm we have a chance of saving her, of saving them all."

"Stop dreaming," the ambassador muttered.

"I'm counting on the pop-eyed man to make a mistake. And Ned French to jump on it."

"Slim goddamned chance, basically."

"Our hands are tied." Connell glanced at the two officers. "Make sure all the Quartermaster Corps people understand the orders, will you? Keep away from the house. Inside, everybody's life depends on it."

An odd sound broke the tense silence. The two officers looked away, embarrassed. Royce realized that the ambassador had made the sound, a tight, strangled moan of sheer anguish.

French and the blond moved inside the great room as if locked together by invisible chains. Across the wide floor, Fownes stared challengingly at them. So did everyone else.

Laverne's big, pale eyes looked wide with questions. Jane, standing tall beside her, gave Ned the guilty, fluttering gaze of a mourner. Behind them, across that infernally huge room, Fownes barked:

"The guests?"

"Nothing yet," the blond called.

"It's a trick."

"Important guests always come late," Ned suggested.

Beside him the blond's muscular body tensed. His hand flew sideways in a looping arc and the Browning smashed into Ned's mouth. Hot salty blood welled up inside the lower lip. Ned knew better than to reach up and touch it.

"Yes," Fownes said, "that mouth needs discipline. Back against the wall, Colonel French. We have to do some more waiting, yes?"

The gun had tasted of exploded cordite. Ned could feel a worm of his own blood writhing down his chin. He sucked in and swallowed what seemed like a choking mouthful. Then he willed himself to stand motionless against the wall next to Max Grieves.

"His Nibs is safe," he muttered without moving his lips.

"Shit to that," Max responded.

But where *were* the guests? The roadway had been absolutely empty of cars or people, as if . . . Ned sucked in more blood from his lip. As if, he thought, this area was contaminated, unsafe, the site of some hideous nuclear disaster.

Ned blinked. His mouth had begun to ache, his lips and teeth throbbing with pain. But he finally understood what was happening outside.

All over town, people were finding something else to do, somewhere else to spend their Fourth of July. Even sit by their TV and watch the world protest this latest attack on unarmed women and children blamed on irresponsible America. Whether it was true or not, why risk showing up at the garden party of such a cowboy nation? Hadn't there been threats of terrorist action all along? Better to stay home. A few latecomers might show, and some of the press. But the big picture was clear.

There would be no guests. America had thrown a party and nobody was coming.

"Look," he called to Fownes. "We must talk."

"That mouth," the pop-eyed man said. "Get rid of it."

The blond took a step toward Ned. He lifted the heavy Parabellum to shoulder height. His finger tightened on the trigger.

The sound of a gun was deafening. The blond clutched his exploded eye as he jerked backward onto the floor.

In front of the French doors, silhouetted like a statue, legs apart, Laverne held one of the flat twin-set Webleys in her right fist, her left cupped under it as if standing alone at her shooting range.

She sent a second bullet through Fownes's throat.

The two men holding silenced Ingrams opened up a deadly crossfire. *Ti-ti. Ti-di-di.*

Red holes opened up across Laverne's bolero vest like a great X. She crumpled to the marble floor.

Ned dived across her and grabbed the Webley. He snapped a shot at the man by the windows and spun him around. The man toppled face first.

Wriggling through blood, Ned squirmed sideways and let off a round at the man guarding the door. He raised the Ingram and fired a burst that crashed into Ned's left shoulder.

Grimacing, Ned fired once more and saw a hole open up over the man's heart. Ned turned quickly to Laverne.

Her pale eyes were open wide. They stared deeply into his. "Did I get him?" Her voice was as thin as a line running off a spool.

"You got him, Verne."

Her eyes stayed open but the life went out of them. They looked as drowned as Chamoun's. They looked as icy as Wyckoff's.

Sudden silence, inside and out. Then, Marine guards running toward the house. And overhead, Ned could hear the muezzin bird singing his heart out.

SUNDAY
JULY 11

EPILOGUE

No one here can love and understand me.
Oh, what hard luck stories they all hand me.
Make my bed and light the light,
I'll arrive late tonight:
Blackbird . . . bye bye.

In the distance, so far away it hurt the eyes to see them, a range of mountains sketched a jagged edge to the horizon. The intense sun beat down like a hammer on the open gong of the desert, lying flat and endless in the reaches above Palm Desert toward the Colorado border.

Nothing grew here except artificially, on water stolen from Colorado. Nothing, that is, but gila monsters and scorpions.

In full uniform, Ned stood bareheaded. The heat of the sun caused the bandages and drains in his splinted left shoulder to ache in long, slow waves of pain. His daughters had ranged themselves on either side of him, somehow managing, all four of them, to get an arm part way around his waist. Next to them stood his father and mother, who had flown in from Wisconsin.

Behind them, flashing bold, brassy slants of sunlight, a military band in Camp Liberty colors, dusty sage green, stood at attention. One of the trumpeters had already played taps as the coffin had been lowered on its tapes into the unfriendly desert grave.

Ned eyed his parents as if they were strangers. His shoulder throbbed. He hadn't seen them in a long time and they looked older than he remembered. Perhaps fatigue from the long air trip? His girls hardly knew them. Come to that, he barely recognized them in their new, submerged early-retirement personalities. They needed livening up. They needed . . . He remembered talking with Jane about that once. What had she said? He'd have to ask her if they—when they—met again.

Ned felt somehow bruised and harassed by the glitter of the hot sun on the brass band. The idea of a military funeral had been the general's. No early retirement for him. A military funeral in this sagebrush prison? Ned's shoulder ached endlessly. He knew his face looked grim. To hell with them all.

Lieutenant General De Cartha Krikowski now stepped forward and handed a small trowel to Ned. Camp Liberty's cemetery was perhaps the greenest spot in this barracks-strewn wilderness of barbed wire, guard towers, and force-grown eucalyptus. It was certainly the only enclosure not surrounded by electrified fence.

Ned took the trowel and bent down. Under the three-inch sod cover of the cemetery the base earth was alkali sand and hardscrabble. He scooped up a trowelful of both and sent it like a projectile, out into the air in a dropping curve that landed with a hollow thud on Laverne's plain pine coffin. Ned handed the trowel to Lou Ann, who did the same thing. His other three daughters followed suit, looking forlorn, their eyes downcast.

Before Sally, his youngest, could hand the trowel back to the general, Ned chucked it into the grave. He stared coldly at the old desk soldier, whose face seemed to break into uncertain lines of doubt. Resplendent in his brass and braid, the old man turned away and took his wife's arm. They were flanked on either side by their sons, who barely kept from glaring at Ned.

He remembered this scene that night, in the barracks he was sharing with his daughters. They had all gone to bed early, some in grim silence, some tearfully. Half an hour later none of them was asleep when Ned went to the bathroom for a glass of water to swallow some painkiller pills.

"Dad," Lou Ann called, "bring some water for us?"

His earliest memories of these girls was of ferrying endless glasses of water to them in the night. What do you suppose, over the years? he asked himself. A thousand gallons of bedtime water? He smiled. He found a tray and brought back brimming glasses of hard, gritty, alkaline Camp Liberty water. His shoulder throbbed steadily.

"Yech," Lou Ann said. "How soon can we get out of here?"

Ned was silent for a moment, sitting in the dark at the foot of her bed. "What do you mean?" he asked at last, all his reactions slowed down, as they had been for the past week. "Don't you like it here?"

"Like it?" De Cartha asked. "Ha."

He stared from one to the other of them. "I thought . . . Your mother . . ."

"How soon?" Lou Ann repeated.

Ned sat there, speechless. Finally he roused himself. "You should know that I'm resigning my commission."

In the darkness none of them spoke. Gloria dipped her hand in her glass of water and, coming up unseen behind Sally, faked a sneeze and flicked water on the back of her bare neck.

"Not funny!"

"Don't resign till we're in London, okay?" De Cartha asked.

Ned sat back, gently massaging his splinted shoulder as he looked at each of them in turn. Only Lou Ann resembled her mother. The rest took after him. By some mysterious intrafamily chemistry, as the oldest and a faint replica of Laverne, Lou Ann had assumed control of the girls. Or, to put it more exactly: if they were under any control, it was hers.

"Why London?" he asked.

"Dad," Lou Ann assured him. "You want Bonn? Rome? Anywhere but here."

"The general won't like it."

"No," Lou Ann said thoughtfully. "He sure as hell won't."

"What about Wisconsin?" Ned asked.

"Hey!" Lou Ann said. "It's a bi-i-ig country."